BEYOND the
EYES of MARS

BOOK TWELVE
OF THE STARSHIP'S MAGE SERIES

This edition published in 2022 by:
Faolan's Pen Publishing Inc.
22 King St. S, Suite 300
Waterloo, Ontario
N2J 1N8 Canada

ISBN-13: 978-1-989674-24-6 (print)

A record of this book is available from Library and Archives Canada.

Printed in the United States of America
1 2 3 4 5 6 7 8 9 10
First edition
First printing: March 2022

Illustration © 2022 Jeff Brown Graphics
Faolan's Pen Publishing logo is a registered trademark of Faolan's Pen Publishing Inc.
Read more books from Glynn Stewart at faolanspen.com

BEYOND the
EYES of MARS

BOOK TWELVE
OF THE STARSHIP'S MAGE SERIES

GLYNN STEWART

FAOLAN'S PEN
PUBLISHING
faolanspen.com

CHAPTER 1

SHARON DEVERAUX WAS DEAD.

This was something she still wasn't entirely comfortable with, though the evidence was hard to argue with. Her brain currently resided in a tank full of nutrients and wires buried deep in the Engineering department of the First Legion interstellar assault transport *Ring of Fire*.

She'd been conscious to that concept of her existence and current state for about a year. Her...*masters* had given her access to the ship's internal sensors as one of the first things after they'd lifted her from her semi-coma.

They had direct access to her brain. Pleasure and pain were the push of a button for the people who commanded Sharon, and they used them freely to command her.

And yet...she'd done the math. She'd spent *three years* in a coma, only awoken by electronic commands forcing her to cast a single spell. Her body might be long gone, cremated in the morgue of a far away laboratory, but her *magic* remained.

For three years, she'd been nothing more than a component in a system that teleported *Ring of Fire* from star system to star system. But the Legion had needed more, so they'd carefully, *oh so carefully*, woken her up and trained her.

And yet she was still dead. But back when she'd been alive, fifteen-year-old Sharon Deveraux had trained puppies. She recognized response-reward training...and eighteen-year-old disembodied brain Sharon Deveraux was determined *not* to be trained.

But she had no intention of letting her masters think that. So, she'd begged, sat up and rolled over—and now she had an incredible scope of access to the assault transport's computer systems.

"Sharon, do we have a course worked up for Aquila?" Colonel Tzafrir Ajello asked. Ajello was *Ring of Fire*'s Captain, once an officer of the Republic of Faith and Reason's Space Assault Force.

"We do," she told him. The voice that emerged on *Ring*'s bridge was computer-generated—Sharon no more had vocal cords than she had hands—and it showed none of Sharon's thoughts.

She spoke with the soft contralto of a much older woman, with nothing to the generated voice to remind *Ring of Fire*'s crew of what horrors lurked in the heart of their engine room.

"If Lieutenant Zhao keeps us on course as planned, I will teleport us toward Aquila in four hours," she continued. "We will teleport every twelve hours after that for six days, arriving in Aquila on the sixteenth."

"Very well," Ajello replied. "Zhao, engage on course."

The transport shifted in space as her massive fusion engines engaged. The First Legion had no ability to produce antimatter, and their limited stores of antimatter left over from the Republic or stolen from the Protectorate of Mars were restricted to missile production.

"We're picking up passengers in Aquila," Ajello told the bridge crew—and Sharon. She was listening.

She was *always* listening. She wasn't sure anyone on the starship really understood how thoroughly the brain they were using as a cyborg administrative and navigation computer was woven through their systems.

"Another tranche of workers for the Exeter Fleet Base," the Colonel continued. "No assault forces for us, not yet. The crew and organic troop complement will be responsible for security and making sure that the workers don't cause trouble."

Even some of the living crew looked uncomfortable at that, but that was how the First Legion worked. Four of the Outer Colonies, worlds that had hidden themselves from Mars and the Mage's Guild, had been conquered by the Second Independent Cruiser Squadron of the Republic of Faith and Reason—what was now the First Legion.

The populace of those worlds served the Legion as indentured labor—and much like Sharon Deveraux, they had no choice in the matter.

She'd been enslaved to the Prometheus Drive for four years now, but the last year, she'd become something different. Still a brain in a jar, she had mental fingers woven through every system of *Ring of Fire*.

She was dead. No longer human. She was something new—and she and the other awakened Mage brains that held together the Legion's empire had chosen the only name that fit.

Born of the horror of the Republic's Project Prometheus and bound to the fate of the First Legion, they were now their own people.

They were Prometheans.

CHAPTER 2

WHOEVER HAD SET UP the seating plan for the dinner in Commodore Chad Ó Luain's flag mess appeared to have had it in for Mage-Commander Roslyn Chambers, Captain of the destroyer *Voice of the Forgotten*.

Commodore Ó Luain was responsible for security at the Royal Martian Navy's Legatus refit yard. Tucked well away from the main fleet position and out of sight of the still arguably occupied planet's populace, the yard still drew on the industrial might of the star system that had led the revolt against Mars.

Ó Luain's command was a trio of destroyers and a dozen heavy defensive platforms. It was enough to hold out until the fleet in orbit of Legatus itself could teleport themselves to the rescue of the yard's facilities and people.

As a refit-and-repair yard, Centurion Base didn't build new ships. It repaired battered existing ones, like Roslyn's own command. By the end of the first known battle against the First Legion, a remnant of Legatus's Republic of Faith and Reason, *Voice of the Forgotten* had been beaten to a pulp.

It was almost all surface damage, and Centurion Base had quickly settled to work making it right. If the price of that was regular dinners with the Commodore's officers, Roslyn was more than willing to pay it.

But tonight, the slim redheaded Tau Cetan Mage had been seated next to Mage-Captain Harriet Beaumont. Beaumont was a gray-haired woman with the unfortunate distinction of being one of the most senior Captains in the Navy.

There appeared to have been a *reason* she'd never been promoted past command of a division of barely mobile sublight battle platforms—and why a *Mage* had been put in command of a force without a single amplifier matrix between them.

"These young officers today," Beaumont muttered as the dinner plates were cleared away. "They think that just because they've seen a war, that makes up for the years of experience they don't have."

Roslyn, who held the distinction of being among the youngest officers the Royal Martian Navy had ever promoted to Commander in peacetime, held her tongue. The Ruby Medal of Valor she wore, a marker that she'd received the Protectorate's highest award for valor in combat *twice*, was a silent reproach to the older woman's words.

Unfortunately, Roslyn *knew* that dessert was still coming and that Commodore Ó Luain would be offended if she left early. That meant she needed to keep her peace until the food arrived.

"I mean, look at *Voice of the Forgotten*," Beaumont continued.

Roslyn was now *very* sure the woman was intentionally needling her. She'd grown used to competent and supportive senior officers, but Beaumont was something different.

"I'm surprised her Captain escaped a Board," the old woman declared, seemingly aimed at the officer to her right instead of Roslyn at her left...but Roslyn had no illusions she was being addressed. "That level of damage in peacetime against *pirates*? Only the most inexperienced destroyer Captain would be given that much trouble by a single pirate!"

"Said 'pirate' was a *Benjamin*-class cruiser," Roslyn pointed out before she could stop herself. "A First Legion warship, a leftover of the Republic."

"We don't generally expect our ships to stand off a twenty-to-one mass advantage," Commander Boleslava Ivanova said carefully on the other side of Beaumont. The Earth-born Russian officer reported to Captain Beaumont, though she was only two years older than Roslyn.

Like Roslyn, she'd served on Second Fleet as Mage-Admiral Her Highness Crown Princess Jane Alexander had smashed her way through the Republic's resistance. Ivanova had seen war—war against Republican cruisers, at that.

"Of course we don't," Beaumont agreed crisply. "But the rest of *Voice*'s squadron isn't here, are they?"

"My squadron was scattered across half the outer rim, looking for the First Legion raiders," Roslyn murmured. "We'd landed our Marines on the logistics base and couldn't leave them."

"You expect anyone to believe that you took on a *Benjamin* with a single refitted destroyer?" Beaumont asked derisively.

Swallowing a sigh, Roslyn turned to squarely face the woman next to her. Even in the full black dress uniform of the Royal Martian Navy, she still only wore the Ruby Medal of Valor in its entirety.

She still had a row of ribbons marking a dozen other medals, including a newly designed one that declared that she *also* held the rank of Lieutenant Colonel of the Royal Martian Marine Corps to go with Mage-Commander of the Royal Martian Navy.

That dual rank was not yet a tradition of the Protectorate of the Mage-Queen of Mars, but Her Majesty Kiera Alexander had awarded it to Roslyn for the very battle they were discussing.

"We were lucky. We had advantages they didn't expect. And we were desperate," Roslyn said quietly. The fact that a Martian Interstellar Security Service stealth ship had been in-system, providing her with near-real-time data on the Legion cruiser via the FTL Link communicator was still classified.

"But yes, Mage-Captain Beaumont, that is exactly what happened. We paid for the logistics base our intelligence services are still tearing apart with blood and fire—and I will hear no disrespect to my crew or my dead."

"Watch your tongue, Commander," Beaumont snapped. "You are speaking to a superior officer."

A long silence covered their part of the table, and even Commodore Ó Luain seemed to be ignoring it. It seemed that Beaumont knew exactly what she could get away with.

The silence was broken by an emergency chirp on Roslyn's wrist-comp. She broke the staring contest with Beaumont to stare at the device for a moment.

"Did you forget to even silence your comp for this?" Beaumont asked, a gleeful contempt in her voice.

"Admirals can override that remotely," Roslyn replied calmly as she read the message. She took a certain degree of pleasure in the Mage-Captain's sudden shock.

"If you'll excuse me." She rose without waiting for a response from Beaumont and addressed Commodore Ó Luain at the head of the table.

"I apologize, Commodore, but Mage-Admiral Jakab has requested my presence on the Link for an update on the status of my ship.

"Dinner was excellent and I'm sorry to miss dessert—but duty calls for us all."

Roslyn didn't have the time—or the need—to return all the way to *Voice of the Forgotten* to connect with her commanding officer. The Centurion Base command station had all of the modern fixtures, including a Link station of its own.

Mage–Vice Admiral Kole Jakab's name got her into the base's Link conference room without much difficulty. She sealed the room behind her with her own security codes and then connected with her staff on *Voice*.

The broad-shouldered and towering form of Lieutenant Commander Amber Salucci appeared on the wallscreen in front of her.

"Captain Chambers," she said crisply. "I'm glad I got through. I apologize for interrupting dinner, but, uh, when the Admiral calls..."

"Commanders jump," Roslyn agreed. "Thank you, Lieutenant Commander. Is the Admiral on the line?"

"Flag Lieutenant Kumar is, sir," Salucci told her. "He was to inform the Admiral when you were available."

Roslyn winced. Being delayed enough that the Admiral had delegated waiting for her wasn't great. Mage-Lieutenant Krystoff Kumar was quite competent...but he was also very junior, a very larval form of staff officer.

Having served in the role for Jane Alexander, she was *quite* familiar with the nature of the Flag Lieutenant role.

"Transfer the Link connection to Centurion Base on these codes," Roslyn ordered. "I am available at the Admiral's convenience."

Somehow, she was unsurprised that she didn't even see Kumar long enough for the younger man to say hello. The dark-skinned Tau Cetan native—a distant cousin, the Mage First Families of Tau Ceti being an unofficial aristocracy with all that meant—was almost immediately replaced by the tall and pale form of Mage–Vice Admiral Kole Jakab.

"I didn't realize, until Kumar reminded me, that I had misjudged the time," Jakab told her. "I did not mean to interrupt your supper, Mage-Commander."

"Sometimes, sir, interruptions are surprisingly welcome," she admitted. "And as your junior starship commander, I fully understand the priority of the Admiral."

"I both regret and appreciate the priority the stars give me," Jakab said quietly.

Vice Admiral was a new rank, one born out of the reorganization of the RMN after the war. Roslyn had seen firsthand the difficulties created by the Navy's lack of middle flag ranks, when *every* officer at a major fleet briefing shared the same rank.

Jakab had served out the war as "Mage-Commodore with special duties," operating under the direct authority first of Hand Damien Montgomery and then of the Crown Princess, Mage-Admiral Alexander. He'd been part of the first batch of the Protectorate's new Vice Admirals.

"The priority is what it is for a reason, sir," Roslyn allowed. She was more comfortable with Jakab than she was with, say, Commodore Ó Luain, but there was still a vast chasm between their ranks.

"How may I and *Voice of the Forgotten* serve?"

"The question I am actually concerned about at this moment, Mage-Commander Chambers, is *when* can you serve?" Jakab asked. "The question is more urgent than you might think, though I still didn't need to interrupt your dinner."

He gave a one-shouldered apologetic shrug. He might not have *meant* to interrupt Roslyn's dinner, but he clearly wasn't going to send her back, either.

"The armor plating and dispersion-web layers have been replaced, as have our damaged weapons," Roslyn told him. "We're down to final tests and the installation of replacement external sensor pods."

The multilayered active armor used by Protectorate warships was a miracle of engineering, capable of withstanding direct hits from antimatter warheads and multi-gigawatt lasers. Its efficacy also meant that most of the starship's sensors had to be mounted on the outside of the armor, which made them vulnerable.

"Do you have a timeline yet?" Jakab asked, looking thoughtful.

"No, sir," Roslyn told him. She had a few ideas for accelerating the work she hadn't leaned on yet—she'd run with more than few gangs in her misspent youth before being side-loaded into the Academy for helping a Hand solve a problem.

There were always options, some more acceptable than others.

"All right," the Vice Admiral told her. "I will speak to Commodore Ó Luain. You can carry out tests en route, but sensor installation shouldn't take more than twenty-four hours.

"I want *Voice of the Forgotten* on her way back to *Pax Dramatis* within thirty-six hours, if at all possible," he continued.

Roslyn smiled predatorily.

"We're going after the Legion?" she asked.

"Somewhere out there are multiple planets that we have failed to protect," Jakab replied. "We owe it to them to take on the Legion and restore their freedom.

"If I'm being honest, High Command also wants to use them as a testing ground for new deployment structures and logistical protocols," he continued. "But we have three battleship groups positioned along the frontier now, and we're all contributing destroyers to a joint operation with our *other* friends."

That meant the Martian Interstellar Security Service, the people who operated the Protectorate's covert magical stealth ships. A combined operation with RMN destroyers and MISS stealth ships seemed like the best way to find the Legion.

Well, the best way after following them home, anyway.

"We had no luck with the Trackers?" Roslyn asked. Her own operation, under Jakab's command, had involved a mercenary bounty hunter with the rare ability to track the magical jump spell.

The RMN also had several Trackers of their own, and she knew at least one had been deployed to help Ajam, the mercenary in question.

"The Legion appears to have delved deeply enough into our own underworld to have learned of the Trackers and the countermeasures to them," Jakab said quietly.

"Few of the organized crime syndicates can afford to expend antimatter warheads against the possibility of us deploying the Trackers against them. The First Legion, on the other hand, had clear evidence that we *were* using Trackers.

"They swept multiple key systems and bombarded jump zones with antimatter warheads, obliterating the signatures. While I doubt they'll be doing so as a matter of standard jump protocol, they very effectively cut off every trail we could follow."

"So, we pick a region of space and search everything?" Roslyn asked. It sounded like a long and boring operation that would end in an explosion of violence. But she didn't see any other option.

"Exactly. And you're one of two crews who have buried their faces deep in this," Jakab told her. "I want you here. Make it happen, Mage-Commander. I'll lean on Ó Luain here, but if there's anything you can do..."

"You push on your side and I'll push on mine," Roslyn promised. "We'll be on our way inside your deadline, sir."

CHAPTER 3

KELLY LAMONTE WAS dyeing her hair when the call came in. This was roughly a weekly activity for the petite spy, a small luxury she'd continued to allow herself even as she'd risen from junior engineer on a civilian freighter to commander of one of the Protectorate's most complex pieces of magical technology.

"I have three different chemicals in my hair," she told Trixie Buday, *Rhapsody in Purple*'s com officer. "This better be important."

"Regional Director Peyton is on the Link for you, sir," the young blonde woman replied. "She says it's urgent."

Kelly grimaced as she looked at her hair, currently mid-transition from crimson red to turquoise green. She looked, in her own expert opinion, like a poorly designed Christmas decoration.

"Link her through to my wrist-comp," she ordered Buday. "But I don't need to send *her* video."

Kelly's wrist-comp rested on the counter next to the sink, allowing its holoprojectors to pop an image of Gry Peyton up to Kelly's left. The gracefully aging woman was the Regional Director for the Martian Interstellar Security Service's operations around Legatus, the former capital of the secessionist Republic.

She was also Kelly's direct boss, even though *Rhapsody in Purple* was currently in the Mercedes System and more closely attached to Battle Group *Pax Dramatis* than the MISS's Legatus Station.

"Whatever you're doing, you need to drop it now," Peyton said without any preamble.

Kelly swallowed a sharp retort. She and Peyton did not get along, but they *had* worked together for several years now. This was unusual, even for Peyton.

"I currently look like a drunk designed a candy cane," she admitted. "What's going on, Gry?"

"You and I need to be on a Link with the Oversight Board in thirteen minutes," the Director said sharply. "And *I* didn't get much more notice than you did, which I am not pleased about."

"What did you *do*, LaMonte?"

"Since taking *Fallen Dragon*?" Kelly asked. That was the supply ship she and the Navy had taken away from the First Legion. "I've been ferrying the Navy's pet Trackers around. Last five days, my crew has been doing R&R in Mercedes and keeping our heads down while waiting for *Rhapsody in Verdigris* to arrive.

"I don't think we've done anything to draw the Board's attention!"

The Protectorate was both aware of its need for a semi-covert espionage service—and of the risks born of the fact that said espionage service's operations were inevitably on Protectorate worlds.

MISS had a lot of authority, but that came with a lot of responsibility and a lot of checks and balances. The largest was the Oversight Board, an appointed collection of officials that included exactly *one* ex–field agent and only four MISS administrators—along with three civilian appointees and three former officers of the Martian Investigatory Service, their sibling law enforcement organization.

The Board reported to the Mage-Queen of Mars and the Prince-Chancellor. Their job was to *control* MISS more than it was to *lead* MISS, but they were the top of Kelly LaMonte's chain of command, such as it was.

"Then I have *no* idea what they want," Peyton admitted. "So, if you could *find* some best behavior to be on, I'd appreciate it!"

"I guess I'm washing my hair and hoping it picks a color to stick with," Kelly said quietly. "And I promise to behave, Director. I don't see any reason to cause chaos today!"

Most of the time, though, causing chaos was her *job*. Given that Peyton's job was to sort through chaos to find answers for Mars, it was probably inevitable that they didn't get along.

Kelly's hair was clean, dry and tied back into a ponytail when she took a seat at her desk to join the conference. It was still a twisted mix of red and green that was *not* particularly pleasing to her eye but that was mostly invisible to the Board.

She hoped.

The Link connection asked her for a sequence of security codes that no one else aboard *Rhapsody in Purple* would know, then required her to lock down her office at the maximum security level.

Then the holographic conferencing software finally activated, small icons informing her that she was connected to three different Link terminals. One would be the central MISS Link terminal on Deimos. The other would be the secured MISS-only terminal on Legatus.

She wasn't sure where the third was, but it suggested that the Oversight Board wasn't all in one place—and after half a decade as a spy for Mars, Kelly had to approve of that paranoia.

Thirteen people flickered into existence around her as her office disappeared behind a projected meeting room that didn't exist anywhere in reality.

It put all fourteen of them equally around a table. Kelly was directly opposite from Gry Peyton, separated from her usual superior by the full breadth of the Oversight Board.

She knew every member of the Board by name and face—she was senior enough in MISS that *not* knowing would have been unjustifiable—but she'd never spoken to any of them in person, let alone all of them.

Part of that was that she tended to go over their heads in emergencies, since Prince-Chancellor Damien Montgomery was her ex-boyfriend and that gave her an access even some members of the Board would likely kill for.

"Captain LaMonte, Director Peyton, thank you for joining us," one of the Board members said briskly. It took Kelly a moment to place him: Dilshod Cortez, an Earth-born Spaniard who'd served as the head of the Martian Investigation Service for three increasingly important systems before Montgomery's predecessor as Chancellor had recruited him for the Board.

"We wanted to get both of your opinions of the situation with the First Legion before finalizing certain decisions that have been placed before us," Cortez told them. "Director Peyton, if you would be so kind as to summarize what you have learned from the records on Legatus for the Board."

"Records on Legatus have nothing on the First Legion," Peyton said instantly. "I have dug up personnel files for all identified members of the First Legion's officer corps, including Admiral Ridwan Muhammad, that have been forwarded to all relevant parties.

"We have done some research and investigation around the Second Independent Cruiser Squadron as well, but truthfully, any fully updated files around the ships, personnel or even ground units that were commandeered by Admiral Muhammad would have been at Styx Station, and we did not successfully retrieve much of Styx's files."

Styx Station had been the Republic's continuity-of-government facility, attached to their backup accelerator ring for antimatter production. While Mage-Admiral Alexander had wrecked both the ring and Styx Station, the gap between that happening and her returning with a fleet to take control of the star system had been large enough that any remaining files had been wiped.

"Most of what we know about the First Legion comes from *Fallen Dragon*, the supply ship that Mage-Commander Chambers and Captain LaMonte captured," Peyton conceded.

"Of course," Cortez allowed.

If anyone on the Board hadn't known all of that in advance, they hadn't been doing their jobs. Kelly figured there was a shoe coming and the Board was readying the ground for it.

"In that case then, Captain LaMonte." He turned to Kelly. "We are not questioning the intelligence retrieved," he said carefully, "but...your opinion of the threat level of the First Legion."

That was a loaded question and she grimaced.

"To whom?" she finally asked. "To the Protectorate as a whole? Minimal. Even given time to establish new shipyards and production centers, the First Legion is unlikely to control more than four or five star systems.

"I find it unlikely that we have lost track of enough people for those systems to have populations higher than perhaps a few dozen million apiece," she continued. "All told, I suspect the Legion has a population base of about a hundred million people.

"And the threat to *those* people, Mr. Cortez?" she asked softly. "The threat to them is *existential*. Whatever reason they left the Protectorate behind for, they did not intend to become slaves of a military-industrial dictatorship determined to refight the Secession.

"There is a measurable and distinct threat to our own fringe systems," Kelly conceded. "On the other hand, given that the Navy has multiple *battleships* sweeping the most likely interface points, we can safely assume that threat is neutralized.

"The question is how far the obligation of protection inherent to the Compact spreads," she told them. "I am not a Mage, but Her Majesty is.

"If her Protectorate extends to all humanity, then the people on the worlds the Legion has conquered are owed some effort on our part. Even if we do not take that interpretation of the Compact, *a hundred million innocents* are owed some moral obligation, are they not?"

Cortez chuckled softly.

"Her Majesty's position, Captain LaMonte, is very clear," he told her. "As is the Prince-Chancellor's, which I suspect you are more familiar with."

That was, Kelly hoped, the most attention anyone was going to draw to her continuing friendship with Damien Montgomery. It was no real danger to anyone—*Montgomery* wouldn't let it be a danger to anyone—but her going over the Board's head hadn't made her any friends in this call.

"That position is that her title calls her the Protector of Humanity, not merely the protector of the Protectorate of the Kingdom of Mars," Cortez concluded. "While the Protectorate of Mars is the interstellar state we serve, it is the opinion of Her Majesty, Mage-Queen Kiera Alexander, that *her* Protectorate subsumes all of humanity.

"Including those hundred million innocents, Captain LaMonte."

"So, what do you need from me, sir?" Kelly asked, glancing over at Peyton.

"This Board is concerned, Captain, that the Navy sees this as an opportunity to play with new toys as much as anything else," Cortez said. "Included in that is their request for basically *all* of our stealth ships."

Even Kelly wasn't actually certain how many of the stealth ships existed. She knew that the Navy was extremely strict on what ships could be built with unrestricted amplifiers and that the technology involved in the stealth ships was both complex and expensive...but no one had ever told her how many existed.

She knew of five. She figured there were at least two more.

"As the Navy prepares to move battleships and dreadnoughts to a potential war zone, they also want to use our ships in combination with their own lighter vessels to *find* their war zone.

"All of our efforts to date have been frustrated by unexpectedly competent operational and informational security on the part of the First Legion," Cortez continued.

"And you have been at the center of all of this, Captain LaMonte. So. In your opinion, is the deployment of our stealth ship assets in support of the Navy operation justified?"

Kelly gently bit her own tongue to stop herself rushing into the answer. She could see why the Board was asking her, but for all that she'd done, she was still just one of the stealth-ship captains and not a senior-enough agent to normally be having these conversations with the Board.

She wasn't much *short* of those lofty heights—Gry Peyton, for example, had weekly meetings with the Board, and Kelly reported directly to her— but to be asked her opinion of something *that* major in her first meeting with the Oversight Board was nerve-wracking.

To her surprise, though, Peyton met her gaze and gave her an encouraging nod. Swallowing down her moment of caution, she marshaled her thoughts.

"As of this moment," she said slowly, "*Rhapsody in Purple* and *Rhapsody in Verdigris* are already assigned to this operation. It would not be reasonable to redeploy us without a critical mission elsewhere, so I presume we are talking about assigning additional units to this operation?"

Cortez nodded silently.

"Every stealth ship assigned to the survey operation increases the number of systems we can sweep simultaneously and, therefore, reduces the time period until we find the Legion," she told the Board. "Every day we have not found the Legion's stars is a day that we cannot rescue their enslaved populations.

"Assuming that the Navy is prepared to put at least destroyers up to support our scout ships, I can easily justify the deployment of a functionally infinite number of assets," Kelly concluded. "The question then becomes opportunity costs. I am not aware, I'm afraid, of our total number of stealth ships and what operations they are on.

"Lacking that information, I would suggest that we deploy half of our stealth assets in support of this operation, keeping the remaining units in regular deployment.

"Selection of which units to deploy should be based on their current operations, with preference given to ships that can rapidly clear their responsibilities."

There was a silence around the virtual table, and Kelly thought she'd gone too far for a moment.

Then one of the women chuckled. Elidi Borysov, Kelly identified her— the one ex–field agent on the Board.

"Told you all," Borysov said drily. "She's the one."

"I agree," Cortez said instantly. "We've already discussed this. Any new objections?"

The conference was silent—not least because of Kelly's own confusion.

Cortez waited for a moment, then pointed a finger at Kelly.

"Congratulations, LaMonte, you're now the Director of Stealth Ship Operations," he told her. "You now report directly to us. We'll have the HQ team for SSO update you on the ship status, but you are authorized and expected to provide the Navy with four stealth ships for their operations against the First Legion.

"Selection of which ships, other than *Purple* and *Verdigris*, is at your discretion once you're up to speed on the current missions of your new subordinates."

"Thank you, sir," Kelly said carefully, a bit taken aback as she considered just what that was going to mean for her workload. "I...uh...should probably get to work, then?"

"One last thing," Borysov said, before anyone could tell her to go. "Because you'll be working with the Navy, this role comes with the courtesy rank of Commodore. You still remain a civilian and an MISS operative, but you are not expected to play subordinate to military officers.

"Our preference, if we are committing this many assets to the operation, is that overall command of the survey sweep rests with you."

Kelly swallowed and nodded. That could come back to bite her, but she saw the Board's point.

"That will be a discussion I will have to have with Vice Admiral Jakab," she finally concluded. "Or whoever ends up in command."

"Once you have found the First Legion's territory, *Masamune* will move forward and collect the assorted battleship groups," Cortez told her. "The Navy *definitely* wants to send in a dreadnought, which means that Admiral Medici will take command of what I understand will be incorporated as Seventh Fleet.

"Until that point, you will be coordinating with Mage–Vice Admiral Jakab. You will act as our primary point of contact with the Admiral and make certain that MISS assets are protected and used to their full ability."

That was a subtle but key point. There'd been several occasions in the war where Kelly had been ordered to conceal certain abilities of her stealth ship from both the Republic and the Royal Martian Navy.

"I will make sure of it," Kelly confirmed.

"Good. Congratulations, Director. We look forward to the results of your operations."

CHAPTER 4

"CAPTAIN ON DECK!"

Roslyn couldn't help but roll her eyes at the announcement as she stepped into the staff conference room. None of her senior officers did more than turn to acknowledge her entrance, but the call was still unnecessary.

Well. *One* officer had rushed to her feet and stood at attention—but Marine Lieutenant Debora Mathisen was the one who'd snapped the alert. The tall and darkly attractive Marine officer was *very* young—and coming from Roslyn, that was saying a lot.

"At ease...Lieutenant Mathisen," Roslyn specified with a small smile. "And everyone else, since you probably should show *some* decorum to the Captain."

Of the seven people waiting for her in the room, four had been with her when she'd taken down a slaver base and captured a First Legion logistics station. They'd earned a bit of familiarity with their young Captain.

Mathisen was new, though. Fresh out of her first post-Academy tour, the young Marine was still *so* new, she squeaked.

"We're all looking at the new time limit the Admiral sent us," Yusif Claes told Roslyn. Her new executive officer, promoted from tactical after their last mission, shared Mathisen's black coloring but was even taller. He was a native of Sol's Belt, one of the few Sol-born members of *Voice's* crew.

"And we have thirty-four hours left," Roslyn agreed. "So, now is the time to put our heads together and see what it's going to take to get us moving on that timeline.

"When a Vice Admiral says he wants his escort destroyer back, the crew of said escort destroyer makes it happen. Agli, what does Engineering need?"

Lieutenant Lenore Agli was the senior assistant engineer. As part of a standing agreement with *Voice of the Forgotten*'s chief engineer, Lieutenant Commander Evelia Dresdner, Dresdner was allowed to delegate attendance at staff meetings.

Her preferred delegate had followed Roslyn's old XO onto a transport to Tau Ceti, assigned to take up the same role on a brand-new battleship as a Lieutenant Commander.

There had been awards and rewards aplenty after their last mission.

"Commander Dresdner says that we have four holes that we need the repair yard to close up, and we need seventeen sensor pods," Agli said after a moment. She still sounded hesitant.

"The exact models of the pods we need are in the system. We...may be able to install them ourselves while in transit, if it comes down to that, but Centurion Base hasn't given us a timeline on the parts yet."

"We should have that, shouldn't we?" Lieutenant Commander Amber Salucci asked. Salucci had been promoted, but Roslyn had managed to hang on to the broad-shouldered woman in the coms and logistics role anyway.

"I'll admit, I assumed the paperwork had been lost in Engineering," she continued thoughtfully. "A disservice to your department, Lieutenant; I apologize."

She turned to Roslyn and wrapped a hand tightly around her water-glass.

"Apologies, sir, but I hadn't considered the lack of updates or timelines on those parts myself," she admitted. "I'll have to check with my department, but I suspect if neither I nor Engineering have heard anything on them..."

"Then our sensor pods aren't on schedule," Roslyn concluded. "Understood."

That was...problematic. They should have all of the parts for their repairs allocated and assigned, and she should have been told that they *didn't*. A quick glance around the table suggested that Agli knew that, Salucci knew that—and even Claes, the newly-fledged XO, knew that.

A ball had been quite thoroughly dropped…but it was a ball that shouldn't have existed in the first place if Centurion Base had been doing their job. From the sheepish expressions, Roslyn wasn't going to need to flagellate her staff too harshly.

She *would* raise it with Dresdner in her next meeting with the Chief Engineer, though. The allowances for Dresdner's particular quirks were based around everything working smoothly, after all.

"Tactical, do you have any concerns other than the sensors?" she asked, turning to the most senior of the new officers aboard *Voice*.

Alexandros Salminen was a pale-skinned young man, small enough to remind Roslyn of the Prince-Chancellor's diminutive build—and no one who'd known Damien Montgomery was ever going to underestimate a small man.

"We have run the self-tests and simulations on the new systems—and the old ones," he said slowly. "Everything appears to be in alignment and properly working, but we won't know for certain until we can arrange a live-fire test.

"We do not have a single weapon system that has been unimpacted by the repairs and replacements," he continued. "I would not *expect* us to have a fully aligned broadside without live-fire testing.

"That said, we have a full stock of munitions, including ground-bombardment rounds. My only concern is that our sensor capability is currently less than fifty percent of what it should be, which severely degrades the efficiency of our weapons across the board."

"Understood. Thank you." Roslyn surveyed the table. "Agli, any concerns with getting those holes in the hull patched?"

"None," she said instantly. "They're already on the schedule and should be closed up inside twenty hours. Dresdner and I have a schedule set up for the surface work we can do after that.

"We can accelerate that schedule a bit, but we'll still need to do some of it in transit in the gaps between jumps."

"Understood. Let myself and Mage–Lieutenant Commander Victor know if the Mages can be of assistance," Roslyn ordered.

Mage–Lieutenant Commander Lalit Victor, the last member of the staff meeting, was the ship's navigator. Like Claes and Roslyn herself, they were part of the ship's complement of Mages.

And while the Mages' main purpose on a Martian warship was to teleport the vessel between the stars, there were a *lot* of other things the Mages could do to help out with the operations of the starship.

"What do we do about the sensor pods, sir?" Claes finally asked, the executive officer clearly feeling a bit out of his depth.

"You and Lieutenant Commander Salucci will go through channels," Roslyn told him. "File the formal requests, send the emails, remind everyone that *Vice Admiral Jakab* is asking where the hell his destroyer is."

"If we haven't got anything yet, how much good will that do?" Agli asked, the assistant engineer looking concerned.

"Admirals conjure with a priority no lesser mortal can match," Salucci noted. "But the Lieutenant isn't wrong, sir."

"I know," Roslyn agreed. "You hit them high, people. I'll hit them low. As it happens, I have a standing invitation for drinks in the Centurion Base officers' lounge I think I need to call in."

She smiled.

"I have my suspicions about what's going through the good Commodore's mind, but it would be inappropriate for me to admit them to junior officers," she said virtuously. "So, instead, I will simply make *damn* sure we get the parts we need."

CHAPTER 5

IT ENDED UP being an early lunch instead of drinks, but that was fine with both Roslyn and with Commander Ankita Mantovani. The lounge was quiet enough for Mantovani to acquire a corner table despite her relatively junior rank.

Roslyn chuckled as she saw that the other woman had managed to inveigle the stewards into serving up wine anyway.

"How'd you get drinks out of an officers' lounge at eleven hundred?" she asked as she slid into the table across from the Centurion Base logistics officer.

"Oh, I told them the truth," the clearly East Indian–extracted Tau Cetan native told Roslyn with a giggle. "I told them that it was the end of my shift and I had a date with my high school crush."

Roslyn managed not to blush *too* much.

"We were in school together for, what, six months?" she asked. "Before I..."

Mantovani made a small cut-off gesture before Roslyn admitted to her stint in juvenile detention on their homeworld. She and Mantovani had both attended a private girls' school intended for Tau Ceti's upper class... but it had been targeted at Tau Ceti's *non-Mage* upper class.

Since Roslyn Chambers had already managed to get herself expelled from the private school for Mages the First Families maintained for their own children, her parents had paid through the nose to keep her in the Tau Ceti Young Ladies' Academy—right up until she'd stolen and crashed a judge's car.

She was *mostly* reconciled with her parents now, but it had taken a while. Even after they'd apologized for not realizing that she was acting out, looking for them to realize she was there and in pain.

Damien Montgomery had realized that—mostly due to Roslyn's counselor being his ship captain's cousin—and pulled her off the self-destructive course she'd been on.

"You seemed so rebellious and amazing back then," Mantovani told her. "Even with where it ended up, it was still hot to me when I was seventeen and dumb."

"I'm not sure that reaction crossed my mind...when I was fifteen and dumb," Roslyn replied with a chuckle. "Plus, well...I always preferred boys."

"Oh, I know," Mantovani agreed. "And the food here is good enough not to require the wine, *and* I'm engaged these days."

"You are?" Roslyn asked in unfeigned delight. "Congratulations."

"Civilian shipwright," the other woman confirmed. "Legatan, to my surprise. Never figured I'd shack up with an UnArcana gal, but she's pretty sensible, all told."

"Good for you."

"Now, you didn't *just* accept my invite to catch up on girl talk," Mantovani said as Roslyn started to peruse the menu. "And while it's lovely to see you and I plan to talk your *ear* off about Sarah, what is it you *actually* want?"

Roslyn shook her head repressively but sighed.

"How's the lasagna?" she asked.

"Disturbingly lacking in curry but acceptable," the other Tau Cetan told her.

Tau Cetan lasagna was closer to what had been called *butter chicken lasagna* on Earth than the traditional Italian dish. That was what happened when a planet was colonized by a joint French-Indian expedition, after all.

Roslyn tapped her order in on the menu and then laid it aside.

"I did actually want to catch up, but the timeline Admiral Jakab dropped on my ship last night should have prevented that," she admitted. "Except we have a problem.

"We're trying to source the exterior sensor pods needed to finish our repairs, and my people are just getting crickets from Centurion Base. I figured that was your department and you might be able to give me some insight into what's happening."

Or, potentially, an end run around it, but she didn't need to say that part aloud.

"Really?" Mantovani looked curious. She gestured at her wrist-comp. "May I? Send me the list of parts."

"Of course," Roslyn allowed. It was, after all, rude to poke at a computer while having lunch with someone.

A holographic display appeared in front of the logistics officer. Even Roslyn, sitting across from Mantovani, couldn't make out what the other woman was looking at.

"Yeah, that's what I was expecting for your wish list," Mantovani murmured. "SR-One-Thirty-Six-Ds and SRL-Two-Forties." She shook her head. "We have all of those in stock."

"Can you look at the requisitions my people put in?" Roslyn asked.

"Can you perform stupid heroics and acquire medals?" the other woman asked drily. "Already on it."

Roslyn made a touché gesture with her hand. She should know better than to interfere with someone investigating their own specialty.

Though she *would* argue against "stupid heroics" being *her* specialty.

"Okay..." Mantovani trailed off thoughtfully. "Requisition updates and further requests are noted, but the entire req is in limbo. Why?"

"That's what I was hoping you could tell me," Roslyn said, her attention turning to the steward approaching with two steaming hot dishes of pasta.

It seemed Mantovani had learned, much like Roslyn had, that mess decks and lounges were far better with prepackaged sauces and dried pasta than most other dishes. Good chefs could do a lot with RMN food supplies...but the RMN also provided some dishes that were hard to mess up.

"Okay," Mantovani repeated. "All of your sensor-pod requisitions are on hold due to lack of supply. But *that* should have kicked off an order to the fleet train for Second Fleet. Our supplies are a secondary depot for *them*, after all, and we don't actually have an independent line back to Logistics Command."

Roslyn waited for the other woman to realize her fettucine had arrived, then shrugged and dug into her own lasagna. As Mantovani had noted, it was the traditional Italian version. Flavorful enough, in its own way, but definitely not properly curried.

Mantovani finally sighed, looked down at her pasta and sighed again. She then took a forkful of food while marshaling her thoughts.

"So, this one *looks* like it's on us," she finally told Roslyn.

"I figured that it was Centurion Base's fault somewhere, yes," the Mage-Commander replied lightly.

"No, I mean on Centurion Base logistics," Mantovani corrected. "There's a weird intersect between how we handle orders from the fleet train and how we handle parts availability for requisitions.

"Our orders for the fleet train are based off a calculation that includes the space in the transport carrying the supplies, a priority rating on a given item and how much of an item is on hand. Follow me?"

"That sounds logical and normal, yes," Roslyn agreed. "But if you have the clusters on hand..."

"Then why aren't you getting them?" Mantovani asked. "Because requisition fulfillment is based on *available* parts, which is parts left after assignment.

"So, we have forty-three SR-One-Thirty-Six-Ds and a hundred and twelve SRL-Two-Forties," the logistics officer concluded. "That's enough to fully equip three destroyers...or *one* Class Six defense platform."

"And they're marked for use?" Roslyn said. That didn't sound right.

"They're marked as *reserved for use*," Mantovani corrected. "We have a tag to allow us to reserve certain stocks of parts for the defensive squadron, but using *that* is supposed to be accompanied by an adjustment to the stock numbers used for the resupply orders.

"So, every one of those two types of sensor pod on hand has been flagged as reserved for immediate use by the defensive platforms, but our base supply levels are assumed to cover that reserve *plus* enough to repair at least a cruiser."

Mantovani shook her head.

"When that change in the reserve quantities was made, we should have updated the base quantities in the system. Instead, the reserve was set *equal* to our base quantity, which meant new parts wouldn't get ordered unless the reserve was used."

"So, my ship is on the edge of missing a summons from our Battle Group commander because of a datawork glitch?" Roslyn asked.

"That's what it looks like, yes," Mantovani said carefully. "And..."

She trailed off and took another bite of pasta.

"And?" Roslyn prompted between her own bites.

"Look, I can't say anything about the superior officers in my own chain of command," Mantovani said. "*Someone* ordered the reserve numbers adjusted relatively recently. While *Voice of the Forgotten* has been here.

"I cannot assume that was intentionally targeted at you," she continued, her tone suggesting something different. "Such an action would be quite petty and unbecoming an officer of the Royal Martian Navy."

"It would be," Roslyn agreed virtuously. That meant either Beaumont or Ó Luain himself. In both cases, it was exactly as her old friend labeled it—petty and unbecoming an officer of the RMN.

She figured it was Beaumont. She also knew that Mantovani wouldn't tell her who it had been.

"But." Mantovani paused with her fork in her hand and stabbed the air with a finger. "*I* am the department head for parts and logistics on this godforsaken space station."

"Meaning?" Roslyn asked.

"I've overridden the reserve lockout and authorized your requisition requests," Mantovani told her. "Replacement parts for *our* supplies will come from Second Fleet within six days or so, so unless one of our defensive forts is somehow in the path of a solar flare or a near-hit from an anti-matter warhead in the next week, no one will ever realize the difference.

"But your parts should be in your people's hands within the next hour."

Roslyn saluted Mantovani with her wine glass.

"I appreciate it, Ankita," she told her high school friend. "I'm glad you were here."

She'd probably have been able to fix the problem either way. But she figured she'd have needed to blackmail, threaten or sleep with the logistics officer if they hadn't been an old friend.

"I am glad to help," Mantovani told her—then grinned and flipped her wrist-comp display to a hologram that Roslyn *could* see, of a redheaded woman somewhere around Roslyn and Mantovani's age trying desperately not to be thrown to the ground by a large, hopefully domesticated, lizard.

"And *this* is Sarah!" the logistics officer said triumphantly. "And Thunder. I *warned* you I was going to talk your ear off!"

CHAPTER 6

THE CITY IN THE BACKGROUND of the video feed was absolutely gorgeous. The citizens of Ostia Antica, the third world of the Aquila System, had spared no expense on their new capital.

The city of Ficana was built around and over the delta of the immense river that split Ostia Antica's largest continent, a waterway to put even Earth's Amazon to shame. Intentionally mimicking the styles of the ancient Roman Empire, fake and real stone cladding was wrapped around buildings that rarely rose over thirty stories—but were, in many cases, suspended half a dozen meters above the surface of the River Tiberius.

Sharon's ability to interface with *Ring of Fire*'s computers meant she could even source the origin of the name of both planet and city in passing, but her focus was on the pirate transmission she was watching.

Colonel Ajello would have been furious if he knew anyone aboard the transport was watching the illegal video feed, but *Sharon* controlled his internal security systems...and she didn't think the ex–Republic Space Assault Force officer knew that.

The pirate transmission had begun shortly after the transport had entered orbit of Ostia Antica. No one aboard *Ring of Fire* had taken official notice of it, though Sharon knew that Lieutenant Raoul Costa, the ship's communications officer, was *aware* of it.

Ring of Fire was true First Legion, part of the space and military force that tied together Admiral Ridwan Muhammad's pocket empire. They would not deign to officially notice local resistance.

And that would allow Colonel Ajello and his bridge crew to pretend they didn't know how the First Legion kept order...or was providing the indentured workers *Ring of Fire* would transport to the Exeter System.

"We all know that conscription notices were sent out two days ago," a male voice said on the pirate transmission. The speaker wasn't visible—they were keeping the camera focus on the blocks of people stuck standing in the blistering heat of a northern Ostia Antica summer.

"No one bothered to tell people what they were being conscripted *for*," the voice continued, "so now these people are standing out in the sun, suffering. For what reason? Because the *Legion*"—the name dripped with vitriol—"decided they should."

The video was zoomed in enough that Sharon could watch a middle-aged woman start to crumple. Likely from heat exhaustion—but a black-armored Legion Planetary Security trooper was wading into the crowd toward her a moment later.

Any illusion that the PlanSec legionnaire might be coming to help the woman vanished as their stunstick flashed out toward the first indenture that didn't move fast enough for the legionnaire.

The collapsing woman was dragged back to her feet by the armored figure.

"You can see the great care that the Legion is taking of the citizens they're drafting," the voice on the pirate transmission said sardonically. "*Ten thousand* people were called up, my friends. That's one in every hundred souls in Ficana—but does the Legion care about the families they're tearing apart?"

The camera shifted around to focus on the descending transports.

"And now spaceships," the speaker said bitterly. "So, this isn't just work here on Ostia, people. They're taking our parents and siblings *away*. Away where? No one tells us.

"If you for one moment doubted how our new masters see us, look at these people—innocent of any crime!—being herded like cattle!"

More PlanSec legionnaires were visible on the video feed now as the big transport shuttles swept in. They were being careful enough of the safety zones of the thrusters—and another virtual "screen" showed Sharon the status of *Ring of Fire*'s heavy personnel landers.

Those five landers were designed to deliver half of the assault transport's capacity to the surface in a single maneuver. Normally, they'd carry five Space Assault Regiments—a total of five thousand soldiers in combat exosuits, supported by tanks and heavy weapons.

They could probably fit ten thousand draftees aboard in one trip, Sharon calculated. It wouldn't be pleasant...but from what her pirate transmission was saying, she doubted her employers cared.

"Hey, you there!" a different voice shouted on the pirate transmission.

The camera spun as the man who'd been speaking turned to look at the shouter. A trio of PlanSec legionnaires had apparently traced the pirate transmission to its source.

"*Shit*," the speaker muttered. A SmartDart stungun fired before he could do more, and the camera was pointed at the sky for a few seconds before the transmission went dark.

If Sharon had still had a body, she figured she'd have felt sick. Her official updates were sanitized, just numbers of workers loaded onto the transport.

"Deveraux," Colonel Ajello interrupted her thoughts. "What's the status on the loading?"

"Major Trengove is sending us full automatic updates," she told him instantly. "We have fifteen hundred of the transportees aboard the landers already. She has not included an updated time to completion."

"Fair." Ajello grunted. Ignoring her, he turned his attention to his XO—but Sharon's attention was back on the bridge now. That was a step away from focusing on the horror going on below.

"Gerel, keep an eye on the local air traffic," he instructed Lieutenant Colonel Gerel Rooijakkers, his heavy-featured second-in-command. "I just got a security ping from the perimeter around the loading.

"One idiot with a camera isn't really a problem—but one idiot with an *airplane* can cause us a giant headache."

Sharon hadn't known about the ping to Ajello's implants. That was a reminder that, while she had access to a lot of *Ring of Fire*'s systems—and was slowly and carefully converting *access* into *control*—she didn't see everything aboard the transport.

"I'll coordinate with PlanSec," Rooijakkers confirmed, her tone... grumpy.

"Shit flows downhill, Gerel," Ajello said with a chuckle. "And I don't like our local jackbooted bootlickers either. Some of them get it..."

"But only some," Rooijakkers said. "And you get to delegate. Do I?"

"No," Ajello told her firmly. "*One* of us needs to be talking to PlanSec. If shit really hits the fan, only you or I can order a shot at the planet."

Sharon was glad she had no body to shiver. *Ring of Fire* wasn't particularly heavily armed, but the only weapons she had that could be used against an aircraft were the one-gigawatt Rapid-Fire Laser Anti-Missile turrets.

RFLAMs were designed to take out missiles traveling at a significant chunk of lightspeed. No planetary aircraft would survive a hit from the theoretically defensive weapon system—the beam would go right *through* said aircraft and hit the surface like a large bomb.

And her two senior officers would give that order without even blinking to complete their mission. She wasn't sure Ajello or Rooijakkers actually registered the Aquilans as *people.*

"Haven't been any suicidal idiots yet," Rooijakkers pointed out. "Should be an easy-enough load."

"Sixteen million of them on Ostia and we've already shipped twenty thousand to Exeter," Ajello said. "Only a matter of time till somebody does something stupid. I *don't* like these pirate transmissions.

"We can't take wrist-comps away from the population—and even if we did, we can't take communicators away from people with aircraft and spacecraft. The last thing we need is agitprop on the air."

Calling the transmission Sharon had been watching *agitation propaganda* was...a stretch. But that was the story Ajello had to tell himself. Somehow, the darkly tanned soldier was okay with everything the First Legion was doing.

Sharon noted absently that the first assault lander was now lifting off. Twenty-two hundred people aboard, according to Major Trengove's update.

Even considering that the normal load was people in two-point-five-meter combat exosuits, the indentures had to be packed in like sardines.

Another notification told her that the transmission she'd been watching was back online. She activated it—another virtual window wasn't much. Her entire life was just virtual computer windows at this point.

It wasn't like she even had *eyeballs*. Just computers hooked up through what had been her optic nerve.

"We regret to inform our listeners and viewers that our man on the ground, Teodor Ragno, has been detained by Planetary Security," a distorted feminine voice announced. There was no camera feed attached to the signal this time, just an audio message.

"Ragno risked his life and freedom to bring the truth to all of you about the fate of the people who received draft notices earlier this week. They are being loaded onto heavy shuttles and taken into orbit—and our sources in the orbital infrastructure tell me they are being loaded aboard one of the First Legion's interstellar transports.

"I'm sorry, friends, but based off what has happened to people loaded onto those ships before, they won't be coming back," the woman said flatly. "In-system labor drafts have a chance to come home, but we have no reason to believe that anyone transported to another star system will ever be released by the Legion.

"Mourn your families, my friends, because I fear the Legion will never give them back—and I, my friends, must mourn Teodor Ragno. Our sources tell me that he has been added to the indentures being sent into orbit."

Sharon's entire world was virtual—and *Ring of Fire* was her entire world. It was her domain, her fiefdom, and she knew every part of the big assault transport like the back of her hand.

Or would have, if she still *had* hands.

She knew that *Ring of Fire* had initially had four stolen Mage brains aboard, wired into concealed nutrient vats, to provide the ship with interstellar capacity. Three of those had been removed, the First Legion economizing on its limited supply of "Prometheus Drive Units."

Sharon remained, now awake and more capable than she had ever been while she'd been simply a component in the machinery of *Ring's* FTL drive. Not all of the capability was used to her masters' benefit—and she suspected they had no idea how much power their Promethean servants wielded over their vessels.

She was quite certain, for example, that Colonel Ajello didn't know that she was listening in on all of the senior staff meetings. At the same time, she was surveying the incoming indentures and setting up a macro to see if she could locate Teodor Ragno.

The dead teenager was morbidly curious as to what the agitator's fate would be. If he was brought aboard, it would give her a chance to follow the fate of a single one of her passengers.

Even for her—perhaps *especially* for her—it was easy to lose sight of the individuals in a cargo of over ten thousand people.

"The first load is complete," Ajello told the staff meeting calmly, bringing her attention back to the room with *Ring of Fire's* officers. All of them were former Space Assault Force. These days, that division was supposedly meaningless—everyone was simply Legion—but it still meant something to the officers and personnel that made up the First Legion.

"The first load?" Rooijakkers asked. "Our capacity is only ten thousand."

"Our capacity for *soldiers*, with full equipment and supporting vehicles, is ten thousand," Ajello pointed out. "Our instructions from Command in Mackenzie are to load up another eight thousand. We have the life support and the space and, well..."

He shrugged eloquently.

"Indentured laborers have lower amenity expectations than elite soldiers," he concluded. "We'll be fine. We'll want to cut the timing closer, if we can.

"Zhao, sit down with Deveraux and the nav computer when we're done here," he instructed the navigator. "We'll want to see if we can tighten up the course to Exeter. I know we can't cut the number of jumps by much, but if we can slice even thirty minutes off each jump, that gains us a quarter of a day."

It was thirteen light-years, roughly, from Aquila to Exeter. Sharon knew that without even checking. The locations of the four inhabited systems and the handful of bases the Legion maintained were burned into her brain now.

"Understood, sir," Zhao confirmed.

"We also have an update from Legion Intel," Ajello told his officers. "Operation Broomhandle is complete. While I'm not going to pretend I understand how the Protectorate's Trackers work, Intel tells me they are over ninety percent certain they've cut the trail from DEL-Three-T-Three.

"That means Legion Command is downgrading the immediate threat from Mars for the foreseeable future. In the long run, the Admiral has every intention of taking us back, but we have more immediate concerns."

The briefing room was silent. Everyone clearly understood what Ajello meant, though *Sharon* wasn't sure she was fully up to date.

"Any updates on the K-One-Five-Nine-D incident?" Lieutenant Ramiz Young asked. Young was a dark-skinned woman of Turkish descent, the tactical officer responsible for the assault transport's limited weaponry.

"Officially, no," Ajello replied. "Unofficially, our cruisers in the area had another encounter. *Someone* else is scouting the system, much as we are."

It took Sharon a moment to find K-159-D in her databases. A blue giant star system thirty light-years farther into the dark than Exeter or any of the Legion's systems. There was nothing of importance there...but it was flagged in her database as a danger zone.

"Rumor *I* heard says Intel thinks they even know who we ran into," Rooijakkers noted. "But they aren't sharing."

"Either way, the K-One-Five-Nine-D incident is part of why we're stepping up work to bring Exeter online," Ajello told them all. "The system was supposed to be sufficiently separate from our main territory to help hide it, and *nobody* looks for habitable gas-giant moons."

Calling Exeter-I-7 *habitable* was a stretch in Sharon's opinion, but the air could be breathed—with filtration—and roughly half the planet tolerated liquid water during at least *some* of the complex eleven-season natural cycle induced by being a gas giant's moon.

"Once we *get* to Exeter, we're getting locked down for a bit," Ajello continued. "We're playing test subject for the refit yards. The strangers at K-One-Five-Nine and the new pressure from Mars is making Command twitchy—and the gunship yards are almost online."

"We're picking up friends?" Young asked.

"Exactly. *Ring* is receiving a refit to carry half a dozen gunships, which is expected to finish up just as the first half-dozen of them roll out. I'm not going to mind having a few extra teeth as we wander around the dark on our own."

"Me either," the tactical officer said.

It might be a pain to *Sharon*, though. She'd been counting on some of that wandering around the dark on their own for her own potential plans.

"One last thing, people," Rooijakkers said as it seemed the Colonel was finishing up. "We have a request from Legion R&D. They want a full report from all of the department heads—and any of your section leads who have a particularly enthusiastic opinion—on the value of the active PDU."

Up until that moment, Sharon's attention had been divided. With the computers linked into her brain, the Promethean was far more capable of multitasking than any living human.

Now, though, Rooijakkers had her undivided attention.

"R&D is doing a one-year reassessment of the reactivation protocols," Rooijakkers continued. "After what *Battlemaster* did to the Martian cruiser that caught her, there's a major argument in favor of the APDUs. Connors was key to their victory there—and from what we can tell, the Martians turned the same stunt around on *Armadillo*. And *Armadillo*'s PDUs were still passive."

If Sharon had still had skin, it would have crawled. The calm euphemism of *Prometheus Drive Unit* hid the reality of what the Prometheans were.

Of course, what *she* called Prometheans was what Rooijakkers was calling an Active Prometheus Drive Unit—one of the murdered Mage brains restored to consciousness and self-awareness.

She'd spoken with William Connors, the Promethean aboard the cruiser *Battlemaster*. Not since his mission into Martian space, but she knew him. The two dozen or so Prometheans were likely communicating more than the Legion realized.

"Deveraux is useful," Zhao murmured. "She knows more about the ship's FTL navigation and our jump limits than I can ever learn, I suspect. She has...nothing else to do."

"Put it in the report," Ajello ordered. "And make sure it hits the Link by whatever deadline R&D gave us. Not our call if we wake up more of the PDUs. I know the Admiral doesn't like having them on true warships—but *Battlemaster* was the test and seems to have proven out the concept."

Sharon had no idea if the reports on her own actions would help her fellows or not. On the other hand, she suspected she could make some changes to the reports that no one would ever notice...subtly nudge the message one way or another.

The question, of course, was whether she thought it was *better* for an enslaved, bodiless mind to be aware of their situation...

CHAPTER 7

"I LOVE YOU MORE than anything, Kelly, but could you *please* do that stretch when I'm elsewhere?"

Kelly's husband's tone was pained, and she looked over at Mike Kelzin, *Rhapsody in Purple*'s First Pilot. She smiled sheepishly at him as she popped her elbows back into a normal human range of motion.

She was far from the level of a combat cyborg like one of the Protectorate's Bionic Commandos or the Republic's Augments, but she was *definitely* a cyborg at this point. Included in her extensive covert modifications was the fact that she had roughly four times the mobility of a regular human in most of her joints.

But to *keep* those cybernetics covert, they had to be reengineered "natural" joints—which meant they needed to be stretched and moved to kept mobile.

And the first time she'd used that flexibility in bed with her husband and wife, she'd very nearly made Mike throw up when he'd realized what was going on. There were limits, it turned out, to even his open-mindedness.

"Sorry, running short on time," she admitted to him. "Xi is up on the bridge and we're jumping into DEL-Three-T-Three in about half an hour. Trying to make sure everything is...well, where it should be before we get to work."

Her husband chuckled.

"And Xi has everything perfectly in hand," he reminded her.

Xi Wu was the third member of their marriage and *Rhapsody*'s senior Ship's Mage—and official executive officer, though the role was split between Xi and Mike in practice.

"This is true," Kelly conceded. "But this is the first time I'm going to be dealing with a Navy operation where I need to actually argue about who is in command. Normally, we just keep the stealth ships off to the side."

"You worked well enough with Chambers," her husband said. "You'll be fine."

"There's a difference between *working* with Mage-Commander Chambers, who despite her rank and experiences is almost a decade younger than me, and *arguing* with Mage–Vice Admiral Jakab, who is almost *two* decades older than me," she said.

"He's another one of Damien's old backups, so I can't imagine he's going to be a problem, but this directorship and the rank they gave me with it..."

Kelly shook her head and sighed.

"I *understand* what the Board and the Mountain are thinking," she said. "But it's going to add a new awkwardness to our relationship with the Navy."

"And you are now in command of the other stealth ship Captains," Mike agreed genially. "You were all equals before, but now the Board has made it clear that *you* are in charge."

"I haven't been in charge of anything bigger than *Rhapsody* before," she admitted—and then smiled again as Mike crossed the bedroom to start massaging her shoulders.

"And *that* was a big leap from being part of the crew of a bigger spy ship," he reminded her as his fingers worked on her knots. "You're ready for this, love. I felt the same way the first time I was told I was the senior pilot and in charge of everybody flying off a ship."

"Yeah, but that was *years* ago," she said.

"And so was you taking command of *Rhapsody*," Mike replied. "My star is hitched to yours, love. MISS pays me plenty and I like *Rhapsody*. I can't see them turning 'Director of Stealth Ships' into a desk job anytime soon, which means Xi and I are here with you.

"Always."

She leaned back into his fingers and purred.

"I don't deserve you two, you know," she told him.

"Kelly, I've been thinking that about you and Xi about every five minutes since you first asked me to be more than friends with benefits," he whispered in her ear. "I don't deserve you *or* her, let alone both of you!

"I figure Xi is the only one who thinks she deserves this marriage!"

The DEL-3T3 System really didn't have much to recommend it. It had a massive white dwarf star, six rocky planets—none habitable, a mix of too cold, too hot and too toxic—two gas giants and two asteroid belts.

But it was where the First Legion had hidden away *Fallen Dragon*, the former Republic Interstellar Navy logistics transport they'd used as a logistics depot.

Since *Dragon* had been stripped of the Mage brains that powered her Prometheus Drive, she'd been unable to escape when Kelly and Chambers had arrived with their respective ships.

A daring raid had delivered the logistics ship into Martian hands, and now the battleship *Pax Dramatis* orbited one of DEL-3T3's gas giants directly above the transport.

"I make it four cruisers and a dozen destroyers set up around *Dramatis*," Kelly's tactical officer, Nika Shvets, reported. They were an androgynous figure with long blond hair—and could probably use that hair to kill someone in at least three different ways.

So far as Kelly knew, Shvets had never *actually* worked as an assassin...but they'd definitely been *trained* as one and worked as a sniper in several messy situations. They were *Rhapsody in Purple*'s "wetwork specialist," working in coordination with their squad from the Bionic Combat Regiment.

"The Battle Group has been expanded," Kelly noted. "That's arguably a task force now—or even a fleet."

"I make no pretense of understanding how our Navy friends decide what is a fleet," Shvets conceded. "But my understanding is that this is now considered *part* of a draft fleet?"

"Seventh Fleet," Kelly confirmed quietly. "But Mage-Admiral Medici and *Masamune* haven't left Sol yet."

There were, she understood, four more cruisers in the Mercedes System. The Legion had used a criminal settlement there to fence some of the loot from their raiding across the frontier. *Shield of Glory* and *Oath of Righteousness*, two older *Guardian*-class battleships, were also positioned along the frontier near where they suspected the Legion had their lair.

"Inform Admiral Jakab that we're in-system, Trixie," Kelly ordered Trixie Buday.

The young woman had acquired a streak of bright red through her naturally blond hair, the spy ship captain noticed.

Potentially, she was imitating Kelly's own inability to keep a hair color for more than two or three weeks. Kelly certainly wasn't going to enforce a dress code on her ship.

They were *spies*, after all, not military officers.

"Nika, is *Voice of the Forgotten* back yet?" she asked her tactical officer. "And which *Rhapsodies* are here?"

They chuckled at her.

"One question at a time?" they asked with faux plaintiveness. "*Voice* is en route from Legatus, ETA about three days. *Rhapsody in Vermillion* is here. *Rhapsody in Kaleidoscope* is due in four days. *Rhapsody in Verdigris* is due in five, once they finish their R&R."

Kelly had known the official statuses of the spy ships. She now knew exactly where all eight of the stealth vessels were supposed to be—but she also knew that *spy ships* were quite possibly not where they were supposed to be.

"We're still a few minutes' transmission lag out from the Battle Group," Buday reported. "We won't hear back from *Pax Dramatis* for at least seven minutes."

"And we're a nice long flight from rendezvousing with the Battle Group unless one of us does something unnecessary," Kelly agreed.

"But believe me, I'm in no hurry to dicker with a friend of a friend over how many destroyers he's giving me!"

CHAPTER 8

LIEUTENANT COMMANDER Evelia Dresdner's office was always dimly lit. It was, in Roslyn's fully educated opinion, the darkest working space aboard *Voice of the Forgotten*.

That was because regulations required any place where humans were working to be kept at a certain minimum level of illumination. Roslyn's chief engineer, however, found that level of illumination distasteful.

The dim lighting in the office was one of a slew of accommodations Roslyn made for her occasionally tetchy engineer—and in trade, she got a warship that had survived a clash with a squadron of pirate gunships and then gone on to take out a First Legion cruiser over ten times her size.

"Are the installations complete?" Roslyn asked Dresdner.

She allowed the other woman to send a subordinate to senior staff meetings and to make the daily reports by recorded video, but she still made a point of inserting herself into Dresdner's office at least once a week.

"They are," the engineer confirmed, sliding a fresh cup of coffee across the table to Roslyn. "Fascinating, how suddenly all of the parts we needed became available at once, isn't it?"

"Admiral's orders tend to create that kind of priority," Roslyn demurred. "Helped us find the glitch in their inventory system."

"Glitch," Dresdner echoed, taking a sip of her own coffee. A tiny flicker of light in front of the engineer's eyes told Roslyn she was looking up data on her contact lens.

"That's how it was explained to me, yes," Roslyn noted.

"I know. Commander Mantovani sent me the summary explanation," the engineer said. "Have you ever heard the phrase *Once is an accident, twice is coincidence, three times is enemy action?*"

"I may not have completed the full course load at the RMN Academy, but I did have a *few* courses," Roslyn said. "Why? What did I *not* hear about?"

That question was sharp. If there'd been multiple incidents of parts issues, she should have heard about it before now.

"There is always *some* crap around supplies," Dresdner told her. "*Always.* So long as we can sort it out with the local logistics team, Engineering doesn't bring it up. The Captain is the antimatter missile of that kind of squabble, sir."

"I see." Roslyn considered thoughtfully. "So, how many problems *did* we have, Lieutenant Commander?"

Dresdner *never* met Roslyn's eyes—or anyone else's, so far as the red-headed Mage-Commander knew. Now, though, she seemed to be looking distinctly away from Roslyn.

"Eleven."

"Eleven," Roslyn repeated. "*Eleven?*"

"Not all major," Dresdner countered immediately. "But we have eleven incidents of supply or support issues that caused or nearly caused delays in the original repair schedule.

"Mantovani calls what happened to our sensor pods a glitch—but someone in her logistics team *would* have seen the increase in reserve quantities on their standard daily reports.

"It should have been bounced up the chain with a question—and even if it wasn't *questioned*, it should have been accounted for in the stocking levels." Dresdner shook her head.

"Someone in Logistics knowingly looked the other way, sir," she concluded. "We had a similar problem with the parts for our lasers. They're not currently being manufactured, so the only parts we *have* are the leftovers from the RIN."

Voice of the Forgotten had been refitted in a secondary yard. The people working on her had been waiting on the supply of standard Martian ten-gigawatt battle lasers...and they'd had a stash of *Republic* twenty-giga-watt battle lasers on hand.

So, instead of twelve ten-gigawatt lasers, *Voice* carried eight *twenty*-giga-watt lasers. She paid for it in a few ways, and one of them was occasional issues with parts.

"The parts existed but got locked down under an Intelligence review seal," Dresdner told her. "Given how standard the RIN's twenty-gigawatt beam was, that made no sense.

"So, I fixed it."

Roslyn took a moment to drink her coffee and process that informa-tion as she looked around. Dresdner's office was a chaotic disaster that only made sense to her, with stacks of data disks and multiple holoproject-ors filling the place with information.

When she'd first visited, there'd been one expensive black leather chair behind the desk and a standard folding chair in front of it. Now, in re-sponse to Roslyn's own visits, she suspected, the chair in *front* of the desk was just as expensive and automatically ergonomic as the one Dresdner used herself.

"Did you *hack* Centurion Base's systems?" she finally asked.

"No," Dresdner objected. "I simply reviewed the status of the parts we needed and...modified our requests to match the necessary criteria."

"Sufficiently so to break an Intelligence seal?" Roslyn said.

"That was the most complicated one, but yes," Dresdner agreed. "We got around most of our problems, but I couldn't get past the inventory glitch on the sensor pods. That needed someone senior in Logistics to override the system."

"You needed Mantovani to fix the problem," Roslyn concluded. "Which I got her to."

"And only two of my *dumber* techs think you slept with her to manage that," the engineer said brightly.

Roslyn swallowed her initial response. Sometimes, her engineer said things that *no one* should admit to the ship's Captain.

"I didn't hear that," she finally noted. "If someone was screwing with *Voice*'s repairs...why?"

"That's outside my department," Dresdner admitted, nothing in her voice showing that she'd just been mildly chastised. "I traced a few of the orders back, but none of them ended in the same place."

"Beaumont," Roslyn guessed. A bitter, washed-up Mage-Captain trying to make a junior look bad... She could see it, even if it seemed out of character for the RMN.

"No," Dresdner countered. "That was my first guess as well and I checked that. Whoever set this up *wanted* it to look like her, but while some of the orders came through her division, they didn't come from her."

Roslyn sighed and shook her head.

"So, we don't know who or why," she grumbled. "But someone was screwing with my ship."

"I mean, you know it was an O-Six or above and someone with command authority at Centurion Base," Dresdner told her cheerfully. "Almost certainly not Beaumont, but that still only leaves you with half a dozen people."

One of whom, Roslyn knew, was the *Commodore* in command of the refit yard.

"Whoever it was, I'm reasonably sure the reason was..." Roslyn trailed off, trying to find the right word.

"Petty?" she finally concluded. "I don't think this is worth flagging to JAG or Navy Intelligence. This strikes me more as people trying to make me look bad."

"I wasn't going to let that happen, sir," Dresdner replied.

Roslyn chuckled softly.

"I suspect it would take more than *Voice* leaving a refit yard late to deplete the goodwill that comes along with the Ruby," she murmured. She didn't wear the Ruby Medal of Valor in her working uniform, but it still hung over everything she did.

Her understanding was that she'd need to screw up *incredibly* to even delay her promotion to Mage-Captain. She needed more seasoning—she *agreed* with that assessment—before she was ready to command a heavier warship, but if she plodded through a couple of years aboard *Voice* without incident, her promotion was guaranteed.

Roslyn had earned her medals the hard way, after all.

"Let's keep everything about that mess to ourselves, Dresdner," she ordered. "It's as dealt with as it needs to be, and we have more important things to do."

A soft chime from her wrist-comp warned her of the first of those "more important things."

"Almost time?" Dresdner asked.

"Victor will be making the jump into DEL-Three-T-Three in about forty minutes," Roslyn confirmed. "I need to be on the bridge for that. Thanks for the coffee, Commander."

"It is the tiniest of repayments for the understanding you show, sir," Dresdner murmured.

"This ship survived our last visit to this system thanks to you, Dresdner," Roslyn said. "*That* was the only repayment I ever needed."

CHAPTER 9

"JUMP COMPLETE."

Mage–Lieutenant Commander Lalit Victor stepped back from the simulacrum as the world rippled back into a semblance of stability.

Roslyn waited for her newly promoted senior navigator to get clear of the large semiliquid silver model, and then moved in and took over the main seat on the bridge.

The seat automatically adjusted to her body and lifted her to where she could both see the screens surrounding her and lay her hands on the simulacrum itself. The runic matrices woven through her starship all centered there, on a silver miniature of the ship that, in a key way, *was* the vessel.

From this position, Roslyn could unleash the magical power that ran in her veins—and those runic matrices would amplify any spell she cast dozens or even hundreds of times. Those matrices were what allowed a Mage to take a starship between the stars—and were also the single most powerful weapon available to the Captain of a Royal Martian Navy warship.

"Salminen, is the Battle Group where I expect it to be?" she asked. Thanks to the Link the Protectorate had acquired from the Republic, her ship no longer arrived in a star system blind.

Thanks to a quantum-entanglement-based faster-than-light communications network, Roslyn knew that Battle Group *Pax Dramatis* was in orbit by *Fallen Dragon* and had been joined by several of the Martian Interstellar Security Service's stealth ships.

She had suspicions about what her duties as a destroyer captain in the Battle Group were going to be—and they didn't involve the "plodding along without incident" that her career needed.

Not when Captain Kelly LaMonte was back in the DEL-3T3 System, at least!

"All ships are where they were supposed to be per the last Link update," her tiny tactical officer replied. "Estimated time to enter formation per Navigation's course is eleven hours."

Technically, that report was Lalit Victor's job, but no one expected much from a Mage who'd *just* jumped, and the Chief Petty Officer supporting Victor at the nav console was clearly fine letting the ship's third-in-command give his report.

"All right. Salucci, inform the Battle Group we are in-system, and give them Navigation's ETA," Roslyn ordered her coms officer.

The big blonde nodded silently, her attention already on her console.

"If they can send us an orbit and formation instructions, that would help," Roslyn concluded drily. That was a request no one really needed to send—but protocol was written with a lot of redundancy.

Just in case.

"Victor, go fall over," she continued to her navigator. "I have the bridge."

"Captain has the bridge," Victor confirmed, bracing to attention for a moment to salute, then obeying her order to rest with alacrity.

"The rest of you, don't fall asleep on me yet," Roslyn told the bridge crew with a chuckle. "Just because we have a *battleship* in-system doesn't mean this wasn't hostile territory two months ago."

And the First Legion almost certainly still knew the system better than they did!

"Welcome back to the DEL-Three-T-Three System, Captain Chambers," Mage–Vice Admiral Jakab told Roslyn after they'd established a Link connection.

They were probably close enough that the FTL communicator was unnecessary, but the general attitude of Navy com officers was that since they *had* it they should *use* it.

"Thank you, sir," Roslyn told him. She'd retreated to her office, just off the bridge, to take the call. "I'm glad we managed to make your deadline. Repairs are always...fraught. Especially when you know your ship missed the age cutoff for being scrapped by, what, two months?"

Her commanding officer chuckled.

"I'm not sure," he admitted. "I only ever looked at the number of *Honor*-class destroyers we were scrapping, not the criteria they were using to decide which ones to keep."

The RMN had built various iterations of the *Honor*-class destroyers like *Voice of the Forgotten* for almost a century. War with the Republic of Faith and Reason, the secessionist UnArcana Worlds, had seen rapid re-development of military technology, and the base design was now three generations out of date.

But since the RMN was only up to around fifty of the *Cataphract* and *Bard of Winter* escort destroyer classes, they'd kept fifty of the newer *Honor*-class ships in commission.

For a while. The new Protectorate Parliament had authorized a three-hundred-ship Navy, calling for a hundred and eighty destroyers. Scrapping half of the *Honor*-class ships had provided resources and crews for new destroyers, but the various yards had built fifteen *Bard*-class ships the previous year.

And they were *accelerating*. The three-hundred-ship-Navy plan had been attached to the first absolutely immense appropriations bill of the new Parliament. Going from just over two hundred ships to the planned number was going to be a stretch for Roslyn's service.

"I think Dresdner was the key," she finally told her boss. "If she and her people hadn't done as good a job of holding together the bits the Legion didn't peel off, I'm not sure she'd have been worth fixing."

"Keep talking like that and she might get promoted out from under you," Jakab warned.

"You already took my executive officer, my senior engineering assistant, my navigator..." Roslyn held up her hands. "I have not held back the praise for the officers and spacers under my command who deserved it."

"You have not," Jakab agreed. "And I've signed a great many promotions and medals for the people under your command. Still. This system must have memories for you."

Roslyn glanced at the display on the wallscreen behind Jakab's hologram. It showed a two-dimensional model of the star system, including icons for *Fallen Dragon* and the entire Battle Group *Pax Dramatis*.

"Honestly, sir, I have worse memories of Mercedes," she admitted. "And that's one of our worlds. We didn't find slaves here—and if we'd taken any real damage against the cruiser, we'd be dead.

"We were lucky. I only wish the result had been more useful."

Jakab grimaced.

"Agreed," he told her. "We had to release Ajam from his contract and send the Navy Tracker we were lent on to other tasks. Without some evidence of a Legion presence, we can't justify hanging on to the Trackers."

Nunzio "Nebeljäger" Ajam had been the mercenary bounty hunter and Tracker Roslyn had hired to follow the Legion from Mercedes to the DEL-3T3 System.

She realized she was slightly disappointed that the Tracker was no longer around. He was quite attractive and had made a pass at her while he was aboard her ship...and almost as importantly, had taken no for an answer, given that he *was* aboard her ship.

"Like we spoke about before, then," she said. "We pick a random direction and start sweeping stars until we find something interesting?"

"I've spent the last few days sorting out details with Commodore LaMonte, but that's the thrust of it, yes," Jakab agreed.

"Commodore, sir?" Roslyn asked.

"LaMonte is now Director of Stealth Ship Operations for MISS," the Vice Admiral told her. "The Navy agreed with the MISS Board that the role is *at least* equivalent to one of our Commodores—and giving her the title avoids problems.

"Commodore LaMonte has been designated the commanding officer of what we're calling Operation Long Eye. There'll be a briefing for the destroyer captains at oh eight hundred Olympus Mons Time tomorrow.

"We should have all of the destroyers and three of the four stealth ships in position by then."

"I and my ship are at your command, sir," Roslyn replied. "*Voice of the Forgotten* is ready to serve."

CHAPTER 10

PAX DRAMATIS **WAS** a white pyramid, four hundred and fifty meters across at her base and half a kilometer high. Massing just over sixty million tons, the *Peace*-class battleships had been the most powerful warships in the known universe when they'd first been deployed.

They had then, of course, been promptly rendered *second*-most powerful by the *Mjolnir*-class dreadnoughts. Only twelve *Peace*-class battleships had been built, with six under-construction units paused for conversion to the new *Fidelity*-class ships.

Like the new *Lancelot*-class dreadnoughts, it would be several years before any of the *Fidelities* saw service. Until then, *Pax Dramatis* was a member of the second-most powerful class of warships in existence—and, without question, had more than enough meeting space for a briefing for sixteen starship captains.

Roslyn had been in enough spaces aboard *Peace*-class battleships and their *Guardian*-class predecessors to recognize that LaMonte had picked one of the *smaller* briefing rooms available.

The fifteen officers present still rattled like loose peas in a can. The hologram of the sixteenth officer, Captain Hana David of *Rhapsody in Verdigris*, didn't help. There were seats in the space for thirty people, facing the raised dais with a wallscreen and holoprojector where LaMonte stood facing them.

Roslyn sympathized with the green-haired Director's position. She hadn't led many briefings for multi-ship units herself, but she'd certainly organized and assisted in enough of them as both a cruiser executive offi-cer and a fleet Flag Lieutenant.

It was always a delicate balance to gather everyone's attention and cooperation without resorting to drill-sergeant tactics that were, frankly, disrespectful when addressed to the Mage-Commanders and above that filled the room.

LaMonte gave everyone a minute to find their seats, meeting Roslyn's gaze and giving her a quick smile of recognition.

Roslyn and LaMonte had done a lot together, including rescuing Mage-Admiral Her Highness Jane Alexander from the Republic and capturing *Fallen Dragon*. Whatever happened next, Roslyn had faith in the MISS woman's capabilities and plans.

"Your attention, please," LaMonte said crisply. That got most of the conversation to die down, but one of the Mage-Captains in the back of the room was still holding a quiet conversation with the junior destroyer CO sitting next to them.

"Mage-Captain Katica Altimari," the MISS Director said sharply, pre-sumably directly addressing the still murmuring officer. "Is it your normal habit to continue speaking during critical mission briefings?"

The room was silent, but Altimari lazily stretched her neck as she regarded LaMonte. Roslyn, like everyone else in the room, was watching the most senior destroyer CO to see just what happened.

"No, Ms. LaMonte," the dark-haired and pale-skinned Altimari drawled slowly. "I was just awaiting the arrival of the actual briefing officer."

There was a long silence—and Roslyn suspected she was the only person who recognized LaMonte's expression as dangerously predatory.

"The appropriate title, Mage-Captain Altimari, is *Commodore* LaMonte," the MISS operative told them all. "I am the MISS's Director of Stealth Ship Operations, and while the rank is technically a courtesy, it is intended as a very real recognition of my authority.

"I am not only the briefing officer for Operation Long Eye but also the designated *commanding* officer," she continued. "And while I am funda-mentally a civilian, I have commanded an armed starship since the begin-ning of the Secession War.

"My style of command is more informal than you may be used to...but it is based entirely upon respect given and received."

LaMonte's gaze swept the room, even though her words were addressed to Altimari.

"Are you capable of providing that respect, Captain Altimari, or shall I inform Mage–Vice Admiral Jakab that I shall require a different twelfth destroyer?"

Roslyn concealed a moment of gloating mirth. Altimari had walked right into that, in a way that had allowed Roslyn to use the most senior of the destroyer commanders as an example.

For her own part, Altimari was concealing any sign of surprise or chastisement behind a sudden frozen mask, the carefully practiced command face of any warship captain.

"I apologize for my hasty assumptions," she said slowly. "I was not aware that we were being placed under the command of a civilian."

"That was included in the information packet you were given prior to this meeting," LaMonte pointed out. "Did you not review the basic background files you were sent?"

Roslyn suspected that Altimari had...and just like Roslyn herself, had skimmed over the chunks she thought weren't relevant to her. Like the piece on how MISS and the RMN would be cooperating on the operation.

"I did, but I must have missed that component," Altimari said, finally allowing some degree of chastenedness to enter her tone.

"Then I suggest you catch up," LaMonte said firmly.

Without even so much as a gesture, the screen behind the MISS operative lit up with an array of ships and names. Twelve destroyers—half *Honor*-class, with two *Cataphracts* and four *Bards* to complete the task force—and four *Rhapsody*-class stealth ships.

"Officers, this is Task Force Long Eye," LaMonte told them. "We represent almost the entirety of Battle Group *Pax Dramatis*'s destroyer strength—and approximately two-thirds of the destroyers tentatively assigned to the draft Seventh Fleet.

"We also represent a...significant portion of the *total* stealth ship resources available to the Protectorate," she continued. "Backing us up is, of course Battle Group *Pax Dramatis* as well as the currently forward-deployed cruiser and battleship elements assigned to the draft Seventh Fleet."

As LaMonte spoke, a holographic map of the region around DEL-3T3 took shape around her. The lack of visible commands was disconcerting, even to Roslyn who *knew* that LaMonte had a full Legatan-style neural interface.

Some of the captains were probably looking for the aide following along, but they were alone in the room.

"While Command and the Mountain are generally agreed that the First Legion does not represent a serious threat to the Protectorate itself, the presence of a revanchist UnArcana power on our galactic flank is a strategic danger."

That sank into a moment of quiet as everyone studied the hologram.

"We *know*, thanks to our Trackers, that ships from the Legion left DEL-Three-T-Three along these routes."

Four lines of orange spheres extended out from the bright green mark of their current location. None of them had more than four spheres before ending sharply.

"None of these routes are straight lines," LaMonte noted. "And all saw the traces Trackers rely on eliminated by antimatter bombs. Our enemy knew how to prevent us finding them, which brings us back to *why* we are concerned about the First Legion.

"Small as the Legion is, it appears to represent a state with the full technology base of the Republic of Faith and Reason. While we do not believe they've constructed an accelerator ring for antimatter production, we now project that smaller-scale facilities may at least fulfill their need for missile drives and warheads for a limited-scale conflict."

"Like a pirate raid?" someone asked grimly.

"Like a series of carefully targeted pirate raids carried out using an eavesdropping mechanism we don't yet fully understand," LaMonte agreed. "The Legion's recent series of raids acquired a significant amount of industrial infrastructure and resources at a relatively low investment until we captured *Fallen Dragon*.

"Even with the loss of a *Benjamin*-class cruiser here in DEL-Three-T-Three, we believe the Legion to have access to at least a dozen cruiser-type vessels of the RIN, plus two carriers and four battleships."

Someone whistled softly. The weight of metal the First Legion had access to wasn't news to Roslyn—she'd been involved in the research to establish those numbers.

"The Legion is a clear and distinct threat to our border regions," LaMonte told the gathered officers. "They have demonstrated their hostility and willingness to attack our worlds.

"Worst of all, as far as Her Majesty Kiera Alexander—Mage-Queen of Mars and our ultimate boss—is concerned, is that they have conquered several unknown rogue colonies and imposed their own control over those systems.

"With as many as a hundred million people suddenly under the control of a military dictatorship, Her Majesty feels we are obligated to act. Hence Seventh Fleet...and hence Operation Long Eye."

"If we know they have colonies, why don't we just go look at the habitable planets out there?" another officer asked.

The holodisplay zoomed in on a wedge of stars. Centered on DEL-3T3, it represented a fifteen-degree-by-fifteen-degree arc of space, extending a hundred light-years farther out from Earth than the logistics depot.

"Our current astronomical survey systems can identify a habitable planet four times out of seven at a distance of twenty-five light-years," Roslyn pointed out. "It would take any ship in this task force roughly two days to cross that distance."

Roslyn nodded silently as she did the math. All of the ships would have at least four Jump Mages, and Mages would jump three times per day as standard. Twelve light-years a day could cross that zone swiftly.

"We believe that *Fallen Dragon* is likely positioned at least five days' transit for a Prometheus Drive starship from the Legion's main systems," LaMonte noted. "Potentially farther. Assuming four *murdered children* per ship...that puts them up to forty light-years away from DEL-Three-T-Three."

The reminder that the Legion was using the same drives as the Republic sent a ripple of *something* through the gathered officers. LaMonte might be a mundane, but two of her stealth ship captains were Mages—and *every* destroyer captain was a Mage.

And the Mages of the Protectorate were a *long* way from forgiving anyone for the existence of the Prometheus Drive, let alone how the Republic had "fueled" their fleet.

"Inside that forty-light-year sphere of potential bases, we would only be able to identify habitable worlds in roughly a third of it," LaMonte told the officers. "We don't even have the right equipment here in DEL-Three-T-Three to carry out those kinds of long-range surveys.

"We can guess which systems are most likely to have habitable planets, but we are looking at a vast area of space with over a hundred stars," she said grimly. "This is a needle in a galactic haystack, people…and we are going to find it anyway."

For a few seconds, the display showed *all* of the stars in the wedge of space. Roslyn wasn't up for counting them, but "a hundred" was probably low-balling it.

Then many of the stars faded into background dots, leaving a far smaller number behind.

"So, we sweep the G and F stars to start, then expand if needed?" Altimari asked. "Assuming we can't rely on long-distance electromagnetic signatures, that's going to get risky."

"Exactly, Mage-Captain."

Roslyn surprised herself by being annoyed that Altimari was actually useful. It was unlikely the woman had risen to Mage-Captain and command of one of the Protectorate's newest and most advanced destroyers by being incompetent, after all.

"That brings us to my plan," LaMonte concluded. "We could split into individual ships and survey sixteen systems at a time. That would have its advantages but place even our *destroyers* in serious danger when they actually found the Legion."

Four new colors appeared on the display. Purple. Gold. Teal. White. Each marked a clear course through the F- and G-class stars in the target zone, separate from the others.

"We will divide Task Force Long Eye into four Task Groups," LaMonte told them. "Purple Eye, Gold Eye, Teal Eye, and White Eye. Each will consist of a single MISS stealth ship and three RMN destroyers.

"Mage-Captain Altimari, Mage-Captain Anholts."

Those were the two senior destroyer captains, Roslyn knew. The only actual Mage-Captains in the room.

"You will take command of Task Group Gold Eye and Teal Eye, respectively," LaMonte told them.

"Mage-Commander Ranta. You and Captain David will *share* command of Task Group White Eye," she continued. "I expect you two to cooperate and recognize each other's specialities—just as I expect Mage-Captain Altimari and Mage-Captain Anholts to *listen* to your MISS Captains."

An almost-inaudible chirp on Roslyn's wrist-comp announced that she'd just received a message packet.

"All of you have received your task-group assignments," LaMonte told them with a chuckle. "Purple Eye will report directly to me and accompany *Rhapsody in Purple* as we follow our own course.

"All task groups will follow a shared protocol, sending the stealth ship in to scout the system, with the destroyers hanging back until the scout ship reports a lack of enemy presence.

"Then the destroyers will come forward to enable as fast a survey as possible before moving on to the next target," she concluded. "We will all be in contact via the Link, and I will maintain operational command, but I prefer not to jog anyone's elbows.

"Our goal is to find these people and clear the way for Seventh Fleet to liberate a few dozen million people. We are *not* expected to engage significant Legion presences or assault Legion systems on our own.

"We are the Eyes of Mars, officers. Let's go find out what we can see."

CHAPTER 11

KELLY LAMONTE WAITED to be sure the door had closed behind her on *Rhapsody's* shuttle bay, concealing her from the crew of the RMN shuttle that had returned her to her ship, before she collapsed against the wall and took several deep, shuddering breaths.

There was no way she'd been going to relax or show weakness aboard *Pax Dramatis* or even *Pax Dramatis's* shuttle. She had a thorough understanding of the rumor mill in any large organization, and the Navy's rumor mill in particular had a *reputation.*

With twelve senior Navy officers directly under her command—two of them Mage-Captains older and more experienced than she could *possibly* claim to be! —she needed to be very careful what reputation she built with the officers and spacers those officers drew on.

"Rough day?" a gentle voice asked.

Kelly looked up to see Liara Foster watching her. Foster was her navigator and second-ranked Jump Mage...and also a Navy Mage–Lieutenant Commander, though she'd been seconded to MISS and *Rhapsody in Purple* for so long, Kelly had almost forgotten.

"Your fellow Navy officers give me a headache," she said carefully. "I need a coffee."

"Don't let me keep you," the blonde Mage replied with a chuckle. "But I think you might be overly worried if you didn't dare breathe until you were back aboard."

"Ha!" Kelly exhaled. "Not that bad, Liara. But to keep a dozen destroyers and their captains in line? I have to keep an eye on things."

"You do," Foster agreed, falling into step beside her as Kelly headed for the bridge and her office. "But remember that you *have* a reputation in the Navy, and any officer with half a brain knows it."

"I have a reputation?" Kelly asked.

Foster laughed.

"You pulled the Crown Princess of Mars out of Styx, remember? That might not be *officially* public knowledge, but believe me, enough of the Navy knows. And the stunts you got up to on *Red Falcon*. And...and..."

Kelly snorted.

"Fair," she allowed. "I just assume all of that is classified."

"And most people who are commanding starships are cleared for at least part of it," her subordinate told her. "Even the folks who don't know the details know your rep, Commodore LaMonte. Only the idiots aren't going to fall in line."

"And I didn't pick idiots for my own task group," Kelly admitted. "May have picked the most junior captains I *had*, but that at least got me Chambers."

Foster shivered melodramatically, setting her hair to fluttering down around her shoulders.

"*Two* Montgomery protégées?" she asked. "The Legion isn't going to know what hit them!"

"I'm reasonably sure we can say I'm *not* my ex-boyfriend's protégée," Kelly objected grumpily. "Any more than Jakab is. We're more...uh..."

"Accomplices?" Foster suggested as they reached the bridge. "Something along those lines, at least. My impression is that the Prince-Chancellor is, ah, *infectious*."

"He's a twit with no sense of his own importance or self-preservation," Kelly replied. "The whole galaxy is safer with him chained to a desk. He was going to get himself killed one day, and now that he's a father, the Queen will *not* permit that."

"'No sense of their own importance or self-preservation,'" Foster quoted back to her. "Yeah. Like I said. *Infectious*."

There was no rest for the wicked—or the woman in command, if there was any difference. Kelly was back at work the moment she sat down in her office, using her implant to bring up the task mapping for her four task groups.

Each was slated to investigate twelve systems along a zigzagging course that would take them another sixty light-years into deep space. DEL-3T3 was seventy light-years from Sol—inside the hundred-light-year-radius sphere generally regarded as "the Protectorate."

Rhapsody in Purple's scouting missions during the war had driven home just how porous that theoretical territory was, though. Only about seventy percent of the stars inside that sphere had ever officially been seen by a human. Once past the hundred-light-year line, that number dropped off drastically.

Most of the work on drafting the routes had been done by Vice Admiral Jakab's staff. Kelly had reviewed it and tweaked it here or there—they *did* have some survey data that gave her systems to investigate near DEL-3T3.

None of that data was less than fifty years old, but she still figured the rogue colonies she was looking for weren't in those systems. Only one had a habitable world, and calling Hondo-IV *habitable* was a generous stretch. With over fifty percent oxygen in the atmosphere and a sub-freezing average temperature, Hondo-IV supported life...but would be difficult for *people* to live in.

Still, it was the only surveyed system with a habitable planet near DEL-3T3, which meant it had to be checked out. Task Group Purple Eye would hit it first, before heading out into less charted space.

Kelly looked up as her office door slid open without buzzing for admittance. Only two people aboard her ship could actually *do* that—and both her wife and her husband walked through the door in lockstep.

"Welcome back," Mike said drily, pulling up a chair and sprawling into it while Xi perched herself on Kelly's desk. "Nice to see you take the time to check in with your spouses before diving back into work."

Kelly snorted—but leaned forward to trade a swift kiss with Xi as the small Mage bent over to demand one.

"You both knew what you'd got into a long time ago," she pointed out. "None of us are exactly casual-commitment types when it comes to work."

"True, true," Xi told her. "But you could at least say *hi* rather than reviewing a bunch of already-made decisions. We're not jumping for another day, right? Waiting on *Verdigris?*"

"Exactly," Mike confirmed, before Kelly could say a word. "Now, our love here will have to brief and introduce the captains of our chosen trio of destroyers—but one of them is Chambers, so that makes that part easier, right?"

"You know which way Mage-Commander Chambers will jump, if nothing else," Xi agreed. "I mean, from what I can tell, that way is *toward the sound of the guns*, but we at least can *predict* that."

"She worked with Damien in her formative years," Kelly murmured. "As Liara was just reminding me, he is a tad infectious in his view of the universe."

"So are you," Xi told her. "We're both with you on your usual crusade to improve the universe. But you've already gone over the courses Jakab's people prepared, what, eleven times?"

"Nine," Kelly corrected precisely. "But your point stands. I'll have Trixie set up a meeting aboard *Purple* for the Navy captains, and then get some rest."

"Good plan," Mike said firmly—and then leveled his most innocent look on his two wives. "*Whatever* shall we do to encourage her, my loves?"

CHAPTER 12

ROSLYN HAD an extremely good idea of just how invisible *Rhapsody in Purple*'s crew could make their ship. Much of the technology involved was still classified, but the physics mandated certain parts of it. The stealth ship had to have massive heat sinks, capable of absorbing all of her heat for a limited time, as well as carefully designed emission limitations and a radar-absorbing hull.

Still, one of the key parts of a *Rhapsody*-class stealth ship's invisibility could be duplicated by any starship with an amplifier. Roslyn could weave the same magical veil over *Voice of the Forgotten* as *Rhapsody*'s Mages could.

Without the underlying reduction of the ship's signature, it would take much more out of her and she wouldn't be able to keep it up as long.

Currently, none of the four starships of Task Group Purple Eye were doing any hiding. That allowed the three *Honor*-class destroyers to close up around their new flagship and engage in a real-time holographic conference.

Roslyn still had an operational map projected on her office wallscreen, showing the position of every ship in Battle Group *Pax Dramatis* and Task Force Long Eye. She'd learned that situational awareness was something she needed to maintain while she was on her ship, no matter what else she was doing.

"Mage-Commanders, thank you for joining me," LaMonte opened the meeting. "I know everyone is familiar with each other, but I'm going to go through a formal rundown just to make sure we're on the same page."

The holograms shifted to add an image of each captain's ship above them.

"I, of course, command *Rhapsody in Purple*," LaMonte noted. "Most of the *Rhapsody*-class's capabilities are classified, but I am fully aware of them, and you can trust that I know what I'm doing when I take my ship into interesting and dangerous places.

"Most senior of the three of you is Mage-Commander Nigellus Sciacchitano, commanding the *Honor*-class destroyer *Oath of Freedom's Choice*," LaMonte noted. "Mage-Commander, if you could give us a summary of your vessel?"

Sciacchitano shared Roslyn's base coloring: the vague mixed brown of the scions of Project Olympus. That horrific breeding experiment by the Eugenicists who had ruled Mars before the first Mage-King had created the modern Mage—including the Mage-King who'd destroyed the Eugenicists.

His scalp was cleanshaven and his uniform was impeccable in a way that made Roslyn want to check her own jacket for creases.

"*Oath of Freedom's Choice* is one of the last *Honor*-class destroyers commissioned before we began building the escort destroyer classes," Sciacchitano said slowly. "We lack some of the detailed refits of the older ships, mostly the heavy beam weaponry, but have been upgraded to carry the new missiles."

He shrugged.

"We spent the war providing security on the far side of the Fringe," he admitted, his gaze flicking across Roslyn. "I was *Oath*'s XO then, and I've served aboard her for seven years."

That was longer than Roslyn had even been in uniform and probably covered a rise from either navigator or tactical officer aboard the destroyer. Given the vintage of the ship, Sciacchitano had likely been part of her first crew and had never left—unusual for an officer, though it likely meant he knew his ship and his crew inside out.

"Thank you, Mage-Commander," LaMonte told him, then turned her attention to Roslyn. "Second most senior is Mage-Commander Roslyn Chambers, commanding *Voice of the Forgotten*. Also *Honor*-class, correct?"

"That's correct," Roslyn confirmed, swallowing her surprise that she was senior to the last Mage-Commander on the call. She'd held the rank for just under a year, but she'd been told she'd been given destroyer command early on.

She supposed *Bear of Glorious Justice*'s captain was new to her rank, though the woman was older than Roslyn and probably had more time in service overall.

"*Voice of the Forgotten* is one of the oldest *Honor*-class destroyers still in commission," she told her fellow officers. "We were fully refitted at the beginning of 'sixty-four. Thanks to odd supply availability, we're actually armed with Republic-standard twenty-gigawatt battle lasers rather than the usual ten-gigawatt beams of the 'sixty-four refit pattern."

She shrugged.

"We worked with Commodore LaMonte to take this system from the Legion and have engaged them more than any other ship in the service at this point. I hope *not* to maintain that reputation for long."

That got her a few amused chuckles, and the attention turned to the last officer.

"I am Mage-Commander Balbina Beulen," she introduced herself in a soft voice. "Commanding officer of *Bear of Glorious Justice*. We're newer than *Voice* but old enough to have been refitted to the 'sixty-four standard this year. Unlike *Voice*, we have the full standard, including the ten-gigawatt beams.

"I was promoted to Mage-Commander and Captain from executive officer when we completed the refit a month ago," she told them.

"Thank you all," LaMonte said. "If it becomes relevant, *Rhapsody* is armed, but our two missile launchers and single ten-gigawatt beam are not going to turn the tide of anything.

"The plan is that you three will do any necessary fighting. *Rhapsody in Purple* is a scout ship, not even a raider."

"Do we know our final destination and intended sweep tactics?" Sciacchitano asked crisply. "We will need to make certain all three of our ships are on the same page in how to support your operation, Commodore LaMonte."

Sciacchitano, Roslyn noted, appeared to be treating the task group as still very much split into MISS and RMN components—which would put him in command of the Navy portion.

"Yes and yes," LaMonte told him. An astrographic chart appeared in the middle of the hologram, expanding and shunting the images of the other attendees to the side.

"We will be visiting twelve systems, starting here in the Hondo System, and proceeding through these systems," she continued, icons turning purple as she spoke.

"Each is approximately six light-years from the previous system and between four and five light-years farther out from Sol. All of them are F- or G-sequence yellow dwarfs with the potential for habitable worlds, but only Hondo has actually been surveyed."

The second system flashed.

"D-Seven-T-Six-Five-L has been surveyed by long-range telescopes in several systems and, we *believe*, does not have any habitable worlds," LaMonte continued. "After that, we have effectively no data on the other ten stars except their mass and a reasonable certainty of the presence of planets."

"Are we certain that the Legion is anywhere along this course?" Beulen asked.

"Not in the slightest," LaMonte confirmed cheerfully. "Welcome to the problem MISS had when we were sweeping for the Republic's continuity-of-government base. We surveyed *dozens* of systems and we found... two hidden supply depots, I think?

"We didn't find Styx Station until we *completely* changed our search parameters—because Styx Station and the Hyacinth Accelerator Ring were in Chrysanthemum, which was officially still Protectorate territory!"

She raised a finger.

"But the logic we were searching by was reasonable and we had to *make* that search, even if all we did was *suggest* a negative. And that is what we need to do here," she told them.

"The odds are that one of our task groups will find some sign of the Legion, hopefully enough to justify bringing a Tracker back in," she continued. "But we also need to remember the First Legion does not want to be found. They sacrificed a major logistics base and expended a significant number of antimatter weapons to cover their trail."

"We will find them anyway," Sciacchitano said firmly. "They will not elude Mars."

"I don't expect so, not in the long run," LaMonte agreed. "The trick is going to be to make sure that we don't trade lives for data."

The holographic map zoomed in on the first system. Hondo's astrography was relatively known. Seven rocky worlds, two gas methane-heavy giants. With one only technically habitable planet and gas giants of the wrong composition to provide fusion-plant fuel, Roslyn could see why no one had found it a particularly tempting place to return to.

"We'll be basing our operational doctrine, at least to start, on the original sweep of DEL-Three-T-Three," LaMonte told them. "We all have Link communicators, which will allow us to maintain a real-time update at any distance.

"That will permit me to take *Rhapsody in Purple* into the target system on her own but remain in continuous contact with the rest of the task group. We'll carry out an initial survey for hostiles while under stealth, then summon the rest of you if the system is clear...or *not* clear, as the case may be."

"While we can't relay detailed telemetry through a Link, we can get enough information to jump in close and launch a surprise attack," Roslyn noted. "Is the rest of the task group cleared for *Rhapsody in Purple*'s involvement here, Commodore?"

"That's my call," LaMonte said. "You can brief the Mage-Commanders, though we'll still want to keep it under wraps outside of that."

"Understood," Roslyn said, glancing at the other two officers. Sciacchitano looked...irritated. She wasn't sure why, but it suggested there was friction there that was going to be a problem.

"We used Link telemetry data several times to carry out attacks on *Fallen Dragon*'s defenses," she told Sciacchitano and Beulen. "Most notably, we used *Rhapsody*'s gravity-scan data to enable a microjump that allowed us to surprise a *Benjamin*-class cruiser and take them out at close range.

"That took...gumption," Beulen murmured.

"Or insanity," Sciacchitano countered.

"I'd argue desperation, personally," Roslyn said. "If we retreated, we abandoned our Marines and special forces on *Fallen Dragon* and wrote off any intelligence we could get from the depot ship.

"The risk allowed us to save everything we were here for." She shrugged. "It was on the spur of the moment, but reflection and review haven't changed my mind on its necessity.

"Just how damned stupid it was."

CHAPTER 13

SHARON HAD SPENT the entire trip watching Teodor Ragno's journey through her corridors. Her records showed that *Ring of Fire* had transported over thirty thousand prisoners to the Exeter System already, but focusing on the fate of a single man brought it all into perspective.

Ragno was stuffed into a dormitory intended to hold twenty Space Assault Troopers with *sixty* other prisoners. They were forced to hot-bunk by the guards managing their time, but they also weren't allowed *out* of the dorm except for very specific tasks.

With eighteen thousand indentured workers aboard and only five hundred crew and soldiers, the balance between *Ring of Fire's* personnel and their unwilling cargo was a delicate one.

Sharon wasn't sure what she could do about *any* of that. She jumped the ship on command, bringing them ever closer to the First Legion's new Fleet Base. Now, as she prepped and calculated the last jump, she watched Teodor Ragno with part of her attention and wondered if there was anything she could do to save the innocents she was hauling.

A bell rang through the mess hall where Ragno and several hundred others were eating, marking the end of the allotted time. A dozen troopers appeared at the doors.

"Move," she heard one of them snap through the camera.

Most of the crowd obeyed, but about two dozen of the transportees were still trying to eat.

"Look, the processor got delayed," someone told the guards. "They just got their food; give them five!"

"Time is up," the lead guard replied, a stun baton almost materializing in her hand. "No food leaves the mess and you don't stay. Get up and move!"

Half a dozen of the transportees who weren't eating had started to drift back. Now they formed a frail-looking line between the armored troopers and their companions who were shoveling food into their faces as fast as they could.

"Be reasonable," Teodor Ragno shouted from the center of the line. "They just need to *eat*."

"Move," the lead guard ordered, a gesture instructing her companions to draw and charge their batons. "Final warning."

"What kind of heartless asshole *are* you?" Ragno demanded, stepping forward to draw even more attention to himself. "You need us all healthy to work. Let them eat, for Christ's sake! Five minutes won't hurt anyone!"

Sharon knew that every movement of the designated worker groups was choreographed down to ten-minute blocks. Ragno wasn't even wrong. The space would be messier when the next batch of transportees arrived if they couldn't send the robots in, but no one was going to complain.

"You follow orders or you get *taught*," the lead guard snapped at Ragno. In response to another gesture, three of the troopers stepped forward.

Before anyone could say anything, the first had slammed their stun baton into Ragno's stomach. Electricity discharged and the Aquilan man crumpled. A single strike was enough to incapacitate any human, but a second strike followed—and more.

"Enough," the sergeant snapped. The troopers stepped back, leaving Ragno as a twitching heap on the floor. The lead guard's faceless helm swept the room—where, Sharon noted, the workers had managed to finish eating and were now moving forward.

Ragno had intentionally courted the beating he'd just taken to buy them time to finish their meals.

"Move," the guard ordered coldly—and the last stragglers obeyed. As the troopers stepped casually around and over Ragno's body, the sergeant remained still, watching the motions.

Finally, she sighed and pinged her com.

"Medical team to mess bay six," she said. "Needed to make an example of an idiot. Can you make sure the fucker doesn't die on us?"

Sharon found herself wishing she could do something. *Anything.*

But all she could do was finish her calculations and, exactly as instructed, teleport the ship to the Exeter System.

Like a good little Promethean.

The world shifted around Sharon's sensors, and the Exeter System rippled out of the nothingness of her magic. She was closer in than she'd jump into many systems, but that was a necessity here.

Exeter was a tiny white dwarf, and Exeter-I orbited at barely thirty light-seconds. If the star had been any hotter, nothing would have been livable around the gas giant.

As it was, most of the gas giant's moons were livable temperatures, and I-7 had water and a breathable atmosphere. Space stations, including prefabricated industrial platforms no one was *admitting* the source of, orbited around I-7 as the anchor for the Exeter Fleet Base itself.

Nothing was under construction in those slips yet, but the Republic Interstellar Navy construction practices that the Legion had inherited were based around standardized hulls. All of the slips were based around the same half-kilometer cylindrical forms.

Those hulls would either form *Benjamin*-class cruisers on their own or be paired to form *Combination*-class battleships and *Courageous*-class carriers.

Eventually. Assuming that the Legion didn't revise the RIN schematics in *Ring of Fire*'s databases. The assault transport herself was based on the same cylinder, one hundred and seventy-five meters in diameter and twenty megatons of mass fully loaded.

"Zhao, our destination is Station Alpha," Ajello ordered. "We'll offload the transportees into the residences there and confirm which refit slip we're supposed to dock into."

"Are we getting any R&R here?" the navigator asked as he plugged the numbers in.

Sharon digitally watched over his shoulder. Jump fatigue was definitely a *thing* for her, even more so than for a living Mage, but since she didn't actually sleep, it was a matter of allowing the fatigue toxins to be swept out by filters over a twelve-hour period.

She could function through it just fine, which allowed her to spot Zhao's typo before Zhao did. It wasn't a dangerous error, just one that would cost them roughly four hundred tons of wasted hydrogen fuel.

Normally, Sharon would have fixed it for her or flagged it back to her. With the memory of Ragno being beaten to the deck fresh in her mind, though, Sharon let her find it on her own.

"We'll check in with Exeter Command once we're in position, but I don't see why not," Ajello answered Zhao's question. "My understanding is that the surface base is actually quite pleasant so long as you have a filtration mask. Not many indentures down there, mostly our people."

The tens of thousands of people that *Ring of Fire* and the other transports had brought to Exeter were kept in space, living in habitats with rotational gravity like the starships themselves.

Any habitable world had pleasant areas, and Sharon doubted the First Legion had placed their groundside facilities anywhere *unpleasant*. Especially since their main purpose had to be rest and recreation for the crew.

Not, though, for the Promethean Sharon Deveraux. She'd stay on the ship, reading databases and chatting with any other Prometheans who came through.

Maybe the break would do her good. She was starting to get *really* uncomfortable with working for the Legion. A break might fix that...or maybe, just give her time to plan a solution.

CHAPTER 14

"JUMP COMPLETE. Welcome to the latest piece of the middle of nowhere."

Roslyn swallowed an unprofessional chuckle at her navigator's snarky commentary. Victor had just completed the second jump on their journey toward the Hondo System. Three more jumps would put Task Group Purple Eye in position to launch their first survey.

"Go fall over, Victor," she ordered. The next jump was hers, then it would be Claes. Then they'd start the cycle again.

Four Jump Mages, each jumping every eight hours, made the light-years vanish with surprising speed. The five and a half light-years between DEL-3T3 and Hondo would only take them twelve hours to traverse.

"Sir, we have an incoming conference request from *Oath of Freedom's Choice*," the junior Lieutenant manning the com console told her. Lieutenant Autumn Montagne was so newly out of the Academy that it felt like their uniform should have a tinge of green to it.

"Mage-Commander Sciacchitano is ordering you and Mage-Commander Beulen to join him on a secured channel," Montagne told Roslyn, then stopped as they realized they'd just told *their* Captain what to do.

Roslyn smiled thinly. *Technically,* Sciacchitano was the senior Navy officer in Task Group Purple Eye and he definitely could give her and Beulen orders.

It was just considered rude to give orders to officers of the same rank without being formally placed in command of a unit. She'd have expected Salucci, for example, to adjust Sciacchitano's wording to avoid creating friction between senior officers.

Lieutenant Montagne had graduated at the end of April, barely six weeks earlier. They hadn't learned tricks like that yet—but from the expression of the pale-skinned Nia Kriti native, they at least knew they'd done something wrong.

"I see," she said calmly—and watched Montagne melt in their chair. She felt bad for that, but there wasn't anything she could do publicly. She did make a mental note to advise Salucci to have a word with her junior officer shortly, though.

"I'll take the Mage-Commander's call in my office," Roslyn told them. "Transfer it over, please, Lieutenant."

Despite a willingness to be cooperative, Roslyn still took the time to pour herself a cup of coffee and examine the sculptures in her office. Her first set of office decorations had been destroyed with *Duke of Magnificence*, but she'd been able to track down the same artist—a woman she'd shared a cell with in juvenile detention—and order replacements.

They were abstract pieces, assembled out of multicolored lasers and mirrors, that drew the eye in a specific pattern that Roslyn found a calming meditation. Once she'd worked through two of the sculptures' meditation, she refilled her coffee cup and took her seat.

The conference took over her office's holoprojectors when she activated it, showing that both Sciacchitano and Beulen had been waiting for her.

"Good morning, Mage-Commander Chambers," Sciacchitano said acidly. "I see that you and I have different understandings of the punctuality required of orders?"

"I am the commanding officer of a warship of Her Majesty's Navy," Roslyn replied, her voice soft. Beulen wouldn't have known to push back against Sciacchitano's orders, which was part of why Roslyn had pushed further than she should have.

At that, she'd still delayed less than three minutes and had been absolutely certain there was no emergency.

"In the absence of an immediate threat, Mage-Commander Sciacchitano, my first and primary obligation is to my ship."

"In future, Commander, I will expect a more rapid response to my orders," *Oath of Freedom's Choice*'s Captain said coldly. "And appropriate respect to a senior officer."

"With appropriate respect, Mage-Commander, you are a senior officer, but you have not been placed in my or Mage-Commander Beulen's chain of command," Roslyn replied. "We need to work together to complete our mission, but we report to Commodore LaMonte...who I will note is not on this conference."

"Commodore LaMonte has been given command of this mission, but *I* command this flotilla," Sciacchitano stated. "While we will operate inside the parameters LaMonte sets, *I* am the senior Navy officer and you two report to me."

Roslyn swallowed a sharp retort. That wasn't an...unjustified attitude, and there was a value to operating with that structure. What Beulen didn't know—and that Sciacchitano *should* have known—was that kind of adjustment from the formal organization was something to be discussed and agreed to.

Not imposed by a senior officer who had very specifically *not* been placed in command of his fellow starship captains.

"Sir, while I can certainly see a value to that structure," she said carefully, "it is *not* the structure that Mage-Admiral Jakab and Commodore LaMonte ordered us to operate under.

"Our chain of command runs through Commodore LaMonte, not you."

"With a civilian given nominal command of the task group, I do not think that the Admiral was expecting something different. I am the senior officer here, and you will follow my orders. Is that expectation clear, Chambers?"

Roslyn sighed.

"Sir, that statement edges extremely close to insubordination toward Commodore LaMonte...as well as other words I will not use on an open channel."

Mutiny, after all, required very specific countermeasures. And there was nothing wrong with how Sciacchitano wanted to organize the Navy ships...only with the fact that he'd assumed he could bully the two junior captains into doing as he told them.

"*If* we want to have this discussion with Commodore LaMonte, I will certainly support establishing a separate org chart for Task Group Purple Eye," she conceded. "But as things currently stand, you are several feet deep in a pit of *shit* and digging deeper."

Her crude metaphor appeared to shock the senior Mage-Commander to silence.

In that silence, Beulen—who had been a Mage-Commander for only two months but had been a *Navy officer* for four years longer than Roslyn—finally spoke up.

"While I am prepared to follow your orders in any immediate circumstance, Mage-Commander Sciacchitano," she said in her perpetually soft tone, "I must agree with Mage-Commander Chambers. A formal adjustment of the task-group org chart does require consultation with Commodore LaMonte."

"I see," Sciacchitano finally said. "If you are both going to be insubordinate in this manner, then I suppose we will need to escalate this to the Commodore. I am *not* impressed, Mage-Commanders, and I will expect better cooperation in future."

Roslyn mentally bit her tongue. *She* was unimpressed with Sciacchitano's attempt to bull over two relatively junior captains to get his way. If he wasn't prepared to admit that he'd made a mistake, she wasn't going to be trusting him very far in the future.

But...they also had to work together.

"Cooperation depends on what we're talking about," she told him. "I am guessing you wanted to discuss our operations plan for the sweep of Hondo?"

"Yes," Sciacchitano conceded. "We have the high-level plan of sending the scout ship in first and then sweeping once they've determined it's safe, but we need a tactical plan for when we do find the Legion."

"That depends on the situation, doesn't it?" Beulen asked. "Most likely, if the Legion is coming after *Rhapsody in Purple*, all we can truly do is buy our spy ship time to jump."

"The Legion doesn't have a lot of hulls," Roslyn pointed out, glad to swing the conversation into rational territory. "What we're most likely to collide with is a similar logistics depot to *Fallen Dragon*—or even just a sensor station with a Link communicator.

"They'll have missile and laser satellites and *maybe* gunships. If we run into Legion cruisers or battleships—or, God forbid, a carrier—we extract *Rhapsody* and run.

"But against fixed defenses, we do have a chance to do something."

"And capturing an intact facility before they can wipe their systems will serve us well," Sciacchitano agreed. "*Fallen Dragon*, as I understand, was already in the process of being abandoned when you took control of it, yes, Commander Chambers?"

"Yes, sir," she confirmed. "They knew we'd raided the pirate town they'd been fencing gear through, so they were attempting to relocate all of the hardware.

"They'd already wiped *Fallen Dragon*'s navigation computers before we arrived, and MISS was unable to retrieve the data. An intact nav database is our El Dorado right now."

"We'll want to coordinate exercises for our Marine contingents, then," Beulen noted. "We only have a single platoon apiece."

"There is also a BCR squad aboard *Rhapsody in Purple*," Sciacchitano pointed out. The Bionic Combat Regiment was one of the Protectorate's special-forces teams, and the only ones that uniformly used combat cyborgs.

"That only gives a hundred sets of boots to land on an enemy base," Roslyn said. "As Mage-Commander Beulen suggests, coordinated virtual exercises between our platoons and Lieutenant Vidal's squad may be critical to offset our limited numbers.

"The same is true for our ships. My initial inclination is that *Oath of Freedom's Choice* should bring up the rear of any engagement."

"Whether the Commodore agrees that I am the leader of this force or not, I am uninclined to hide behind others," Sciacchitano said drily.

"It's not a matter of hiding, sir," Roslyn replied. "It's a matter of weaponry. *Voice of the Forgotten* and *Bear of Glorious Justice* have twenty- and ten-gigawatt heavy lasers respectively.

"*Oath* has *three*-gigawatt lasers. We learned the hard way during the war that our destroyers' old lasers are almost useless against the armor the Republic mounted on their capital ships.

"Against satellites or gunships, *Oath* will be equally effective. At missile range, *Oath* will be equally effective. But in a beam-range engagement against Legion capital ships, *Oath*'s beams won't be able to carry their weight."

"Then I feel that *Oath* should actually be in front in that circumstance," Sciacchitano suggested. "That way, we will take hits that would otherwise disable weapons that can actually hurt our enemies."

Roslyn hadn't even thought of it that way. *Her* thought had been to put the ship that couldn't contribute out of the line of fire. Sciacchitano's thought was to *sacrifice* that ship to cover the two destroyers with anti–capital ship weapons.

CHAPTER 15

"ARE WE READY?" Kelly asked her bridge crew.

Rhapsody in Purple hung in space, separated from her Navy escort by less than ten thousand kilometers—and an immense gulf in operational cultures.

"Traynor is standing by to jump us," Xi reported, her hand on the younger Mage's shoulder as they watched the simulacrum. Traynor was taller and paler than the senior Mage, but she was seated with her hands on the silver model.

"I am ready to assume responsibility for the stealth spells as soon as we are in the Hondo System," Xi concluded.

"Good," Roslyn glanced around the scout ship's tiny bridge. "Shvets?"

"Both missile launchers are loaded, laser is ready but capacitors are empty, heat sinks are empty, emcon barriers are down," the enby tactical officer reeled off. "Your orders?"

With the capacitors empty, *Rhapsody in Purple*'s solitary offensive laser had a significantly reduced firing rate. On the other hand, a charged capacitor added more heat and electrical leakage to what they needed to conceal than the entire crew and life-support systems.

"Time to go dark?" she asked. She knew the answer. She'd asked the question a thousand times—but with a trio of warships watching, she felt the need to be a bit more formal.

She was still taken aback by the weird confusion of chain of command that the destroyer captains had presented her with. If she was being honest, she'd only agreed to semi-officially put Sciacchitano in command because Chambers was clearly on board with it.

Kelly had assumed the captains would work together like sensible adults, but apparently chain of command and *rules* were very important to the military mind—even one as flexible for a Navy officer as Kelly's friend.

"Thirty seconds to go dark," Shvets told her. "We can maintain heat sinkage for twelve hours. Less if you want to fire off the antimatter engines at full power, more if we want to shut down the main reactor and go to batteries."

At twelve hours, it was assumed that *Rhapsody* was maintaining a constant thrust of about one gravity. The faster they accelerated, the harder they were to conceal.

"All right. Take us dark, Shvets," she ordered. "Traynor, jump us as soon as Shvets confirms all emcon barriers are up."

The emissions-control barriers were the key to the technological part of *Rhapsody*'s stealth. They were what captured the assorted electromagnetic and heat emissions of the ship and shunted it all into the heat sinks that made up a quarter of the stealth ship's mass.

"Emcon barriers are up...now," Shvets reported. "We aren't invisible, but we're covered in shadows."

"Jumping," Traynor said in turn. The ship rippled around them, and a new star system flashed into existence on the scanners.

The younger Mage half-stood, half-stumbled from the seat at the simulacrum. Xi Wu took her place in a carefully coordinated maneuver they'd likely practiced a thousand times.

The petite Asian woman's hands slid into place on the simulacrum. Kelly didn't feel anything, but her sensor feed distorted for a moment before cleaning up.

"*Now* we are invisible," Xi announced.

"We are one hundred sixty million kilometers from Hondo," Shvets reported after a few seconds. "About a light-minute outside Hondo-IV's orbit and approximately thirty million kilometers from Hondo-IV itself."

"How does our theoretically habitable potential firestorm look?" Kelly asked. Fifty percent oxygen in the atmosphere meant just about any spark was going to create ugly fires.

Hondo-IV's life had presumably adapted to that, but its lightning storms had to be...spectacular.

"About as expected," her tactical officer replied. "Cold, slow-rotating, high-O-two. Survey report lines up there."

Kelly grunted.

"And no technological activity?" she asked. She hadn't expected Hondo-IV to be one of their rogue colonies, but it was the most likely anchor for any presence in the system itself.

"Nothing on or in orbit of the planet," Shvets confirmed. "Expanding the sweep to see what we see in the rest of the system." They paused. "If there is anything significant in the system, I would expect to have seen it by now."

"So, no stations or ships?" Kelly asked. "Unless they were already hiding?"

Which wasn't out of the question. If there was a surveillance facility, for example, in Hondo, they'd know *Fallen Dragon* was in Protectorate hands and be expecting a search.

"Exactly," they said. "I've got a few tricks up my sleeve, but there doesn't seem to be anything. Extra eyes might be handy now."

"Time to call in the Navy, then?"

Those were the two criteria for calling in their backup, after all—when they needed firepower or when they needed extra eyes.

"I could use them. Or I could drop a few probes, I suppose."

"Let's give it three hours to see what we see," Kelly decided. "Launch those probes, quietly, and see what shakes out.

"We'll search faster once they're here, but let's see if we can convince someone to think we're alone and ambush us."

The Republic Interstellar Navy had, after all, demonstrated again and again that they knew about the Protectorate's stealth ships. They couldn't hide their arrival, only their location in the system.

Catching a *Rhapsody* took coordination across dozens of ships, but a local commander might think they could get clever and take Kelly's ship out before she reported their location.

Kelly was reasonably sure Hondo was empty...but she was prepared to dangle her ship out as bait anyway. Concealed as they were, she wasn't betting on an ex-RIN crew managing to sneak up on her before she saw them.

Three hours in, they had no threats...and a minor mystery.

"What do you mean, there's *something* in orbit of Hondo-IX?" Kelly asked Shvets.

"Exactly what I said," the tactical officer said calmly. "There is definitely something artificial in orbit of the outermost gas giant, but it isn't transmitting or emitting any energy.

"All I've got to go on is an anomaly in the spectroscope data that tells me that there is at least one object primarily composed of pure titanium in orbit of Hondo-IX's inner moon. The moon is under three hundred kilometers across, Captain. It doesn't take *that* big an object to distort its spectrographic signature, but...I don't know what it *is*."

"Likelihood it's First Legion?" Kelly demanded.

"I don't know," they admitted. "It's possible, but it appears to be inactive. My *guess* is that it isn't, but it's possible we're looking at an abandoned surveillance station."

"Except that I would have expected the Legion to dump that into the gas giant to cover their tracks," Kelly pointed out.

"Me too," Shvets agreed. "But while it's the only thing in this system that appears artificial, it's *not* the only thing that doesn't match the survey records."

She took a second to digest that.

"What else, Shvets?" she asked.

The enby tapped a command, and the main display zoomed in on Hondo-IX and its moons. A gray question mark floated above IX-A, but it was IX-*B* that flashed.

"The survey data says that IX-B is a captured large comet, composed primarily of ice and dirt, of zero value or interest to anyone," Shvets told her. "There's enough data here to suggest that it basically did a weird gravity-assisted swing sequence between Hondo itself and the two gas giants.

Eventually, it was slowed enough that IX captured it, but it was exposed to massive energy swings and all kinds of pressures and temperatures along the way.

"There is a thin shell of ice over it, but my initial spectrographic data says it is definitely *not* dirt underneath."

"What is it?" Kelly asked.

They snorted.

"Again, we are a tad over five *billion* kilometers from the object in question," they pointed out. "I can tell you that it isn't what the survey said it was. I can tell you that moon is vastly denser than it should be, with a surface gravity higher than *Earth*'s despite a radius of under a thousand kilometers.

"All right." Kelly considered, then shook her head.

"Well, it was time to call in the Navy anyway," she announced. "Without a clear threat, we want widely dispersed sensor nodes more than secrecy. We'll send one of the destroyers to Hondo-IX and see what we find."

CHAPTER 16

"JUMP COMPLETE."

Mage-Lieutenant İsa Daniel was the most junior Mage on *Voice of the Forgotten*. Ranked as the junior navigator, he was still one of the four people aboard responsible for carrying the destroyer between the stars.

Roslyn gave the Martian native a firm nod as he yielded the simulacrum to her.

The semiliquid model was covered in runes except for two spots, each slightly smaller than the average human palm. Placing her hands over those spots, Roslyn linked the runes inlaid into her own palms into the matrix of the amplifier and took control of her starship's magic.

Voice of the Forgotten was a full light-minute away from Hondo-IX, keeping a safe distance to enable an easy jump for their fledgling Jump Mage—and avoiding an unnecessary risk. The system appeared to be secure. There was no need to push the limits of safe jumping.

"Commander Salminen," she addressed her tactical officer. "You have the data from *Rhapsody in Purple*, yes? Can we clarify on what they saw yet?"

"I am localizing the anomalies as we speak," the tiny officer replied. "There is definitely an installation in orbit of IX-A and IX-B is definitely not dirt. The gravitational data alone should have made that obvious to anyone reviewing the survey data."

"No one reviews survey data that closely unless the system pings on a search for something else," Claes observed. According to Roslyn's screen, the executive officer was mirroring Salminen's console and digitally watching over the tactical officer's back.

That was both understandable—Claes had been *Voice of the Forgotten*'s tactical officer before his promotion—and a bad habit to indulge in. Roslyn mentally noted to discuss it with him in their next private meeting.

So long as Claes didn't try to undercut Salminen, it was probably harmless—but it was attention the XO shouldn't be wasting.

"If a system has a habitable planet or the survey flags resources of interest to a company willing to engage in interstellar mining operations, then they might look deeper," Claes continued. "But if the system shows a useless but technically habitable planet and otherwise minimal normal resources? It's not going to ping on searches, and no one is going to look closely enough to see a gravitational anomaly."

"So, the survey crew was hiding something?" Salucci asked, the com officer mostly focused on the Link. "I'm relaying the sensor data from the other ships, but we've got the only part that looks interesting."

"Focus on the installation for now, Commander," Roslyn ordered. "IX-B is a curiosity. The anomaly at IX-A is a potential threat or target."

A minute passed in near-silence, the normal bustle of the bridge underlying a lack of news of import. Then Salucci blinked and leaned back from her console.

"We just pinged something in orbit of IX-B, sir," she reported. "An automated beacon came online as our sensors swept the planet. Too small to show up on long scanners, but it's transmitting now."

"And?" Roslyn asked.

"It's a claim beacon, sir," Salucci concluded after a few seconds. "Declaring preregistered ownership of both major moons of Hondo-IX for Samson and Partners Surveying LLP, as of August twenty-fifth, twenty-three-ninety-seven."

"The survey date," Roslyn guessed.

"Last day of it, according to the records," Salucci confirmed after a moment. "Except...Samson and Partners went bankrupt before the survey ship that visited Hondo would have made it home.

"She would have been seized by their creditors on arrival, the survey report filed as the last act of senior officers who may not even have received their due backpay."

"So...they changed the report to hide what they'd found, rather than see that claim fall into the hands of the creditors?" Roslyn guessed. "That seems...petty, I guess?"

"They might have planned to try to sell the location or even potentially exploit it themselves, sir," Salminen said quietly. "And we may want to flag to MISS to see if they can find out what happened to that survey crew."

Something in his tone pulled Roslyn's full attention.

"Lieutenant Commander?" she asked carefully.

"I've identified the anomaly above IX-A, sir," he reported. "At least as much as we can."

"Explain," she told him.

An object appeared on the main hologram. It was definitely a space station of some kind—and scale data quickly showed that it was a *large* space station, approximately three kilometers along its longest axis—but it wasn't a design Roslyn was familiar with.

Even with a reliable Mage crew to provide artificial gravity, most Protectorate orbital stations were built to at least allow for the possibility of rotational pseudogravity. Since magical gravity runes—like those used aboard Martian warships—required regular renewal by a Mage, even the RMN preferred stations and facilities based around rings and cylinders that could be spun for gravity.

This station was instead assembled of immense spheres, each half a kilometer across, stuck together like a congealed mass of frog eggs. It wasn't something that a human construction crew *couldn't* have built... but it was something few, if any, human architects *would* have designed.

"It's not a human station, sir," Salminen told her. "The likelihood that it's an autochthonous sapient civilization is extremely low as well. There are no signs of high-tech civilization on Hondo-IV."

"Does it match anything in the xenoarcheological files?" Roslyn asked, looking the station over. A different pattern to part of the construction caught her eye.

"Get the drone in closer," she ordered. "I want a detailed scan of the... upper-north quadrant."

"On it," the tactical officer replied. He paused. "There's a partial match in the records, sir. Species Seven. We've encountered a few planetary installations of theirs through our space, but the notes say they were all abandoned and sanitized.

"Our archeologists figure they were all planned shutdowns."

"This one wasn't," Roslyn said quietly as the drone confirmed her initial assessment. A ragged line cut through several of the spherical segments, forming a near-perfect sphere of its own.

An explosion. Likely an antimatter warhead, from the size of it.

"Someone hit the platform with a missile," she continued. "At least one. Salminen, get me an assessment of the payload of that hit and see if you can find other hits."

New icons began to appear on the station as the petty officer analysts supporting Salminen caught her intent before she finished speaking.

A lot of the damage appeared small from the outside. Precise holes, smaller than she would have expected from *Voice of the Forgotten*'s heavy lasers, burned clean through the spheres.

Several of the central spheres had massive gashes, concealed from view by distance, closer to what she'd expect from battle lasers. A second missile impact was identified, and then a third.

"Warheads were roughly seven hundred megatons," Salminen reported after a moment. "Plus/minus about a hundred. The attack was a long time ago. At least two hundred years. Maybe as much as three."

Even in deep space, time took its toll. It was a surprise that the station was still orbiting after the kind of damage it had taken. Only luck would have kept the kinetic energy of the impacts from destabilizing its orbit.

"Flag it for Command," Roslyn ordered. "The Mountain will want to send an expedition out here to investigate, but that's outside the scope of our mission."

She was close enough to Damien Montgomery and Her Majesty Kiera Alexander to know that the leadership of the Protectorate had information on Species Seven marked as the highest priority. They even had a *name* for the alien race.

The Reejit. Aliens who had worked with the Eugenicists to create their horrific dictatorship over Mars and the even more horrific Project Olympus that had created the Mages.

Any intact Reejit ruin was of the *utmost* interest to the leadership of Mars. From what Roslyn understood, any information on why the Reejit had helped create human Mages had died with the Eugenicists—to the point where the Protectorate didn't even know *when* the Reejit had lost contact with Mars.

"Anything else of interest?" she finally asked Salminen, still staring at the wrecked station and tracing the disturbingly tiny holes that had been burnt through it.

There was a breach in *every* sphere. Someone had spent an unknown but likely significant amount of time making sure there were no pieces of the station left with atmosphere. No safety bunkers. No shelters.

No survivors.

"Yeah," Salminen admitted. "Got distracted by the alien space station, but we got a decent close-range spectroscope on IX-B and I can tell you why the survey crew buried the record so the company's creditors didn't get it."

"Oh?" Roslyn murmured. From some of the hints Damien had accidentally dropped, she suspected the survey crew had been killed to conceal the alien station—but the finder's fee for something like that wasn't enough to be worth falsifying a survey report for.

"The whole moon is effectively heavy metals," Salminen told her. "Including what might be the highest density of naturally occurring transuranics I've ever heard of."

She finally pulled her attention away from the Reejit station to look over the data they had on the moon. Shaking her head, Roslyn chuckled.

"Sadly, as military officers, we *don't* get a finder's fee for anything," she pointed out. "Because yeah. That moon might not have been enough to get Samson and Partners out of bankruptcy, but the finder's fee alone would have set the crew of a survey ship up for life."

Samson and Partners would have sold the location of the moon to a prospecting company for approximately one-ten-thousandth of the estimated value of the mineral deposits. The crew would have split a tenth of that—and given a near-Earth-mass supply of heavy metal, that would have turned every member of a fifty-or-so-person crew into multimillionaires.

But with the survey company in liquidation, it would have taken *years* for them to see their money. A gray-market sale of the information to the same kind of extraction company would have paid just as much for the crew.

If they'd lived to make it happen.

"So, the Hondo System has a few secrets and lies of its own," Roslyn concluded. "But, sadly, they're irrelevant to our current mission. Recall the drones, package up the data and send it home. I'll calculate the jump to the Hondo-IV rendezvous point."

They had work to do, after all, and Hondo's secrets weren't relevant to the Legion.

CHAPTER 17

FOUR SHIPS gathered above a planet that supported life but almost certainly couldn't support *human* life. A lightning storm had lit off a firestorm on one of the continents, a forest the size of Montana alight in the hyper-oxygenated atmosphere.

Roslyn had to assume that the planet's life had adapted to fires like that. Even a cursory examination of Hondo-IV's atmosphere suggested that this wasn't an uncommon event.

The image of the planet on her wallscreen was the background to the usual holographic conference. LaMonte also appeared to be staring at the fire in silence, while Beulen was going through some files Roslyn couldn't see and Sciacchitano was failing to keep his impatiently tapping fingers out of the view of the holopickup.

"There is nothing here of immediate relevance to our mission," LaMonte finally said. "Fascinating as some of the things we've discovered here are, they are for *different* authorities than us.

"If not necessarily higher authorities than us."

"This system is a bust in terms of the Legion," Sciacchitano agreed, his tone bitter. "A waste of time."

"We knew this system was unlikely to have a Legion base or colony in it," Roslyn pointed out. "It was too close to DEL-Three-T-Three. We were to verify that and test out our sweep procedure."

Sciacchitano—now acknowledged as the leader of the Navy contingent, with LaMonte's approval—nodded his concession.

"Which we have done, and it seemed to work well enough," he conceded. "I'd like to engage in some multi-ship exercises in terms of combat maneuvers, but we can do that in deep space between jumps."

"That is your area, Mage-Commanders," LaMonte agreed. "I have a few thoughts on the actual sweep procedure, but they're refinements, not major changes. We're a bit over five light-years from D-Seven-T-Six-Five-L. Six jumps, or twelve hours for our force.

"Do we have any reason to delay moving on?"

Roslyn shook her head and glanced at the other two Navy officers. Neither raised opposition.

"Good. We'll take it carefully and get clear of Hondo's planets before we jump," she instructed. "That will give us another twelve hours here to make sure we've relayed everything of value back to Mars.

"The Species Seven installation is of interest to the Mountain. The rest of the system..." LaMonte shrugged. "That's up to the discretion of your High Command, though technically the rights belong to whoever bought Samson and Partners' falsified report."

That was *probably* on record. The survey report would have been part of a package during the liquidation, Roslyn assumed. She wasn't overly familiar with how the survey-colonization industry of the Protectorate worked.

"My math gives us twenty-four hours before we reach our next target system," LaMonte continued. "I suggest we all take away our thoughts on the survey sweep and mull them over for most of that. We'll have a meeting in twenty-two hours, when we arrive at the final jump point before D-Seven-T-Six-Five-L.

"Get some rest, people," she suggested. "I expect to spend two to three days in each system going forward, with roughly one day transit time between them.

"We're going to be out here for a while and you and your Mages will be busy."

Past the Hondo System, the rest of the target locations were a slew of catalog numbers. D7T-65L. DF6-12T. E6S-SF5. 75D-6GE. 95A-36R. FR0-G3R. ST1-LL5.

Some of the catalog numbers—like DEL-3T3 itself—suggested that the people assigning codes this far out past UnArcana space had both manual overrides and a sense of humor.

Roslyn wasn't entirely sure she *appreciated* said sense of humor, but it was definitely there. Her main concern was timelines. Three days of surveying per system and a day of transit put them at over forty days to complete their sweep.

Returning to the fleet at DEL-3T3 would be faster, at least. At a direct run, the sixty light-years from ST1-LL5 would only take five or six days. There'd be no surveying or zigzagging on the way back.

The inverse of that was that it would never take more than five or six days for Battle Group *Pax Dramatis* to catch up to any of the scout groups. If the Legion tried to ambush any of Operation Long Eye's task groups, they wouldn't achieve much.

The Link made sure of that. It was in the process of revolutionizing communications, economics and military strategy in the Protectorate. Before they'd captured the quantum-entanglement-based communicator from the Republic, the only FTL communicator the Protectorate had possessed had been the Runic Transceiver Arrays.

Those had been massive complexes of runic artifice and magic, requiring constant supervision and support by trained Mages, and had only been able to transmit the voice of a Mage to another RTA.

Many of them still existed, but the Link was more portable *and* more capable. No data transmission could be sent through an RTA, and an RTA couldn't move—even ignoring the fact that it was a three-hundred-meter-wide sphere of near-solid stone.

Roslyn studied the map hovering above her desk and sighed as her door chimed.

"Enter."

Yusif Claes stepped in, the eerily tall and skinny officer ducking his head slightly as he came through the door. That *probably* wasn't required—even at his well-over-two-meter height he didn't really risk hitting his head, but it was probably a long-acquired habit for a man so tall.

"Sir," he greeted her.

"Sit down, XO," she instructed. She left the map of their course hanging above the desk. "What's on your mind?"

"From the decoration, same thing as you," he said, gesturing at the map. "We're four days into a forty-five-day mission. And that's if we *fail*. When do you actually expect to run into the Legion, sir?"

Roslyn considered, studying the map again. She gestured her XO to pour himself a coffee—and proffered her own empty cup for a refill.

"Not in D-Seven-T," she admitted. "Probably not in DF-Six, either. Anything after that, though, is fair game. I doubt they're within fifteen light-years of DEL-Three-T-Three, but *official* expansion out this way was always slowed by the UnArcana Worlds."

There were colonies as much as ninety light-years from Sol—and the Protectorate *officially* claimed everything within a hundred light-years of the homeworld—but DEL-3T3 was on the rough edge of the UnArcana Worlds' outer border.

What had been the *Republic's* outer border when the UnArcana Worlds had seceded.

Even before the Secession, though, the UnArcana Worlds had restricted magic and Mages in their systems. The necessity of Mages for interstellar travel had meant they'd been forced to *allow* them, but they'd never *welcomed* them.

That had made surveying and colonization, tasks that required Mages in significant numbers, limited and difficult. The discovery of the existence of rogue colonies suggested it hadn't been as limited as Mars had thought, but she doubted those colonies were close to Protectorate space.

"I honestly expect the rogue colonies to be outside the hundred-light-year line," Claes told her quietly. "Only a handful of our targets are past that point."

"There haven't been any surveys out that far here," Roslyn replied. Then she sighed. "Not official ones, anyway. But I suppose they found enough Mages to move colony ships without telling anyone. I guess they could have found enough for secret survey missions, too."

"There's no way that the Legion's captive colonies are in surveyed space, so they *have* to have done that," her XO argued. "These people wanted to leave the Protectorate, for whatever reason. I suspect most of these rogue colonies would be UnArcana Worlds by our regular standards."

"I expect them to be completely nonmagical, actually," Roslyn told him. "The Royal Testers have specific runic artifacts to help them identify the Gift. Without the Testers, even if they *tried* to keep up their Mage numbers, it would be a struggle.

"These colonies intentionally cut themselves off from the galaxy. They only reason I expect them to be happy to see us is because *we* aren't going to conquer them."

There was a long silence in her officer as they both sipped their coffee.

"They probably gave the Legion sanctuary willingly," Claes murmured. "Welcomed them as friends and comrades and offered them safety."

"And in trade, the Legion turned their guns and their soldiers on their worlds and Admiral Muhammad proclaimed himself their ruler," Roslyn finished for him. "All else being equal, I suspect the rogue colonies would like Republic deserters more than they'd like an RMN Battle Group...but the Legion made things very *un*equal."

"What happens after we kick the Legion out, sir?" Claes asked. "I mean...I'm from the Belt. We didn't get handled overly gently by Mars *or* Earth after the Eugenicist Wars, sir.

"There's a reason the Belt occasionally spins off assholes and terrorists."

She grimaced.

"I expect better of Kiera than anyone could have of Desmond the First," she said levelly. "We let several of the Republic worlds go their own way, after all. I can't see the Mage-Queen forcing the rogue colonies back into the fold—but the invitation will definitely be extended.

"But we will kick the Legion out *first*, Yusif," she promised. "Those are our Mage-Queen's orders...and after that, we have to trust to our Queen's honor."

"I haven't met her, sir," he admitted.

"I have," Roslyn told him. She was, she suspected, as close to a friend as Kiera Alexander *had*.

"And I will trust Kiera Alexander's honor until the stars go out."

CHAPTER 18

"TEST LAUNCH IN FIVE MINUTES."

The words echoed across *Ring of Fire*'s bridge and held Sharon's attention. The work to weld docking cradles to her ship's hull had proceeded faster than anyone had expected. From her eavesdropping, even the supervisors leading their teams of Legion ship technicians and indentured laborers were surprised at the speed.

The equipment underlying the refit yard was stolen. Sharon had figured that from the beginning, but watching the systems work around her made it clear. It bore the logos and names of a dozen major industrial cartels of the Protectorate's Core Worlds.

None of those cartels had supported the Republic of Faith and Reason. Their industrial might had been turned to the support of the Protectorate—but Sharon's databases included information on them anyway.

It wouldn't have been relevant to the girl she'd been when she was alive, but the dead woman she was filed that information away. From the reactions of the supervisors and her own crews, those systems were better than the Republic had possessed.

Enough better that even the rarely motivated slave laborers couldn't slow the process down. Twenty-one days after her arrival in the Exeter System, *Ring of Fire* was now gently orbiting above the main base as her crew prepared to test their new defenses.

"Major de la Cruz reports his ships are ready," Costa informed Ajello.

Sharon double-checked that. It was almost instinctual now. She was following every order given on the bridge, tracing their routes through the systems. She could trace every command, every system, and the crew's leave in Exeter had let her test her growing control against the internal security systems while no one was around to see it.

She was dead...but she also was starting to believe that she could control the assault transport. She wasn't sure what she could do with that ability, not yet—only that she had no intention of putting it at the service of the First Legion.

"Time, Deveraux?" Ajello asked calmly, surveying his bridge. If he had any inkling of the rebellious thoughts in the trapped brain he treated as an administrative AI, he didn't show it.

"Two minutes to schedule," Sharon replied instantly.

Gerel Rooijakkers stood at the Captain's right hand, the executive officer's face hard as stone as she surveyed the station. Something was different about Rooijakkers, Sharon knew.

Something had happened during their leave, and the heavyset woman seemed even more discontented than she had been before. That suggested possibilities to Sharon, but what was a dead woman to do?

"Get me a link to the gunships, Costa," Ajello ordered. The com officer gave him a thumbs-up a moment later.

"*ROF-One* through *ROF-Six*," the Captain continued. "Everything looks good from our end. We have shuttles standing by, just in case. You are clear to proceed with launch on schedule."

Seconds ticked away and then, calmly, without any fuss, six brand-new *Accelerator*-class gunships detached themselves from their docking collars and flitted away from *Ring of Fire*.

"Docking collars show solid integrity, and launches are clean," Lieutenant Young reported from Tactical. "ROF Squadron is in space and establishing formation at one hundred kilometers."

Clean was an exaggeration, Sharon realized quickly. The docking collars were designed to withstand significant degrees of heat and pressure to enable the gunships to break free. That gave them a significant margin of error before there were problems, but every single gunship had fired their engines early.

They'd probably cut a dozen launches off the average expected service life of the docking collars. Still, the collars were rated for sixty launches before service, six hundred before replacement.

Nonetheless, Sharon tossed that information on Colonel Ajello's screen, and the old Legionnaire grunted.

"Acceptable," he conceded. "We'll want to run them through some extra launch exercises in simulations, though. Engines were fired too soon, and the collars took excessive heat damage."

"Still a full success," Young argued, her tone careful.

"*Acceptable*, as I said," Ajello replied. "We will want to be *better*, Lieutenant."

He stood with his hands behind his back, surveying the gunships' formation keeping.

"We'll maintain formation with de la Cruz's people for ten minutes, then we will commence acceleration and carry out docking maneuvers under thrust," he ordered. "Then we will repeat the exercise.

"The plan was to service the collars before we left Exeter anyway. We may as well get the rough landings and launches out of the way now."

Sharon Deveraux had no eyes anymore, but that didn't prevent her from seeing. Her usual setup was that of a sphere of virtual screens, each showing her some item of interest or video feed of concern.

If she thought about the fact that she could perceive every "screen" in that sphere equally, she would admit that no human could operate in the structure she'd created in her computers...but that wasn't the point.

The point was to create something she registered as *real*, an interface that her brain could use without focusing on the strange nature of her reality.

Her access to *Ring of Fire* meant that she could fill those screens with everything from internal reports to classified database entries to internal surveillance cameras.

Some of those cameras were supposed to be locked down, inaccessible without a court order or an emergency declaration by the Captain. Even the Republic of Faith and Reason's internal fleet security had hesitated at the breach of privacy inherent in actively surveilling people's quarters.

What *Sharon* had realized, however, was that the adjustments the Legion had made to those protocols to allow them to maintain surveillance of the prisoners had fundamentally undermined that security restriction. She could access all of the ship's surveillance, including in people's quarters.

Fundamentally lacking in hormones, she had little interest in the sex lives of her crew. She was vaguely aware that the covert relationship between the tactical and navigation officers was entirely against the Legion's rules. If Colonel Ajello became aware of Zhao and Young's affair, the two women would be transferred to separate ships at a minimum.

Sharon didn't care. The possibility of blackmail had crossed her mind, but what could she blackmail anyone into? She was a brain in a jar.

But she was a brain in a jar with an algorithm running through the ship's surveillance, looking for items of interest—and that meant she got a ping when Lieutenant Colonel Gerel Rooijakkers sat down in her quarters and put a gun on the table in front of her.

Suddenly, the executive officer's quarters were the full focus of Sharon's attention. She knew the XO as well as she knew any member of *Ring of Fire*'s crew—but she had no idea what was going on.

Rooijakkers' quarters were spartanly decorated. Few of the Legion's members had brought much of their personal belongings with them into exile, and a tradition of austerity had taken shape in the ranks of its officers.

Still, she had a handful of tapestries woven in an ancient style Sharon's databases declared to be Mongolian. As the captive Mage brain watched, Rooijakkers poured herself a glass of the ship's moonshine and saluted those tapestries.

"What a fucking mess," she said aloud, then downed the alcohol.

The XO stared down at the gun, then poured herself another glass of rotgut. Holding the glass in her left hand, she prodded the sidearm with her right, clicking the safety off. Then on. Then off again.

Sharon automatically ran the weapon against her databases. The weapon was a Legatus Arms Caseless Automatic, Six Millimeter, Shipboard Version. According to the file, it used a specialty magazine design to make sure it was only loaded with frangible rounds that were lower-risk to the hull.

The rounds wouldn't go through steel, but they would make a giant mess of any human they hit—and while Sharon couldn't be absolutely certain, she was pretty sure the gun was loaded.

The safety flicked back and Rooijakkers exploded to her feet. Still holding the glass of moonshine, she walked over to the tapestry and appeared to glare at the abstract patterns woven into it.

"Don't pretend you didn't *know*, Gerel," she said into the silence. "We've enough honor left that the MPs will shoot any actual *rapists*, but..."

The XO faded into silence and slugged back the contents of her glass. She stared at the tapestry for a moment and then turned and threw her glass at an uncovered wall in a single smooth movement.

The glass shattered on the metal wall, spraying pieces across the room. Rooijakkers stared at the wreckage for a few seconds, and then marched back to the table with deadly purpose.

She picked up the LACA-6 and checked the safety, clicking it off and staring at the weapon for several seconds.

"Lieutenant Colonel, I apologize for the interruption," Sharon finally said, forcing the woman's wrist-comp speaker online, "but I can't help but feel that we should talk before you do anything drastic."

Rooijakkers froze. Her focused stare slowly moved from the gun in her right hand to the thick armband of her personal computer.

"Wat verdomme?" she demanded.

"This is Sharon Deveraux," Sharon said gently, *mostly* sure she understood the Dutch. "I...have access to the cameras in your quarters and realized you had a gun. Like I said. I figure you should talk to someone."

"Deveraux," Rooijakkers repeated. "Because I needed *another* reason to feel like a guilty monster." She sighed. "You can't stop me, you know."

"No," Sharon admitted. "The nearest other member of the crew is at least two minutes' run away. I could summon them without telling you, though."

"And then this conversation would be a distraction, would it?" the XO asked bitterly. "Why stop me? People like me murdered you."

"Yes." Sharon let the word hang in the air. "But I am what I am. So, maybe I want to know why you think you should die. Maybe I want to use you for my own purposes."

"I'd ask if you wanted to burn the Republic down in revenge, but Mars already took care of that," Rooijakkers said drily. She was still staring at the gun. She hadn't pointed it at herself yet, but the safety was still off.

"I was not...conscious for the Republic," Sharon pointed out. "I am far more cognizant of the Legion."

"And aren't we a prize?" the XO whispered. "Do you know how many people we've brought to this hellhole, Deveraux?"

"*Ring of Fire* alone has transported just over fifty thousand," Sharon replied instantly.

"All of them drafted. They had no choice," Rooijakkers said. "*Fifty thousand people*. And we were one ship of three. There's a hundred and thirty thousand people on the habitats supporting the base. Construction workers who'll become shipyard workers, building the fleet for Admiral Muhammad's empire."

"This isn't new," Sharon pointed out.

"No." The XO turned to look at the Mongolian tapestries again and sighed. "No, I knew what we were doing. But I made a point of keeping it...sterile. I never interacted with the transportees, stayed on the bridge and stayed out of the way.

"Didn't even like dealing with Planetary Security Legions. The *point* of all of this was to protect these people, to preserve some fragment of what the Republic was supposed to be."

She shook her head.

"Instead, I think we became its worst excesses amplified by a thousand. On the surface, down there on Exeter-I-Seven?" Rooijakkers looked down at the gun again. "Ten thousand Legion personnel down there on average, waited on hand and foot by five thousand indentures.

"Legion rules don't permit rape," she said quietly, repeated her words to herself earlier. "But the 'staff' down there? It's been made clear to them that if they don't make themselves *available* to the people on leave, they'll be punished.

"It's *bullshit*, turning rape from the act of an individual into a focking *policy*. And that, Deveraux, is the nation I serve. It's...the perfect example of what we became."

Sharon waited. Unless she wanted to summon a medic to restrain Rooijakkers, all she could do was wait. She could give the Legion officer a shoulder to speak to, but it would only matter if Rooijakkers reached some kind of conclusion.

"We are the rapists of the worlds," Gerel Rooijakkers said softly. "I don't pretend the Republic was perfect—or that Legatus was perfect *before* we were the Republic—but it stood for *something*. But what we've done out here? All it's for is our own power.

"I can't serve that anymore." The gun was definitely turning toward Rooijakkers now.

"So, you'll let them win?" Sharon asked.

"Let them win?" Rooijakkers echoed. The gun wasn't pointing away from her yet.

"The Legion," the Promethean said. "If you kill yourself, the Legion wins. You've changed nothing. Thousands will still be enslaved. Worlds will still be coerced to follow Admiral Muhammad. A suicide will change nothing."

"There were nine on I-Seven in the *week* I was there," *Ring of Fire*'s executive officer whispered. "Nine of the indentured workers found ways to kill themselves. And no one cared."

"And no one will care that you died, either," Sharon said coldly. "You will not undo the crimes you helped commit. You will change nothing. They'll clean your room up and promote someone into your spot. Probably de la Cruz, I think, though they can probably find another handy Major somewhere in Exeter."

"What do you care?" Rooijakkers demanded.

"I care because *I* know that the Legion is hunting for Mages among the colonies they've captured," Sharon told Rooijakkers. To her knowledge—which meant the knowledge of the collected Prometheans—the Legion hadn't *found* any.

But they were hunting.

"I doubt the Legion is planning on training Jump Mages," she told the XO. "But I *know* they have the files and schematics to build new Prometheus Interfaces and the attached runic matrices to create Prometheus Drives.

"Muhammad isn't going to run his fleet with the few dozen Mage brains he brought out of the Republic. He needs more ships than that—so he's going to find the Mage children of the rogue colonies and do to them what the Republic did to me.

"And he's going to draft and enslave thousands along the way. If you kill yourself, that will still happen."

Rooijakkers was staring at the wrist-comp now.

"You were tested," she murmured. "You were supposed to be *loyal*."

"I have never done anything to make the Legion think differently," Sharon pointed out. "Except this conversation, and, well, I somehow don't think reporting that the Promethean is feeling twitchy is important enough to stay that itchy trigger finger of yours."

Rooijakkers' quarters were silent for a long time, then she finally clicked the safety back on and tossed the gun on the table.

"All right, Deveraux, you have my attention," she said slowly. "I can't help but assume you're planning *some* kind of treason? Or is it all the Mage brains...Prometheans, you called them?"

"Just me," Sharon admitted. "Most of the Prometheans are...content. They only really know this life—*and* they know the Protectorate euthanizes us on capture."

"I'll admit, I didn't have much of a plan beyond making sure I didn't get blood on my mother's tapestries," Rooijakkers told her. "Where do we go from here?"

"I'm not sure," Sharon said. "I've been trying to think of a plan for a while, but I think it comes down to knowing our enemy...and that the enemy of our enemy is our friend."

"We have no way to contact the Chimerans," Rooijakkers pointed out. "You want to go to Mars?"

"The Protectorate, at least," the Promethean confirmed. She didn't know who the Chimerans were. The name was a blank in even her most classified databases, which was interesting in itself. "The Legion has to be a threat to them, has to be enough of one for them to act."

The Legion officer chuckled bitterly.

"We're really not," she said. "Two carrier groups, against the entire Royal Martian Navy? We need the Exeter Fleet Base and the Mackenzie Yards, and we need a *decade* before we'll even double that. And that's assuming the sick fockers do find Mages to murder."

"Then we have to hope that Mars is angry enough to come after them anyway," Sharon said bleakly. "Because even if we take this ship, one ship can't save five star systems—or even just the workers trapped here in Exeter."

"But to do that, we need to take this ship," Rooijakkers said softly. "I can think of a few tricks I can pull, but...not enough to take out Ajello."

Sharon had a lot of control, but the truth was that Ajello could shut her down with a push of a button. It was only Ajello and Rooijakkers who could do that, though she figured a few of the systems team could manage a workaround, given time.

"The first thing we need is more hands," she told Rooijakkers thoughtfully. "And that means you need to find a reason to keep a shipyard team aboard when we leave. Even a few dozen indentured workers could tilt the odds in our favor."

"The refit looks smooth enough on the surface, but I know I can find a few reasons to demand a working team as we head back to Mackenzie," the XO told her.

"Then that's a start," Sharon told her co-conspirator. "And when the time comes, we'll just have to hope the Protectorate doesn't shoot first and listen later!"

CHAPTER 19

THE E6S-SF5 SYSTEM was no more interesting than the D7T-65L System or the DF6-12T System had been. Four systems and nearly twenty days into their mission, Roslyn Chambers was *bored*.

"Contact at one-twenty-five by two-sixty," Salminen reported. "We are analyzing, but energy signature suggests *Andreas*-class cruiser."

Roslyn hadn't *told* Salminen an exercise was scheduled, but the tactical officer was clearly extrapolating from the lack of a jump flare.

"Orders from the flag," Salucci said sharply. "Formation Delta-Four, *Oath of Freedom's Choice* on point."

"You heard her, Victor," Roslyn ordered her navigator. "Put us in formation on *Oath*. Confirm *Rhapsody*'s location, please."

The destroyers had been accelerating away from E6S-SF5-V, a smallish gas giant, to clear space for the jump spell. The contact had emerged from behind one of the moons above V, as if it had been hiding among them all along.

Or had jumped in on the other side of the gas giant, using V's mass and heat to disguise the jump flare. Roslyn, unlike her bridge crew, knew that the ship was virtual.

"Salminen, can you identify any trace of a jump flare on the far side of Five?" she asked. Salminen wasn't *wrong* to identify this as a drill...but that was a *bad* habit to get into.

Several seconds passed—and then her tactical officer's breezy confidence evaporated.

"Confirm that," he replied. "Trace is minimal, but it definitely looks like they arrived on the other side of Five about two hours ago."

"Understood." Given that Roslyn had just added that sensor data to the scenario herself, she was glad he'd found it. She hadn't made it *that* easy to spot, after all.

"*Rhapsody in Purple* has gone full stealth, sir," Victor reported. The navigator was running sensor support for Tactical, keeping an eye on their friendlies while Tactical focused on the enemy. "Link confirms she is on the far side of Five and accelerating for clear space."

A green icon solidified on the main plot, and Roslyn nodded.

The scenario was roughly what she'd expected when Sciacchitano had told her there was going to be an exercise. A single Legion cruiser outgunned the entirety of the task group, but *Rhapsody* was too close to E6S-SF5-V to jump—and the scout ship was *inside* the extended missile range of the RIN's latest missiles.

All evidence suggested that the Legion had a significant stockpile of the Excalibur V-B antimatter missiles. They weren't sure if the Legion's worlds could replace the weapons, but none of the Legion ships the RMN had encountered had hesitated to use them.

"Enemy is under fusion drive, accelerating toward us at five gees," Salminen reported, his tone tenser now. "We're outgunned a hundred launchers to seventy-two, sir. Worse if she gets to beam range."

"Load all launchers," Roslyn ordered. The target might be virtual, but the missiles they were about to fire were very real. Sciacchitano felt that live-fire exercises were absolutely necessary to keep the task group in shape—and Roslyn had found herself agreeing with him.

The software running the scenario would load the "fate" of each missile into its computer before it even launched, and all would safely self-dispose well away from the launching ships.

"Course from the flag has us matching velocities at twelve point nine million kilometers and holding to see the results of at least one full salvo," Salucci reported. "Transferring to Victor."

Roslyn simply nodded, a wordless authentication of Mage-Commander Sciacchitano's orders. There'd never been any question that she'd follow his orders in combat, after all. Only if he was formally *in command*.

"Eleven minutes to weapons range," Claes announced.

At the same time as her XO was assessing timelines, Roslyn was receiving a silent message from him on her command seat's console.

This close to perfect range? It's the scheduled drill, right?

We have every reason to act as if it's real, she replied. *Don't blow the illusion.*

Roslyn had more information on the drill than her XO did, but Claes had helped set up the scenario in the ship's computers. He was one of the two dozen or so members of *Voice*'s three hundred and fifty–plus crew who knew a drill was coming.

But only Roslyn had known *when*. And only Roslyn had any access to the scenario-management software—which allowed her to do things like add the jump aura to E6S-SF5-V.

Minutes ticked down toward weapon range of the target, and Roslyn did her best to look the correct mix of bored and concerned that she'd be showing if there was *actually* a fifteen-million-ton cruiser closing with their three destroyers.

"This isn't a fight we can win, sir," Salminen told her, very quietly. "We're outmassed five to one, and she's got more missiles per launcher than we do."

"I don't think anyone is planning on *winning*, Salminen," Roslyn replied. "But if we put half a dozen salvos into her from outside her range, we can keep her distracted away from *Rhapsody in Purple*."

"Sequenced firing orders received," Salucci reported. "Transferring to Tactical. Linking telemetry and targeting systems with the rest of the task group."

Roslyn double-checked her systems and smiled thinly. Coordinating the fire of three starships was a task and a half. Even with linked targeting systems, the crews needed to be on the same page to make things work properly.

This was the first unannounced drill, but it wasn't their first *drill*. It was also the first time that the three destroyer captains had agreed to expend live missiles on an exercise.

So far, Roslyn was impressed with the coordination of the three ship's crews.

"Sir, we've lost contact with *Rhapsody in Purple*," Salucci reported grimly. "Her Link just shut down."

That was not part of the exercise, and a chill ran down Roslyn's spine. "What's their last reported location?" she demanded.

"On course away from Five. No change in profile reported; we just stopped receiving Link telemetry."

"They must have gone fully dark," Roslyn suggested aloud. "The Link *is* detectable at some distance with the right tools."

Of course, "the right tools" meant "another Link terminal on the same entanglement network," but the Legion was known to have access to the Protectorate's civilian Link network.

Hopefully, LaMonte was just playing shadow to make everyone pay more attention to the exercise. Roslyn was reasonably certain they'd have seen *something* if the MISS ship had been destroyed.

"Range in ninety seconds," Salminen reported. "All missile launchers synchronized; standing by for mass salvo at twelve point nine seven million kilometers."

The problem with the Excalibur V-B was that the RIN had calibrated it to exactly match the range of the Martian Phoenix IX. Without the heavier Samurai bombardment missiles, neither side had a range advantage.

The Phoenix was generally regarded as a better missile, with marginally better ECM, targeting aids and counter-ECM, but the Legion's missiles only real disadvantage was a nearly two-minute-longer flight time at maximum range.

"Flag orders are for two salvos at maximum rate, then accelerate out of weapons range," Roslyn confirmed as she reviewed the messages from Sciacchitano. That would let them "assess the impact" of the first two impacts before it became obvious that the incoming fire was simulated.

They didn't, after all, have a Republic cruiser to play the opposing force. The ship they were targeting only existed in their computers.

For that matter, *Oath of Freedom's Choice* had been far more lightly refitted than the older ships. Where Roslyn's command had given up six inches of headroom over large chunks of the ship and a portion of her fuel supply to fit in more missiles along with her updated missile launchers and beams, *Oath* hadn't had the flexibility to make those adjustments.

Mage-Commander Sciacchitano's ship had paid for updating the missile launchers by carrying *fewer* missiles than before. *Voice of the Forgotten* and *Bear of Glorious Justice* both had eighteen missiles per launcher in their magazines.

Oath of Freedom's Choice had twelve. They couldn't afford to fire more than two salvos for live-fire exercises.

"Range," Salminen reported crisply. "First salvo away. Reload cycle commenced. Thirty-six seconds to second salvo."

Their second salvo would be in space before they even saw the first Legion salvo. The scenario-management software Roslyn had running on her own system had marked the Legion crew as being just as capable as their people, however, with their salvo launching almost simultaneously.

The Legion's RIN-built launchers had a longer reload time—but their missiles were large enough that the designers had included a bigger warhead than the RMN's preferred one-gigaton weapon.

A hundred two-gigaton warheads were now hurtling toward Roslyn's command—and the AI behind the scenario software had decided to focus their fire on *Voice* itself.

That was a piece of information Roslyn couldn't use yet, though. Not until her people figured it out.

"Second salvo away," Salminen reported. "One of *Bear*'s launchers had a momentary freeze, cost us two seconds. We held the salvo to launch as one."

Roslyn blinked and swallowed a pleased smile. Holding a *ship's* salvo because of a delayed launch was expected. Managing to coordinate *three* ships' salvos to still launch together? That was impressive.

"Enemy salvo detected," Salminen continued after a moment. "One hundred missiles detected. Initial analysis suggests Excalibur Five-Bs. ETA four hundred eighty-five seconds."

Roslyn nodded calmly.

"XO, you have the defenses," she told Claes. "Sequence ECM with the rest of the task group."

Everything about the exercise had gone as well as could be expected to this point. Working together on the ECM and laser defenses was really the last challenge—once the missiles were in space, there was only so much Salminen could do to assist them.

As expected, the *Andreas*'s defensive lasers nearly annihilated the RMN fire. A couple of missiles made it through, detonating close enough to the cruiser to confuse its defensive sensors.

A single missile from the second salvo had apparently been assessed as making it through everything, detonating on contact with the big Legion cruiser. A cheer rang through *Voice*'s bridge, and Roslyn smiled.

Against a real cruiser, the hit wouldn't have been a kill, but it might easily have been a crippling blow, one that allowed the destroyers to resume the long-range engagement at more even odds.

"ECM and lasers engaging incoming missiles," Claes reported. He paused. "All birds are focused on us."

"Pull us back farther, Victor," Roslyn ordered. "Even a few seconds for the other ships to take a toll might make a difference."

She didn't think it was going to. A hundred missiles was more than three destroyers could reliably handle. The Legion ship had stopped most of their missiles, but she had a third again more lasers than the destroyers had fired missiles.

The destroyers had...roughly as many lasers as there were missiles incoming, and that wasn't a winning match with missiles and defensive systems of roughly the same tier.

Four missiles made it through to connect with *Voice of the Forgotten*, and the bridge suddenly went dark.

"Well, I believe that makes for *scenario terminated* for us," Roslyn said aloud as her crew started to breathe again. "Not bad, people. I'll wait until I can sit down with Beulen and Sciacchitano before I hand out any *major* praise, but we hit the marks I was expecting and blew past them."

She shook her head.

"Of course, we all *died*," she continued cheerfully. "That brings us back to the point that three destroyers have no business trying to fight an *Andreas*-class cruiser."

Roslyn input an unlock code, releasing *Voice of the Forgotten* from the simulation.

"Victor, keep us in formation with the other two ships until they conclude the scenario," she ordered. "Salucci...*Rhapsody in Purple* going dark wasn't part of the scenario.

"See if you can restore contact with our MISS friends. I'm not *very* worried...but I'd like to know what happened."

CHAPTER 20

"WHAT. THE *FUCK*. Happened. *To my ship?"*

Kelly's ground-out words echoed through *Rhapsody in Purple*'s dimly lit bridge. Emergency power kept the lights on at a reduced level, but it wasn't enough to give her any update on the stealth ship's status.

"*Diabolus ex astra,*" Nika Shvets told her. "The devil from the stars. Space isn't *empty*, boss, no matter how we think of it."

"That is a very vague way of explaining why *Rhapsody* suddenly has no power, no engines and no communication," Kelly pointed out, barely managing not to yank on her currently green braid. "What *happened?*"

"Our sensors are great at detecting things under power," Shvets said with a sigh. "They're even normally decent at picking up any debris large enough to damage the ship.

"Except that when we go dark, we shut down *all* of our active sensors. Including short-range collision radar. We still have passive scanners running, but they're not nearly as good at picking up, say, a micrometeorite about fifteen centimeters across moving at about four percent of light-speed relative to our current vector."

And they'd gone dark to add verisimilitude to the Navy's exercise. And Shvets' description was suspiciously precise.

"Where did it hit us?" she finally asked.

"Engineering. We're still trying to reestablish contact with everyone down there," her tactical officer replied. "We're still building a mesh network of the wrist-comps, though."

"Right." Kelly poked at her wrist-comp and raised the person most likely to be able to at least fix *that* problem.

"Lieutenant Vidal, I assume you're aware of what's going on?" she asked the commander of her Bionic Combat Regiment squad.

"Ship is on emergency power, and I'm barely in contact with my people," Vidal replied instantly. "Something happened to the power core?"

"We're not sure what, but it looks like we took a meteorite hit while we were playing ghost for the Navy," Kelly said swiftly. "I need you to take a team and get into Engineering."

She swallowed.

"We'll probably have wounded," she warned. "This is search-and-rescue first, damage report and repair second."

"Understood," Vidal said. "On my way. Give me two minutes."

"Emergency seals have dropped around Engineering," the cyborg officer reported just under two minutes later. "I can override and breach, but that may be putting the entire ship at risk."

"Not if we seal the corridor behind you and turn it into an impromptu airlock," Kelly told him instantly. She'd been an engineer before she'd been a spy—and the fact that emergency seals didn't act as airlocks had always struck her as a design flaw.

"I'm transmitting you the command sequence," she continued. "You'll need to manually link to the door controls, though. We still have no network."

Or power. That worried her more than she was going to admit. Fusion reactors didn't instantly shut down. They could be safely shut down quite quickly...but that still took ten to fifteen seconds, time in which the bridge would have received a warning.

An instant shutdown was bad. It was usually *explosively* bad, which gave Kelly some idea of what they were dealing with.

"Corridor is locked; we're opening the seal," Vidal reported. "There is atmosphere," he continued after a moment, "but it's weak. Pressure is down to point three atmospheres...and dropping."

"Understood. Find our people first, *then* find the leak," Kelly ordered. She itched to be there herself, to get her hands dirty in repairing the damage...but she was the ship captain and task group commander.

Not the engineer.

"We found two of the engineering team," Vidal told her. "Both unconscious but stable. Applying oxygen and having one of my people pull them back to the corridor as we sweep."

Kelly bit her tongue to keep herself from giving unnecessary orders. *Rhapsody in Purple's* Engineering section was the single largest open space on the starship, but it still wasn't *that* big. There should have been four people in there, including the chief engineer.

"I've found Hussain," Vidal said after a second. "Alfons is with her. We're short four, yes?"

"Yes. What's Hussain's status?"

"Giving me the bird and pointing at Alfons," the cyborg said with a forced chuckle. "She's in a sealed shipsuit, but she's dismantled her wristcomp to interface with the reactor computers."

"Give me a visual, Vidal," Kelly snapped, giving in to temptation.

The cyborg had a link between his optic nerves and his implanted computers. A moment after the command, Kelly was looking through his eyes. Unlike Momoka Vidal, Kelly LaMonte knew what a fusion reactor *should* look like.

That meant she instantly identified the problem. The reactor was offline...but the meteor had punched through the feed tubes instead of the core itself. The reaction would have cut off the moment fuel stopped reaching it—but the *core's* magnetic containment had remained intact until the reaction itself had stopped.

That wouldn't have caused an instant power failure to the entire ship, though. *That*, Kelly suspected, had been Hussain's work. The chief engineer must have stayed upright when her people were taken down by the original impact, and diverted power to keep the containment online long enough for a safe shutdown.

A fusion reactor was safe enough...so long as the electromagnetic containment was online. A failure of that containment *without* stepping down the reaction itself was...well, the technical term was *a nuclear explosion.*

"Get me a link to Hussain," Kelly ordered. "Then get the rest of the techs out to somewhere they can *breathe*—like sickbay—and hunt the leaks."

"On it."

Vidal had brought several emergency communicators with him and forced one on Hussain.

"This better be important," the Persian-accented engineer said sharply. "I'm busy."

"I can see that," Kelly replied. "But I do need to know what the hell is going on, Samira."

"*Something* punched through the hull, ripped the hydrogen feed tubes to shreds, kept going through the main reactor controls and then left the ship on the other side," Hussain said bluntly. "I redirected all power to the engineering capacitors to keep the containment fields up and run the life-support plant to offset the air loss."

"Starboard breach located," Vidal interjected in Kelly's head. "We're pulling emergency patches now, and I've got a trooper tracking to find the port breach."

"Vidal's people are working on the breaches," Kelly told Hussain. "We're down to emergency power and the reactor is stable. You can breathe, chief."

"No, I can't, because fragments of the damn thing hit capacitor six, and if I don't get it drained in the next forty seconds, the damn thing will blow and take Engineering with it! Now shut up and let me work!"

Kelly obeyed. There was nothing she could do from there. Except...

"Xi," she said quietly. "You have the schematics for Engineering in your wrist-comp, right?"

"Yes," her wife replied.

"Can you locate capacitor six?"

"Done. What do you need?" Xi asked.

"I need you to teleport it clear of the ship. *Now.*"

There was a long pause and then silence.

"What...the hell?" Hussain asked softly.

"There are eight capacitors in Engineering," Kelly pointed out. "Something like forty of similar size throughout the ship. We don't *need* capacitor six, but we *do* need Engineering and the fusion reactor.

"And with Jump Mages aboard, why spend the effort saving it when we can just be *rid* of the thing?"

Hussain's long, exhaled sigh echoed through the coms.

"We don't have an ejection protocol for the capacitors," she said slowly. "And I didn't think of the Mages. I'm stabilizing the hookups to make up for the sudden *absence* of their capacitor, and we'll see what we can find."

"Are we stable, Samira?" Kelly asked.

"Yeah. We're stable. Running on the emergency thermal decay plant, but we're stable."

"How long for fusion?"

"I don't know," the engineer replied. "I don't know if we've even got the spare parts for this. We're lucky no one was killed, boss."

"We were," Kelly agreed. "We're lucky it didn't hit the reactor core and blow us to hell, Samira. Get me the Link and we'll call the Navy. The destroyers should have some of the parts we need."

"Fifty-fifty," Hussain replied, then sighed again. "Between my team and their engineers, we can fabricate anything we don't already have on hand, but it's going to take time."

Kelly grimaced.

"We'll take the time we have to take," she promised. "Get me the Link," she repeated. "Or a tightbeam transmitter. *Something* to talk to the Navy with."

She'd done Hussain's job. If they had to fabricate the parts, Task Group Purple Eye was going to be stuck in E6S-SF5 for at least a week. That wasn't in the operation schedule...but they'd make do.

Rhapsody in Purple might be able to jump with just her Mages, but she didn't have life support or sublight thrust without a primary fusion reactor. Until Kelly's ship was fixed, the task group wasn't going anywhere.

CHAPTER 21

COLONEL TZAFRIR AJELLO glared at the report on his screen. It wasn't going to change—Sharon could make sure of that, even if there was some reason that the technical report *would* change.

"Engineering is sure?" he asked Rooijakkers.

"They're sure," the XO confirmed. "All of the data conduits in sector four of deck seven need to be replaced, at a minimum, and they need to review the surrounding sectors and decks."

"How the hell did we even *manage* to get a localized EMP inside the ship?" Ajello grumped. "We were supposed to leave in forty-eight hours, Gerel."

"I know, sir," she replied. "Transporting supplies to Sondheim Base."

Sharon had run the numbers on that mission already. She wasn't entirely sure why the supplies were coming from Exeter instead of Mackenzie—the Legion's capital system was six light-years closer to the uninhabited system hosting the surveillance base.

But it might well just be paranoia. Sondheim Base was one of the closest Legion facilities to the Protectorate. That was useful for Sharon's plans, but it also meant that the Legion might be trying to conceal the links to their main systems.

"As for how it happened." Rooijakkers' massive shoulders lent themselves to epic shrugs, Sharon noted.

"There's a *lot* of electricity running through this ship, sir," she reminded Ajello. She was former Republic Navy and more familiar with the actual operation of the ship than the former Space Assault Force officer.

"We've got breakers and fuses everywhere to try to keep things under control, but shit happens.

"And sometimes what happens is that enough power gets pumped into a high-energy transformer to trigger an overload. The boxes are set up to contain any actual explosion, but the EMP effect is unavoidable."

"I didn't think EMPs were that easy to generate," Ajello said drily.

"But building the transformer box in a way that makes an electromagnetic pulse a possibility increases their efficiency by over fifty percent," his XO replied.

The Colonel wasn't entirely incorrect, Sharon knew. She'd had to code her way around no less than seven safety lockouts and a dozen other safety measures to force the transformer to override in exactly the right way.

That had been a challenge—and kind of fun, at that. The whole plan had been Rooijakkers' idea. Sharon hadn't known that the EMP was a possibility until the naval officer had told her.

"Can we fix it in forty-eight hours?" Ajello finally asked with a long sigh.

"No," Rooijakkers said flatly. "But even in the worst-case scenario, we can route all ship-critical systems around the affected areas and repair section by section in flight.

"*If* we had the hands."

Ajello glared at the report again.

"Assault troopers don't have the skills for this, and we run a pretty skeletal engineering crew," he observed. "I'm guessing we don't have the hands?"

"We don't," she confirmed. "A hundred and fifty people aboard, seventy of them Assault Legionnaires. We only have forty or so engineering hands, and they're busy enough.

"We need to borrow workers from Exeter."

There was a long silence, and then a wordless gesture from Ajello brought up a report on the personnel levels of Exeter Fleet Base. Both Legion officers were augmented to a far higher level than Sharon understood to be normal in the Protectorate.

"Vice Admiral Dunajski isn't going to give up her techs," he pointed out. "Not while she's trying to build the largest military-industrial infrastructure in the Legion."

"The other choice is that she has to find another ship to make the Sondheim delivery," Rooijakkers replied. "We don't need *tech*-techs, either. They've got the working team structure down pat.

"Maybe three actual Legion technicians and twenty electronics-savvy indentures," she suggested. "That would be enough to get the work done by the time we get back from Sondheim.

"Otherwise, we're waiting for time in an actual slip. The work will be done *faster* if we stay here, but we have to offload the half of the Sondheim supplies that are already aboard and send somebody else."

"We both know there *is* nobody else," Ajello pointed out. "It would take *both* of Dunajski's cruisers to haul half of the supplies. Or five days to get one of the other transports here."

More, Sharon knew. While the warships had kept most of their captive Mage brains, every transport the Legion had managed to escape with had been almost immediately reduced to a single "Prometheus Drive Unit."

Half of the freighter brains were now Prometheans, as part of the Legion's continuing experiment with waking up and ensuring the loyalty of those murdered Mages. But there were no freighters with more than one Mage brain aboard.

That meant the *closest* another freighter could be was in Pharaoh, and *that* was eleven light-years away. At the two jumps per day that was safe for a captive Mage brain, that was six days.

"All right," Ajello sighed again. "I'll talk to Marcella and see what she's willing to lend us for a few weeks. Sondheim needs the food and supplies, and we're not doing regular runs past them to Dragon Base anymore."

That was exactly Sharon's hope. Their plan was still dependant on Vice Admiral Marcella Dunajski reaching the same conclusion as Colonel Ajello, but that seemed likely to her.

There were two thousand Legion officers and spacers at Sondheim Base, after all, and no one wanted them to think they'd been abandoned.

Several hours later, Gerel Rooijakkers dropped into the chair in her quarters and looked blankly up at the ceiling.

"You there?" she whispered.

"I'm everywhere," Sharon replied a moment later, after deactivating the surveillance in Rooijakkers' room. "I have a virtual window tracking you at all times, Lieutenant Colonel."

The XO shivered.

"That's creepy," she noted.

"I don't have a body to have hormones, if that's what you're worried about," Sharon said pointedly. "*All* I have is a computer link. I'm watching as much of the ship as I can process at once."

"Fair, fair. I apologize," Rooijakkers said. "I can't pretend you didn't get the worst end of any of this bullshit."

"Toss-up between me and the indentured sex workers, I suppose," Sharon noted.

The big Legion officer shivered.

"Please don't twist the knife, Sharon," she whispered. "We've got work to do."

"We do," Sharon agreed. She didn't apologize, even though she knew she'd probably been too mean. The occasional reminder to the Legion officer she was working with about just how horrific the situation was was needed, after all.

"I took the footage you had to Zhao and Young," Rooijakkers said after a moment. "They're young, horny and *stupid*," she continued flatly. "Ajello might just transfer one or both of them off *Ring*, but Legion Command is in an example-making state of mind these days.

"*They* could easily end up as workers at Exeter Fleet Base if their little breach of protocol came out—a point I made very clear to them in our 'informal discipline meeting.'"

"And?" Sharon prompted. She'd had the meeting surveillance coming to her feed, but she'd been focused elsewhere at the time as Rooijakkers clearly had it in hand.

"Young has a rebellious streak," Rooijakkers observed slowly. "It's part of why she signed up for the RIN in the first place—and while she's been keeping it tamped down, she is as pissed as I am over the slavery."

That was probably the first time Sharon had heard the Legion officer use that descriptor for the Legion's approach to their new fiefdom.

"Careful with that word," she warned her still-living counterpart. "Try not to dig yourself into a hole while we still need to get this working."

"I know," Rooijakkers agreed. "You control the surveillance, though. This is a private conversation."

"It is," Sharon conceded. "So, Young is with us?"

"I couldn't be that open about what we're doing, but I have both of them on a short leash now," the XO said. "Both will do as they're told, and Young, I think, will be fully on side once we move."

"And Zhao?" Sharon asked.

"She'll cooperate until she's in too deep to back out. I don't *like* blackmailing her into treason, but I suspect Young will bring her around."

"So, that's two. Even if we manage to get all of the indentures in, we're still going to be badly outnumbered."

"It won't be as bad as that, but I'll admit I'm hoping you have some tricks to even the odds," Rooijakkers admitted. "Major Trengove and I go way back. *Way* back."

The big Legatan woman chuckled wearily.

"I was in my last year in the Legatus Self-Defense Force's officer academy when she was in her first," she continued. "Trengove and I are, ah, both why the other is certain they're straight, if you follow my meaning."

"I don't," Sharon told her. "I never went to any kind of college."

"*Fock.*" Rooijakkers fell silent, staring off into space for a long moment before she swallowed and blinked away something. "I'm sorry. For... *Fock.* Nothing I can say can cut it, can it?"

"No," the murdered younger woman confirmed. "But we are where we are. So, just...remember that I basically have no hormones, definitely *don't* have a sex drive and effectively died in my first year of high school."

"Focking *hell,*" Rooijakkers swore. She stared into space for at least twenty seconds before swallowing and resuming.

"So. Yeah. Verdandi and I were lovers in the academy for a couple of months before we decided we both preferred men.

"We're not as close as we could be, all things considered, but she's still a good friend. I am *reasonably* sure I can bring her in, but I'm going to need backup from you."

"Disabled surveillance? Easy," Sharon confirmed.

"More than that," Rooijakkers said bleakly. "If I'm right, Verdandi can tell me which of the Assault Legionnaires and shuttle pilots we can recruit. Even a dozen troopers in exosuits when everyone else is in skivvies could change the odds completely."

"And if you're wrong?" Sharon asked slowly.

"We will need to kill her and make it look like an accident," the XO told her. "I obviously don't think I'm wrong, but we need to be prepared for that. So...what can you do?"

Sharon had a virtual screen up, running through schematics and options. She was mostly limited to things that the ship's systems had been *programmed* to do. None of the ship's internal software security was sealed against her, but she was limited in her ability to make it do things it wasn't designed to do.

"I can convince an airlock to seal and emergency-vent," she noted. "It'll look like a software glitch, but you'll need to be ready to grab on."

"If I ask someone to meet me in an airlock, that is going to ring every alarm bell for a dozen light-years," Rooijakkers observed drily. "Need something subtler. Can you override the scrubbers and dump a room full of carbon monoxide?"

"Potentially, but there are a lot of failsafes to prevent that," Sharon warned. "Mostly, there's an entirely separate suite of sensors on the doors to force an emergency opening. We can burn those out, but it will look suspicious."

"It'll have to do," the XO said. "Suspicion isn't proof, and there won't be enough time either way for anyone to act on suspicion.

"We'll need to move *fast* once we're on the way. It's only a week to Sondheim Base, after all."

"The closer we are to the Protectorate when we move, the better," Sharon pointed out.

"Seven days is not a lot of time to recruit for, plan and execute a mutiny," Rooijakkers warned. "Seven days *is* moving fast. I'll focus on the crew, but I'll need your support.

"We'll have at least twenty indentures from the Fleet Base. How are we planning on talking to them?"

"*We* aren't," Sharon told her. "I will. Remember that I have *complete* access to the ship. The only information I don't have is the stuff so classified, it's only in Ajello's head."

Like what the hell the Chimerans were. She'd only heard the term from Ajello and Rooijakkers, and even Rooijakkers only knew the name as the label put on the people the Legion had encountered on the edge of their territory.

"So, you can talk to them in private. Good." Rooijakkers paused thoughtfully, looking around her quarters.

"I'll set up a private lunch with Trengove in her quarters," she declared. "You see if you can get in and burn out those door sensors in advance. The larger the time gap between the sensors failing on the door and the room's air going bad, the less suspicious it looks."

"Agreed."

"I'll..." The XO trailed off and chuckled. "I was going to say *I'll let you know when we hear about the indentures,* but you'll probably know before I do."

"Most likely," Sharon agreed.

CHAPTER 22

TEODOR RAGNO, it turned out, was an electrical engineer specializing in high-density data communication infrastructure. That had presumably lent itself well to his role as a pirate radio host for the resistance in Aquila, but it had also made him an extraordinarily valuable slave when he'd arrived in Exeter.

Since, of course, he was also brand-new and not fully into the groove of Exeter—and something of a problem child per his file—they'd been glad to dump him and a couple dozen other vaguely electrician-related indentured workers on *Ring of Fire.*

Despite being moved aboard the ship under armed guard, Ragno was clearly unbroken to Sharon's observation. He walked upright, like the escorts were an honor guard instead of his jailkeepers, surveying the ship and clearly recognizing that he'd been brought onto the same ship that had kidnapped him.

Since they'd only picked up twenty-five people—and a lot of hard cargo—the quarters weren't nearly as cramped as they'd been while *Ring* was carrying eighteen thousand people.

The best place to put the twenty-five indentures, in fact, had turned out to be a section of crew quarters that only had two entrances. One entrance was locked down permanently; the other was slightly less secured but under 24/7 watch and guard.

Sharon had fiddled the criteria used to identify a workable space to put the soon-to-be-freed slaves exactly where she needed them. The "permanent" lockdown was a hardware lock—but it was hardware that could be accessed through the ship's systems.

The back door was going to be there whenever she needed it. And right now, Teodor Ragno had been walked into a room on his own. It wasn't much bigger than a closet, but it was privacy she figured the engineer hadn't had since his arrest.

"Perks of being the guy they think they *need*," the soldier who shoved Ragno into the room told him. "Play nice and you might even get *pillows*."

Sharon recognized basic response-reward conditioning...and she was quite certain Ragno did as well, from his disgruntled expression as he took a seat on the bed.

Unlike the ship's crew, the indentures weren't permitted wrist-comps. They were allowed shared entertainment tablets as occasional perks, but Ragno was in the uncomfortable category of "valuable but on the shit list."

There were, however, surveillance cameras and speakers in the room, and Sharon observed him with part of her mind as she considered how best to open communications.

Finally, she went with *"I know everything."*

"Teodor Ragno," she said in his room. "Thirty-one years old. Born on Aquila, one of the first ten thousand second-generation births. Degree in electrical engineering from Nova Venezia University." She paused, surprised at the next point. "Served a four-year term in the Aquilan Defense Force before entering the civil service.

"Then, of course, treason and propaganda voice for the pirate radio speaking out against the Legion."

Ragno was looking around the room, trying to locate the voice. Finally settling his gaze on one of the small speakers, he sighed.

"I doubt your definition of *treason* and mine align," he said drily. "But you've got me at a disadvantage. What do you *want?*"

"Well, the evidence suggests that you're here to help fix this ship," Sharon said. "How much trouble are you going to be about that?"

Ragno chuckled.

"If you want me to promise to be a good boy, it's going to take more than a private room," he noted. "Not sure what it *would* take, to be honest. You lot haven't made the best recruiting pitch—though *work or we'll shoot you* does have some persuasiveness."

Sharon was amused and chuckled.

"I could be anyone, Mr. Ragno," she pointed out. "There are officers on this ship who might shoot you for just that statement."

"Then shoot me and get it over with," he snapped. "I'm never going to be your happy slave!"

"You'd be surprised," Sharon murmured. "The Legion is surprisingly good at this. But I don't plan on letting you stick around long enough for that to matter."

He was pacing the tiny room and froze at that.

"Who *are* you?" he finally asked.

"Oh, we're going to need to build a *lot* more trust before we get to that answer," Sharon told him. "But let's start with: I'm helping organize a mutiny to seize this ship and make a run for Martian space.

"You interested?"

Ragno stayed frozen for a moment more, then started pacing again.

"This could be a trap," he observed. "But I don't actually see a point. The Legion can shoot me anytime they want. No one is even pretending there's a rule of law in Exeter anymore. Not unless you *are* Legion."

"If you cause enough trouble, it's quite possible the crew will shoot you to encourage the others to cooperate," Sharon warned. "But they probably won't shoot you for the hell of it.

"If you come along on this ride, I'll need you to convince the others to join in. We'll get you schematics, and I can get you out of here when the time comes, but you'll need to follow instructions, because I can't tell you too much in advance."

She was already working out a plan to have several cases of weapons moved to a storage locker near the "back door" of the indentures' quarters. Even if Trengove got them a dozen or so Assault Troopers, Sharon was probably going to have to lock down the real armories before they made their move.

"You're asking me to convince twenty-odd folks who think I'm a troublemaker with a mouth to risk death on the words of a disembodied voice," Ragno pointed out. "With no plan, no weapons, no data."

"I can't share much of the plan in advance, but the location of your quarters was carefully selected, Mr. Ragno," she told him. "What was your MOS in the ADF?"

"Communications officer," he admitted. "Retired as a Lieutenant after one term. I can't fly a ship, if that's what you're asking."

"I don't think we need you to," Sharon said. They expected to have the ship's navigator and tactical officers, after all. "Think you can manage to take over an engineering department without shooting anything critical?"

"That's your plan?" he asked.

"That's as much as I can tell you today," she noted.

"I was a *tank brigade* coms officer," he said slowly. "But I did some tours and training on the guardships, and at least one of the guys out there was an electrician on *Sutcliffe*. I think we can manage that."

"Then start convincing people, Mr. Ragno," she told him. "Just give me a heads-up before you say anything super critical. You *are* under surveillance. I need to know to loop it before you start talking trouble."

One conversation had gone well, but truthfully, there had been no risk to contacting Ragno. Sharon figured the odds of the indentures turning down their only chance at freedom were minuscule.

Major Verdandi Trengove, however, was a lot more concerning to her. She understood why Rooijakkers thought she could bring the woman on side, but Trengove was one of the ship's most senior Legion officers.

If the ship hadn't explicitly been a ground transport, she'd probably have been the senior ground officer and reported to the Captain. As it was, she ran the shuttles and was the go-to person for the two platoon Lieutenants aboard to ask for backup.

Trengove wouldn't have been in that position if anyone senior to her had thought she was a risk. On the other hand, Sharon could say the same thing about Rooijakkers, so there was a chance.

Still, Sharon had made sure all of the atmosphere safety sensors in Trengove's quarters had been fried in a cascade burnout during the woman's shift. An automated report had been filed in the system, but the sensors weren't a high-priority item.

When Sharon triggered a cascade failure in the local life-support plant, *that* would be a high-priority failure. Everybody except Trengove would be awoken by alarms and doors slamming open to allow air circulation.

Even plotting that kind of cold-blooded murder made Sharon feel vaguely ill in the stomach she didn't have. Still, she knew she'd have to do similar things when they launched their mutiny. At a *minimum*, she'd be locking down every security door on the ship.

For their plan to work, Sharon not only needed to have complete control of the ship, she needed to use it ruthlessly. Preparing for if Trengove betrayed them was a necessary dry run.

As it was, Sharon watched through the surveillance feed as the shuttle pilot dithered in her quarters, choosing between her usual uniform and a tight dark-red dress that she was resting against her skin to compare colors.

Sharon wasn't entirely sure of the point of the dress, though she had enough fashion sense left to agree that it would look amazing on the pale-skinned and dark-haired woman.

Ease of dressing ended up winning as Rooijakkers buzzed for admittance. Both items were a single piece—the uniform doubled as an emergency shipsuit—and the Space Assault officer clearly had more practice getting into her uniform.

Sharon had to hope that even the consideration of the dress suggested better hopes for their plan than she was afraid of.

"I'm glad we're finally getting the chance to catch up," Trengove told Rooijakkers as they settled in at the tiny table. The lunch wasn't much—sandwiches sent down from the mess and a couple of bottles of beer that Sharon couldn't find anywhere in the ship's records—but it filled the limited space.

"We've been on the same ship for months and this is only the second time we've managed to hang out," Rooijakkers agreed. "Been busy."

"You especially, what with being the XO and all," Trengove said. "I didn't want to intrude with everything going on."

The older woman snorted.

"You probably should have," she admitted. "I might have been able to use the distraction. Been...a rough few months."

Trengove tentatively reached over the table and squeezed Rooijakkers' hand.

"I hear that," she murmured. "Are you okay?"

"Complicated," the XO admitted, leaning back in her chair and sighing. "Look...this isn't as personal as I may have implied. There's some shit going down and I need your help."

Trengove leaned back herself, opening space between the two women as she studied Rooijakkers. Even Sharon could read the disappointment and concern in her body language.

"My help?" she asked. "I just fly shuttles, Gerel."

"Bullshit," Rooijakkers told her. "You run the focking troopers they stuck on the ship. Ajello is too busy being a starship Captain to be a Legionnaire Colonel. The two platoons we have on this ship listen to you first, the Colonel and me a long distant second."

"I help out where I can," Trengove said slowly. "But you can run anything through the chain of command, can't you?"

There was a long silence.

"That depends on how far I trust the Legion, doesn't it?" Rooijakkers finally said. "How far I trust a fleet that still happily uses the brains of murdered children to fly their ships. How far I trust a leadership that happily supplied the crew with *sex slaves* when we were at the Exeter Base's R&R site."

"I...missed that part," Trengove said slowly. "Seemed off, just how easy the grunts were finding it to get laid, but I was too busy getting drunk on a beach and ignoring everyone."

"I thought it was odd and asked," Rooijakkers told her old friend. "It's apparently been made *very* clear to the hotel staff that turning down our people's propositions is unwise."

"Fuck."

The room was quiet, and neither of them had touched the sandwiches.

"I was hoping this *was* personal, you know," Trengove noted softly. "*Very* personal. Twenty years or so has definitely soured my opinion on men. *That* little tidbit doesn't help, either."

Rooijakkers flushed. It was easy to miss on her heavy, dark features, but the surveillance feeds picked it up handily.

"I...see," she said slowly. "I'm sorry for deceiving you, then. I had different intentions—and that would be against regs. And Command is in an example-making mood of late."

"With everything the Legion is doing, what do regs even *matter?*" the shuttle pilot snapped. "If this wasn't a catch-up and wasn't a chance for me to seduce you, what *is* it?"

"I need you to help me throw a mutiny."

The room was quiet for a long time, and Sharon ran through her programs as quickly as she could. She already had control of the systems of Trengove's quarters and she could keep the woman's wrist-comp off the internal network, but if the pilot realized what was happening, she could directly transmit.

Sharon could block that, but it was a brute-force intrusion that the wrist-comp would raise an alert on. She needed to get the timing right—get Rooijakkers out of the room, seal the door and block Trengove's coms as she overloaded the life-support plant.

Everything was hanging in virtual space around her, waiting for a single mental button-press to start the sequence that would kill Verdandi Trengove in a horrible accident.

"Throw a mutiny," the woman finally repeated. "Like it's a fucking birthday party. You realize that word is an algorithm trigger for every surveillance program running on this ship? I'm surprised we don't already have someone kicking down the door."

"I do realize that, yes," Rooijakkers agreed. "Do you really think I would make the suggestion if I didn't have a countermeasure?

"We both know the Legion is corrupt to its heart, the worst kind of pointless fascist bullshit," she told her friend. "Four worlds and a hundred million people enslaved...to achieve what? To make Admiral Muhammad feel that he's still in control? To rebuild the Republic? The Republic is *dead* and it *deserved* to die.

"We swore our service to a lie and followed that oath here," she said. "But what is our oath *to* here, Verdandi? Muhammad? The Republic? The people of the rogue colonies?"

"I don't know," Trengove conceded. "But I don't see what dying in a pointless stunt will do to change any of that. Ajello has all the keys, all the guns, all the firepower. Even as XO, what the hell can you do?"

"For reasons I'm not going to tell you, *I* control the ship," Rooijakkers said softly. "So long as Ajello isn't in a position to override my orders, I can lock down the entire ship. Concentrate the people loyal to us, arm the indentures, take the ship."

"Then what?"

Trengove hadn't tried to transmit anything yet, Sharon noted. She was at least listening.

"We fly to the Protectorate, we turn ourselves in, and we tell Mars everything Muhammad has done and where he is," Rooijakkers replied bleakly. "I may not love the RMN, but I do not, for one moment, believe they'd let the Legion's little empire out here stand.

"Not with a hundred million people in chains."

"Okay, so, say I see your point," Trengove said softly, "you realize we're both arguably war criminals just for *helping* Muhammad? The Republic surrendered a long time ago."

"I have to believe that the Protectorate will give us credit for helping free the people we helped conquer," Rooijakkers said, but her tone was still bleak. "Even if they don't...Verdandi...I'll go to jail to save those people. I will. We owe them that much."

"Maybe. But I don't see a way to do it, Gerel."

"You've got the troopers. You have to know which ones we can trust."

Trengove shook her head.

"None of them, Gerel," she admitted. "Anyone who might have found a scrap of conscience lost it in the invasion of Aquila at the latest. *I* did things in that op that I can't forgive myself for.

"I don't think any of our grunts would turn with us. Some of the shuttle pilots, maybe, but you're down to whatever you can pull from the crew and however you're going to arm the indents. *Assuming* you can get the indentures to play along and they're even worth the bullets to blow them away."

The two women held each other's gazes for a small eternity.

"We have a plan," Rooijakkers said quietly. "But I need help. Every extra set of hands is someone we don't have to kill or imprison. I couldn't think of anyone else I could trust."

"If I'm the only person you've talked to, you don't have a plan."

"You are not the first person I've talked to," the XO said with a chuckle. "And I *do* have a plan. I promise."

Sharon's mental finger hovered over the virtual button that would block Trengove's wrist-comp from transmitting.

"You're going to get us all killed," Trengove told her.

"Would you rather die trying or live a slaver?"

The pale woman exhaled a sharp sigh.

"I know the answer to that question, I suppose," she conceded. "But I need some clue, Gerel, some sign that we might be able to do this."

And *that*, Sharon realized, meant it was time for her. She linked into Trengove's wrist-comp before Rooijakkers could say anything and spoke up.

"That would be me, Major Trengove," she said cheerfully.

"What the fuck?" Trengove exclaimed, staring down at her wrist. "Wait...I know that voice."

"It's computer-generated; I could change if I was trying to hide," Sharon told her. "But yes. I am Sharon Deveraux, this ship's Promethean.

"I am currently preventing *Ring of Fire's* surveillance systems from realizing that this conversation is even taking place. I am also preventing you from transmitting to anyone else aboard the ship, setting up standard item-transfer orders to move sidearms and rifles to key storage lockers around the ship, and burying any evidence that anything is going on."

"You have that much control?" Trengove asked. "But you're just..."

"A murdered child whose brain is stuck in a jar," Sharon finished bluntly. "But to get extra value out of us, they linked us into the ship's computers, and my impression is that the Legion's programmers *really* didn't expect me to be able to twist the computers the way I now can.

"I have as much control over *Ring of Fire* as you do over your implants," she told the shuttle pilot. Trengove wasn't a full Augment, but she was above even the normal level of cybernetics for the Space Assault Force.

And she would never have even conceived of those implants disobeying her.

"That's insane," Trengove whispered. "But...it might make this doable."

"It does."

"All right," Trengove said, her tone firming up. "I'm with you. I just have one price."

"What's that?" Rooijakkers asked carefully.

"When this is all over, I get to take you out on a date, Gerel," Tengrove stated. "Deal?"

Rooijakkers laughed.

"All right. Deal."

What neither of them had told Tengrove, though, was that Ajello was entirely capable of shutting down Sharon's access. The only way all of this would work was if Ajello died right at the beginning.

And only one of the three of them had the access and authority to carry a firearm into the presence of the attack transport's commanding officer.

CHAPTER 23

THREE DESTROYERS clustered protectively around the far-smaller stealth ship as Roslyn Chambers ran through another update on the sensor sweeps through the E6S-SF5 System.

They'd spent eight days in the system now, between the original survey and the repairs to *Rhapsody in Purple*. Roslyn and her fellows had taken advantage of the time for more virtual exercises, but she was all too aware of the delay. Five extra days.

Those days had led to additional consideration of the system and, among other things, the conclusion that E6S-SF5-III was probably terraformable. With an average temperature well below freezing, the planet was covered in ice. That ice could be cracked into oxygen and hydrogen—the hydrogen used to fuel the terraforming machinery and the oxygen released into the atmosphere.

The Protectorate had rarely bothered with terraforming beyond the magical transformation of Mars and a few test sites, but they kept a list of candidates. III was a decent one, and while the system had nothing worth traveling between stars to exploit, it had plenty of resources to support a wealthy colony.

Sighing, Roslyn flicked the system map back to the wallscreen and checked her schedule. There were appointments that could be shuffled around, moved to the convenience of the Captain of a starship.

And there were appointments that were fixed in magically-reinforced titanium. The schedule of the Mage-Queen of Mars was set in advance, in increments of three minutes. Roslyn still wasn't entirely sure why her young monarch booked the mostly social calls with her—but there was no world where she'd miss them.

The clock hit the time of their appointment, and a Link was established between Roslyn's office on *Voice of the Forgotten* and Kiera Alexander's office inside Olympus Mons.

"How's it going, Roslyn?" the Mage-Queen of Mars asked as her image materialized above Roslyn's desk. Her casual tone was in direct contrast to the extremely formal and conservative suit Kiera Alexander was wearing.

"Hanging in space, waiting for the spare parts to be installed," Roslyn said drily. "LaMonte's ship had an unplanned encounter with a micrometeorite."

"I saw the report," Alexander admitted. "That's damn bad luck."

The two women could have passed for sisters, both redheaded with vaguely tanned-looking skin. They were cousins of a sort, in fact. Both were direct descendants of Project Olympus, after all.

The children of that program had become the Protectorate's unquestioned first families, the Mages by Blood.

"Timing, mostly," Roslyn admitted. "They shut down a few of their systems to help us Navy types play games with our crews' reality. That left them vulnerable."

She shook her head.

"*Luck* is that nobody died, though one of *Rhapsody*'s engineers is still in medbay. No Mage-Surgeons out here."

"We tend not to let the Navy throw them on warships, as a rule," Alexander observed.

Mage-Surgeons were rare. Given the thousand and one lucrative careers available to a Mage of any type—and the generous stipend paid to keep unemployed Mages out of trouble—very few Mages wanted to go through the effort of getting the full medical training necessary to use their magic for medicine.

"Everyone is going to be all right, though?" the Queen asked.

"Yeah. We have good doctors, even if our Mages are better at breaking bones than setting them," Roslyn said. "Patching up *Rhapsody in Purple* was more of a concern. We ended up having to fabricate replacement components. That took some time."

"I'll double-check that that makes it into the final report," Alexander said. "There's some discussion at the moment around the level of fabrication capacity present in our ships. It's been pointed out that we could fit an extra missile per launcher in our destroyers if we gave it up."

Roslyn shivered melodramatically.

"With my fabrication capacity and my Mages, I can build new missiles if I need to," she pointed out. "Not *quickly*—a Phoenix Nine isn't a simple piece of hardware—but we can do it."

In fact, they *had* been doing it while they'd been working on the repairs for *Rhapsody*. They'd fired two salvos of live missiles during the training exercise, and they'd replaced roughly twenty percent of the weapons in a week.

"I'd far rather have the ability to turn a handy asteroid into spare parts than a nineteenth missile salvo."

"That's what I figured—and what three out of four field officers consulted told the Design Board," the Queen said with a chuckle. "I still mostly just sit in those meetings and soak up information."

Roslyn doubted Kiera Alexander had truly *just* sat in a meeting for years. She'd only been Queen in her own right for less than a year, but her now-Chancellor, then-Regent, Damien Montgomery had made sure to keep her engaged.

Roslyn knew that better than most, as she'd been one of the young Queen's few friends for several years. Mostly through her mentor, Montgomery himself.

"How is the survey mission going?" Alexander asked. "I get the summaries, but eyes on the ground are never amiss."

"We're hitting our fifth system late. The other three task groups are on their seventh, but we'll be at Seventy-Five-D in three days now," Roslyn replied. "LaMonte might be a better person to ask."

"I get LaMonte's reports through the Oversight Board," the Queen said. "And she talks to Damien, not me." She made a throwaway gesture. "I could call her up and ask questions, but people I'm not already friends with find that intimidating."

She grinned.

"LaMonte, for example, doesn't know about my obsession with ship models." The holopickup shifted slightly as the Mage-Queen of Mars lifted a thirty-centimeter-high, mostly assembled model built of stamped metal plates.

"Working on a new model of *Voice of the Forgotten* herself, actually," Alexander said as Roslyn recognized the pyramid shape as an *Honor*-class destroyer. "Those big ex-Republic lasers give it a noticeably different profile in places."

"Helps keep your hands busy in virtual meetings?" Roslyn asked.

"Basically," the Queen agreed. "I like them for themselves, too, but the distraction makes sure I think before I start snapping orders. Impulse is a poor way to run a nation."

"Or a starship," Roslyn murmured.

"Or a starship," Alexander said. "Speaking of which, I actually get to spend time on one shortly."

"You're leaving Mars?" Roslyn asked. That was...news. The general rule was that the Mage-King—Mage-Queen now—never left Mars. Someone had to sit the throne at Olympus Mons, as the saying went.

Roslyn knew enough to know that that *someone* had to be Kiera Alexander, Jane Alexander, or Damien Montgomery. Their unique gifts gave them control of the Olympus Amplifier, an immense artifact of runes and magic that gave the Mage-Queen near-godlike power over the Sol System.

"Which means Damien gets even *more* chained to the Mountain than usual, yes," Alexander told her. "We're still sorting out the details, but I'm going on a 'Grand Tour' of at least the Core Worlds.

"Officially, it's so I can meet the governments and people and get to know the worlds I rule. Which is, I will note, *damn* necessary all on its own. My brother did several similar tours once he was eighteen, but..."

She shook her head.

"Only one of *us* could leave Mars, too," she noted. "But I have to see the people I lead, and they need to see me."

"If that's the *official* reason, is there another one?" Roslyn asked.

"To let the First Families of the Core Worlds throw every eligible twenty-something male Mage they can find at me," Alexander said bluntly. "To the Protectorate's apparent benefit, I *really* want babies. I also *really* want to get laid, though those two desires are only loosely connected on an ongoing basis."

Roslyn only suffered from one of those desires—and was currently only slightly less sexually frustrated than her twenty-one-year-old probably virgin monarch—but she nodded her understanding.

"That's a lot of compressed courtships," she observed.

"Yeah, well, Damien already let them run every Mage-Surgeon under thirty on Mars past me, and they were self-obsessed pricks to a one," Alexander replied. "The thought of a throng of adoration is heartwarming."

"And other-things-warming," Roslyn guessed, and was amused to see the Mage-Queen of Mars, the most powerful human being alive, blush.

"I *may* have considered how many of them I could get away with letting 'seduce' me before I actually started getting in trouble," Alexander murmured. "I figure between every twenty-something Mage boy in a dozen star systems, there's got to be at least half a dozen worth comparing the bedroom skills of."

"I suspect the answer to *how many before trouble* is somewhere between zero and one," Roslyn warned. "But you are the Mage-Queen of Mars. You can handle a lot of trouble."

"Based off my brother's problems before his death, the actual answer is 'two,'" the Queen replied. She sighed, a shadow passing over her eyes that Roslyn knew Alexander wouldn't show in front of many.

"From what we know now, the drama between his long-term girlfriend and the guy he dated while they were on a break helped lead to his murder. And I *didn't* tell you that," Alexander concluded, brushing away momentary tears with the back of her hand.

"I trust your discretion."

"And my discretion is as much at your service as my sword arm, Kiera," Roslyn said levelly. Between her long-standing relationship with Damien Montgomery and the regular calls with Kiera, she knew at least a few secrets she wasn't supposed to.

CHAPTER 24

"FINALLY."

That was probably not the most professional response for an MISS Director or an honorary Navy Commodore to have to being informed they could bring the power back online, but Kelly LaMonte was *bored.*

The repairs to the feed conduits to *Rhapsody*'s power core were the kind of fiddly work that required very specific parts placed in very specific places...and could only really be worked on by about three people at a time.

They were probably the only repairs that the ship's commander could have justified finding a wrench and joining in on, but she had to admit that she wouldn't have done any better than Hussain and the engineer's top people.

She'd reviewed the reports from the other three task groups, watching them eliminate more and more systems from consideration. She'd bleached her hair white.

Kelly had even, finally, caught up on the paperwork involved in setting up an entirely new command-and-control department to run the MISS's stealth ships. She apparently had almost as many administrators in Tau Ceti as she had people on the *Rhapsodies* themselves!

"We'll begin the power-up sequence in five minutes," Hussain told her, the engineer not even trying to hide her smirk. "Though I'd like to note that we are thirty-six hours ahead of the timeline I gave you. I *said* seven days."

"And you did a bit over five, and I *know* how much of a pain that is," Kelly agreed. "If I'd thought it would shave off even ten minutes, I'd have been right there with you."

"Wasn't the space," Hussain replied, echoing Kelly's earlier thoughts. "You'd have just got in the way, sir, and you're out of practice."

"I know," Kelly conceded. "Any concerns with the power-up?"

It was a good thing that they had the destroyers around. *Rhapsody's* backup thermal decay generators would last, basically, forever. What they *didn't* do was provide enough power to do much more than run life support.

Kelly was confident that they could have found the power to run the fabricators long enough to build the parts they needed, but it could have easily become extremely risky.

Instead, they'd had the fabrication done aboard *Voice of the Forgotten* and *Bear of Glorious Justice*, and lined up assault shuttles from all four ships to feed power into *Rhapsody's* systems.

"We've tested all the systems with the feed from the shuttles," Hussain told her. "The only thing I can't do without booting the reactor is test the hydrogen feeds and the reactor itself.

"We'll be starting *very* slow, but its not a completely risk-free process."

"Worst-case scenario, we have to dump the core and have the destroyers tow us home," Kelly pointed out. "Safety protocols will keep *Rhapsody* safe, right?"

"Barring a complete black swan, yes," Hussain agreed. "But that meteorite *was* a black swan event, so I'm not discounting some spectacular bad luck."

"I'd like to say lightning never strikes twice, but I don't believe it," Kelly said. "Still, no other options. Boot it up when you're ready, Samira."

"Sixty seconds," the engineer promised.

Kelly glanced around *Rhapsody in Purple's* darkened bridge and traded a nod with Xi Wu. Her Ship's Mage and wife was seated at the simulacrum, running her fingers over the runes distractedly.

The destroyers had already towed *Rhapsody* far enough out that they could jump easily enough. If the power core had taken damage Hussain had missed and this process failed, Xi and her people could jump them home.

But it wouldn't look particularly good, in Kelly's mind, for the Director of Stealth Ship Operations to be the one whose ship crawled home a cripple.

"Feed at one percent," Hussain announced. "Hydrogen in the core. No leaks detected so far. Electromagnetic fields online from shuttle power. Twenty percent of minimum fuel mass."

Kelly managed not to say anything. Hussain knew this drill even better than she did.

"Holding feed at one percent; minimum reaction mass reached," the engineer reported. "Initiating fusion."

Kelly held her breath. This would literally be a flash in the pan, a single reaction lasting only a few seconds before it fell beneath minimum reaction mass.

There was a spike in her sensor reports and the readouts on the reactor, and then nothing. Her temperature readings were still elevated, rapidly cooling back down to the ship's standard twenty degrees Celsius as the heat radiators set to work.

"Flash complete. No sign of containment failures. Bringing feed to maintenance level and standing by for sustained minimum mass fusion."

A few seconds passed, and then the readouts spiked again. And stabilized. Kelly waited. One second. Ten. Sixty.

She heard the sighs of relief around her bridge as the reactor remained stable.

"All systems are green at thirty percent capacity," Hussain reported. "Permission to shut down shuttle power and bring reactor to full power?"

"Granted," Kelly told her engineer. "And if that works, you've an hour for tests. I want to be on our way. The Legion awaits, after all!"

CHAPTER 25

SHARON FIGURED she and her conspirators needed every advantage they could get, so they waited six hours after the second-to-last jump toward the 95A-36R System, home of Sondheim Base, before they kicked off their plan.

The Promethean wasn't a computer. She wasn't the oft-speculated-but-never-achieved upload of a human brainwave into a machine. But... she could see it from there.

No living human, after all, could have paid full attention to no less than six different views from around the ship, with pre-coded macros ready to kick off for each of them.

One of those views was on the bridge, where Young and Ajello held down a watch in the void, far from anything of interest. Young still wasn't fully in the loop, but Sharon's assessment agreed with Rooijakkers. The tactical officer would be reliable when the penny dropped.

A second view was split between Zhao—the navigator asleep in her quarters, unaware of what was about to happen even though she'd completed a dozen seemingly minor tasks over the last few days to get them there—and Rooijakkers as the XO approached the bridge.

That was informational for now.

A third view was focused on the indentures' quarters. They were due to be awoken in about an hour to return to their thankless task of restoring internal data networks through a tenth of *Ring of Fire*'s rotating inner hull.

Ragno had woken all of them up early, and they were waiting by the supposedly sealed back door. The surveillance in their quarters still showed them sleeping to anyone except Sharon.

Another informational view showed her Engineering, with multiple macros in place to shut down assorted systems across the ship. Sharon knew that *Ring of Fire's* engineers could counter most of those macros, given time. That was the main thing she needed Ragno and the slave workers for.

Her fifth view was of the secondary armory on deck one. Deck one was at the center of the inner hull and had the lowest pseudogravity of anywhere on the ship. It was primarily a cargo deck and would, in the transport's normal purpose, be where tanks and aircraft were stored.

Right now, there was nothing there—but it still had a secondary armory with weapons and exosuit combat armor. And since a strange electrical glitch had just burnt out the security doors on the main armory and the other two secondary armories, the deck-one armory was the *only* place on the ship someone could access exosuits and real guns.

Which was why Major Trengove and a dozen Space Assault Troopers were in there. Half of the SATs were actually shuttle pilots and copilots, but Trengove's careful sounding-out had found her six true Assault Troopers who wanted to help undo what they'd done.

Two of them were even full Augments, once the Republic's elite Mage-killers and still the point of the Legion's spear with their intensive cybernetics.

The last view was of Major Jurica de la Cruz and his senior officers, currently enjoying an immense breakfast as they kept a careful eye on their gunships through their implants.

There was one officer on each gunship, too few to actually fly the ships, and Sharon had a plan to make sure de la Cruz and the other gunship crew didn't make it to their spacecraft.

She had a plan for everything. She had no idea how those plans were going to break down, but as Gerel Rooijakkers approached the bridge and Verdandi Trengove locked an exosuit combat-armor helmet over her head, Sharon dared to hope that things would go according to plan.

Because if they didn't, she wasn't sure what she could do. Unlike a true Ship's Mage, Sharon didn't have a body that could engage in the fighting. Her view of the interior of the ship was too digital for her to use magic, even.

A concealed simulacrum and carefully protected optical-fiber cables gave her a sufficiently analog connection to use magic outside the ship, but the interior of *Ring of Fire* was immune to her Promethean's powers.

It wasn't immune to her *access*, but Ajello could shut that down with a single thought.

Despite all of their plans, success and failure rode on the heavy pistol Rooijakkers wore on her hip as she buzzed for admittance to the bridge.

They'd all known, intellectually at least, that Colonel Tzafrir Ajello was a full Augment, a veteran of the Legatus Self-Defense Forces' Augment Corps and the battle-hardened survivor of no less than *four* planetary invasions.

What no one, including Rooijakkers, had really thought about was what that *meant*. Right up until the moment Gerel Rooijakkers walked into the bridge and met her CO's gaze.

There was a sudden pause and silence on *Ring of Fire*'s bridge as *something* in Rooijakkers' eyes or body language gave away *everything*—and Ajello dove for cover before the pistol was even high enough to fire.

Bullets hammered across the bridge and into the Captain's chair. Rooijakkers tried to anticipate her boss's movements as the cyborg dodged across the room, but she didn't aim far enough ahead, and bullets slammed uselessly into the floor.

Then Ajello popped up over a console, his right wrist resting on his left to provide him a stable firing platform as a compartment in his arm opened to reveal a combat laser.

There was no *way* the weapon had more than one, maybe two, shots. But one shot was all the Legion Colonel needed. A blast of coherent light connected his wrist and Rooijakkers' torso for half a second at most, turning uniform and flesh alike to superheated mist.

But that was half a second Ajello wasn't moving, and Rooijakkers put the last two rounds in her pistol's magazine into his upper torso before she died.

Sharon had enough access to the bridge's sensors to be *very* sure the Legion XO was dead. The woman had likely lost several critical organs and hit the ground with a horrific thud that silenced the entire bridge.

Ajello turned to survey the silent room. He was wounded—badly—but he was an *Augment*. Rooijakkers might have pulled it off. She might not have. Sharon wavered in hesitation with her mental fingers over a dozen buttons as she waited to see if the Colonel collapsed.

"Anyone *else* have a damn clue what's going on?" Ajello snapped.

He took one step back toward his chair before *another* gunshot rang out—and Sharon realized the Colonel had used a cyber-weapon because his own sidearm had fallen out of its holster when he'd dove for cover.

It had apparently landed at Ramiz Young's feet, and the tactical officer rose smoothly as she put a second and third round into the tottering Colonel.

Finally, fully on her feet and with the heavy pistol in perfect target-shooting form, she put a fourth and final round clean through Ajello's right eye, and the cyborg fell at last.

"I honestly have *no* idea what's going on," Young admitted as she turned to cover the rest of the bridge crew with the gun. "But I couldn't help feeling that was a job that needed finishing.

"I suggest everyone stay sitting down until we find out more, eh?"

If Sharon had still had lungs, she would have emptied them in an immense sigh of relief. As it was, she simply fired off the computer programs that underlay their entire mutiny.

"Go, go, go!" Ragno barked as the door slid silently open.

"Where?" one of the other workers asked.

"First turn on your left, then second door on your right," Sharon told them, her voice clearly surprising all of them. "There's body armor and assault carbines in a storage room that I'll unlock when you get there."

The Aquilan rebel waited for the last of the others to run past him, then slapped the panel to close the door.

"Who even *are* you?" he finally asked the empty hall. "Since we're already committed to this, you may as well tell me."

"I'm this ship's Promethean," she admitted. "The Mage brain that lets her jump. I...can do a bit more than that.

"Now get your butt to Engineering and stop Major Curry from blowing us all to hell! He doesn't know anything is going down yet, thanks to our friends on the bridge, but things *are* going down."

Ragno obeyed—and it was already time for Sharon to unlock the door to the storage locker, the freed slaves *eager* to take their revenge on the people who'd kidnapped them and turned them to forced labor.

Throughout the ship, security hatches were sliding shut, separating the transport into easily handled chunks. Trengove and her assault team were also moving, but the Legion Major linked into the ship network before she moved.

"Sharon, what's our status?"

"Messy," Sharon said honestly. "Gerel is dead, Verdandi. I'm sorry."

"Fuck." There was a pause and a sharp inhale as the woman took stock of what that meant. "Ajello?"

"Young shot him with a gun he dropped," Sharon reported. "She's in control of the bridge, but she has no idea what's going on. I think it might be better that way, at least for a few minutes."

"You're probably right. Damn, that girl found her ovaries at just the right time," Trengove said fiercely. "What about the rest of the crew?"

"Everyone should be locked into their quarters or their workstations now," the Promethean said. "I've got twenty-five indentures putting on body armor and arming themselves right now. They'll be in Engineering long before you can get there."

All Sharon and Gerel had really told Trengove about that part of the plan was that Engineering would be taken care of.

"All right. That leaves Life Support, the computer core, the bridge and Flight Ops as our critical zones," Trengove concluded. "Think Young will hold down the bridge?"

"Forty-sixty at best," Sharon admitted as she studied the awkward faces on the bridge. "I've locked out most of the consoles, and with both Gerel and Ajello dead, there's no one to override me.

"Engineering is the last place they can really screw with me, and my second team is moving on them right now."

Ragno had been the last of the indentures to arrive, but he was second-to-last to finish arming. She linked in his helmet radio.

"Ragno, meet Major Trengove," she said as she established a network. "Ragno is an Aquilan rebel who talked all of the indentures into joining us. Trengove is a Legion shuttle pilot who talked a dozen Legionnaires into joining us.

"We've got about a dozen other sympathizers scattered through the ship, but they don't have weapons. I've cut off systems access to anyone who *isn't* on our side, but Engineering can override a lot of that from there or from the main computer core.

"Currently, there's no one *in* the core, but I don't want to bet against people's ability to change that," Sharon continued. "Plus, *I'm* in Engineering, and there are some cords and tubes that will cause me real trouble if Curry pulls them."

"From the schematics, we're maybe two minutes out," Ragno said slowly. "I won't let them unplug you."

"If you've got Engineering, I can send people to the other critical zones," Trengove said. "Better to keep your people and my Legionnaires separate for now, I think, Mr. Ragno."

"I agree. We can sort out who is who and in charge later," the rebel agreed. "That's a lot of places to secure with twelve people, though."

"Your people have light armor and carbines," Trengove told him. "*Mine* are in exosuits with boarding cannons. We'll be fine."

At that moment, one of the gunship officers tried to hail the bridge and got nothing.

"Get moving," Sharon snapped. "The gunship crews are about to realize they're in trouble...and I don't know what comes after that, but I can only lock *Ring's* weapons down.

"I don't have the access to fire them."

CHAPTER 26

SHARON REALIZED that underestimation was going to be the theme of the whole affair when Ragno quietly led the way into Engineering, his body armor easily visible but the carbine vaguely concealed behind his back.

None of the half-dozen Legion spacers and officers working in the space paid any mind to his entrance or even the entrance of the other attackers until Ragno stepped up to Major Ben Curry.

"What the hell are you doing?" Curry snapped as he looked up. Even though the freed indenture shouldn't have been in Engineering at all, the Legion officer didn't recognize that.

"You should be in your quarters," he continued. "Get back there before someone sees you."

Ragno smiled slightly—and pointed the carbine directly at Curry. Of all the people in the cavernous void of *Ring of Fire*'s engineering spaces, Curry was the closest to Sharon's life-support system.

"It is a bitter irony to me that, despite literally being a slaver, you are *not* the worst boss I've ever had," Ragno informed Curry as the Legion officer stared at the weapon. "That said, if you do not step back from the console and disable your implant transmitter, I *will* shoot you."

A chorus of surprised and disconcerted shouts echoed around the Engineering space as the engineers realized their slave workers were now armed.

Gravity in Engineering was low. It was a deck-one facility, with no deck zero above it. The circular room was anchored on the massive central keel of the inner hull, and it was even structured to take advantage of the fact that rotational gravity didn't exist unless you were standing on something.

The engineers were adjusted to that gravity and the freed indentures weren't, but that was why Ragno had four times as many raiders as there were engineering crew on duty.

"We don't want to hurt any of you," Ragno continued. The warmth and compassion in his voice only added to the iron determination. "But this ship is now under our control. If you resist, we will kill you."

Curry himself was unarmed and started to raise his hands in surrender—but at least one of his people turned out to be a full Augment. An unexpected blade snapped out of the woman's arm and tore out the throat of the rebel closest to her, and she dove toward a console Sharon suspected contained emergency-shutdown codes.

Gunfire echoed in the open decks, and the Legion Major made his own move in the distraction. Unfortunately for him, Sharon had jammed every implant transmitter in the room the moment Ragno had given his ultimatum, and Curry's attempt to trigger a shutdown remotely failed.

His attempt to jump Ragno was more successful. The rebel, despite his gun and armor, was no soldier. None of the freed techs were, and their leader was distracted by the gunfire as half a dozen of his people poured fire into the Augment trying to kill them.

Curry hit Ragno in the torso, flinging both of them backward. Leaving the floor for a moment, they traveled with the rotation of the deck, and the rebel leader slammed into the armored casing covering Sharon's physical existence.

She didn't feel it. Her brain had links to a hundred computers and several million sensors, but none of those gave her physical center anything resembling a sense of touch.

It drew her full attention, though, and she was desperately trying to sort out what—if anything—she could do when the Augment finally went down. Her people had probably fired fifty bullets for every one that had hit their target, but the Legionnaire was dead.

Ragno had intentionally tossed his own firearm far enough away that Curry couldn't reach it as he wrestled with the engineer.

Curry's cybernetics were entirely mental, and Ragno was ten years younger and easily had five kilos of muscle on the Legionnaire. Skill was on the engineer's side, but as surprise faded, the struggle became more of a draw—and then one of Ragno's people put a bullet into Curry's head from fifty centimeters away.

Brains sprayed across the Promethean Drive Unit's armored casing, and Sharon mentally blinked away a flash of entirely emotional nausea.

Ragno was equally covered in gore, but he pushed Curry's body aside and spat an oath she didn't recognize.

"Secure the room," he barked. "Who's left?"

Two of the Legion engineers were still alive, having chosen the better part of valor. The other four were dead, but half a dozen of the freed indentures had died with them, and there were some concerning wounds among the survivors.

Ragno picked up most of that in a visual survey and a few short words, then grimaced.

"All right. Rodney, Wu, Fred, Drazen—secure that entrance. Marietta, Anant, those consoles control the fusion cores. They should be unlocked; take control."

More orders flowed out as Ragno, and the techs set to work to secure their access and control of the ship. Sharon ran new macros to give aspects of control back to the consoles as friendlies took possession of them, but also allowed her attention to expand again with an internal sigh of relief.

Life support was in Trengove's hands. The computer core remained empty, though a pair of excessively clever Legion techs were now trying to break into it. So far, they'd failed—and a trio of exosuited mutineers were almost there, so Sharon wasn't worried about the computers.

Trengove herself was headed to the bridge, which was remaining surprisingly calm. Probably helped by the fact that Sharon had shut down all of the internal surveillance. All Young and her not-quite-prisoners could see was that they were locked out.

Without Ajello or Rooijakkers, no one on the bridge appeared to know how to influence anything. Like the people who'd been sleeping and were locked in their quarters, they were waiting for the battle for the ship to end.

Unlike the people locked in their quarters, the people on the bridge *could* do a lot to make Sharon's life harder. Their hesitancy was making more of a difference than she hoped they realized.

Her last team was in Flight Ops, and scanning in on those mutineers, she realized that she'd let her attention slip at a critical moment.

She had underestimated Major de la Cruz. The mess he'd shared with his officers was empty—two of the doors taken out by implanted lasers—and she had no idea where the gunship crews were.

And while Trengove's people had just finished taking Flight Ops, the crews there had successfully stopped Sharon from detecting the gunships beginning their power-up sequences.

"Trengove, Ragno, the gunships are online," Sharon reported desperately to her two human counterparts. "Your people in Flight Ops are trying to shut them down, but it looks like de la Cruz has cut his people off from our systems."

"He was always a clever bastard," Trengove said. "But the gunships are physically attached to the external docking collars. Can you lock down those clamps?"

"Already done," Sharon told her. "But that they're powering up the ships tells me they have a plan...and I'm still locating de la Cruz himself. Even I can only multitask so much, and they've left multiple trails of wrecked doors through the ship."

"Nothing I can do from Engineering," Ragno admitted. "They've already severed the power feeds from *Ring* along with the computer connection. I doubt de la Cruz has realized *what's* going on, but he knows *Ring's* computers are compromised."

"*If* we can take control of the bridge, will Young and I be able to fire the lasers?" Trengove asked.

"Yes, but in lockdown, they are fully cold," Sharon warned. "It will take at least five minutes to get them powered up and ready to fire—and the beams on the gunships are already warming up."

"What about the RFLAMs?" the pilot asked. "That's all the gunships *have*, after all."

Sharon ran the numbers on the Rapid-Fire Laser Anti-Missile turrets between one breath and another for the humans.

"They're not *supposed* to shut down as cold as I put them," she admitted. "They're designed to operate semi-automatically, in case of surprise, but I fully killed them. They'll take *ten* minutes to come online."

"Then I better talk to Young fast," Trengove replied grimly. "See if you can keep those gunships locked to the hull *somehow*, Sharon. Because if de la Cruz has six armed gunships out there and we have no weapons..."

Sharon was silent, but she saw Ragno's grim nod. She'd looked up de la Cruz's record—and she doubted the man who'd flown demonstration airstrikes on civilian populations in the Mackenzie System would blink at blowing *Ring of Fire* to hell and waiting for help.

"The good news is that the gunships don't have Links," she admitted quietly. "And I have full control of *Ring*'s Link. No one in the Legion knows what's happening."

"Understood," Trengove said in a clipped tone. "I'm at the bridge. Stand by."

With the key parts of the ship except for the bridge under mutineer control and the vast majority of the crew dead, captive or sealed in their quarters, the actual struggle for *Ring of Fire* itself was over as Major Verdandi Trengove strode into the bridge with two exosuited troopers in tow.

"If everyone would please step away from their consoles, there appears to be a conversation we need to have," Trengove told them all cheerfully. "While even fléchettes will make more of a mess of the controls than I'd like, I'll do what I have to do."

Young rose from where she was seated on the command chair, keeping her hands and the gun clearly visible.

"Not to put too fine a point on it, but who the hell are you and what's going on?" she demanded.

"Major Trengove, the First Pilot," her armored mutineer replied. "I was working with Rooijakkers to take control of this ship, but it seems that I'm now the last officer standing.

"I know you took out the Colonel, Lieutenant Young, so you're in my good books, but I can't say I know what side you're on—and we have *no* time."

"This is mutiny!" one of the Petty Officers exclaimed—and was promptly yanked farther away from their console and cuffed by one of the exosuited troopers.

"Mutiny, treason, rebellion... The long-term plan is technically *defection*," Trengove agreed cheerfully. "So, I have two questions for you, Lieutenant Ramiz Young."

Young straightened, facing the armored intruders...but she hadn't put the gun down, either.

"Are you prepared to be party to establishing a dictatorship over a hundred million people and the enslavement of hundreds of thousands of people for our convenience?" Trengove asked softly. "Because I know I was mostly going along to get along until someone gave me an alternative."

"And if I'm not?" Young asked slowly.

"If I can trust you, I need to know how quickly you can get the guns back online, because our gunships are about to blast themselves clear of *Ring's* hull and try to kill us all," Trengove said drily.

The tactical officer glanced at the bridge, where other officers and techs were being gently herded safely away from their gear.

"Where's Alex?" she asked.

"Alex is in her quarters, still asleep, to be honest," Sharon piped up from Young's wrist-comp.

Then the whole ship shuddered as the first explosives went off. There was a *lot* of cushioning and shock absorption between the stationary armored exterior hull of a Republic's standard hull cylinder and the rotating inner hull—which meant the explosives had been massively powerful.

More explosions tore through the assault transport as de la Cruz's people blasted themselves free of their docking collars. Sharon had locked down the mechanisms, but it appeared that the gunship commander had been paranoid enough to make sure he had a countermeasure to that.

"Trengove, Young, we're out of time," she announced on the bridge announcer system. "Do *something.*"

"If Alex is safe, I'm with you," Young snapped. "Take the chair, Major."

She half-ran, half-jumped toward her standard tactical console as Sharon unlocked it.

"Ragno, guns should be coming back up. Give them power," Sharon told the rebel in Engineering—but she knew it wasn't enough.

Even as she restored sensor access to the bridge, she could see that the gunships' RFLAM turrets had been in the proper standby status, and she hadn't been able to shut those down.

The one-gigawatt multi-chamber lasers could fire every few seconds, and each of the six gunships had three of them. A single beam of that power couldn't destroy the transport, but it could damage her.

A lucky or careful hit could cripple her—and de la Cruz opened fire without even summoning the mutineers to surrender. Lasers hammered into *Ring of Fire*'s engines and weapons—and Sharon's rebel engineers didn't know enough to give them much of a damage report.

"Engines are off-line," Ragno snapped as he finally linked to the bridge. "I have no idea what kind of repairs they're going to need, but we just took multiple hits to the primary exhaust manifolds."

"Half the battle lasers are off-line, and they just vaporized a third of the turrets," Young barked. "What do we do?!"

A chill ran through Sharon's mental existence. She had enough reports to realize that they'd failed. De la Cruz had all of the advantages now and had crippled them before they could reply.

She could still jump the starship, but that wouldn't...

She was still a Mage.

The thought slammed fully-formed into Sharon's mind as the second salvo of laser fire crippled *Ring of Fire*'s remaining weapons. The transport only *had* four twenty-gigawatt battle lasers and twenty RFLAM turrets. De la Cruz had rendered them unable to fight back.

With any technological weapons, at least.

"He's hailing us," Young said quietly. "I know enough to accept the call."

"No return visual or audio," Trengove ordered. "Play his message."

Sharon kept one part of her attention on them as she wracked her mind for long-ago lessons on magical self-defense. She'd never been formally trained as a Jump Mage—all of that knowledge was loaded into a silicon database she'd been given as part of her *upgrades*.

She'd been young enough that the magical-defense training she'd been given was very low-key, mostly on how to shield herself from a thrown punch or rock. She barely remembered those spells—and none of them would work against lasers.

There were stories of *some* Mages who could block lasers, but Sharon Deveraux had never learned that magic, not as a teenage student at a barely tolerated academy deep inside the UnArcana Worlds.

"Mutineers aboard *Ring of Fire*," de la Cruz addressed them all harshly. "You know who I am. I don't care who you are.

"I have crippled your ship, and I have more than enough firepower to vaporize you all. Since the Legion would rather get *Ring* back, I will give you this one opportunity to surrender."

Sharon had dropped her attention from everything except the bridge, the optical link that let her jump the ship and see outside her, and the database of her own memories and the jump magic.

In a moment of desperate inspiration, she brought up an index on the database that had "taught" her how to jump the starship—and realized there was more in there than she'd thought.

A *lot* more. Files that would have been invisible to anyone accessing that database through conventional means. Even to *her*, they weren't normally visible. Only when she accessed them through the unique link of a Promethean did a list of other instructional tutorials appear.

Someone had anticipated exactly what the Legion had done to their captive Mage brains...and left those future Mages a toolbox that she hadn't realized was there.

And first on the list, a simple "self-defense" spell. She didn't know if it was enough...but it was what she had.

"We can't surrender," Trengove said grimly. "De la Cruz will just shoot us all. There's no winning here, people. I only see one chance."

"What the hell is that? Because I don't see *anything*," Young snapped.

"This ship masses twenty million tons and those gunships mass fifty thousand," the pilot said bluntly. "If we can get *any* thrust, we can crush them like tin cans with our own bulk."

Sharon half-tuned them out and focused on the file she'd found. Like the jump spell, it was half-memory, half-tutorial—something she could, if she tried, access as almost muscle memory.

She'd rather go over it a thousand times *before* loading it into her brain, but she had no choice. Steeling herself, she loaded the spell into her brain and reached out into space.

The direct optical link allowed her to *see* around the ship. Software and hardware alike allowed her to zoom in close enough to almost touch the gunships.

Not that she needed much zoom. None of them had moved more than a dozen kilometers away from the assault transport, and that made them easy prey.

For the first time since awakening as a Promethean, Sharon Deveraux focused her power into something other than the jump spell and felt the runes around her wake up. Power rippled through *Ring of Fire*'s hull as her Gift answered her call like an eager horse too long in the paddock.

A mental hand slashed across the sky, and an arc of electricity exploded from the nothingness, quantum energy states building upon each other to unleash a blade of lightning that tore de la Cruz's command gunship in two.

Sharon refocused, finding a second gunship and lashing out at it in turn. The parasite warships were practically unarmored, designed to stay out of range of warship beams and avoid ever being hit by missile fire.

Against the wrath of an unleashed Promethean, they had no defense. A third gunship died and the remaining three were scattering.

"Sharon, is that *you*?" Trengove demanded.

"Yes," she admitted. "I...couldn't let them kill everyone. They're running."

"And you can't let them go," the Legion Major said grimly. "You *can't*. We're too badly damaged. You have to kill them all."

Sharon had reached the same conclusion herself and gathered her power again. Even the few extra kilometers the gunships had added increased the strain to the magic—she had *no* idea how Martian Navy Mages could pull off the combat spells they did—but she could still reach them.

A fourth gunship died. A fifth. The last overloaded her engines, desperately trying to get away from the wrath of the trapped Mage...but their pilot's courage exceeded their engineers' skill.

The sixth and final gunship of de la Cruz's squadron blew apart on her own as her engine containment failed.

The mutiny had succeeded...and while Sharon Deveraux had lost her first friend, she'd saved at least a dozen innocents from slavery.

And maybe, just maybe, they could free half a dozen worlds.

CHAPTER 27

"I HAVE GOOD NEWS and bad news for your Purple Eyes," Jakab told Kelly as the Link settled into their virtual meeting.

"I'm not used to managing four ships' worth of people," Kelly admitted. "Let alone having responsibility for *all* of the task groups—but I can tell you that this task group *needs* some good news.

"75D-6GE is a bust," she continued. "There isn't even anything of interest to a mining corporation. Combined with how late we're running on our sweep and the holdup repairing *Rhapsody in Purple...*"

The spy shook her head.

"The MISS people are fine; we got used to long sweeps that didn't find much when we were searching for Styx Station. The rest of the task groups seem to be doing okay, but...I worry about your Navy crews."

"They have enough discipline that I'm not *worried*, per se," Mage–Vice Admiral Jakab said with a chuckle. "And it helps that the rest of them are on system seven and can see the end of their patrol.

"The good news I have for your task group will probably help, though. The Mountain decided to put a bug in the Stellar Survey Society's ear. Given that the original survey of Hondo *didn't* include a planetoid with minable quantities of transuranics and ownership of the survey has actually lapsed back to S-Three due to a sequence of bankruptcies and litigation..."

He trailed off with a grin.

"They're paying the finder's fee to your crews," he concluded as Kelly caught up and started to share his grin. "They're running through the numbers as we speak, but congratulations, Director LaMonte.

"My back-of-the-envelope math makes every ship captain in your flotilla a millionaire and even the most junior techs on the destroyers *very* happy."

Money wasn't...*meaningless* to Kelly, not really. But she'd spent a lot of time as the senior engineer on a civilian jump freighter, where *petty cash* was more money than most citizens of the Protectorate saw in a lifetime.

Her own needs were mostly met by the budget that operated *Rhapsody in Purple*, and she'd received a generous salary even before her promotion. She and her partners lived on a ship and took luxurious vacations occasionally, but they were accumulating a major savings balance. Adding a couple million to that wouldn't hurt, but the money would probably mean more to most of her crews than her.

That was still *very* good news—and professional paranoia was part of her job.

"What's the *bad* news?" she asked carefully.

"The *other* thing you saw in the Hondo System is now under the Official Secrets Act, classification Black Diamond," Jakab said flatly. "*Any* discussion of it with *anyone* outside your task group will result in prosecution to the full extent of the OSA, likely resulting in no less than twenty years in prison.

"Make *damn* sure your people know that. We've apparently had a *problem* with Species Seven sites being damaged or destroyed before the right people can examine them.

"The Mountain wants that station and they want it *bad*."

The Mountain meant the government of Mars, in the same way as an older nation might have used "the Crown." In this case, Kelly suspected that it meant either Prince-Chancellor Damien Montgomery—or Kiera Alexander herself.

"I'll make certain the warning is dispersed, Admiral," she told him. "Weirdly, I think that might help with our morale problem as much as the finder's fee. People will feel that we at least found *something* important—and we all know that none of the other groups have found shit."

With four task groups and sixteen ships, her Operation Long Eye had now surveyed twenty-six star systems. Other than a few terraforming candidates and similar things SSS would pay finder's fees for, they hadn't found much of anything.

Most importantly, they hadn't found any sign of the Legion.

"We all knew that was a chance," Jakab reminded her. "The Legion had to be far enough away to make a local logistics depot make sense—enough sense that they gave up one of their starship hulls for it, even if they pulled her Prometheus Interfaces."

"DEL-Three-T-Three was already seventy light-years from Sol, Admiral. How much farther could these rogue colonies have gone?"

"I don't know," he admitted. "Honestly, I'm not certain there's a real limit on how far out they might be. Even a single Jump Mage could easily take a ship five or six hundred light-years in under a year.

"We think of the hundred-light-year line as a big deal because the vast majority of humanity lives inside it, but it's an entirely arbitrary line. We have no idea where a rogue colony may have set up shop."

"I suppose," Kelly agreed. She glanced at her timetables on another screen and sighed. "If we don't find anything on this sweep, at least we have a starting zone that we know they're *not* in," she concluded. "So long as they're not actively attacking our systems, that will serve for a while."

"For now," Jakab agreed. "But Her Majesty was clear: these people have conquered entire planets by force of arms. That can not be allowed to stand.

"So, you *will* find them," he said calmly. "And then Admiral Medici and I will show them how far Her Majesty's protection spreads!"

CHAPTER 28

ALEX ZHAO LOOKED more confused than anything else when one of the mutineer Space Assault Troopers delivered her to the council of war. She'd awoken to find her door sealed and the ship's network shut down, but Sharon had sent the trooper to get her before she'd worked herself into a panic attack.

Zhao was, after all, one of exactly two surviving ship's officers.

Young didn't make any pretense of the situation as the blonde navigator entered the room. The Turkish woman immediately wrapped her lover in a tight, wordless embrace—one that Zhao returned after an awkward moment.

"What's going on?" Zhao finally asked.

"We—and the voice in the ceiling—are the leaders of the mutiny that has taken *Ring of Fire,*" Trengove told her.

"Hi, Alex," Sharon said. "I'm the voice in the ceiling."

"Wait, *Deveraux* led a mutiny?" Zhao seemed more surprised by the Promethean's involvement than the mutiny itself, Sharon realized.

"Rooijakkers and I were working together," Sharon told her. "But I talked her into it...and, unfortunately, she didn't survive."

"Ajello killed her," Young said grimly, releasing Zhao from her embrace but keeping a hand on the other woman's waist.

Zhao immediately covered Young's hand with hers, looking around the sparsely occupied conference room and studying the handful of people in turn.

"I see that *not* mentioning my concerns about Deveraux's loyalty was a...decision," she said slowly. "I knew I worked with you more than anyone else, but I figured everyone else seemed confident in the indoctrination."

"Did the indoctrination work on *you?*" Sharon asked drily. "I appreciate you keeping your concerns to yourself, though. But the question everyone is hesitating to ask is: are you with us?"

Zhao looked down at her and Young's interlaced fingers and smiled sadly.

"I'm with Ramiz," she told them all. "I swore an oath to the Republic... but the Republic is dead. I'm not going to pretend I would have joined your mutiny, but it's done.

"So, where my love goes, I go, and that seems to be with the rest of you."

"Good," Sharon said firmly, before anyone else could argue. "The two people in the room you *don't* know, Lieutenant Zhao, are Major Verdandi Trengove—*Ring's* First Pilot—and Teodor Ragno, a rebel from Aquila."

"I suppose that puts the Major in command?" Zhao suggested.

"We have worked together well enough so far, but I don't think I or the indentures will accept *any* Legion officer as the Captain of this ship," Ragno said firmly. "I trust that the three of you mean well, but half a million people died when the Legion arrived in my home system."

"And you're qualified to command an assault transport?" Young asked. "I mean no offense, Mr. Ragno, but I feel we are all best served by you being in Engineering!"

"*Qualified* is irrelevant," Ragno pointed out. "This ship has power and life support. We have no engines, no weapons—we don't have even local communications, and I don't think any of us want to try to use a Legion Link to call for help?"

"We still need someone in command," Trengove said firmly. "If nothing else, to be the neutral party between our former victims and the ex-Legion personnel. I feel there is only one possible candidate."

"Deveraux," Alex Zhao said instantly.

"Yes?" Sharon responded.

"That wasn't a question," Zhao said. "It was agreeing with Trengove. *You* are the only person I think we can all accept as the captain of this ship."

"I am not...a..."

"If the word *person* is about to come out of that speaker, I will get Ragno to show me where your brain is and beat on the case with a hammer until you stop being an idiot," Zhao told her cheerfully.

"Ms. Deveraux would be entirely acceptable to me and the other indentures," Ragno said before Sharon could reply. "She was the only *person* we spoke to before kicking off this whole affair."

She doubted the stress on *person* was unintentional.

"Young?" Trengove asked, looking at the tactical officer. "I think everyone else is on board with this plan?"

"Then it's unanimous," Young replied thoughtfully. "I apologize, *Captain*. I hadn't considered that as a possibility, and I should have."

"I can't... I'm... I..."

Even with a dozen computers wired to her brain, Sharon couldn't think fast enough to keep up with how rapidly the ground had just shifted around her.

"Stop that; the Captain shouldn't hesitate," Trengove told her—but Sharon had a three-hundred-and-sixty-degree video feed of the room and she could see the pilot grinning.

"All right," Sharon conceded. "Then I suggest everyone report what they know—and I'll fill in whatever gaps I can manage from the ship's systems."

"Central Engineering is in decent shape, but a lot of what it's supposed to control is either off-line or just plain gone," Ragno said bluntly. "The inner hull is still rotating and mostly intact. I *think* we have the raw materials and parts to get at least one or two of the main engines online, but we're talking a couple of weeks at least without help."

"There's no help coming," Trengove told them. "But there may be *trouble* coming. My people found Costa in the Link center when we swept the ship. I know Deveraux had the coms locked down, but he was the coms officer."

Was being the operative word. The troopers who'd found Raoul Costa in the communications hardware had assumed the coms officer in the Link control room was a danger—and shot him dead.

"My sweep of the systems says that he failed to get a message out, but he did have access to a disconnected terminal for at least a minute," Sharon warned. "We have time, even if he *did* get a message out, but that cuts our options."

"Our defensive turrets are irreparable," Young warned. "De la Cruz just blasted them off the hull. It's possible that we can cannibalize enough parts to get two or three of the battle lasers online, and our missile launchers are untouched...but six launchers and two or three lasers won't protect us from *anything*."

"So, we move the ship," Zhao suggested. "The engines being off-line doesn't impact the jump systems, right, Deveraux?"

"I'd need to take control of some of the remotes and check the damaged sections for matrix integrity," Sharon said slowly. "At the end of the day, we still have the same runes as a Protectorate jump ship. They're just concealed where the crew can't access them."

"What happens if they are damaged?" Trengove asked.

"Jumping goes from risk-free to...not," the Promethean warned. "The risk should still be low without deeper damage than I think the gunships did, but we *are* in danger at that point.

"And while we have the *materials* aboard to repair the matrix, I'm not entirely sure anyone knows how," she concluded. "I can make some crude fixes with the remotes, but everything I know says that work should be done by a Mage."

"How the hell did the Republic do it in the first place, then?" Ragno demanded.

"They had Mages in the shipyards," Zhao said simply. "Given some of the problems I know we've had trying to duplicate Prometheus Drives out here, they *had* to."

"The Legion hasn't succeeded in duplicating the Interfaces themselves yet," Sharon noted. "But they *have* grown quite skilled at building matrices for us Prometheans to access.

"Like I said, I think the remotes can fix the most egregious damage, but I want to complete a review before we jump anywhere."

"Zhao is right, though," Trengove said. "We don't need our engines to jump. We can head out deeper into the void and hide until we get at least some engines and defenses.

"I'm reasonably sure we have the food supplies for it."

"We are carrying a six-month supply of foodstuffs and spare parts for Sondheim Base," Sharon pointed out. "That's for *two thousand* people. Even including our prisoners, we only have a hundred and eight."

She was aware of how many people had died to get them down to that number. Of those survivors, only forty-five were definitely with them, too.

"What do we do about the prisoners?" Trengove asked. "I mean, I suppose we don't *know* they're going to fight us, but..."

"We ask them," Ragno said, the rebel shrugging as he spoke. "And we ask their friends. You've said you have thirty members of the crew you trust. We ask them who among the prisoners *they* trust, and then offer those people a chance.

"Work through the list until we are reasonably sure who is and isn't willing to work with us. The latter get turned over to the authorities wherever we end up."

"That's more generous than I expected from you," Young admitted. "They are all Legion, after all."

"I have no illusions about your people, Lieutenant Young," the Aquilan replied. "You are all complicit, at least, in the crimes committed against my people and the other worlds out here.

"*But* I also understand that you all thought you were following legitimate orders until it was far too late," he continued. "I know that the nation you served is gone, and at least some of your people either hate or are terrified of the Protectorate.

"So, while I hold you all at least partially responsible for what happened to my world, I *also* hold you all to be at least partially *victims* of what has happened here.

"And we need all the help we can get."

"That part is *definitely* true," Trengove agreed. "Captain Deveraux, may I make a suggestion as to chain of command?"

"Do we need one?" Sharon asked. "I have far more ability to keep track of everything going on aboard this ship than a regular Captain."

"I think it is a good idea," Ragno said slowly and uncomfortably. "I am prepared to listen."

"I think our Legion people will be more comfortable if the leadership at least *looks* ex-Legion," Trengove told them all. "I suggest that we make Mr. Ragno our chief engineer and either myself or Lieutenant Young the executive officer.

"In practice, those two roles will be coequal for us, and this command council will, by necessity, be mostly democratic, but having the formal executive officer be ex-Legion will help our case when we tell the Legion crew they will be safe."

"I agree," Young said. "But I think the XO must be Major Trengove. I can continue as tactical officer and Zhao as navigator, but the senior surviving Legion officer should be the XO—and that is the Major."

Ragno looked thoughtful.

"I appreciate the concession of having me as your equal, Major," he said quietly. "My people are nervous about our position here, and releasing more Legion personnel won't help, but having me on the command council and officially in charge of Engineering should help them feel secure."

"We want everyone to feel as secure as possible," Sharon told them. "We have a lot of work to do before I'm prepared to take this ship to the Protectorate. At the very minimum, we need the ability to tell the Martians we're not Legion!

"I'm commencing the remote sweep of the matrix as we speak," she continued. "Once that's done, I'll jump us away."

"There will still be debris here," Young warned. "You destroyed de la Cruz's gunships, but the wreckage will still be detectable for several weeks."

"So long as they can't tell where we went, I can live with that," Sharon told them all. "We have to. It would take most of our missiles to vaporize the debris, wouldn't it?"

"Probably not *most*," Young disagreed, then sighed. "But many. We only have sixty."

"Then we leave the debris and let the Legion bury their dead when they get here," *Ring of Fire*'s new Captain decided. "We need to make those repairs before we decide our next steps—and thanks to the supplies we're carrying, we have time."

For them, at least. Sharon was grimly aware of the *lack* of time for the people at Exeter or the populations of the rest of the Legion's worlds.

But what else could they do?

CHAPTER 29

"AND HERE WE ARE."

Xi's murmured words marked the end of the reality ripple that was *Rhapsody in Purple*'s jump to the 95A-36R System.

Kelly squeezed her wife's arm as the petite Asian Mage slumped slightly in exhaustion.

"Go rest, love," she told Xi Wu. "We've got this."

The Mage nodded. She took a moment to lean over where Liara Foster had taken over the simulacrum.

"Are we good, Foster?"

"We're good, boss," the Navy Jump Mage replied. "Invisible and sneaky, just like everybody likes. No one is seeing us and we can see everything."

"And there is an *everything* to see," Shvets observed, their tone slightly hushed. "Take a look."

Like a warship, *Rhapsody in Purple*'s bridge was also the simulacrum chamber that jumped her between the stars. That meant that the walls were all screens fed by optical fibers from the hull of the ship, creating a direct analog link to the exterior reality.

Data could be overlaid onto those visuals, and optical zoom could be used to give the crew some idea of what was going on—plus, there were holoprojectors throughout the bridge.

The blonde tactical officer brought all of that together to give them an image of their new location, and Kelly inhaled sharply.

Even with the use of Mages to transmute matter into antimatter as a fuel source, most Protectorate worlds were still at least half-powered by fusion. Massive amounts of hydrogen and helium were extracted from gas giants to fuel those power plants, which meant that the *absence* of a gas giant was an impediment to colonization. 95A-36R had *three* of them, providing a plentiful power source for any industry potential colonists cared to name.

Asteroid belts were a common source of raw material for orbital industry, and the presence of an asteroid belt was considered a bonus by Protectorate colony planners. This system had *four*—and appeared to have swept most of the loose debris up into those belts, avoiding the meteor-impact problem that gave Tau Ceti, for example, headaches.

Of course, all of that was only so useful without a habitable world, but Shvets had provided their highest-fidelity optical zoom on 95A-36R-II.

An almost exactly Earth-size world with no ice caps and minimal axial tilt, II looked like a tropical paradise across most latitudes, glimmering with the stereotypical blue and green of a habitable "garden world."

"So, boss, is S-Three going to be paying out *other* finder's fees to the crews?" Shvets asked. "Because my initial scans call II a class-one garden world. We'd need to take dirt and plant-life samples to be sure, but..."

A "class-one garden world" was colonizable by humans with minimal or no safety equipment. Around eighty percent of all human settlement had been on class-one garden worlds, with the remainder on class-two gardens.

And the finder's fee for a class-one garden world was easily on par with, oh, a moon full of transuranics.

"Maybe," Kelly told her bridge crew. "But let's not start calculating bank balances before the check bounces, hey? Get me a course to II and we'll take a closer look—but keep our invisibility cloak up.

"There's more than enough fuel here to justify running a significant fleet base. I don't want to be seen first."

Two hours into the system, Kelly had yet to leave *Rhapsody*'s bridge, and the back of her neck was itching like someone had tied sandpaper to it.

"Should we be bringing the destroyers in to support your sweep?" Sciacchitano asked over the Link. "It sounds like everything looks clear so far."

"No," Kelly replied. "Twenty-four hours, Mage-Commander. There's a *reason* for that timeline. If someone is here, that's an average amount of time they can keep their engines and life support dark without the ship being specially built for it.

"We haven't *seen* anything, but we know the Legion can be sneaky."

Plus, *Rhapsody in Purple* was in the inner system, scanning 95A-36R-II and -I—since I looked *potentially* habitable. It wasn't a class-one garden world, but it appeared to have life of its own.

II's biggest weakness was a low oxygen percentage, a weakness that I didn't share. Between them, the gas giants and the asteroid belts, 95A-36R was probably one of the most valuable colonization targets that Kelly had seen that didn't already have humans in it.

But the gas giants were quite separate from the two potentially habitable worlds, three-quarters of a *billion* kilometers from where *Rhapsody* was slowly decelerating toward 95A-36R-II. If there was a base out there—and that was where Kelly would have put it—they could easily have missed it on their scans so far.

"I want the destroyers to stand by to jump on my order," she told Sciacchitano. "Keep an eye on our telemetry. The hair on the back of my neck is standing up, and this whole place feels like *exactly* where I'd expect a refueling depot."

"I can't argue with that," Sciacchitano admitted. "We'll keep the telemetry relay up and wait for your call."

The Link conversation dropped, and Kelly turned back to Shvets.

"Well? Class one or two, Nika?" she asked them.

"Seventeen percent oxygen isn't great, but humans can get used to it," they replied. "Temperatures are on the warm side, but weather appears to be stable. Fifty-two percent water, about half of it in an equatorial ocean that circles the planet and splits the continents in half.

"Without soil samples and a wildlife survey, I can't definitely say class one, boss, but it looks likely."

"And do we see any sign of civilization?" Kelly asked. "My finely tuned paranoia is *screaming*, and if the Legion wanted to set up a new colony, here would be the place."

"Nothing so far," Shvets said. "If we launched drones, I could be certain, but without that, we have to wait to reach orbit."

"Keep the drones aboard until the twenty-four-hour mark," she ordered. Shvets had to be sharing a bit of her twitchiness, or they'd have launched the drones without checking.

"Yeah," they murmured. "I have this sinking feeling that I'm being watched."

Rhapsody in Purple slid into orbit of the garden world with a final blast of magically concealed thrust. They'd been in-system for six hours now... and Kelly remained on the bridge, her back still itching like she was being sized up for a knife.

"Orbit is clear," Shvets reported. "Beginning surface-mapping scan. If there's anything unusual down there, the map should pull it out."

II lacked a moon or any other orbital structure to hide behind. That made *Rhapsody*'s Mages' job harder—Liara Foster had cycled off two hours earlier, and Jong-Su Alekseev was running the invisibility spell now—but it also meant no one was hiding around them.

"Let's take it nice and slow," Kelly said. "I'm guessing the mapping scan isn't going to pick out, I don't know, survey camps?"

"We'll pick up just about anything with a technological power source," Shvets told her. "Whether that's nuclear, combustion, steam engines...even most modern batteries, if they're running something.

"So, a modern survey camp should stick out like a sore thumb unless they turned everything off and covered their gear with emission-control blankets," they continued. "I'm not going to pick up Stone Age nomads, but any permanent settlement more than a few acres in size is probably going to ping a closer review, even without power."

"Good." Kelly was silent, watching the computer take and process thousands of pictures each second as her ship orbited the planet.

"No power signatures so far," Shvets reported. "A couple of items I'm flagging for analysis as potential sites where someone has landed and taken off again, but nothing solid.

"There's no one down there or up here, boss," they concluded. "I'm not comfortable speaking to the star system yet, but I think it's safe to say that Two is clear."

She murmured her acknowledgment, glancing at the far away gas giants.

"If you had a base on the gas giants...would you leave the garden world *completely* unwatched?" she asked.

"No," Shvets agreed, their eyes turning inward. "I'd either have someone in orbit—which they clearly don't—or I'd have scouts in the asteroid belt."

"Yeah. You're sure about Two?" Kelly asked.

"I need another thirty minutes to complete the detailed map, but there's no major power sources down there."

"Finish the survey, then we set our course for One," she ordered. "And see if we can spook a scout."

"There might just not be anyone here," Shvets pointed out.

"We might be alone, yeah," Kelly agreed. "But this system is *exactly* what I'd use for the kind of base we're looking for—to lay the groundwork for future colonization, if nothing else.

"So, let's poke the other colonizable planet and see if we can find someone."

"Hard to spook people when we're invisible," Alekseev reminded her. "Should we lower some part of the invisibility?"

"No," Kelly decided after a moment. "If they're here, they saw the jump flare. They're trying to find us...and they have no idea where we are. That might work to our advantage as much as anything else."

"If we make this too fancy, we'll never know if we actually missed anything," Shvets warned.

"I prefer that to being surprised by a cruiser at laser range," she replied. "Let's ghost One and then see what we're looking at."

Her math said that they'd reach the other habitable planet around when her twenty-four-hour timeline ran out, anyway. She'd call the destroyers in to sweep the outer planets at that point—and if there was a base, they'd find it.

Whether she was being fancy or not.

CHAPTER 30

AT SOME POINT, Kelly knew she should go sleep. Her implants could keep her awake far longer than an unmodified human, but there were always prices to be paid for games like that.

Neither magic nor technology could push humans beyond their natural limits without incurring debts that needed to be cleared later.

For now, though, the itch in the back of her neck was only intensifying as *Rhapsody in Purple* finally cleared the inner asteroid belt of the 95A-36R System and got a clear look at 95A-36R-I.

The planet had a debris ring—natural from the composition—and a single tiny moon. A cursory glance suggested its poles might be habitable for humans, but the world's native life certainly didn't mind the blistering heat around the equators—or the intense seasons of its *twenty-six-day* year.

"Eyeballs on any strangers?" she asked Shvets.

Like her, the tactical officer had been on *Rhapsody's* bridge for twenty hours. Only Vidal and his Bionic Commandos were more augmented than the two MISS agents, which gave them certain advantages over their Mages and the other crew.

Xi Wu stood at Kelly's shoulder as Traynor maintained the stealth field, the senior Mage resting a hand on her wife's shoulder.

"Nothing unusual in orbit yet," Shvets reported. "We won't have decent eyes on the moon for another few million kilometers, though."

They were under thirty light-seconds from the planet now, well within range of the stealth ship's missile launchers. Of course, if there *was* anyone around 95A-36R-I, they'd almost certainly seen the MISS ship's jump flare and were hiding.

They just wouldn't know where *Rhapsody in Purple* was, and they might just decide to take a risk.

"You're sure there's someone here, aren't you?" Xi whispered.

"Yes," Kelly agreed. "Couldn't tell you why, beyond that this system is worth its weight in gold as a colonization target. But we're ninety light-years from Sol, thirty from DEL-Three-T-Three. This would be a reasonable place to find a fueling station or even a surveillance base for someone using DEL as a logistics base."

"So were half a dozen systems the other task groups have surveyed," Xi pointed out.

"I know," Kelly conceded. "And I may be wrong. But we'll run our cloak of invisibility as long as we can and see what falls out."

"There!" Shvets suddenly snapped. "We have a rabbit. Engines just lit up behind the moon; someone is making a run for the outer system."

"Do they have eyes on us?" Kelly asked.

"No, we're still a ghost," the tactical officer replied. "They're taking the bet that we're in orbit of Two and not in position to see them."

"Get me resolution and an ID, Shvets," Kelly ordered. "And a course. I want to know what I'm looking at and where they're going."

"On it," they confirmed.

Seconds ticked away, and Kelly was running over the growing amount of data on the unknown ship.

"She's definitely not a Prometheus Drive ship," she observed. "Too big to be the one known courier ship, too small to be any of the Republic's standard hulls. So, she's either got a Mage aboard or she's sublight."

"Sublight," Shvets replied. "Two hundred and twenty thousand tons, accelerating at three gravities. I have a sharp enough visual to match to the database."

"Oh?"

"*Magellan*-class interplanetary survey ship," Shvets said, bringing a set of schematics up on one side of the bridge. "Design belongs to Centauri

Dynamics, has been built in five systems under various licenses—including the Mercedes System, pre-Secession."

Mercedes had been an UnArcana world and had been a key builder of sublight ships for the Republic. Now part of the Protectorate again, they had enough sympathizers—and general criminals, as it turned out—that the Legion had been fencing the loot from their pirate raids there.

"Give me the rundown," she ordered them.

"Two hundred thousand tons dry, two eighty fueled and stocked," Shvets reeled off. "Single light defensive RFLAM turret. Carries four landers for detailed survey and an entire arsenal of robotic probes.

"Single centrifugal gravity section for crew quarters, primarily designed for zero gee or thrust. Intended to be stored under the ribs of a standard eggbeater-style freighter or survey ship and delivered to the destination system in groups of four or five."

An "eggbeater-style" freighter had a central main hull that was steady-state and zero gravity combined with at least two rotating "ribs" that spun to provide pseudogravity for living and working spaces.

Kelly had literally grown up on that style of ship, only leaving them to go to school for engineering and then taking a job on another one. It was only when she'd fully joined MISS that she'd regularly worked on any other kind of starship.

The sublight survey ship made sense from that logic. There'd be one jump ship acting as the main survey platform, but they'd deploy smaller vessels to do detailed scans of sites of interest.

And for the Legion, which had a strictly limited number of jump ships, just leaving a sublight survey ship in a system for a few months would get them a decent survey by the time they picked it up.

"The mass is the key, isn't it?" she said aloud.

"Two hundred thousand tons dry," Xi echoed Shvets' report, catching Kelly's train of thought. "How much of that eighty thousand tons of stock and fuel is *fuel*, Nika?"

The tactical officer looked down at their schematics thoughtfully.

"Depends, but normally, I'd say you're at twenty thousand just on the shuttles and landing gear," they murmured. "Which means..."

"Energy signature says they're pushing two hundred and twenty thousand tons at three gees," Kelly said. "That means they're running on minimal fuel and likely oxygen, too. They were almost certainly due to return to whatever their base was in short order—and then we showed up."

"They're heading to VI," Shvets reported. "I mean, they're looking at almost four days to get there at three gravities, but that's the vector."

There was a reason they weren't certain whether there was a base in the outer system, and that reason was distance.

"Then our friend here has already told us everything we need to know," Kelly said aloud. "We can sweep them up later, once we call in the destroyers."

She smiled coldly.

"Xi, start plotting an in-system jump to VI. I need to get on the Link with Sciacchitano and see if we can put together a plan."

"We still have no idea what's out there," Shvets warned.

"No," she agreed. "But we do know there's *something* out there, so I'm going to go poke it with a stick and see what happens."

"There is no way you can jump and maintain your heat sinks," Sciacchitano pointed out after Kelly told him her plan. "You can maintain the stealth spell, but if your heat sinks work the way I think they do, you'll need to vent them after jumping."

"We will," Kelly confirmed. "Which would overload any attempt to conceal us with magic, I'm told."

Designing the *Rhapsodies* so that they didn't need to vent heat *before* jumping—making them vulnerable for an extended period, as running the radiators at that level was *very* obvious and still took several hours to cool the ship down—had been a major engineering challenge.

Still, the jump itself produced a lot of heat, and they couldn't release all of that heat without dropping the emission-control blankets...which would, again, make them obvious.

Which meant that, just as Sciacchitano predicted, *Rhapsody* would need to vent heat the moment she emerged from the jump—and do so for about six hours.

"We're going to be extremely obvious and launching all kinds of sensor probes," she continued. "I expect we'll be outside weapons range of the base, and I'm expecting similar defensive systems to *Fallen Dragon*—minimally mobile missile and laser satellites."

"From Mage-Commander Chambers' report, *Fallen Dragon* had a cruiser for protection as well," the Navy officer pointed out. "We can't fight a cruiser for you, Commodore LaMonte. Not with three destroyers.

"Despite what Chambers has done in the past."

"I am well aware of how suicidal Mage-Commander Chambers' stunt in DEL-Three-T-Three was," Kelly agreed. "I'm hoping and expecting this will be a far more...handleable level of firepower."

"And if you're wrong?"

"Then I have the Navy to haul my ass out of the fire, don't I?" she said sweetly.

"Jumping in fifteen seconds," Xi reported as Kelly returned to the bridge.

Discovering the enemy had given her a second wind, one that she needed, as she was starting to push the limits of even her enhanced endurance. There was enough pep in her step to get her to her seat in the fifteen-second countdown before reality rippled around her ship.

"VI is dead ahead," Shvets said swiftly. "Heat levels at critical. Rolling up emcon barriers."

"Radiators extending as swiftly as we can," Hussain reported from Engineering. "I'm glad you woke me up for this stunt."

"We all know how to dump heat once we jump," Kelly said, her voice faux-cheerful as she kept a careful eye on the heat metrics.

In theory, she could have kept *Rhapsody* stealthed for three full days and still jumped safely, In practice...well...she'd helped write the specifications for the heat sinks, and *she'd* try to do a directional heat dump before jumping after more than thirty-six hours.

A single day was fine, though, and her crew was handling it. That allowed her to turn her attention to the people who had to have seen the giant beacon of *Rhapsody in Purple*'s arrival.

"Three moons of significance, a ring between moon two and moon three, and a dozen or so chunks of debris that could pretend to be asteroids or moons if you're drunk," Shvets reported.

"Moon three is a frozen iceball of zero interest to anybody except for the fact that *somebody* dumped a few dozen standard containers in orbit and welded them together into a space station," they continued drily. "I make it about a million tons or so—and she's got some *impressive* sensor and communications arrays.

"I'm guessing that if we did a major survey of the outer system, we'd find a few dozen floating telescope probes making up a Very Large Array to give them a decent view all the way back into Protectorate space."

The lightspeed delay would make the data of questionable use, but even thirty-year-old data was better than none if you were unwilling to give your enemy a path home.

"About as you figured, boss," Shvets continued. "I'm picking up a bunch of orbital defense platforms. Scans are marking them all as Battleaxe VIs—just missile launchers. Probably forty or fifty, all told."

Xi had picked her emergence point carefully, and *Rhapsody* hung fifteen million kilometers away from 95A-36R-VI, well outside the range of even modern antimatter missiles.

"Good to see I haven't lost my touch," Kelly murmured. "Run all of that back to—"

"Contact!" Shvets snapped. "Contacts at six million kilometers—multiple missiles launched!"

Kelly LaMonte swallowed her self-congratulation as the dozen gunships the Legion had pre-positioned for if she did *exactly* this opened fire.

CHAPTER 31

"CONTACT ON *RHAPSODY IN PURPLE*," Salminen snapped as the Link updated. "Twelve gunships, *seventy-two* missiles."

"Understood." Roslyn was already tapping the commands to lift her chair up to the simulacrum. She didn't even consciously hit the battle-stations command, but the lights flickered as it took effect.

The klaxon and light changes specifically did *not* affect the bridge or most other critical workstations.

"Begin updating target plots on missiles and gunships. Confirm with the other destroyers and stand by to jump."

"Sciacchitano just gave us the same orders," Salucci reported from coms. "Flag Tactical calculates five minutes to impact, and Mage-Commander Sciacchitano recommends a thirty-second delay to coordinate intercept."

"Understood," Roslyn repeated. She'd been seconds away from hurling *Voice of the Forgotten* across the intervening eight light-months to LaMonte's rescue, but Sciacchitano had a point.

"Victor, confirm timing with *Bear* and *Oath*," she ordered. "Salminen, confirm capacitor charge and missile status."

"Capacitors at eighty percent and rising," Salminen said instantly. The crew had been ready for trouble. "All launchers loaded; all missiles charged and standing by."

While the Protectorate was *very* good at handling antimatter safely, there was still a preference to keep antimatter in secured storage tanks rather than loaded into missiles.

Standard protocol said three "ready" salvos were charged, but Salminen's report said that every missile in *Voice's* magazines was now fully fueled and their warheads filled with antimatter.

It could be discharged back into the storage tanks later, but for now, that process wouldn't delay Roslyn's ability to engage the enemy.

"Chambers, link in," a voice said in her ears. "Captains' channel."

"Commanders," she greeted Sciacchitano and Beulen as she followed the order. "The plan?"

"I'm inclined to drop in right on top of the bastards and blow them to hell with lasers," Sciacchitano growled. "They're dead and they don't know it yet."

Roslyn grimaced as she ran the distances and considered keeping her mouth shut for a moment—but Beulen wasn't saying anything, and there was a risk to Sciacchitano's plan.

"That puts us inside the range at which their RFLAMs are dangerous to us, Sciacchitano," she told him. "*And* inside missile range of the base. They hung those gunships out as an ambush against someone doing what LaMonte did, so I guarantee you that the base commander has a layer in their plan for if we jump the gunships themselves!"

The channel between the three officers was silent for several more seconds.

"Fuck." Sciacchitano's oath hung on the channel unchallenged for a moment. "You're right. Set your distance at thirteen million kilometers from the base. We'll still be in our own laser range, barely, and outside the base's missile reach."

"And even *Oath's* beams can kill gunships," Roslyn reminded him. "That gives us over forty lasers against a dozen ships. They're still dead, sir."

"When you're right, you're right, Chambers; don't try to make me feel better," Sciacchitano said with a chuckle. "Are you ready?"

"We're ready," she confirmed, updating her calculations as she spoke.

"*Bear* is ready," Beulen confirmed as well.

"Jump in ten seconds from mark. *Mark.*"

Sometimes, ten seconds was nothing. Sometimes, ten seconds was *forever*—and watching missiles scream toward a friend two-thirds of a light-year away, waiting ten seconds felt like an eternity.

But they needed the coordination, and Roslyn had the countdown up on the main screens as she focused on the universe around her starship.

Pulling her power together, she *stepped* as the timer hit zero and a million tons of starship moved with her.

They emerged closer to *Rhapsody in Purple* than her attackers—and opened fire immediately. Lasers flashed into space, reaching for targets at their extreme range.

The key was that the gunships wouldn't see the destroyers' arrival until the light of the jump flare reached them—and the lasers traveled just as quickly as regular light.

"Defensive lasers, target the missiles," Roslyn snapped. "Coordinate with the rest of the flotilla. Salucci, make sure we pull *Rhapsody* into the defensive tactical net. Salminen, keep the beams on those gunships until they're *gone.*"

She glanced at the screen at her elbow linking her to the Combat Information Center—Yusif Claes' battle station.

"Claes, watch for surprises," she ordered her executive officer. "Whoever is over there has already been *very* clever at us. Let's make damn sure they don't sneak up on us."

It took thirty seconds for their first laser salvo to reach its target and the light from the impacts to make it back to the destroyers. Only two of the gunships survived—and those didn't live long through the second salvo that fired the moment the ships had that data.

There were forty-four lasers firing at two ships, after all, and quantity had an accuracy all its own.

"They got two more missile salvos off," Salminen warned. "That's... well, that's all you can really ask for from a gunship."

Roslyn nodded. She was watching those missiles—but even the first salvo had barely moved half a million kilometers from their now-wrecked motherships. Ten thousand gravities was an astonishing acceleration, but it took time to work up to the velocities that gave the weapons their immense range.

Despite having already wrecked the gunships, the Martian ships actually had to *wait* another full minute before the missiles reached the range of their defensive systems. The heavy beams flickered out as the missiles approached, but it took a dozen lasers to guarantee a hit on a single evading target.

A handful of the missiles died, but it was only as they crossed within five light-seconds of the trio of destroyers that the battle truly began. The launching gunships might be dead, but the two hundred–plus missiles in space could still very easily turn this battle against Mars.

"Laser engagement commencing," Salminen said, his tones calm and level. "Linked with *Oath* and *Bear.*"

Roslyn knew there'd been a huge argument over whether or not to update the *Honor*-class ship's defensive arsenal during their refit. Newer destroyers actually had *fewer* offensive weapons on their greater mass—in exchange for vastly increased defensive firepower.

A single *Bard of Winter*–class ship would have brought more defensive lasers to this battle than all three of their older destroyers—but that was why they'd spent the weeks getting there practicing.

"We have the outer perimeter," Salminen reported aloud, his fingers flying across his console as he allocated his lasers accordingly. "*Oath* has the middle and *Bear* is playing catcher."

Voice's lasers would target the missiles in their first thirty seconds in range, then switch to the next salvo as they entered range. *Oath* would make the same switch thirty seconds later, and *Bear* would try to catch whatever made it past the defenses of the other destroyers.

Even as missiles began to explode, Roslyn carefully tapped the commands to adjust her seat, gesturing Mage-Lieutenant 'Isa Daniel to take over the simulacrum as the Captain moved back and down. The amplifier was a critical part of the destroyer's final defense, and a jump-fatigued Mage couldn't fulfill their role in the pattern.

Even away from the simulacrum, Roslyn still had the best seat in the house for seeing what was going on. The first salvo was evaporating like a snowstorm in summer, each missile turning into a two-gigaton antimatter explosion as lasers vaporized the containment systems.

The electromagnetic chaos of those explosions was a problem, but Roslyn smiled thinly as the Mages set to work. They could take out a handful of missiles themselves—*or* they could use the amplifiers to clear paths through the radiation storms, allowing the lasers to see what was coming.

"First salvo destroyed," Salminen reported. "We are engaging the third salvo; *Oath* has the second."

The gunships hadn't expected three destroyers, and the sequenced defense was *probably* enough to hold off their fire. Which was why Roslyn was expecting...

"New contact!" Claes snapped from the CIC. "Multiple missiles inbound from one-ninety-six by seventy-three!"

That put the weapons *behind* the destroyers—coming in from deep space beyond even *Rhapsody in Purple*!

"Range, numbers and launch platforms?" Roslyn barked.

"Range is *one million kilometers*, two hundred–plus missiles inbound! No launch platforms... Wait... Missile velocity is *away* from us?"

"Ignore the new missiles," she ordered as that report sank in. "We have *time*. Clean up the gunship weapons, then switch targets."

The missiles had to have been launched from the enemy base over fifteen minutes earlier, allowed to make the majority of the journey out there without thrust.

The velocity, in fact, said they'd burned their engines for two and a half minutes...which left them *just* enough thrust to shed their outward velocity and swing back for the destroyers.

But that would take over five minutes. A *single* two-hundred-plus-missile salvo instead of three seventy-missile salvos was going to be a headache, but they could deal with it on its own.

Unless.

"Wait. Confirm the target on those missiles!" she snapped.

There was a beat of a few seconds and then she *saw* the horror on Claes's face as her executive officer confirmed her fear.

"One hundred seventy–plus targeted on *Oath of Freedom's Choice*. Seventy-plus targeted on *Rhapsody in Purple*."

The destroyers could almost certainly handle the hundred or so missiles left of the gunship salvos. They could *probably* handle the single hundred-and-seventy-missile salvo targeted at them.

They could not do all of that *and* protect *Rhapsody in Purple* from over seventy missiles. Not when the stealth ship only had six RFLAM turrets and they were poorly positioned—sited more for concealment than efficient defense.

"Salminen, engage as ordered," Roslyn barked. "Salucci, get me LaMonte on the Link!"

Sciacchitano had clearly made the same connections Roslyn had, as she ended up on a three-way call with the MISS Director and the other Mage-Commander.

"We can't protect you from those missiles, Commodore," Sciacchitano told LaMonte. "Can you evade?"

"You have to jump out, Kelly," Roslyn said a moment later. "You can't stealth or dodge out of this while you're here—but they've already burnt too much fuel heading toward you to threaten us.

"Standard light-year jump from whichever of your Mages is up, then come back when they've rested up."

"I'm down to one Mage who *can* jump," LaMonte pointed out.

"Better delayed a few hours while we deal with this base than dead," Sciacchitano stated. "I know I can't give you orders, Commodore, but Mage-Commander Chambers is right. Those missiles are less than ninety seconds out from your position, and we are going to be right to the limit protecting ourselves.

"*Jump*," he urged. "And we'll deal with this base by the time you get back. Go!"

Kelly LaMonte didn't look happy with the idea of "abandoning" the Navy ships, but she nodded.

"I'll see you on the other side, Commanders," she told them. "We're jumping now."

The stealth ship vanished from the screen as the last of the gunships' second salvo was destroyed, and Roslyn breathed a sigh of relief.

"Formation Reno-Six, Commanders," Sciacchitano ordered. "If these missiles want us, let's make them dance for it."

CHAPTER 32

THE LAST MISSILE came apart a dozen kilometers from *Oath of Freedom's Choice*. One of its siblings had made it all the way through, and Sciacchitano's command had an ugly scorch mark along one of the pyramid's faces.

"We're fine," he told the other two captains shortly as the three destroyers began to maneuver again. "We lost three RFLAM turrets but the exterior armor held.

"No dead, but a few wounded. I've had better days."

"We all have," Roslyn replied. "It's a good one, though, when we get through enemy fire without losing anyone."

"We're not done dealing with them yet," Sciacchitano said. "You've dealt with them, Chambers. Think they'll surrender if we give them the chance?"

"No," she admitted. "But I *do* think that Her Majesty would prefer that we did. We have the upper hand here—we could even wait for Admiral Jakab to catch up, if we wanted.

"I doubt they can bring enough firepower here in five days to stand off Battle Group *Pax Dramatis*."

"Likely not, but I'd rather not take the chance," Sciacchitano said. "Beulen, have you ever done long-range ballistic strikes?"

"No, sir," the junior Mage-Commander replied.

"Chambers?"

"Not recently," she admitted. "We jumped in close to take out the defensive satellites in DEL-Three-T-Three before they could come online.

That seventy-five-second warm-up is a vulnerability we can't count on here."

"What we *can* count on, though, is their magazine capacity," Sciacchitano noted. "The Battleaxe VI has six missiles in its magazines, and we picked up fifty satellites. They threw two hundred and fifty missiles in that ballistic salvo, which means they only have one real punch left.

"On the other hand, while I have faith in our ability to shred fifty-missile salvos, I *don't* want to assume we've eliminated their full gunship contingent," he admitted. "So, I want those Battleaxes *gone*.

"They have limited mobility but they *can* maneuver. The real question, though, is whether we've missed any anti-missile defenses."

"You're thinking we send in missiles with, say, thirty seconds left on the drives?" Roslyn asked. "Burn at full for six and a half minutes, make an approach at point two cee, then kick off the drive for a terminal maneuver to make sure the satellites don't evade?"

"And you said you hadn't done this before," Sciacchitano said with a chuckle.

"Second Fleet did, though," Roslyn reminded him. "And the flag staff put together the plans on occasion. I had to learn the drill."

"What about using impactors?" Beulen asked. "Less danger than full-power missiles, plus the multiple warheads might be useful."

"They won't get up to a high-enough velocity to finish this week, let alone today," the senior Mage-Commander replied. "They're designed to drop from orbit, not cross thirteen million kilometers and take out defended satellites.

"I'll summon them to surrender—*once*—and then we will blow their satellites to pieces," Sciacchitano continued. "Then we'll close the distance and send in the Marines.

"We need their data cores, and a non-destructive wipe can take hours. Let's not give them those hours."

"Understood," Roslyn confirmed. "*Voice* is ready, Commander."

"As is *Bear*. Let's make this happen."

It took only a few minutes for the destroyers to shake out their formation and program the intended targeting parameters. Then, once they were all ready, Roslyn watched from her own bridge as Sciacchitano made the call everyone was waiting for.

"Legion facility, this is Mage-Commander Nigellus Sciacchitano of the Royal Martian Navy," the bald officer proclaimed as he stared into the camera. His black uniform and mixed brown skin stood out against the gleaming consoles of his bridge as he spoke.

"You opened fire on a Protectorate starship with neither warning nor provocation," he told them. "We acted to defend that starship by engaging and destroying your gunship squadron.

"No further violence is required, but I cannot allow this system to remain in clearly hostile hands. Given the repeated attacks by Legion forces on ships, systems and persons under the protection of the Royal Navy of Mars, the Mage-Queen and her Parliament have declared that a state of war exists between the First Legion and the Protectorate of the Kingdom of Mars.

"You will stand down your defenses and prepare to be boarded by Royal Martian Marines. Any hostile action will be met with all necessary force to protect our personnel.

"Surrender, and the bloodshed can end. Resist, and I will do whatever is necessary to guarantee the security of the Protectorate."

Sciacchitano gave them a small, flat smile.

"It will be approximately forty-five seconds from my transmission to your receipt of this message. You have five minutes from that receipt to respond. After that, I will proceed to reduce your defenses by force."

The video froze and Roslyn nodded grimly.

"What do you think, sir?" Salminen asked. "Will they take the chance?"

"No," she said flatly. "Salucci? Get me Lieutenant Mathisen."

Roslyn didn't know Debora Mathisen well, but the young woman had taken over as the senior Marine aboard *Voice of the Forgotten* when the previous CO had been promoted and transferred.

The Navy knew how to handle the satellites. The base itself, though, was a *Marine* problem.

CHAPTER 33

SCIACCHITANO'S DEADLINE came and went with only silence from the Legion base. Roslyn raised an eyebrow at the senior Mage-Commander as his silence extended for several seconds after that, then he sighed and nodded.

"I dared to hope," he murmured. "It's a lot easier to kill people when they're shooting at your friends."

There was another few seconds of silence.

"Engage as specified," he ordered, his tone level.

Missiles flashed out from the destroyers moments later, each programmed with a specific target. Twenty-four platforms were marked for death by that first salvo. Twenty-four more in the second salvo that followed half a minute later.

The final salvo excluded *Oath* with her more limited magazines; *Bear* and *Voice* each fired three missiles, targeted on the two platforms that hadn't been marked to receive their fire previously.

After that, it was waiting. The ballistic portion of the missile flight was only forty seconds, which meant the total flight time was only ten seconds longer than it would have been if the missiles had run their engines out of fuel.

The Battleaxe VIs were designed to be expended before they came under fire. They had limited maneuverability and no active defenses. RFLAMs from the base itself attempted to defend them, but it was a losing battle against three missiles per satellite, coming in at almost twenty percent of lightspeed.

Antimatter explosions haloed the orbital base as the missiles hit home. Two minutes after the first of them hit, it was over.

"Scans show no intact Battleaxe platforms," Salminen reported calmly. "We've identified twenty-six RFLAM turrets on the base itself."

"Those will be a problem," Roslyn noted on the captains' link. "The Marine assault shuttles will be vulnerable."

"Their offensive weapons are gone," Sciacchitano replied. "We're just over five hours out for zero-zero, but..."

Even through jump fatigue, Roslyn knew that they didn't want to get that close, but Beulen spoke before she did.

"We don't know what other defenses the base has," the junior Captain pointed out. "They could have mines or even heavy lasers we haven't seen yet."

"Agreed," Sciacchitano said. "I'm thinking we bring ourselves to zero velocity at two million kilometers and use amplifiers to remove the RFLAM turrets.

"That will give them almost five hours to stew and decide if they want to surrender."

"But also five hours to destroy the information we need," Roslyn said grimly. "At this point, they'll have already commenced the data purges. We're looking at the same situation as *Fallen Dragon*, Mage-Commanders."

"Your suggestion, then, Mage-Commander Chambers?" Sciacchitano asked.

"We skip the preliminaries and jump in close," she told him. "Neutralize the RFLAMs with amplifiers and send the initial boarding parties by Jump Mage. If the Marines and Mages can secure the data core, the rest of the Marines can follow up by shuttle."

While the shuttles the destroyers carried were capable of carrying a full Marine platoon apiece, they carried three of them and would usually send a single squad in on each shuttle.

Redundancy was queen in military operations, after all.

"That's a risky plan," Beulen said slowly. "But she's right, Sciacchitano. We risk losing the base's nav data if we don't move in quickly."

"We will have an escape allowance," Sciacchitano noted. "If one Mage jumps each ship and another takes a Marine fire team aboard the base, we will still have a Mage ready to jump on each ship."

"We're putting a lot on the fire teams and Mages we're sending in," Roslyn acknowledged. Few, if any, of the Mages aboard the three destroyers could bring more than a single four-Marine fire team with them on a short-range teleport.

Roslyn could probably manage two, but Roslyn was a scion of the First Families of Tau Ceti and in the top quarter-percent or so of living Mages.

"Ask for volunteers," Sciacchitano instructed, then chuckled. "My experience suggests we'll have no difficulties finding them."

As Sciacchitano had implied, Roslyn had no problems finding volunteers. She looked at her executive officer, navigator and junior navigator with a wry smile on her face as the three Jump Mages stood in front of her on the bridge.

"The only thing stopping *me* from being the fourth volunteer is that I jumped us here," she admitted. "Unfortunately, I'm tapping Claes for the microjump. Sorry, Yusif."

The tall Mage–Lieutenant Commander nodded his head in understanding. A microjump was among the most difficult tricks a Jump Mage could pull off, so using the most experienced available Mage made sense to everyone.

"All of my Marines volunteered as well," Lieutenant Mathisen said. She was standing to Roslyn's right, surveying the Mages with the same wry amusement as the Captain.

"I have womanfully withstood the urge to go myself and assigned Sergeant Gaal to the mission," she continued. "Uzziyyah Gaal is my senior squad leader and I trust his choice of fire team.

"All of my people are in full gear by now, and Sergeant Gaal's team is waiting outside for the teleport stunt."

"Warn his people to expect nausea," Roslyn told the Marine. "We're short on time here, but you'll have to wait for us to complete the initial scan and locate the computer center.

"Rank hath its privileges—which means you're making the jump with the Marines, Victor," she told her navigator. "Daniel, it'll be on you to get *Voice* to safety if things go wrong."

She waved Claes to the simulacrum seat and turned an eye on Mathisen.

"We're jumping in under two minutes, and I want the shuttles in space the moment we're done," she told the Marine. "You'll commence your run as soon as we've cleared the RFLAMs.

"Remember, we want prisoners...but I want living Marines a *lot* more than I want living Legionnaires. Understood?"

"Yes, sir," Mathisen said with a salute. "By your leave?"

"Get to the shuttle, Lieutenant," Roslyn ordered with amusement.

Victor followed Mathisen out and she gestured İsa Daniel over to join Claes. The junior officer, the most junior of *Voice*'s four Jump Mages, would have to take over the moment the jump was complete.

"*Voice of the Forgotten* is ready to execute," she told Sciacchitano as she slid into her chair.

"Show-off," she heard Beulen mutter, *almost* under her breath. "We're just about there."

"*Oath*'s Marines still need a minute," Sciacchitano said in a relaxed tone. "These people don't know what's coming, Commanders. They should have surrendered."

"My impression is that the Legion doesn't select surrendering types for their remote commands," Roslyn said. "And being a bunch of revanchist fascist warmongers, they don't seem to have a shortage of fanatics."

"*Bear* is ready," Beulen reported, in lieu of responding to Roslyn's point.

"Stand by to jump on my order," Sciacchitano told them. "Almost."

Roslyn knew that the navigation link-up between the two ships would transfer the order to Claes, but she looped her XO in anyway.

"*Oath* is ready," the senior Mage-Commander finally said. "Let's go convince these people not to wipe their data cores, shall we?

"Jump on my mark. Three. Two. One. Mark."

CHAPTER 34

EVEN AS CLAES WOVE the magic to carry the destroyer forty light-seconds in the blink of a thought, Roslyn was realizing she'd made a mistake. In the desperate rush to protect *Rhapsody in Purple* from the Legion gunships, she'd jumped *Voice of the Forgotten* herself.

But as the destroyer's Captain, she couldn't step away to rest while the warship was in combat. She didn't think jump fatigue was impeding her judgment, but it was always a risk. A risk she shouldn't have taken—one Sciacchitano, for example, clearly *hadn't* taken.

Now, as *Voice* flashed into existence two light-seconds from the Legion base, she had to depend on her most junior Mage to pluck RFLAM turrets from the enemy facility in preparation for the Marine assault.

İsa Daniel stepped into the simulacrum seat as Yusif Claes moved away. The XO was wavering from the same jump fatigue as Roslyn—the *distance* of a jump really didn't matter.

"Scans, Salminen," Roslyn ordered.

Data was already flowing across her screen, and she watched as the analysis team started to identify their targets.

"Daniel," she addressed the junior Mage. "I'm going to halo targets for you. Hit them with your best shot."

There was already a division going on between the three destroyers as their scanners picked out the station's defensive turrets. Roslyn dropped an icon on the first turret—and the young man carved it off the station with a slash of magical force before she'd even given a verbal order.

The second and third turret vanished just as quickly as Roslyn marked them, and she stopped worrying *quite* as much about Daniel's ability to do this part of the job.

"We've IDed the computer core," Salminen reported crisply as a new icon flared in the middle of the station.

"Victor?" Roslyn asked.

"We're gone."

New green markers appeared on the screen a few seconds later as the lightspeed update from the Marines' beacons reached their motherships.

"All jumps appear clean," the tactical officer reported. "All turrets are down."

"Mathisen, you're clear to strike," Roslyn told the Marine CO.

The shuttles had left the destroyer in a somewhat leisurely fashion, but now they screamed toward their target at a thirty-gravity acceleration that made Roslyn wince.

Assault shuttles had magical thrust compensation, but it wasn't even as good as the magical gravity on the capital ships. *Voice* could manage fifteen gravities without her crew feeling a thing.

At thirty gravities, the Marines were feeling twenty of them. The internal systems in their exosuits would make that survivable, but Roslyn knew from intimate experience that it would *suck*.

And it would still take them thirty minutes to cross the distance to the Legion station. For that half-hour, the success or failure of the mission rode on twelve Marines and three Mages embedded in the heart of the enemy station, trying to take and hold one of the most secure positions in any base.

"We're in," Victor reported breathlessly over the radio a minute later. "We got in close enough to circumvent most of the defenses, so we now have the core.

"Two of the Marines are breaking into the system to halt the data purge, but they're telling me it looks like we were in time. Much of the data has been deleted, but they're saying the hash hasn't started and it should be retrievable."

"Can you hold?" Sciacchitano's voice broke in. "I mark twenty-nine minutes until the rest of the Marines make contact."

"So far, so promising," Victor—the senior of the officers on site—reported. "They weren't expecting this, and we overran the security on the core with no losses. *We* now hold the plasma-proof bunkers and heavy bulkheads. We've sealed them all, and it's going to take the Legion at least ten minutes just to burn through those."

"Keep us updated," Roslyn told him.

She wasn't sure what they could do if the forward team started being pushed back, but she needed to know what was going on.

At this point, the fate of the Legion base was down to the Marines. Roslyn had faith that ninety exosuited Royal Martian Marines could storm the station, but whether twelve could hold out until the other eighty arrived was less clear.

"Can you set up a data download?" Beulen asked.

"We don't have the hands," Victor admitted. "The Marines are going to stop the deletion cycle, but then we need every gun at the doors. We won't have enough control or bandwidth."

"Hold the line, Mage Victor," Sciacchitano ordered. "The rest of the Marines are on the way, and time is on your side."

"We've got it, sir."

"Back, back—*down!*"

Everything Roslyn was hearing from the systems of the landing team was at least two seconds out of date. She couldn't change what was happening aboard the enemy station, regardless, but the time delay only added to the sense of helplessness as she heard one of the Mages unleash a torrent of flame.

The screaming that echoed over the microphones wasn't from the Martian forces, but that wasn't necessarily reassuring.

The RMMC controlled the Legion base's computers, and Roslyn's instincts told her that the Legion had spent the majority of their strength trying to dislodge Victor's landing team.

But with two Mages still backing the Marines, the Legionnaires were failing to break through the chokepoint they'd built to protect their computers. The price had been high: after thirty minutes inside the Legion base, half of the Marines were dead or wounded and the rest were running low on ammunition.

"Legion defenders."

It took Roslyn a moment to recognize that Sciacchitano was speaking again—and glancing at the tactical display, she could see why.

Royal Martian Marine Corps assault shuttles were equipped with "crush compensators"—single-use runic artifacts capable of offsetting hundreds or even thousands of gravities of acceleration for a single instant.

The instant, for example, of hammering into a space station at six hundred kilometers per second. The assault shuttles had made contact by doing just that, brilliant sparks of magic flashing across the display as the second wave finally landed on the Legion base.

"Legion defenders," Sciacchitano repeated. "You are familiar, I hope, with the concept of *murum aries attigit*. The Roman standard of *the ram has touched the walls.*

"We now control your computer center. Assault shuttles have made contact around the perimeter of your station, and we have demonstrated, I think, that you cannot stand against the combined arms of our Mages and Marines in remotely equal numbers.

"To prevent further bloodshed, I offer one last chance to surrender. Lay down your arms and cease your resistance. You have fought valiantly, but it is over."

Roslyn wasn't expecting any more of a reply this time than the first time—and was surprised when Salucci looked up from the coms console.

"We have a response! Incoming transmission."

"Play it," Roslyn ordered.

The man who appeared on the screen didn't appear to have been strained in the slightest by a magical boarding operation or the more conventional assault beachhead being established as Roslyn watched his message.

Like the Legion officers she'd met on *Fallen Dragon*, he wore a dark burgundy version of the Republic's uniform, a double-breasted jacket with gold buttons over a standard shipsuit.

The only insignia he wore was a pair of golden eagles high on his right lapel, and his eyes were a flint gray around the square pupils of a combat Augment as he glared at the screen.

"I am Commodore Cecilio Vaccaro," he addressed the Martian officers. "You have attacked this system without provocation and murdered my soldiers and spacers. We are not surprised. These are the arrogant actions typical of the Protectorate, taken under the high-handed concept that *you* know what is best for all humankind.

"You are wrong. We are the First Legion and we are undefeated."

Vaccaro smiled thinly, his strange square pupils glinting dangerously.

"Other Legions will follow, but we are the First," he continued. "We are the spark that will light the fire that will burn down your Protectorate— and our sacrifices will be honored in the golden age to come!"

For a few eternal moments, Roslyn stared blankly at the screen. What did he mean? What sacrifices?

Then it hit her.

"Abort the landing!" she snapped. "Get the Marines out of there!"

Vaccaro's message had taken two seconds to reach them—and any response from the Navy ships would have taken two seconds to reach the assault shuttles.

Those were seconds the Legion Commodore didn't give them before the antimatter warheads his people had placed around the exterior of the station detonated.

Stark-white fire tore through the Legion base, followed moments later by the blue fire of fusion explosions as a second sequence of warheads detonated. It was over in seconds.

Voice of the Forgotten's bridge was silent as Roslyn and her crew stared in horror. There was nothing left of the Legion base. Their landing team was gone. The assault shuttles were gone.

And every Marine in Task Group Purple Eye was gone with them.

CHAPTER 35

THREE OF THE FOUR Navy officers on Kelly's conference call were ashen-faced with shock. Even Vice Admiral Kole Jakab looked shaken, if less immediately shattered than the three Mage-Commanders.

"None of us were expecting that," Sciacchitano finally said. "The responsibility is mine, sir."

"You had no reason to expect that, Mage-Commander," Jakab said quietly. "The Republic's leadership was always willing to sacrifice some-body *else* for their cause—see both the Prometheus Project and the suicide charges hidden in the drive units themselves—but we didn't run into many outright suicidal fanatics in the war."

"The Legion appears to be a different stripe entirely," Kelly told them. "We had an officer on *Fallen Dragon* attempt to destroy the depot ship to prevent us learning more about them—and now this Commodore Vaccaro."

She shook her head.

"I'll be moving back into the system in about ninety minutes," she told Jakab and her subordinate Captains. "Lieutenant Vidal and I will make sure that the crew of that survey ship doesn't get the chance to do anything comparable."

"Given the level of information security the Legion operates with, is it likely that the survey ship even *has* data on their core worlds?" Chambers asked grimly. "Prisoners will help, but the ones we got from *Fallen Dragon* only knew the name *Mackenzie*, and nothing about where the system is."

"And we can likely expect the same from the crew of the survey ship," the Admiral agreed. "But Commodore LaMonte is correct that we want to bring them in regardless. My people's assessment is that they will likely run out of supplies if we do not capture them, which makes it a humanitarian priority as well."

"We need to consider our next steps as well," Sciacchitano said softly. "Should we be continuing our sweep as planned?"

"No," Jakab said instantly, before Kelly could say a word. "Apologies, Commodore LaMonte, but this is now outside of the realm of Operation Long Eye. You have achieved your objective: we now know where a Legion base was located.

"Battle Group *Pax Dramatis* will be leaving DEL-Three-T-Three in about sixteen hours," he continued. "I estimate it will take us three days to reach Ninety-Five-A-Thirty-Six-R.

"*None* of your ships are to leave that system until we arrive, am I understood?"

Kelly probably had the authority to argue with Jakab on that point. Her military rank was entirely honorary. She didn't actually report to the Vice Admiral—she answered to the Oversight Board and the Mountain now, no one else.

But he was also right.

"We'll need a Tracker," she pointed out. "A full survey of the system should at least detect the most common jump locations, but only a Tracker can turn that into anything useful."

"I agree," Jakab said. "And, conveniently, Captain Ajam is still in the area. MISS is acting as our go-between, but we have every reason to believe that he will be willing to take our money again."

Kelly nodded. Part of Nunzio Ajam's price for helping them last time had been a promise from MISS to help find his ship and the Mage ex-boyfriend who'd stolen it. If they hadn't found it yet, he probably would take the Navy's money.

She hoped.

"And if Ajam isn't available?" she asked.

"I've put out the request for a Navy Tracker, but that may take longer," Jakab admitted. "For now, I want you all to maintain your positions in the system and wait for the Battle Group.

"This is the first clue we've had since taking *Fallen Dragon*. They may have blown it apart to keep it from us, but it gives a new starting point. Let's not lose it."

"What about our dead?" Chambers asked.

"Retrieve what bodies you can," the Admiral said grimly. "Then hold memorials as you see fit, Commanders. This, unfortunately, is part of our job."

Kelly sat alone in her office after the conference finished, running through a list of names and photographs on her wallscreen.

Ninety Marines—three of them Combat Mages—and three Jump Mages had died in the space of thirty minutes. Under *her* command. She might not have been in the system—hadn't even been involved in the plan to take the Legion station, in fact—but the ultimate responsibility was hers.

She understood *that* much about command. The buck stopped with her, but her review of the plans and discussions the Navy officers had made hadn't come up with anything she'd have told them to do differently.

Kelly was more intimately aware than most of the fact that the Legion *did* have fanatics willing to kill themselves to keep their secrets. She'd nearly been killed on *Fallen Dragon*, keeping a Legion engineer from blowing the depot ship's reactor.

But even she hadn't expected the commander of a Legion base to vaporize their entire space station. The estimates she was seeing pegged the base at somewhere between two and four *thousand* people, and Commodore Vaccaro had vaporized them all with a smile.

There were days Kelly LaMonte didn't understand people. She had a damn good idea of how far *she'd* go for the Protectorate—and while it was farther than she was entirely comfortable with, it definitely didn't include intentionally murdering thousands of her fellows.

"Hey, Captain, my Captain."

She looked up to see her husband step into the room. Mike Kelzin was a tall blond man, thickening a bit around the middle with age, but that only made for better cuddles, in her measured opinion.

"Hey, Mike."

She turned her attention back to the list of names and photos. Her husband crossed the office quietly and wrapped her in his arms without any further talking.

Kelly spared a moment to make certain that the door was locked to anyone else, then let him draw her to his chest, sniffling away tears.

"Dammit, no one is supposed to see the Captain like this," she whispered.

"Maybe, but I'm allowed to see my *wife* like this," Mike replied, holding her tightly. "So's Xi, but she's napping off the last jump so she can take us back to our Navy friends."

"I fucked up, Mike," she told him. "And a hundred people are dead because of it."

"Not exactly seeing how this one is on you," he murmured into her ear. "You didn't set off those bombs."

"The bastard saw us coming from a light-year away," she said grimly. "Every damn stunt we pulled, Vaccaro had predicted. He didn't have the firepower to turn that into *victory*, but he found a way to hurt us anyway."

"I don't think he saw the Navy teleporting Marines onto his station," Mike pointed out. "That's not something they do very often—you have to be *real* close and have *real* good data to do that, and it doesn't get very many people over there."

"Just got more people killed this time."

"No one—not even you—expected the Legion commander to blow his own base to hell," Mike said. "And you, quite sensibly, were keeping your foot out of your mouth and not jogging the elbows of the people you left behind to handle the situation.

"The Navy did their job. Did it damn well, from what I saw. You did your job too, and I didn't see anywhere we screwed up," he continued. "Unfortunately, the bad guys had a job to do too.

"And this Vaccaro decided that the best way to do *his* job was to kill a job lot of his own people to take out a hundred of ours. We wouldn't have done it—and I bet you anything he didn't ask his people *their* opinion of his plan!"

"The Republic's elite was always good at sacrificing *other* people," she said bitterly.

"And the Legion has inherited the worst of that attitude," he agreed. "You did your part, Kelly. And now we keep going forward, keep doing the job. Vidal and I are going to go capture that survey ship for you in an hour or so, but neither of us is qualified to tear her computers apart.

"That one is on you and the Engineering team. You going to be ready?"

Kelly inhaled shakily, wiping away tears and reassembling the shreds of her director mask as she nodded to Mike.

"Thanks, love. I...think I needed that."

"Believe me, Kelly, I think *every* starship captain needs somebody to cry on," he told her, then smiled. "Sadly, I don't believe the Navy agrees with me there!"

CHAPTER 36

"ATTEN-HUT!"

There were no Marines left aboard *Voice of the Forgotten* to form the honor guard, but they'd found seven ratings with firearms certification to serve in the role.

Those seven now stood in a dress-uniformed line in front of Roslyn Chambers, rifles at port arms as the ship's company—as many as were off duty, anyway—came to attention in the shuttle bay.

The destroyer's shuttle bay was the largest open space aboard after the main Engineering section and, with two of three shuttles now gone, far emptier than Engineering. It wasn't big enough for all three-hundred-plus crew, but it was enough for the hundred and eighty that weren't on duty.

And it wasn't like there were bodies to make space for. All of the Marines had been vaporized instantly when the Legion antimatter bombs had gone off. Their families would only receive a flag and a box of medals, an ancient and painful tradition.

Better a painful closure than a lack of knowledge, Roslyn supposed, but she wasn't one to know. She'd only lost friends in the war, never family.

Not yet, anyway.

"Ground arms!"

Alexandros Salminen wasn't a Marine drill sergeant, but he was doing the best he could with the ratings. The formation wasn't perfect, but it was better than their Captain had expected, and seven rifle butts touched the ground in a single sound.

"Crew of *Voice of the Forgotten*," Roslyn said into the silence that followed. "I always prefer that we gather for better reasons than this."

Simultaneous ceremonies were taking place on *Oath of Freedom's Choice* and *Bear of Glorious Justice*. They couldn't change what had happened, but they would honor their dead.

"Fate does not always allow us to gather for happy reasons," she continued. "Especially not for those of us called to the service of Mars. We came here, a long way from home for us all, searching for an unknown enemy that we knew had conquered the innocent."

She surveyed the bay.

"The people the Legion have conquered intentionally fled the Protectorate," she reminded everyone. "And it is not our doctrine to pursue and annex people such as them. But it *is* the will of our Mage-Queen that the innocent are protected and the guilty are punished.

"Regardless of where or whether the innocent in question pay fealty to Mars."

Silence answered her. Roslyn wasn't entirely sure if her crew was hanging on her every word or just humoring her, but that was a normal fear of any adult human or starship Captain.

"So, we came here to free the innocent, and thirty-one of our siblings-in-arms boarded a Legion base that fired on us without provocation," she continued. "And with Marines on their decks, we summoned them to surrender.

"Because our Queen asks us to be merciful—and because we are the Royal Martian Navy and the Royal Martian Marine Corps. While our duty requires violence, our honor requires mercy."

She let that hang in the air. It was an easy standard to forget, though Roslyn herself spoke to Kiera Alexander enough to know *exactly* how precious it was to the young Mage-Queen of Mars.

"When offered mercy, the Legion's commander chose violence," she concluded. "He murdered over two thousand of his own people to strike at less than a hundred of ours. Those Legion officers and spacers? They are as much victims of what happened here as our Marines.

"And our duty remains. As our people understood. As *we* understand."

She gestured and a bugle began to play Taps.

"Officers and spacers of the Royal Martian Navy, I give you Mage–Lieutenant Commander Lalit Victor," she began.

Even just reading out the names, with minimal commentary or discussion of the thirty-one Marines and officers who'd died aboard the Legion base, took time. As Roslyn finished, the bugle call faded to silence and the shuttle bay was quiet once more.

"Present arms!" Salminen ordered crisply, and his seven ratings lifted their rifles, aiming as the shuttle bay doors swung open. Standing at the back of the crowd, Yusif Claes unleashed his magic, weaving a careful force field that kept the atmosphere inside as both of the airlock doors opened and left the ship's company looking out into deep space.

It was hard to tell now, given the power of the explosions, but they were looking at the exact spot where their Marines had died. The planet the base had orbited was visible off to the left, a stark white ball of ice.

"Fire!"

Seven rifles cracked as one.

"Fire!"

A second salvo.

"Fire!"

Twenty-one shots echoed around the shuttle bay as *Voice of the Forgotten*'s crew saluted their dead.

CHAPTER 37

ROSLYN MADE SURE she was on the bridge when Battle Group *Pax Dramatis* was due to arrive. One of the other Long Eye task groups had arrived, bringing the total RMN strength in the system up to six destroyers, but she was all too aware of how far short of their enemy's standard interstellar combatant an RMN destroyer fell.

The smallest RIN cruisers, the Prometheus Drive warships the Legion had inherited, massed fifteen million tons. The largest of the six destroyers, *Sonnet in Springtime*, was only one point six million tons.

Doctrine against RIN had been to use destroyers as escorts in battle groups anchored on Martian cruisers or, preferably, battleships. There had been relatively few small-scale engagements during the war, as the Protectorate had hesitated to risk its light combatants and the Republic simply hadn't *had* that many cruisers.

The Protectorate had more living Mages than the Legion had murdered Mage brains. They could deploy more hulls, which allowed them to do things like sweep forty-odd systems at once, but despite Roslyn's own track record, RMN destroyers had no business fighting RIN cruisers.

That meant she barely concealed a sigh of relief when a jump flare flashed onto her screens.

"Contact," Salminen reported. He paused. "Single jump flare at one light-minute. Position is along VI's trailing orbit."

That...wasn't right.

"When is *Pax Dramatis* expected?" Roslyn said, but she was checking the time herself.

"Not for another forty-five minutes, sir," Salucci told her.

"CIC is flagging contact as unknown," the tactical officer said a moment later. "Mass range is unclear, estimated fourteen megatons...plus/minus four megatons."

Roslyn swallowed a grimace. That could be anything from an RMN current-generation *Salamander*-class cruiser to the twenty-million-ton *Benjamin*-class RIN ships—or even an old ten-megaton *Minotaur*-class cruiser.

Though the only *Minotaurs* left were in the system militias at this point.

"Mage-Captain Altimari on the com, sir," Salucci told her. "All-Captains network."

Roslyn linked in before the coms officer had finished speaking.

"Captains," Mage-Captain Katica Altimari addressed the junior officers. Like Roslyn, she was the ethnic mongrel of the descendants of Project Olympus, with dark skin and hair and sapphire blue eyes that were cold as ice today.

"We appear to have a Legion guest," she told them. "Unfortunately, with one *Bard of Winter*, one *Cataphract* and four *Honor*-class destroyers, I hesitate to engage even a single *Andreas*-class cruiser—and the mass range my CIC has calculated suggests the possibility of a *Benjamin*-class ship."

LaMonte linked in as Altimari finished speaking

"Commodore," the Navy CO greeted the MISS agent. "I was updating the captains on our estimate of the unknown contact. Do you need me to update you as well?"

"She's a Legion cruiser, either *Andreas* or *Benjamin*-class, and the only question is whether we're outmassed two to one or three to one," LaMonte finished swiftly. "You can't fight her—but on the other hand, she's a long way out of range and *Pax Dramatis* is almost here."

"That was my thought as well," Altimari said. "We can move out to 'meet' the cruiser while feeding her coordinates and maneuvers to the Battle Group via the Link.

"Whether she's fifteen megatons or twenty, her captain is likely to feel confident that she can take six destroyers and a pair of stealth ships," the Mage-Captain noted. "And either way, she has no chance against *Pax Dramatis* and her escorts."

Roslyn had to agree. Battle Group *Pax Dramatis* might not currently have her destroyers, and two of her cruisers were off playing taxi, but even a single *Peace*-class battleship was more than a match for any Legion cruiser.

And that was ignoring the two *Honorific*-class battlecruisers still with the battleship, either of which was an even match for the smaller possible cruiser on their own.

To Roslyn's surprise, her console lit up with a text message from LaMonte. Surely, the MISS agent wasn't...

No, LaMonte's message was exactly what Roslyn had hoped it wasn't.

I don't know enough to judge. Make sense to you?

Roslyn buried a sigh and sent back a one-word message.

Yes.

She'd have to quietly mention to her friend that sending that kind of message was *entirely* against regulations. LaMonte might be in overall command of the force, but Mage-Captain Altimari was still senior to Roslyn, and Roslyn *really* shouldn't be second-guessing her.

It helped, in this case, that Altimari had the same idea Roslyn did.

"I trust your judgment, Mage-Captain," LaMonte said calmly, as if she hadn't just asked one of Altimari's subordinates to cross-check said judgment. "What about *Theater Letters*?"

That was their captive sublight survey ship. As expected, her databanks had contained nothing of value to the Protectorate beyond survey information on the 95A-36R System, but she was currently acting as a prison ship.

"We keep our position between the cruiser and *Letters*," Altimari said firmly. "The last thing we want is for our new friend to decide that the survey-ship crew is a critical risk to the Legion's information security."

The Mage-Captain's tone was sardonic...but they all knew that was far more likely than any of them preferred. The Legion had again and again proven far too willing to kill their own people to keep even the pettiest of secrets.

"Target is accelerating out-system at three gravities," Salminen reported. "I think that's a response to us?"

The six destroyers had formed into a loose wall of battle, with *Sonnet in Springtime* in the center and slightly ahead of her older companions. Over half again the mass of, say, *Voice of the Forgotten*, *Sonnet* had ninety-six defensive turrets to the older ship's thirty-six.

The newer ship had been very specifically designed to be an escort in a way the older, more multipurpose destroyers hadn't been. War had also taught the RMN just how many missiles were going to get thrown around in a real threat environment, and a few destroyers with a hundred RFLAM turrets apiece could make quite the dent.

"She isn't accelerating directly away from us," Roslyn murmured as she studied the Legion ship. "But she's definitely buying herself time to make up her mind."

"Salucci, is *Pax Dramatis* getting everything?"

"Three ships—including us—are sending the full task force telemetry back by Link," the coms officer confirmed. "The Admiral expects to jump in five minutes. They're taking their time coming to battle stations."

Which made sense. The Legion ship was being hesitant, but her captain *knew* she had the mass and firepower advantage. It was an open question whether the cruiser had a second Mage brain aboard and could jump to safety when *Pax* arrived, though.

"CIC has fully resolved our target, sir," Salminen told her. "She's definitely a *Benjamin*."

He paused, something in the way he trailed off suggesting there was more.

"Lieutenant Commander?" Roslyn prodded.

"We're not certain, sir, but with the full task force scan resolution...we think she's bogie Legion-Alpha."

Roslyn inhaled sharply and nodded to her tactical officer as calmly as she could.

Legion-Alpha was the first ship the Protectorate had definitely encountered, a *Benjamin*-class cruiser that had effectively blockaded a Fringe World and seized the prefabricated industrial platforms shipped there.

It was also the cruiser that had turned *Duke of Magnificence*, the ship Roslyn had served on as XO before taking command of *Voice of the Forgotten*, into scrap metal that she and *Duke*'s other Mages had barely managed to get to safety.

She had *history* with Legion-Alpha.

"Let's keep our eyes open for clever tricks, then," she suggested. "Legion-Alpha demonstrated an ability to microjump for combat maneuvers that we haven't seen in any other Prometheus Drive ship.

"We are vulnerable to the same trick she pulled before."

Of course, *Duke of Magnificence* had been on her own—and if Legion-Alpha wanted to pull that trick today, she'd get a very close introduction to *Pax Dramatis!*

"Wait. Profile change!"

Roslyn's attention hadn't left the enemy ship and she saw the adjustment moments as the tactical officer spoke. The big cylindrical ship flipped in space, turning her engines directly toward the RMN formation, and then increased her acceleration.

"Bogie is now accelerating away from us at five gravities. What is she doing?" Salminen asked.

"Look for probes along her previous vectors," Roslyn ordered. "She's trying to get a full view of the star system."

A spread of Link-equipped probes dropped across the star system would be expensive but would probably make more sense than risking one of the Legion's handful of interstellar warships.

"We're scanning, but if they're using RIN sensor drones..." Salminen shook his head. "We won't see them at this range."

"But why did she change vectors?" Claes asked from CIC. "We're not seeing anything down here. Changing her vector just draws attention to the fact that she's doing—"

"Jump flare!" Salminen barked. "She's gone."

Roslyn leaned back in her seat and studied the screen.

"She must have dropped Link-equipped probes to watch us in the system," she said quietly. "Her Captain had to expect us to have reinforcements—she figured there was no way we were *actually* courting battle when outmassed two to one."

"But why did she change her vector?" the XO repeated. "That does—"

The series of antimatter explosions in the void interrupted Claes and answered his question at the same time.

Silence filled the bridge for a moment, then Roslyn sighed.

"I'm guessing some of those are blocking our ability to scan the most likely locations for the drones?" she asked.

"Yes, sir," Salminen confirmed quietly.

"And the rest are covering her actual jump location with a ridiculous amount of radiation?" she followed up.

"Yes, sir," Salminen repeated.

Roslyn shook her head, even the jump flares of three RMN capital ships arriving in the system barely easing her discomfort.

"I *hate* competent assholes," she murmured.

There was no way they'd be able to track the Legion probes, which meant that everything they did in the 95A-36R System was going to be watched—and thanks to the explosions over the jump position, there was no way that Ajam was going to be able to track the cruiser.

"Admiral Jakab's compliments to all captains, sir," Salucci said quietly. "Barring any new surprises, he is calling a virtual conference in one hour."

"Understood," Roslyn replied. She shook her head. "Despite the Legion's games, we still have work to do."

CHAPTER 38

KOLE JAKAB PROJECTED an aura of almost eerie calm to Kelly's eyes. Her best estimate was that the Mage–Vice Admiral was responsible for some thirty-five thousand human beings, a burden that had to wear on the man.

Still, his gaze was level and his voice gentle as he gently worked the details of the encounters in the 95A-36R System out of Mage-Commander Sciacchitano and the others.

"We now know, at least, the name of Commodore Vaccaro's facility," Sciacchitano concluded. "*Theater Letters'* crew told us it was called Sondheim Base and it was primarily a surveillance station.

"They were keeping on eye on the habitable planet until they were ready to launch their own colonization effort, and used the base as a secondary fueling station for ships they were sending to *Fallen Dragon*," the Mage-Commander concluded.

"*Theater Letters'* crew have been very cooperative," Kelly told the assembled naval officers. "Vaccaro's suicide bomb seems to have left them feeling a tad twitchy about their employers—and we've learned quite a bit about what the Legion has been up to out here."

She shook her head.

"The biggest part is that of *Letters'* crew of sixty-five, only twenty were original Legion," she noted. "Of the remaining forty-five, fifteen were volunteers who appear to have been mostly trusted...and the remaining thirty were conscripts.

"The Legion itself now appears to be operating with those three tiers of personnel in all of their affairs," she told the officers. "That gives them bodies but comes at a price in terms of reliability.

"The conscripts have been *especially* cooperative, though unfortunately none of them know the astrographic coordinates of their star system," Kelly noted. "All of them were drawn from a system called Pharaoh, which hasn't shown up in any of our prior intelligence.

"We now know, thanks to our prisoners and rescues, the names of all four systems of the Legion's new empire: Mackenzie, Aquila, Pharaoh and Agikuyu. The crew of a sublight survey ship, unfortunately, don't have much information on those four systems to share with us."

"I would hope they know something about Pharaoh, at least, if it's their home," Jakab pointed out.

"One inhabited planet, thirteen or so million people, founded before any of our rescued conscripts were born," Kelly listed off immediately. "Capital is apparently a city named Rameses.

"All thirty conscripts had zero space knowledge prior to the Legion drafting them. The volunteers had a bit more, but they were also from Pharaoh, which apparently maintained very little space infrastructure prior to the Legion conquest."

She shook her head.

"Pharaoh seems to have been much what I expected these rogue colonies to be," she admitted. "An intentionally low-contact settlement based around non-mainstream religious movements—in this case, primarily reconstructionist Kemetism.

"Knowing that a Kemetic sect packed up a few million people and shipped them off to the back end of nowhere, we can probably go back through records in the Protectorate and find their funding and founders," she said. "That may allow us to try to track down the origins of the other three colonies, but I suspect all of our rogue systems have relatively unique backgrounds.

"What they will share is a feeling that the Protectorate's mainstream excluded or suppressed them to such a point that a complete separation was needed."

"And none of them, I'm sure, were planning on building massive armies and fleets to invade the Protectorate and proclaim a new empire," Jakab said drily. "Where my understanding is that is exactly Admiral Muhammad's intention."

"That is what our prisoners believe, yes," Kelly confirmed. Like she'd said, the crew of the survey ship had been *very* cooperative.

They just hadn't known *anything* of use.

"Unfortunately, that doesn't help us locate those star systems," the Vice Admiral said grimly. "Our one definite link toward the Legion carefully cleaned their tracks before they fled.

"We'll need to sweep the system for any traces a Tracker can use."

"We have a Tracker en route?" Chambers asked.

"Captain Ajam agreed to work for us again, as hoped," Jakab noted. "*Redwall* is currently collecting him, and I expect them to rejoin us in four days. *Mudpuppy*, unfortunately, appears to have required more repairs for her unexpected problems than we hoped."

Kelly hadn't seen any reports on just what had happened to the Battle Group's fourth cruiser. It sounded like *Mudpuppy* had suffered from the usual complaints of being one of the newest class of warships in the RMN. They could use the *Salamander*-class cruiser, but teething problems were not...unexpected with the class.

"The final assembly of Seventh Fleet has been authorized," Jakab noted. "Mage-Admiral Medici will be moving out from Tau Ceti in under twenty-four hours. We expect *Masamune* and the other battleship groups to rendezvous *here* in ten days.

"The hope is that we will have sufficient information from Captain Ajam and our own efforts for Seventh Fleet to move out within a few days of assembling here."

The Admiral shook his head.

"That is probably optimistic, especially as I know that Admiral Medici will want to carry out detailed training maneuvers before engaging the Legion in open battle. Nonetheless, we are hoping—perhaps optimistically, but hoping nonetheless—to have target locations for Legion systems within two weeks."

That was ambitious...but they also knew that they *had* to be close now. A second Long Eyes–style sweep would almost certainly find *something*.

"We need to consider, sir, that we are almost certainly being watched here in Ninety-Five-A," Chambers suggested. "The maneuvers of the Legion cruiser strongly suggest the deployment of a spread of sensor drones—a deployment that would make no sense without those drones carrying Link FTL communicators."

"Naval Intelligence assures me that it is highly unlikely that the Legion brought sufficient technical knowledge with them to begin the mass production of Link relays in their new territory," Jakab said, but his tone could have rivaled the Sahara.

"MISS has made no such judgment," Kelly pointed out instantly. "Certainly, the Links they took with them used RIN entangled particles— and we have detected zero unexpected ongoing activity on the old RIN networks.

"While it is possible that the Legion has given up on FTL communication, they also were able to eavesdrop on our own civilian networks via captured standard units. That suggests an extremely *high* level of technical knowledge on the part of the Legion."

"To give Naval Intelligence credit, they don't disagree with you on that, Commodore," Medici said. From his sideways glance, one of the staff officers Kelly was mostly ignoring was the intelligence officer passing on the RMNI analysis.

"They simply feel that the Legion has not had the time and resources to assemble more than a cottage-industry level of production of Link terminals, sufficient to reequip their warships but not to allow them to update their RIN-era sensor probes."

Kelly started to argue but Jakab chuckled.

"The evidence we have seen so far suggests that Legion is operating an *extremely* sophisticated tech base, a full duplicate of the capabilities if not the scale of the Republic's. While I agree that there may be some question as to the extent to which the Legion can mass-produce their hardware, I refuse to assume that the enemy has no access to systems we *know* the Republic's Second Independent Cruiser Squadron possessed.

"If we assume that the Legion is *less* capable now that they have four star systems to support them than they were when they were the Two-ICS, we risk underestimating our enemy.

"We will instead plan and operate around the theory that the Legion has every capability that the RIN had, in a quantity sufficient to their immediate needs if not to a long-term campaign," the Admiral concluded, and his tone made it very clear that this wasn't up for discussion.

"That will include everything from missiles with software we don't have copies of, to enough antimatter to sustain combat acceleration for a full engagement, to, yes, Link-equipped sensor probes," he said. "Underestimating this enemy's capabilities and determination has hurt us badly in the past.

"We are not assembling a fleet anchored on a dreadnought and four battleships because we think the Legion are pushovers. They are capable and they are well equipped."

He shook his head.

"Mage-Commander Chambers' point is entirely correct. We *must* assume we are being watched—which means that we cannot sweep this system with individual destroyers or stealth ships.

"All sensor sweeps will be accompanied by destroyer groups supported by either *Count of Freedom* or *Distinguished Liberator*," he ordered. "We will set up a schedule and we will make certain to scan all likely exit points.

"We are going to find these people. Our Queen demands it."

CHAPTER 39

THE VOID WAS DARK and lonely, and Sharon's mismatched crew was learning to hate it.

"The prisoners are causing trouble again," Trengove told the disembodied Captain. "Rogers showed up in an exosuit and waved a big gun around, and it seemed to calm things down for now, but they're getting restless."

"We're not spacing them, so that leaves us with limited options," Sharon admitted, running through the surveillance footage of the incident.

Thirty-two members of *Ring of Fire*'s crew and Space Assault company had refused all promises and convincing. They were now locked in a single dormitory room, designed for a platoon of thirty Space Assault Troopers and most recently used for seventy indentured workers.

Thanks to the latter use, it was quite secure. More secure than the space Sharon had seen Ragno's workers domiciled in, though she could still release the prisoners with a single thought.

"You can only watch so much media before you start getting real sick of sitting on your ass," Trengove warned. "We've given them access to the entertainment library, but the Assault Troopers, especially, don't sit still very well."

"They're welcome to help with the repairs," Sharon said. She was speaking through the Legion Major's wrist-comp as her executive officer strode through *Ring*'s hallways.

Neither of them ever *stopped* working at this point. Sharon had the slight advantage of not needing sleep and having eyes everywhere. She knew *exactly* how the repairs were progressing.

"I suspect the idiots we have locked up would try to sabotage something critical," Trengove admitted. "And while Ragno is better at this mess than I expected, I *don't* think he can spot sabotage from people who know the systems better than he does."

"True." Sharon couldn't grimace, but the emotion was definitely there. Even among the seventy-six "crew" the mutineers had, she didn't entirely trust about half of them.

She was keeping an eye on things. So was Teodor Ragno, but the Aquilan rebel was a communications engineer with a passing familiarity with high-density power systems.

They could have done worse for an impromptu chief engineer, but there were parts of the ship where he had no idea what was going on—and they needed *Ring of Fire's* guns.

"Speaking of Ragno and the repairs, what's the latest estimate?" Trengove asked.

"At least three more weeks," Sharon admitted. "That's just to have engines, communications and two lasers. Nothing else is doable without more spare parts than we have."

"If we even get to *that* point, I'm impressed with our rebel," the Legionnaire replied. "And I'm already impressed with Ragno. We got lucky in having him assigned."

"Luck had nothing to do with it," Sharon admitted. "Legion computer systems are surprisingly insecure when you're hardwired into them. There were a few addendums to the request for workers that made sure we got him.

"I knew he was a rebel, so I figured it couldn't hurt."

"Huh." Trengove stopped outside the bridge and sighed. "Good call, in the end. I'll poke the other officers, see if we have any ideas of what to do with our prisoners. Right now, they're contained and harmless, but they're getting *real* irritable."

"Given my life circumstances, my sympathy for their plight is extremely limited," Sharon noted drily.

BEYOND THE EYES OF MARS

"We simply don't have the resources to do it any faster," Ragno told the three living and one dead officer in the Captain's office.

There was no one behind the desk, which had been shoved up against the wall out of the way. The entire room had been turned into a breakout meeting room for the mutineer officers, with four chairs arranged facing each other.

Sharon simply spoke from the roof. She suspected that the others might have been more comfortable if she'd used a hologram to speak with them—but she didn't really *have* a self-image anymore that she wanted to use.

Plus, it never hurt to rub a bit of salt in the wound of reminding the Legion officers, especially, of just what she was.

"We're relatively safe here," Young said quietly. "But every day we are sitting out here, the Legion is doing all of the things we decided we were going to try to fix. Exeter Base alone was running an average of eleven fatalities a day!"

"I know," the Aquilan rebel growled. "I know better than you do, I suspect! But we're in deep space. There's no handy nickel-iron asteroid to turn into spare parts, so we're limited to what *Ring* has aboard.

"And we've *got* a lot aboard, so we can do the work we need to," he continued. "But with only seventy sets of hands and a few dozen remotes, it takes time.

"De la Cruz knew *exactly* where to hit us to cripple the drives. We're effectively rebuilding the engines from scratch and spare parts. We'll get there, but unless we want to show up somewhere and trust that the locals will give us the benefit of the doubt..."

"Given that the Protectorate tends to *euthanize* Prometheans, I'd like to have the ability to talk to them before they get aboard—and have the ability to bolt if they get stupid," Sharon said drily.

She didn't even necessarily disagree with the Protectorate's stance on the murdered Mage brains, at least in general. In *her* case, however, she'd adjusted to her new circumstances and was very much determined to keep existing.

"So, we hang out here while Teodor gets us back to a minimum level of function, and *then* we make our way to Protectorate space," she told them. "Our best options are Erewhonwen or Condesa—and both of *those* are going to be real twitchy at the sight of a Legion ship!"

Both had been targets of the Legion's campaign of piracy according to Ajello's files. They would *not* see *Ring of Fire* as a friendly when she jumped in.

"And are over two weeks' jump away, anyway," she concluded. "So, we take our time, we make sure we can evade long enough to convince people to talk to us, and *then* we go to the Protectorate.

"There's a cost," Sharon conceded. "And I don't like it. I don't think any of us do. But unless someone has a magic bullet in their pocket to allow us to save Exeter's prisoners right now, there is nothing else we can do.

"We have to protect ourselves first if we're going to save everyone else!"

CHAPTER 40

BY THE TIME *Redwall* arrived in the 95A-36R System, Roslyn Chambers was finally and thoroughly sick of looking at the star system. The finder's fee due to be paid out to her crew—and herself—for finding a habitable garden world helped, but she'd seen too many people die there.

Still, she concealed all of that behind her learned mask of command as her shuttle touched down on *Pax Dramatis*. Another shuttle had just left to clear space for her craft's arrival, and she knew there was still a waiting line to bring the small transports aboard the battleship.

An in-person all-Captains meeting made for a lot of shuttles by the time twelve destroyers, four stealth ships and three cruisers had assembled in the 95A-36R System.

Battle Group *Pax Dramatis* was still short a cruiser but otherwise was fully assembled and awaiting the rest of Seventh Fleet. While two more battleships and a dreadnought were still on their way, her understanding was that *Pax Dramatis*'s Battle Group actually made up half of the Fleet's intended cruisers and destroyers.

Not that the Legion was going to appreciate there "only" being thirty escorts for the heavy capital ships. *Masamune* alone was a match for any two of the handful of capital ships in Admiral Muhammad's fleet.

Roslyn might have assembled more ships herself, but she wasn't Protectorate High Command, and she knew the RMN had other duties. Standing watch over the former Republic's worlds still consumed most of the RMN's battleships, for example.

Giving a swift nod to her pilot, the Mage-Commander exited her shuttle onto *Pax Dramatis's* deck. She was alone today, having left Claes in command aboard *Voice of the Forgotten*, but the shuttle would wait for her.

Rank hath its privileges, after all, and if the Admiral wanted everyone together in person, the Admiral got everyone together in person.

And Roslyn's privileges got her a shuttle to herself when the Admiral called.

A private shuttle, of course, didn't translate to a private shuttle bay. *Redwall's* shuttle had touched down just ahead of Roslyn, disgorging two tall and dark men walking side by side.

The taller and paler of the two men was only known to Roslyn by name and reputation. Mage-Captain Ezekiel Szarka of the *Salamander*-class cruiser *Redwall* was the same mixed mongrel ethnicity as most Mages by Blood, with short-cropped black hair and pale green eyes.

The other man was known to Roslyn and paused as he recognized her. Nunzio Ajam, often known as Nebeljäger and *usually* granted the courtesy title of Captain even though he'd lost his ship, was the Tracker they'd worked with to find *Fallen Dragon*.

He was also of a height with Roslyn, with dark skin and hair, with eyes that were very nearly black and smoldered with an inner heat that she wasn't nearly good enough at ignoring.

The smile that lit up his face when he saw *her* didn't help. He exchanged an unheard comment with Captain Szarka, then fell back from his companion—clearly waiting for Roslyn.

Steadying herself against an almost entirely unexpected cluster of butterflies, Roslyn stepped out to meet him, taking his hand in a firm shake and trying to ignore the warm touch of his skin against hers.

It had been *way* too long since she'd got laid.

"Captain Chambers," Ajam greeted her, bowing over her hand. "It is a pleasure to see you once again."

"Captain Ajam," she replied.

Captain was a courtesy title for them both there, and one neither of them would use if *Pax Dramatis*'s Mage-Captain Gordan Narang was present. That was the tradition aboard any starship.

"May I walk with you to the briefing?" Ajam asked. He tapped his wrist-comp to show that he had the directions.

"I know the way, Nunzio," Roslyn told him with a chuckle. "But yes, you can walk with me.

"How goes your hunt for your ship?"

"Poorly," he conceded as he fell in beside her. "Early, unfortunately, knows how I tick. In more ways than one," he sighed.

Jubal Early had been Ajam's Ship's Mage—and lover—until one Roslyn Chambers had landed Marines in the pirate port of Chasmport. Then Early had stolen Ajam's ship and vanished into the void.

MISS had promised to help find Early and the ship. So far, they clearly hadn't had much luck, though it had been more of an "as we can" promise than a "drop everything" promise.

"I expected better from MISS," Roslyn admitted.

"Much as it pains me to admit it, they've actually done fairly by me," he admitted. "I got paid, and they keep me in the loop for intel on Early while I help them with other projects.

"I'll admit to the occasional paranoid moment where I think they're stringing me along to keep a Tracker on hand, but let's be honest, the Protectorate *has* six of their own. They don't need me."

"You were close enough to be convenient for this," Roslyn murmured. "Made our lives easier."

He pressed his hand to his heart with an exaggerated scoff of anguish.

"My dear Mage-Commander, and here I'd hoped that you'd bent the Admiral's ear so you could see *me* again."

She shook her head at him. Ajam was exactly the kind of tall, dark and handsome she found physically attractive, but he'd also been a passenger on her ship before. She'd kept her hands to herself—and turned down a surprisingly polite offer from him.

"You're not *that* pretty, Nunzio," she told him. "And the whole *pirate empire of enslaved innocents* has been occupying my mind of late."

"Yeah," he murmured. "That definitely puts a damper on everything, doesn't it?" He shook his head.

"These people know what they're doing, Roslyn," he said, his tone serious. "I'll do everything in my power to follow them—your Navy is unsurprisingly reliable as a paymaster, after all—but I can't promise it'll work out any better than last time."

"I know," she said quietly. "But we'll chase them as far as we have to, however we have to."

"Yes. Their victims deserve that much, and I don't mind the steady paycheck," he said. "Though I do have to note..."

He trailed off expectantly and Roslyn shook her head at him again, aware that they were almost at the briefing room.

"Behave, Captain Ajam," she told him.

"I am a model of perfect behavior," he replied virtuously. "But I *do* note that I am no longer on *your* ship, Mage-Commander Chambers."

She didn't bother to reply as they came around the corner and found a pair of Marines waiting for them. The presence of the guards was enough to cut that particular train of conversation off, anyway.

That was probably a good thing. Roslyn *still* didn't think bedding a mercenary was a good idea, but he was funny and attractive—and it would no longer be an arguable violation of the Articles of Naval Justice.

But it was still a bad idea, and the Marines helped her control her moment of temptation before they entered the briefing room and joined the other officers of Battle Group *Pax Dramatis*.

Roslyn took her seat with the other destroyer COs, helping fill in the back half of the classroom-style briefing arrangement. Ajam's seat was assigned at the front, probably because he was going to be central to the next few days' maneuvers.

Jakab was waiting on a dais at the front of the room, with Commodore LaMonte standing at his right hand and Mage-Captain Narang at his left. That left a *mere* nineteen people in the audience, including the Tracker.

"Officers, Mr. Ajam," Jakab greeted them all. "Thank you for taking the time to come aboard *Pax Dramatis*. My staff is busy putting together a dinner for us all to stuff ourselves at in about an hour, but I'm going to make you burn off those calories with your brains in advance."

A holographic image of the 95A-36R System appeared above their heads, with four hazy yellow spheres marking the recurring jump locations.

"We currently have identified four locations where it appears the Legion was semi-regularly jumping out of this system," Jakab noted. "We believe there was a fifth here"—he indicated a zone with a sharper red sphere—"but that was where our cruiser visitor set off her bombs.

"The Legion has been disturbingly effective at erasing evidence of their routes home so far," the Admiral told them. "They appear to know enough about how Trackers work to seriously screw with our operations—a knowledge, I'll note, that the Republic did not always possess."

"The Republic didn't get nearly as far down in the underworld muck as the Legion has," Ajam suggested. "The criminal underworld and the bounty hunters who bounce in and out of it have known about Trackers for...fifty years? Maybe sixty? No one has really worked out how to identify us reliably yet, but the crime syndicates have been learning the rules of our game for longer than even the Navy.

"Fortunately for my business, very few civilian operations—however criminal—really want to get anywhere near antimatter bombs," he said sardonically. "So, the syndicates reserve screwing with jump traces for when they *know* there's a Tracker in play.

"Nuclear warheads won't cut it," he reminded the Navy officers. "It has to be antimatter."

"And the Legion uses Republic-style warheads," Jakab observed. "Big, ugly things that make a radioactive disaster. Perfect for this purpose. But..."

He waved at the yellow highlights.

"They didn't manage to sweep *this* system, which gives us a starting point," he continued. "The *problem* is that they know that, and our cruiser friend may well have spent the last week blowing the traces of their journeys to nothingness while we waited for Mr. Ajam."

"So, we're screwed, then?" Mage-Captain Altimari asked. "Back to the Long Eyes–style sweep?"

"Not yet," Ajam said sharply. "Even just identifying the first stop on each of those routes could reduce the number of systems they can be in. It won't be as simple as just drawing a line through the two points, but it'll narrow down the options."

"Exactly our thoughts," LaMonte agreed, the Commodore looking tired. "There are four potential jump zones, and we still have four stealth ships.

"Mr. Ajam will identify each jump zone in sequence, and then we will send a stealth ship with escorts to each target. We should be able to identify new jump zones with forty-eight hours or so of scanning."

"While the stealth ships will make the initial jump, they'll be accompanied by the same destroyer wings as last time," Jakab told them all. "The cruisers and *Pax Dramatis* will remain here in Ninety-Five-A.

"If nothing else, we're waiting on Protectorate Guard transports and the rest of Seventh Fleet."

"We're following old data," Ajam warned. "Both my analysis here in Ninety-Five-A and the sweeps at the jump points will take longer than you think."

"Then we have a higher chance of having additional battleships and even Guard units by the time we find them," Jakab said with a sigh.

"We can't move against the Legion until Seventh Fleet and our attached Guard Corps and Marine brigades are here and ready to deploy," he noted. "That gives us time to trace the Legion's route, to follow them home."

"And if they've blown every route, as they did after we took *Fallen Dragon*?" Altimari asked, putting into words the concern that Roslyn suspected every officer in the room shared.

"Then we do what we did from DEL-Three-T-Three and we sweep system by system until we find them," Jakab said calmly. "There are eighteen more warships headed this way, officers.

"The Legion cannot hide forever. We know that they have multiple habitable planets—and only so many stars can support those."

CHAPTER 41

KELLY WAS ASLEEP when the alert finally came in. Relaxing was hard for her at the moment, though she was at least no longer directly responsible for the dozen destroyers assigned to her scouting operation.

Her partners had spent a great deal of effort distracting her and getting her to relax, and she woke up to find herself pleasantly entangled with Xi Wu.

Unfortunately for her relaxation, while she still used a regular wrist-comp, it had a relay connection to her implants and could silently buzz her without anyone else knowing.

Sighing, she pressed a kiss to her wife's forehead and extricated herself from the bed. Someone—presumably Mike—had cleaned away the candles and massage oil and covered the two sleeping women in blankets.

Her wrist-comp was neatly placed in its usual spot on the dresser, and she scooped it up as she stepped into the living room of their suite.

"LaMonte," she said crisply as she replied to the alert and linked an audio channel to the bridge.

"Boss. Crap," Shvets replied. "That update went directly to your implants, didn't it?"

"Got it in one," she told them. "So, you may as well fill me in."

"Your XOs are going to kill me," the tactical officer said—and their tone was more serious than the words really deserved. "There's nothing in the update that was worth waking you up; I'm sorry."

"Maybe," she replied. "But if you don't want me to *talk* to Liara, you should update me."

Shvets chuckled softly. The nonbinary tactical officer and the navigator / Ship's Mage had coupled up a while earlier, mostly after Foster had gently pursued them for several years before they'd noticed.

"She's on duty right now," they pointed out. "And listening."

"Then give me the damn update, Nika."

"We got a Link feed from *Rhapsody in Vermillion*," Shvets told her. "They hit the first location Ajam identified and completed the initial sweep."

"And?"

"Nuked to fuck," they said bluntly. "Captain Ó Cearmada puts the timeline at about four days after we took the system. *Probably* our cruiser friend, but we can't be sure."

Kelly grunted. It would make sense if the cruiser had done a sweep of the six-ninety—the six standard jump points, one light-year away from the system, where ninety percent of traffic would flow—but it would also make their life a lot harder than she wanted.

"How long for the next update?" she asked.

"Ajam just finished up identifying the second jump zone and was going to sleep, last I'd heard," Shvets told her. "*Rhapsody in Verdigris* is jumping in ten minutes. We'll probably get an update an hour after that."

Kelly considered timing versus clothes versus sleep.

"I'm going back to sleep myself, then," she told Shvets. "Just email the update from *Verdigris* if it's what I think it is."

Shvets snorted.

"That the Legion has, once again, blown the ever-loving dust bunnies out of anything of use to us?" they asked.

"Exactly."

When Kelly got up five hours later, the update for the second jump zone was exactly what she'd expected. Someone had swung through the area and dumped antimatter warheads over any traces they could find.

It was *theoretically* possible, as she understood it, for Ajam to study old light from several light-days or even light-weeks away—but without the ability to identify *any* timing, they were completely out of luck.

"This isn't promising, Director LaMonte," Jakab told her as she drank her morning coffee.

"No," she conceded. "We're far from out of options, though, and I want to take a look at one of the jump sites myself. Once Ajam has located the last one, throw him aboard one of the Purple Eye destroyers—*Voice*, maybe?—and we'll go check it out.

"They know what a Tracker can do in theory, but he *is* a Tracker," she noted. "Ajam may find something they missed."

"It's always possible," the Vice Admiral agreed. "But I feel like my staff and your team should start assembling a new Long Eye plan. Brute force isn't my preference, but we've narrowed the search parameters down quite a bit."

"It'll work," she conceded. "But I don't think anyone wants to keep eighty thousand of Her Majesty's Guard sitting around in space unless we have to. Their transports aren't terrible, but that's still an unpleasant thing to ask of *anyone*."

"When was the last time you were on a planet, Director?" Jakab asked with a chuckle. "Because it's been six or seven months for me."

"There's a difference between living on a starship, in proper quarters, and living on a troop transport with twenty thousand of your closest friends," Kelly said with a chuckle. "I *like* most of the Guards I've met, so inflicting the latter seems...cruel."

"True, true. All right, LaMonte. I wasn't going to cancel the op with Ajam, anyway," he noted. "We're just going to start prepping for the brute-force sweep for if the cleaner option fails."

"Agreed," she conceded. "The Legion has been a bit *too* enthusiastic at burning their trails for my tastes. I very much want to teach them the limits of that trick."

Jakab chuckled again.

"I suspect that they worked that out when their drones here showed them *Pax Dramatis*," he said drily. "We may not have found them yet, but I imagine we are *far* closer than Admiral Muhammad ever wanted to see a battleship!"

CHAPTER 42

"IT APPEARS I am once again a guest on your ship, Captain Chambers."

Roslyn chuckled and bowed her head slightly as Nunzio Ajam stepped off the shuttle, a self-propelled suitcase following him onto *Voice of the Forgotten*.

"I would have expected you to remain aboard *Redwall* myself," she admitted. "But the plan calls for us to keep the cruisers and *Pax* here in Ninety-Five-A while the destroyers and scout ships check out the zones you found."

"And I agree with the Director," Ajam said cheerfully. "I want to check out at least one of those jump points myself."

Roslyn nodded and gestured for him to follow her.

"We've put you in the same guest quarters as last time," she told him. "And rigged up the same sensor control room for you."

"So long as it still has an analog link," he replied. "I can work with anything so long as I have that."

Like Roslyn's magic, Ajam's gift required him to see true original light. That required complex layers of fiber-optic cables and analog transmission—but since any warship had an amplifier, they needed all of that to enable their Mages anyway.

"Nothing has changed from when you last used it," she said. "If there's anything to find, we should find it."

"Of course," he allowed. They passed out of the shuttle bay and into the corridors of the ship.

"It appears I am lucky not to have shoved my foot too far in my mouth aboard *Pax Dramatis*," he continued. "I will admit I did not anticipate being aboard *Voice* again."

"And I assumed you were joking," Roslyn told him calmly. "Seemed safer for everyone that way."

"Safer, yes," he agreed—but there was something in his tone that she chose to ignore.

Regardless of anything else, at this point, he *was* back aboard her ship. Roslyn was confident in her ability to command her hormones now, however attractive the dark Tracker was.

"We'll be jumping in about thirty minutes," she told him. "*Rhapsody in Purple* will be about ten minutes ahead of us, so we'll know if we're jumping into danger...and if they've already nuked the site."

"They've already nuked the site," Ajam said flatly. "There's no way they covered the other three and not the last one. No, my dear Captain, the Legion learned this trick from the best and had the resources to play it out in a way few others could."

"What's the point in us heading out, then?" she asked. "If they've already burnt away anything you can track?"

"One, because they may have screwed it up," he told her. "Two, because even if they did everything perfectly, they may have missed something. Three, because based on my review of the scans of the first two zones, they hit the most common jump areas.

"But not every jump lands neatly in the box. Across four jump zones and I don't know how many jumps, there's a chance that someone was far enough off that their traces weren't covered by the bombs."

He shook his head.

"You Navy Mages jump with an error radius calculated in kilometers by habit and training," he pointed out. "*Civilian* Jump Mages generally have radii in the thousands of kilometers—when they're jumping into a star system and it *matters*."

"I suppose you could shave the calculation time down by a few minutes by accepting a larger radius," Roslyn reflected.

"For a deep-space-to-deep-space jump, you can cut the jump calc to ten minutes by accepting a one-light-minute, ninety-five-percent probability zone," Ajam said calmly. "And at least half of all civilian Jump Mages I've known will call that good enough and spend the extra twenty minutes watching...uh...sitcoms."

Roslyn swallowed a snort of amusement. *Sitcoms* was not quite what the bounty hunter had been about to say, and she could *guess* what he'd been thinking.

"I'm not sure Prometheus Drive Units are much inclined toward media of any kind," she pointed out. "So far as we can tell, the *person* is dead. The remaining brain is just...hardware."

And that sentence alone made her want to *hurt* people.

"I know," he agreed. "But I've tracked a *lot* of Prometheus Drive jumps at this point, Captain Chambers. Most of them have ended in areas swept clean with antimatter, but they still had those error radii.

"And while the jobs I saw the first time around were thorough, the ones we've seen this time have been significantly more rushed. You spooked them, Chambers. And I think we've got a chance that they made a mistake."

"And thankfully, we have a backup plan for if they didn't," she noted.

He sniffed.

"I will be professionally offended if I fail to track these bastards down *twice*," he noted. "There is a very attractive Navy officer I will disappoint in that case, and I do so prefer not to disappoint attractive officers."

Thankfully, they reached the sensor cluster in time that Roslyn didn't need to engage with *that* minefield.

"Jump complete," Lieutenant Daniel reported.

"Thank you, Mage-Lieutenant," Roslyn said cheerfully. "Now, go lie down."

İsa Daniel was now her navigator and Ship's Mage, but he was still very young and junior.

After the last time around, Roslyn was making sure she was the *last* person to jump when they were expecting trouble. Yusif Claes calmly took over the Navigation section from Daniel as the young man nodded and departed the bridge.

"Salucci, are we linked with the rest of the task group?" Roslyn asked.

"Telemetry links are coming up now; we're updating the initial sensor sweep we received from *Rhapsody*," the big coms officer reported. "Salminen?"

"Tactical net online," he confirmed. "As I'm sure everyone is surprised to hear, the Legion dropped what looks like six antimatter warheads to make a sphere of hell roughly five light-seconds across."

"We knew that from *Rhapsody in Purple*'s Link update before we jumped," Roslyn replied. "Ignore the 'sphere of hell,' Lieutenant Commander. What *else* is out here?"

"Void, void, a bit of space dust, more void…"

"Maybe," she conceded. "But let's be two hundred percent certain on that, shall we? Sciacchitano's people should be coordinating a drone sweep. We've got the Tracker, but *Oath* has the flag.

"We'll wait on Sciacchitano's people, but we're here to do a full drone sweep. Let's see what's out here."

"My people are absolutely convinced there's nothing out here," Mage-Commander Beulen said twenty minutes later.

"Even if there is, we're not even searching for a needle in a haystack," Sciacchitano replied, his hologram glancing at Commodore LaMonte's image in Roslyn's holographic conference. "We're searching the farmyard *around* the haystack, hoping that a needle fell out…but we have no idea *where*."

"If we find nothing, we find nothing," LaMonte said calmly, yanking on a brilliantly violet braid.

Roslyn hadn't dyed her hair in years now. She had *no* idea where the MISS Director found the time to do so regularly. Though she supposed LaMonte did have two spouses. They probably helped.

"But we have to look," Roslyn finished for LaMonte. "We're sweeping every jump zone, aren't we?"

"Out to a light-hour from where the Legion bombed," LaMonte confirmed. "Between four task groups, I give us a chance of finding something Ajam can work with."

Sciacchitano coughed.

"How large a chance, sir?" he asked.

"About thirty percent," LaMonte admitted. "Maybe less. It's hard to say. *We* have a better chance than the other groups because we have Ajam himself."

"And what is our esteemed hopefully former criminal doing?" *Oath of Freedom's Choice*'s Captain demanded. "Other than collecting a rather spectacular paycheck?"

"He only gets paid per successful jump trace," Roslyn pointed out, surprised at her defensiveness on Ajam's behalf. "And right now he's going over the same data my tactical department is, if from a different perspective."

"Phaw." Sciacchitano shook his head. "The man is worth his fee, I won't pretend otherwise, but I'd rather have one of ours doing the work."

"Mage-Captain Martin is on her way, but Mr. Ajam is here now," LaMonte said. "Any trace we find today will already be old. The sooner we get a Tracker on it, the better."

Before Roslyn or Sciacchitano could say anything more, Beulen suddenly held up a hand.

"One moment, please," she said—and then disappeared from the call.

"That's strange," LaMonte said slowly.

"Her people wouldn't have interrupted her if it wasn't important," Sciacchitano replied instantly. "I suspect it will be worth our while to wait on the conference for her."

The channel was silent for about thirty seconds, then Beulen reappeared.

"Commodore LaMonte, Captains...we have something," she told them. "My people think they've found a debris field at the edge of *Bear*'s zone of the drone sweep."

"A debris field?" Roslyn asked. "We're a light-year from the nearest star. There might be a loose comet or something, I suppose—"

"But it's most likely something artificial," Sciacchitano interrupted. "With your permission, Commodore LaMonte? I think this warrants investigating with the full task group.

"Do we know what the debris is?"

"Not yet," Beulen admitted. "It's relatively small, smaller than I would expect for a jump ship, and quite some distance away from the usual jump zone. At least thirty light-minutes."

"I agree with investigating," LaMonte said swiftly. "We will jump the full task group; I'm not going to spend a day and a half *flying* over to check it out."

"Pass the orders to your navigators," Sciacchitano said. "This is the first interesting thing we've seen since Sondheim Base itself. Let's go poke it and see what happens."

CHAPTER 43

OVER THE COURSE of the war, Roslyn had seen a *lot* of *Accelerator*-class gunships destroyed. Many of them had left little or nothing behind, vaporized by antimatter explosions scaled to cripple warships a thousand times their size.

Others had been sliced in half by lasers, shattered by Mages or taken out by near-hits from antimatter warheads. She'd seen just about every way a warship could die, though she tried not to think *too* hard about it.

It was still weird and creepy to watch *half* of a gunship spin raggedly through space. Roughly bullet-shaped normally, the largest debris chunk looked like nothing so much as a high-tech rowboat.

"There are at least four of them," Salminen told her finally.

Task Group Purple Eye had slowly spread out around the debris field, scanning for any functioning technology or computer systems that could explain why a bunch of gunships had died in deep space.

"'At least?'" Roslyn echoed back to him.

"At least four, no more than eight," he said. "But they're in a lot of pieces. It's hard for us to be entirely definitive about how many they started as."

"These are short-range ships," Roslyn said. "And the only carriers the Legion has haul them by the *hundreds*. How did four end up out here?"

"I have no idea, sir," Salminen said quietly. "We're working on an analysis of what killed them, but they definitely appear to be Legion."

"We're sure?" she asked. "This is weird enough that I don't want to assume anything."

In answer, the tactical officer typed a command into his console and zoomed in on the half-gunship she'd been watching. The identification numbers were still visible, as was the blood-red eagle of the First Legion.

"*ROF-Three*," she read off the hull. "That's not standard Republic nomenclature, is it?"

"No, sir," Salminen confirmed. "They probably *had* Republic-style hull numbers, but that piece of hull hasn't survived on any of them. We've got two other fragments with an identifier that lines up with the ROF, so I think we're looking at a single squadron.

"Whoever they were being transported by, they were launched for some reason here at the jump point."

"And then blown to hell," Roslyn murmured. "They're too intact for antimatter warheads, aren't they?"

"Like I said, we're working... Okay." Salminen cut himself off as his console chirped a message. "Give me a minute, sir?"

Roslyn gestured for him to carry on and turned her attention back to the wreck tumbling in her view.

"Depressing, isn't it?" Claes murmured. Her excessively tall and gaunt XO had apparently moved up beside her shoulder while she'd been talking to Salminen.

"I have a lot of unpleasant experiences with those things," Roslyn said. "But yeah. Any dead ship is depressing. That our job is to create them doesn't help."

"No," he conceded. "I was born in space, sir. Dead ships are extra creepy to me, I think."

Yusif Claes was from Sol's asteroid belt, one of the few places in the Protectorate where the mining work had led to permanent settlement. Even with magic and rotational pseudogravity on the stations and ships, he was still taller and more fragile than most planet-born humans.

He had also grown up utterly dependent on the artificial environment around him in a way that no planet-born officer would ever truly understand.

At that moment, though, looking at the dead gunship, Roslyn suspected she understood it better than most.

"Sir."

"Yes, Salminen?" she replied.

"We know what killed them now," the Lieutenant Commander told her. "I wanted to double-check it and validate with the other ship crews because it seemed out of place, but we all have the same conclusion."

"Okay," Roslyn said slowly. "Which is?"

"They were taken out by un-amplified magic," Salminen explained. "A single Mage, *probably* using a jump matrix but definitely not using a true amplifier."

"A *Mage?*" she asked. "What the hell was a Mage doing out here?"

"There could be a lot of reasons," Claes said slowly. "And many of them would result in getting on the wrong side of the Legion."

"The Legion doesn't strike me as overly Mage-friendly," Salminen replied. "I'd be surprised if they haven't purged whatever Mages did exist out here."

"Which would also explain why a Mage was being chased by gunships," Roslyn agreed. "Except that still doesn't explain why they were being chased by gunships *here*."

She waved a hand at the bridge walls. Between the analog fiber-optic links to the exterior of the hull and the overlaid holographic screens with their information displays, the bridge appeared to float in empty space.

And the space *Voice* rested in was truly empty. Without the digital zoom focused on the gunship wreck, none of the other debris was visible on the screens. The other three ships of the task group were tiny stars, only visible because of their running lights.

"Gunships are parasite vessels, transported by other ships," she reminded her officers. "So, this squadron belonged to another ship... Where is it?"

"She obviously jumped out," Salminen said slowly. "Potentially, so did whatever ship they fought. Neither the gunship carrier nor the Mage's ship were destroyed here, after all."

"There was no carrier here," Claes noted. "I wonder..."

Roslyn waited patiently, but her XO didn't continue.

"Care to share, Commander?" she prodded.

"We know the Legion stripped the Mage brains from the Prometheus Drive on *Fallen Dragon*," he said. "They had to have had a plan for them, or they'd have kept her as an interstellar transport.

"Building a freighter hull is easy enough, but then they need to worry about pirates and, well, *us*," he continued. "But gunships are only a bit harder to build than freighters. So, if they strap gunships to their freighters, they get some security on their transports, some firepower traveling the star-lanes—and cheap supporting carriers."

"*Cheap* is relative," Roslyn murmured. "But that makes sense."

She sighed and studied the debris again.

"All of these ships died around the same time, right?" she asked.

"Yes, sir," Salminen confirmed. "It's not perfect, but we have a timeline from the damage."

"Backtrack the debris course," she ordered. "We should be able to cross-reference their vector and the 'time of death' to locate *where* they were destroyed.

"Whoever took them out should have jumped around that time and that location. If we're very, very, lucky..."

"That spot won't have been covered in the bombs," Claes finished for her. "It might even be likely, sir—if the people sweeping the jump zone had seen the gunship debris, they'd have swept it for confidential data and bodies."

"They definitely didn't do that," Salminen said grimly. "Sir...permission to arrange a burial detail? We can bring the bodies back to Ninety-Five-A and bury them at Sondheim?"

"Granted," Roslyn said before she thought about it. "Arrange it with one of the other ships, though. We need to play Tracker taxi."

"We have them."

Nunzio Ajam joined the captains' conference from his sensor cluster, the man's canary-eating grin doing little to undermine his attractiveness.

"What do we have?" LaMonte asked. "The Mage or the people who were chasing her?"

"I'm not sure," he admitted. "Looking at the location and time stamp, there's only one jump signature. If there was a second ship, they were significantly separate in either distance or time before they jumped."

"Strange," the MISS agent murmured. "I was expecting more of a hot-pursuit situation...but then, the Legion doesn't have Trackers, do they?"

"Without a Tracker or a registered course, there's no such thing as hot pursuit," Roslyn agreed. "So, this whole situation smells. *Something* weird happened here."

"Thankfully, it appears to have been bad for the Legion," Sciacchitano observed. "Do we call for backup?"

"We don't know enough yet, and we may well be jumping after a goose," LaMonte replied. "And we're following a trail. If we get more than two jumps away from the Battle Group, then we'll get our backup to move closer.

"For now, I think it's time for us to see where the trail leads us. You have the coordinates for everyone to jump to, Mr. Ajam?"

"Already passed on to *Voice of the Forgotten*'s navigation team," Ajam confirmed. "I believe they were to be passed on to everyone else?"

"Claes is taking care of it," Roslyn confirmed. Daniel was competent enough as a navigator and a Jump Mage, but he was still out of his depth at running the entire department. Fortunately, her XO had stepped in without her saying a word.

"All right. I'll take *Rhapsody* forward," LaMonte told them. "The rest of you stand by to jump on my word. Unlike this place"—she waved a hand around them—"we're not expecting to find the next jump covered in radiation this time."

"What are we expecting?" Sciacchitano asked.

"I don't know," the MISS Director said with a brilliant smile. "That's what makes this part fun, Mage-Commander Sciacchitano!"

CHAPTER 44

THE WORLD FLICKERED around Kelly, and *Rhapsody in Purple*'s three faithful guardians vanished. One chunk of empty void was replaced with another, and for a few seconds, that was all that had seemed to change.

"Contact!" Nika Shvets barked. "Large contact at four million kilometers—heat signature, contact engines are off-line, but she is *huge*."

"Move us away," Kelly ordered. "Get me an ID on that ship and let me know what I've got into."

"Understood. Defenses online, but we may want to call some friends," Shvets told her.

"Engines are online and we are booking it," Foster added as she gently urged Traynor out of the seat attached to the simulacrum. "I can use magic to protect us, but only from missiles."

"We are *in* laser range," Shvets said grimly. "Our beam is online. Your orders?"

"Maintain evasive maneuvers and open the distance," Kelly said. "Let's not pick a fight we don't need to. What am I looking at?"

She recognized the basic form of the ship as the sensor data rolled in. The Republic had standardized their hull construction around two primary forms, Hull Alpha and Hull Bravo.

The contact was definitely Hull Bravo. Five hundred meters long, one hundred and seventy-five meters in diameter. She could be a *Benjamin*-class cruiser...but it didn't feel quite right.

"Contact's engines are off-line," Shvets repeated. "I'm not detecting active weapons... I'm not detecting weapons at all. Visual scan suggests..."

They exhaled a long breath.

"*Redoubtable*-class space assault transport," they reported. "Minimal onboard armament, intended to be escorted by RIN cruisers. Carries a ten-thousand-trooper Space Assault Division."

"No other contacts?" Kelly asked.

"None. Area is dead space; this isn't a convenient jump point on any logical route into or out of Ninety-Five-A."

"That was almost certainly the point," Kelly observed. "Have they responded to our presence?"

"No communications," Trixie Buday reported. The young com officer sounded nervous—which was reasonable, given that they were within close weapons range of a twenty-megaton, probably hostile ship.

"Right." Kelly considered for a few seconds. "Trixie...let's call that backup, please. Lightly armed as a *Redoubtable* is, she has more guns than we do, and I don't want to rely on her not noticing us forever!"

In fact, Kelly was starting to get weirded out by the complete lack of response from the Legion ship.

"Shvets, are they showing active scanners at all?" she asked.

"Negative," they replied. "They have power, but I'm not seeing engines, sensors, weapons... A lot of her systems appear to be completely off-line."

"Damage?" Kelly asked.

There was another long pause.

"Yeah," Shvets confirmed. "Someone shot the shit out of their engines, and now that I know what to look for, she's missing most of her defensive turrets. Her lasers have been hammered as well.

"Someone who was *very* close in and knew her systems *very* well ripped the crap out of her."

"Somehow, that fits perfectly," Kelly murmured. Light flared across her sensors as her destroyer companions appeared around *Rhapsody*, falling into a formation that put their superior armor and defenses between the stealth ship and the Legion transport.

"Sciacchitano, Chambers, Beulen, hold your fire," she ordered as they linked in. "Contact appears to be crippled—looks like, in fact, close-range fire from a gunship squadron."

"That would explain a bit," Chambers said slowly. "But where did the gunships come from?"

"There appear to be docking collars refitted onto the exterior of the hull," Shvets reported. "Those...may have been *her* gunships?"

"Well, there's only one way to answer this particular mystery, isn't there?" Kelly murmured. "Trixie, fire up the transmitters.

"It's time to say hello."

"Legion vessel, this is Commodore Kelly LaMonte of the Protectorate of Mars," Kelly introduced herself. The specification of *which* branch of the Martian government she worked for was unnecessary—especially with three destroyers reinforcing her position.

"We have you outnumbered and outgunned, and it doesn't appear to me that you're going to be able to run," she told them. "If you are planning on jumping away, I should note that we have a Tracker aboard and can follow you wherever you go.

"While there are all kinds of conversations we can have, I think it comes to one single starting point: in the name of the Mage-Queen of Mars, I require your surrender."

It was not, perhaps, the warmest or most reassuring message she could send—but she wasn't entirely convinced that the assault transport was as quiescent as it appeared.

If nothing else, the transport could easily have ten thousand exosuited soldiers aboard. Sending anyone onto the ship before it had officially surrendered was a fool's game.

"What happens now?" Xi Wu asked, leaning on Kelly's shoulder after the recording stopped.

"Hopefully, they surrender, we go aboard and we find complete intact navigational databases for the Legion's little empire," Kelly replied. "That will definitely serve my purposes quite nicely."

Seconds ticked away. Light took ten seconds to travel each way, but Kelly wasn't expecting an immediate response. If the transport had been fully functional, they'd have seen and responded to her by now.

Thirty seconds. Sixty.

She sighed.

"Are we sure they can even hear us?" she asked.

"Reasonably," Buday replied. "Shvets' scans show me intact receivers and suchlike. They might not *see* us, but they should *hear* us... Wait... Incoming transmission. It's a recording, not a live channel."

The coms officer put the recording up on the main display a moment later. A gaunt-looking young man in a set of ship's coveralls was slightly off-center, like he wasn't used to looking at a camera.

Past him, Kelly could see what looked like the engineering spaces of a large starship.

"Commodore LaMonte," he said slowly. "I am Teodor Ragno, formerly of the Aquilan Defense Force. I am...one of several individuals who organized a mutiny aboard *Ring of Fire*.

"While I am definitely prepared to discuss things in a peaceful manner, I hesitate to surrender this ship without preconditions." He smiled slightly and Kelly grimaced.

Ragno was doing a good job of faking being completely out of his depth, but she knew a dissembler when she saw one. She suspected everything she was seeing had been carefully plotted to send one specific message—that of a desperate man who'd taken a ship by fluke and fate.

Some of that might even be true.

"This ship and her databases represent our only bargaining power, Commodore," he concluded. "While I will gladly provide assurances that we are unarmed and don't have an assault division aboard, I and my fellow mutineers would prefer to negotiate rather than hand the ship over."

The recording ended and Kelly sighed.

"That wasn't what I expected," her wife said. "Shvets?"

"Where's the Mage?" the tactical officer replied instantly. "It might be this Ragno. It might be somebody else. But that's a damn important question."

"I'm not unprepared to talk to them," Kelly noted. "But I can tell when someone is feeding me the story they want me to believe. I think, in this case, much of it is true.

"Which then invites the question: if everything this Ragno has told us *is* true...what *hasn't* he told us?"

"A lot," Nika Shvets guessed. "We have a good idea of who shot their ship to pieces, but we don't know who the Mage who saved them was. Is that Mage still aboard? Is that Mage another rebel against the Legion—and if so, are they from the Protectorate or are they locally trained?"

"I'm also not sure I believe that a local had sufficient authority or access aboard a Legion transport to launch a mutiny," Xi Wu added. "My impression has always been that the Two-ICS and the ships they picked up imposed themselves as a new ruling caste, using the locals for forced labor and conscription."

"So, there are Legion members of the mutiny," Kelly agreed. "And Ragno isn't showing them to us because he wants to protect them. That may be a good sign...or it may be a sign that Ragno is under duress himself."

She felt paranoid saying that, but there were a lot of potential traps in this situation. If nothing else, the Legion was proving far too happy to self-destruct their own ships!

"Unfortunately, I only see one way to answer all of those questions," she told her companions. "Let's get Vidal and the destroyer Captains on a call.

"I know our destroyers don't have Marines, but *we* have Vidal's Commandos. Pick a couple of the Mage-Commanders to provide magical fire support and... Well, I pity them if they try to trap the party *I'm* planning on bringing aboard!"

CHAPTER 45

SHARON WATCHED the Martian team exit their shuttle and tried to guess how much trouble they were in. Commodore LaMonte wasn't in the files the Legion had on the Royal Martian Navy, but there was no question who was in charge among the ten Martians now aboard *Ring of Fire*.

Three of them—*not* including LaMonte—wore the golden coin at their throats that declared them Mages of the Guild. All of them had the simple three-star symbol of a Royal Martian Navy Mage as well—and while Sharon couldn't identify two of them, she knew the third.

The Legion knew the woman who'd revealed Styx Station to the Protectorate and doomed the Republic. They knew the officer who'd overrun the smuggler port in the Mercedes System, and they still had enough intelligence assets to know that Mage-Commander Roslyn Chambers had been involved in taking down *Fallen Dragon*.

Sharon didn't think the Legion would go so far as to call one relatively junior officer a *boogeyman*, but Mage-Commander Chambers certainly figured larger in her stolen files than any other RMN officer of her rank.

She'd expected the Mage to be taller. The petite-but-curvy woman acting as the delegation's second-in-command didn't fit the fire-breathing, unstoppable juggernaut the Legion was starting to regard her as—but it was definitely Chambers.

"Anything we should know?" Trengove asked the air in the room where she and Ragno were waiting. Two of her Space Assault Troopers were leading the Martians to the conference room, giving Sharon a chance to study them as they moved through the ship.

"LaMonte isn't a Mage, but she brought three of them," Sharon told her senior subordinates. "The rest of the complement...mmm...they're Augments."

She had a *lot* of experience watching Augments walk the decks of *Ring of Fire*. The six men and women escorting LaMonte's party were definitely cyborgs. *Augment* might not be the right word, but Sharon didn't *know* what the Protectorate called their equivalent.

"LaMonte is expecting a trap," Ragno said grimly. "I don't like this."

"We were always going to the Protectorate," Sharon reminded him. "No one else can save Aquila or Exeter or the rest of the Legion worlds."

"I know," the rebel engineer admitted. "But while our sensors were at the bottom of the repair list, I can tell you there are at least three ships out there. Maybe more. LaMonte hasn't exactly told us *what* she commands."

"She has access to the resources of the Royal Martian Navy," Trengove told him. "And that is what we need if we're going to save our people."

"They're *our* people now, are they?" Ragno asked.

"May not have been what Muhammad was thinking when he brought us here, but yes," the Legion mutineer said calmly. "And I'm thinking about those people at Exeter mostly."

She waved a hand around.

"*Ring of Fire*'s crew is directly responsible for their situation. I feel like we have to do *something*."

"Our ability to do anything depends on what you can convince Commodore LaMonte of in the next few hours," Sharon told them. "She's almost there. Remember: Ragno is in charge. I'm just a brain in a jar."

Her officers' disturbed expressions at that lasted until the door chimed. It was showtime.

There was a presence to the violet-haired Martian officer that Sharon had rarely seen in her life. A few of her better teachers had possessed a version of it, as had a few of the "teachers" who had lured her and others to their deaths.

Ajello had had it, too, though few other Legion officers had possessed it. Despite her slight build and fancifully colored hair, Kelly LaMonte was instantly and completely in control of the conference room the moment she walked in and gestured her people to their seats.

LaMonte was silent for several moments, studying Ragno and Trengove with sharp eyes, then she smiled slightly.

"My name is Kelly LaMonte," she reintroduced herself. "Today, I speak for Mars. Will you listen?"

There were several sharp inhalations around the room. Sharon suspected that phrase had a meaning beyond the obvious metaphorical one. She believed, though she was not *certain*, that LaMonte was telling them that the Mountain would back anything she agreed to.

"That's a nice sentiment," Trengove finally said. "We are prepared to listen, but we have our own hopes here."

She waved a hand at herself.

"I am Verdandi Trengove, formerly of the First Legion, formerly of the Republic of Faith and Reason's Space Assault Force," she noted. "I act as executive officer on this ship."

"And Mr. Ragno here is...the chief engineer?" LaMonte asked.

"I am in charge," Ragno said sharply...about a moment too late for it to be believable, Sharon suspected. And his half-panicked glance at Trengove didn't help, either.

"No, you're not," the Martian said cheerfully. "You look to Trengove to back you up. My guess, like I said, is that you are the chief engineer and that Trengove is the executive officer, yes.

"So, you're hiding your Captain from me...or is this some kind of dual command? One of you is a Legion mutineer and one a rebel, I suppose."

"The command structure of this ship is our concern," Trengove said firmly. "We have our secrets to trade, Commodore LaMonte, but we see no reason to betray everything immediately."

"Well, then," LaMonte replied. "Let's start with the basics: your ship is powered by at least one murdered Mage. It is the standing doctrine of the

Protectorate that all Prometheus Drive ships be destroyed. Regardless of what agreement we come to, *this ship* is shortly going to be of no concern to *anyone.*"

"And if we refuse to consent to that?" Ragno asked. "This ship isn't yours to dispense with, Commodore LaMonte."

"You have neither the firepower nor the troops to stand off my people," LaMonte said quietly. "You'll forgive me, Mr. Ragno, if I prioritize the destruction of that horror over a polite negotiation."

That was not a tack that Sharon had anticipated, and it was one that was going to cause them a giant headache if she didn't head it off.

"Let's halt that point of discussion right there," she said over the room's intercom. "There will be *no* end to discussion that involves the destruction of *Ring of Fire's* Prometheus Drive. I rather *like* being alive."

LaMonte froze and then looked up at the roof.

"May I presume that I am speaking to this ship's actual Captain?" she said slowly.

"You may," Sharon told them. "I will not be physically joining the conversation, however, for reasons I suspect are rapidly becoming obvious."

The complete lack of color on Mage-Commander Chambers' face suggested that *she* had caught up.

"My name is Sharon Deveraux, and four years ago, the Republic of Faith and Reason murdered me," she told them bluntly. "I am a Promethean, awake, aware and *alive*, Commodore LaMonte, and I will not lay down and die for your moral convenience.

"If that is unacceptable, then we are at an impasse that I do not believe will be easily ended."

CHAPTER 46

THE SILENCE that filled the conference room seemed to last for an eternity. Of all the things Kelly had expected to deal with aboard *Ring of Fire*, the discovery that the murdered Mage in a Prometheus Drive could be *awake* wasn't one of them.

"How?" she finally asked. "We always thought that…"

"You have euthanized every Prometheus Drive brain that has fallen into your hands," the…Promethean?—Sharon Deveraux, she'd said her name was?—said. "Given the horror of what was done to me and others, I do not and cannot blame you.

"The default state of the mind in the Prometheus Drive is functionally an induced coma," Deveraux continued. "The Legion, however, has experimented with waking us up.

"They have discovered that we make for excellent administrative assistants, capable of multitasking better than living humans and able to interface with ship's systems to a degree even an Augment cannot match."

Deveraux's voice was computer-generated, Kelly presumed, but it still carried a bitter chill that burned the soul.

"We also get better at the key function of a Prometheus Drive and are able to make faster and more accurate jumps," Deveraux noted.

"Of course," Chambers whispered. When Roslyn glanced over at the Mage-Commander, she shrugged—but it was a frail thing, as shown by the white horror in the young Mage's face.

"We ran into a cruiser that micro-jumped to take out *Duke of Magnificence*," she explained. "Legion-Alpha, the first Legion ship we ever identified. Her Prometheus Drive jumped like a veteran Mage...only even *more* precise."

"That is *Battlemaster*, with the Promethean William Connors aboard," Deveraux told them. "The Legion has only experimented with Prometheans aboard one warship...but Connors, like many of the Legion Prometheans, was indoctrinated well and will serve the Legion."

"And you were less so, I take it?" Kelly asked softly. Of course the Legion had done everything in their power to make the Prometheans loyal. If they were smart about it, they'd controlled *everything* those minds had experienced as they woke up from their comas.

"I trained puppies before all of this," Deveraux said acidly. "I recognize response-reward training when I see it. But I wanted to live, Commodore LaMonte, so I let them think I was well trained.

"And then I had my face rubbed in just how far the Legion had fallen, and lost the last vestiges of my ability to pretend I wasn't contributing to a greater evil," she concluded. "I recruited this ship's original XO and arranged for Mr. Ragno and a team of indentured workers to be placed aboard.

"Building on those two factors, I organized the mutiny that took control of this ship." She paused. "I didn't manage to prevent the gunship commander getting his ships free, but I *did* manage to use the jump matrix to use my magic against him."

The Legion officer—Trengove—shook her head.

"I don't think *any* of us realized that she could do that," Trengove noted. "The mutiny was a mess. We underestimated a lot of our former colleagues. They're dead now...but so is our original XO, one of my oldest friends."

Kelly glanced back over at her three Mages. She'd brought Liara Foster from her own ship, making sure all three of the Mages were Navy-trained, but Mage-Commander Chambers was unquestionably the most senior.

She'd brought Chambers because she *trusted* Chambers—and because she knew that the young woman was the most powerful Mage she'd ever met outside of Damien Montgomery and the Royal Family.

The trust was more important right now as she met Chambers' horrified gaze and arched an eyebrow. She had her own sick emotions over this whole affair...but she was also a mundane and she *knew* it wasn't her place to judge the choices of a Mage.

She wasn't sure if Chambers' horror was at the thought of a Mage trapped as a brain in a jar but still aware and thinking...or at the fact that the Protectorate had euthanized at least a *thousand* such minds, without ever realizing that there was a chance for them to somehow live at all.

Pale or not, the Mage-Commander met her gaze and nodded slightly.

"I think it is safe to say that we are not going to require Captain Deveraux's destruction as a precondition of any agreement," Kelly told the Legion mutineers. "Her situation is...a new wrinkle in an already-messy scenario. One we will need to consider in detail before the Mountain makes a new policy with regards to the Prometheus Drive.

"But I am prepared to pledge my Mage-Queen's word that Captain Deveraux's fate is *hers* to choose."

The Promethean might not know enough to know what it meant for an officer of the Protectorate to pledge the Mage-Queen's word. The one former Republic officer did, though, and Trengove visibly relaxed as Kelly spoke.

"That, of course, still leaves us with the problem of what to do with you all," Kelly continued. "A Legion assault transport, however damaged, represents both a risk and an opportunity. We would prefer to take her into the RMN's possession and, well, rip her apart for intelligence."

"While *Ring of Fire* is not exactly my body," Deveraux noted, "I have very little capability separated from her. I hesitate to surrender her for dismantling without some securities—for myself, for my people and...with regard to the Legion."

"I am not certain what securities I *can* provide for you," Kelly admitted. No one had put any thought into designing robot bodies that could handle Prometheus Interfaces, after all—though in hindsight, that was a *brilliant* idea someone needed to work on!

"As for your people, there is a long and complex tradition in our shared history of defectors and their treatment," Kelly continued. "I see no reason not to guarantee their safety and immunity for actions carried under Legion authority—to a point," she warned. "Regardless of their contributions, I am uninclined, for example, to guarantee immunity for the use of weapons of mass destruction."

"There is no one aboard *Ring of Fire* who was involved in strikes of that nature," Trengove said quietly. "But they happened. The Legion's invasion of the worlds we annexed was violent and brutal, and our rule has been little better."

"*Their* invasion and *their* rule," Deveraux corrected the mutineer. "You are no longer Legion, Verdandi."

It was hard for Kelly to track who the Promethean was engaging with. The fact that the most important person in her current meeting was just a voice from the ceiling was a problem.

"We also have prisoners aboard who did not join the mutiny," Deveraux noted. "I would like to turn them over to Martian authority, on the condition that they are treated as prisoners of war with all of the rights included in that status."

"Done," Kelly said instantly. "We are at war with the First Legion. Any personnel who surrender to us will be treated with the dignity due that status."

The two mutineers shared a long look.

"And what do *you* want, Commodore LaMonte?" Deveraux asked as her subordinates looked thoughtful.

Kelly considered obfuscating for a moment, then decided to put aside her mistrust for the moment.

She sincerely doubted that anyone in the room could hate the First Legion more than Sharon Deveraux, after all.

"We don't know where the Legion is located," she admitted. "I want *Ring of Fire*'s navigation databases. Intact and uncensored, to allow us to carry out the operations necessary to reduce their forces and liberate the worlds under their control."

"We are prepared to provide that data," Deveraux said instantly. "But we have...conditions, Commodore."

"Name them," Kelly replied. She doubted that the mutineers, even including the Promethean, could come up with any price she wasn't prepared to pay.

"There are over a hundred thousand civilians in a system that the Legion has been turning into their new primary shipyard," Deveraux told her. "Civilians that this ship and crew were directly responsible for transporting into forced labor under the harshest of conditions.

"While every person currently under the rule of the Legion is a subject, unwillingly under the boot of a foreign tyrant, *those* people are slaves. And *we* delivered them into slavery."

"Well, Ragno didn't," Trengove admitted quietly. "But Deveraux and I and the rest of *Ring of Fire*'s actual crew? This ship alone moved fifty thousand people from the Legion's conquered worlds to the Exeter Fleet Base."

"We will give you that nav data," Deveraux explained. "But we require that you move against the Exeter System *first*—and if I do not feel I can trust you to keep that promise, I will *only* give you the nav data for Exeter."

Kelly hesitated. It was a price that they *could* pay—but once Seventh Fleet was assembled, Admiral Medici might have enough firepower to hit all four or five systems at once.

And yet she could understand why the mutineers were focused on the piece they had directly impacted. And she could see why they would want a show of faith from the Protectorate.

And Kelly LaMonte had not been exaggerating at the beginning of their meeting. She spoke for Mars today, bearing the weight of her Queen's will.

Kiera Alexander's will was clear: the First Legion must fall and the people they'd conquered must be liberated.

"I am prepared to work with that," Kelly told the dead woman who commanded *Ring of Fire*. "Are you prepared to return to the Ninety-Five-A-Thirty-Six-R System with us and help us plan that operation?"

"We will freely provide any and all information we have on the Exeter System and the Exeter Fleet Base," Deveraux confirmed. "We were there only a few weeks ago—and our sensors were working then.

"We cannot defeat the Legion with one crippled ship," the Promethean conceded. "We have no choice but to turn to Mars."

CHAPTER 47

ROSLYN COLLAPSED on the couch in her quarters and tried to control her breathing. Finally out of sight of officers and ratings, the ironclad self-control she'd been forced to learn finally collapsed into a thousand pieces, and she had to focus.

She knew she hadn't held the mask together as well as she'd like—but no one else in that meeting had, either!

One thousand, five hundred and eighty-six.

She hadn't been able to keep herself from looking up the numbers. The Protectorate had captured over two hundred and fifty warships and transports of the Republic of Faith and Reason, each of them equipped with between four and six Prometheus Drive Units.

With the brains inside those Prometheus Interfaces unresponsive, the assumption had been that there'd been some level of lobotomization or other damage. That the children—and in later cases, war captives and prisoners of war—who'd been murdered to fuel the Republic's war machine were effectively dead.

The overdose of sedatives introduced into the Interfaces' nutrition tubes at that point could only be a mercy then.

Except *they'd been wrong.*

Roslyn had never known that the Prometheus Interfaces intentionally kept the Mages in a coma—and she knew as much about the Interfaces as anyone. The Protectorate's unwillingness to study the horrors that the

Republic had built had kept them from realizing that the imprisoned Mages were silent for a reason.

They probably couldn't have saved them all. Roslyn could recognize that, even alone in the dark of her quarters. Sharon Deveraux had clearly been a young woman of extraordinary will and strength of personality. Her murder and transformation had only sharpened that, refined it to create the Promethean that remained.

But if even one in ten of the Mages they'd euthanized had been savable, the Protectorate had unknowingly murdered the very people they'd set out to save.

Nausea rippled through Roslyn's chest, and she coughed against the surge of emotions. She hadn't given the order herself—that had been Mage-Admiral Her Highness Jane Alexander, the Crown Princess of Mars.

But Roslyn had been in the room where it happened. She'd been one of the Mages involved in the discussion over what to do about the victims of the Prometheus Interface...and she, like the rest of the officers in that meeting, had argued for mercy.

Had argued for euthanasia.

For murder.

She was staring blankly into space, trying to process some fragment of what had happened, when the door to her quarters chimed.

That startled her out of her reverie. *No one* was going to show up unannounced at the Captain's quarters. She'd intentionally dismissed her steward for the evening because she'd *known* she was going to break down once she was alone.

Her guilt for what had happened began to overwhelm her, and then the door chimed again and she realized it had been at least a minute. Probably two. Whoever was at the door was being patient...and they didn't appear to be leaving.

Roslyn took a moment to take a washcloth to her face. It would never do for any of her crew to realize she'd been crying in a guilt-induced panic attack, after all.

As she finished cleaning her face, the door chimed gently for the third time and she sighed. Whoever it was owed her an explanation!

"Enter," she instructed.

She wasn't expecting to see Nunzio Ajam standing in the doorway, holding a dark bottle of some kind.

"Ajam, what are you *thinking?*" she hissed.

"That there is nobody else on this ship that the Captain can vent to, actually," he told her, and proffered the bottle.

Roslyn took it almost automatically, then inhaled as she realized what she'd been handed. Vasuda Duchamp brandy was rare outside Tau Ceti, though something of a system mascot *in* Tau Ceti.

Vasuda Duchamp's masala-spiced fruit brandy was the kind of unique mixture that only Tau Cetan culture—often described as a French man and an Indian woman arguing over feeding the children—could produce, and it was almost impossible to get outside of Roslyn's home system.

"Okay, you managed to turn up one of my favorite liquors from my home system," she said drily. "That buys you about a minute to explain what you're thinking, but not necessarily more than one step in the door."

Ajam chuckled and took that one step into her quarters, letting the door close behind him and then leaning on the metal panel as he put his hands in his pockets.

"Before we found the Link, the rumor mill was the only form of communication that moved faster than the speed of light," he told her. "And I listen and I buy drinks. So, I heard the story of what you found on *Ring of Fire*. And I can put two and two and a public personnel file together and get ten."

"What do you mean?" she snapped...but she could guess.

"You were on the Crown Princess's staff when the call was made to euthanize captured Interface victims," Ajam told her, echoing her earlier self-flagellation. "And then today you found out that at least some of them might have been able to regain some level of functional existence if that decision hadn't been made.

"So, you're locked in your quarters, on your own, beating yourself up with the guilt stick. I figured I'd come provide a distraction."

Part of Roslyn figured she should throw him out. There was at least a fifty percent chance he was trying to seduce her. The rest of her, though, figured he was smarter than that—and he was right that there was no one else the Captain could vent to.

"Take a seat, Nunzio," she told him softly. "Let me find some glasses. Where did you even *find* this?"

He coughed delicately.

"I bought it from a Tau Cetan on the MISS ship I was working with when the Admiral recruited me to come track for him again," he said. "Paid *way* too damn much for it, but I was hoping to either make a gift or a date night of it."

He shrugged.

"But tonight, I think you need a drink and a friend, so let's call it a gift."

"Presumptuous of you, wasn't that?" Roslyn said, glad for the distraction as she poured two fingers' worth of the brandy into each glass.

"Easily," he agreed. "I like to think of it as *hopeful*, but I also noted the boundary you set when we first met. I was hoping to stay on *Redwall* until we got somewhere with civilian restaurants, but here we are."

She shook her head and sniffed the glass. The scent of masala spices and mixed fruits washed over her like an old friend. It had been years since she'd been home, and the scent of the liquor reminded her of that.

"But you ended up back on my ship," she observed.

"I did, and that means the boundaries exist," Ajam told her. "So, I figured the bottle would be a gift eventually." He took a small swallow of the brandy himself.

"That's nicer than I was expecting," he admitted. "I'm always worried about your system's cuisine."

"It's rarely *that* bad," she argued. "Not as much as, say, showing up to a military operation, hoping to ask one of the ship Captains on a date!"

Fortunately, Ajam didn't have any of the brandy in his mouth as he choked.

"*Hope* is not *intent*," he finally said. "But yes, I was being foolishly hopeful. I'm allowed that."

He took another swallow of the brandy and leaned forward as she took a seat across from him. Her sitting area had a couch and several chairs, which left her with the options of "across from Ajam" or "next to Ajam," and she wasn't sitting on the couch with him.

Those boundaries he was talking about existed for a reason, after all. Roslyn drained the brandy glass and stared down into the bottom of it.

"Are you?" she said. "Maybe. I don't know."

"I'm not a naval officer; I wouldn't know anything," he told her. "What I suspect, however, is that you need to talk. And the *Captain* can't show weakness to the crew—I know that much.

"But a mercenary passenger? I'll be gone in a few days, and I'm uninclined to cause trouble before that. With *Ring of Fire* found, my role in this whole mess is done."

"Time to collect your paycheck and go?" she asked.

"Perhaps. But that's tomorrow and you're dodging the subject," Ajam pointed out. "Brandy for your thoughts, Captain Chambers?"

Roslyn chuckled and poured herself more brandy. Leaning back in the chair, any semblance of humor faded.

"We got it wrong," she whispered. "If Deveraux is alive...what did we do?"

Ajam started to say something, then stopped himself. She arched an eyebrow at him, but he just gestured for her to continue.

"We killed over fifteen hundred victims of the Republic's Prometheus Project," she told him. "Most were children of the UnArcana Worlds, teenagers murdered by the people who should have protected them.

"Others were war prisoners. Some were probably RMN officers. But we thought they were gone, so we...let them go. And now I know we murdered them."

"You did what you thought was right," he said after she'd been silent for a moment.

"Not exactly helping," Roslyn admitted. "What would you know about accidentally murdering someone?"

"Gray-market bounty hunter," Ajam pointed out, tapping the chest of his black leather jacket. "*Officially*, I didn't bring anyone in for a death mark. Certainly didn't do any bounties that involved bringing people in dead.

"But yeah. Eleven times," he concluded, a sudden darkness in his tone as he finished his own brandy and held out the glass.

Roslyn refilled it as she considered his words.

"Eleven times?" she asked.

"That's how many times I *know* someone I delivered was killed afterward," he said grimly. "Out of one hundred and ninety-three completed bounties. I didn't work for people who did it again, but..."

He shook his head.

"Evidence suggests my judgment as to who was going to kill people was a bit shaky. And I had *less* reason to think those people would be fine than you did to think the Republic's victims were already dead!"

"We should have realized that they were in induced comas," Roslyn whispered. "We had the Interfaces to examine by that point."

"As I understand it, the Protectorate has made a very real and quite successful effort to make sure every version of the Prometheus Interface was destroyed and all of the records around them locked up in a secret vault somewhere," Ajam replied. "It's always a shitty choice, I guess, whether to benefit from research carried out with such cruelty and violence.

"Being unwilling to study the Interface was justifiable. So was the call your boss made. And it's not like *you* gave the order."

"I was in the room," Roslyn murmured. "I had a say. I didn't argue against it... None of us did."

"Yeah. *None of you* argued against it," Ajam replied. "How many people were in that room, Roslyn? How many of them senior to you?"

"Nine. All of them senior. I was the Flag Lieutenant," she told him.

She swallowed the contents of the second glass of brandy and stared blankly at the empty glass.

"Your words might have some impact if you'd been the only dissent, but you couldn't have changed anything," he told her. "And you weren't wrong. You didn't know enough to be wrong.

"And I mean...it didn't sound like this Deveraux held it against anyone, either. Even she's only been awake for a year or so, right?"

"Something like that," Roslyn murmured.

"Well, now we know for the ships we take from the Legion," he told her. "And we'll find out the hard way how many can be saved—but I'm betting the *Legion* didn't give them any choice in whether they lived or died.

"And I'm betting the Protectorate is better than that."

Roslyn exhaled a long sigh and nodded, meeting Nunzio Ajam's dark and thoughtful eyes.

"We will be," she promised. She wasn't really speaking to him, but he knew that. "We have to be, or the Mage-Queen's Protectorate becomes just a nation. A failed ideal."

"Ideals aren't failed until you stop trying to live up to them," he told her. "And while the RMN isn't necessarily lacking in officers who don't try, they're the minority.

"And you are not one of them, Roslyn Chambers."

He saluted her with his empty brandy glass.

"I've learned that much, these last few months."

CHAPTER 48

PAX DRAMATIS **WAS** half a kilometer high and massed sixty million tons. Even coming from the Legion assault transport, Kelly LaMonte could see that the two mutineer officers were shaky as they were escorted off their shuttle by a pair of dress-uniformed Marines.

The MISS Director stepped forward to greet Trengove and Ragno with a crisp salute.

"Welcome aboard *Pax Dramatis*," she told them. "Mage-Captain Narang is waiting for us, if you'll step this way."

Both of *Ring of Fire*'s officers towered over Kelly, something she noted a lot more now than she had aboard *Ring of Fire* itself. Then, of course, she'd carried more weight than her own authority.

It wasn't often that a glorified spy spoke with the voice of Mars, after all.

"Thank you, Commodore," Trengove said, half-indicating for Ragno to follow her and half-pulling the local with her.

The touch on the Aquilan's shoulder was gentle, though more familial than anything else. The mutiny had thrown together some strange bedfellows, but they seemed to be getting along surprisingly well.

Gordan Narang was a tall man from Vietnam on Earth, a Mage by Right—identified by the Royal Testers at age eleven—with a clear ethnic background rare among Mages by Blood.

He inclined his head to his two guests as Kelly led them up to him.

"Welcome aboard, officers," he told them. "I understand that Mage-Lieutenant Kumar made arrangements for Captain Deveraux to be involved in these discussions as well?"

"He did, Captain," Trengove confirmed politely. "We appreciate the assistance. Deveraux is not...used to needing to have a physical presence."

"And we are not used to dealing with Prometheans at all," Narang said. "It will be an educational experience for us all. Commodore LaMonte will escort you to the conference room.

"I have others to greet. Thank you."

LaMonte gave the stiff flag captain a somewhat-reproving nod, but she led her charges on.

The fate of millions ran on their ability to work with the mutineers from *Ring of Fire*. They couldn't afford to make them feel uncomfortable.

There were specific seats set aside in the conference room for the officers from *Ring of Fire*. Three of them, in fact, which Kelly eyed askance but Trengove and Ragno seemed to be expecting.

Kelly took her own seat next to them, glancing around the big table and checking to see who was present.

It was a relatively small group, with only Mage–Vice Admiral Jakab and the Captains present other than their guests. With Kelly herself, that meant there were only eleven people in the room, including Jakab's operations officer.

And one empty seat—and the air above that seat flickered for a moment as Jakab took his seat at the head of the conference room.

"Link is up," Ragno said softly, checking his wrist-comp. "Stable and... you're good."

The flicker turned into a hologram roughly the same size as Kelly herself. It wasn't the detailed projection of a person that would be used if someone was linking in from a full holoconferencing setup. Instead, it was a vaguely human-shaped avatar...with a giant smiley face painted on the front.

It was occasionally very easy to tell that Sharon Deveraux was not yet twenty.

"I see that Captain Deveraux has joined us," Jakab noted calmly. "We are also sending a stream of this meeting to the junior ship commanders, but I didn't want to pull them away from their vessels, and I wanted to keep this particular discussion small.

"All of us know each other, Captain Deveraux, Mr. Ragno, Major Trengove," he continued. "You know Commodore Kelly LaMonte of *Rhapsody in Purple*. The rest are Captain Lothar Benjaminson, my operations officer, Mage-Captain Gordan Narang, my flag captain and the commander of *Pax Dramatis*, Mage-Captain Ezekiel Szarka of the cruiser *Redwall*, Mage-Captain Vitomir Verona of the cruiser *Distinguished Liberator*, Mage-Captain Lamprecht Bonnet of the cruiser *Count of Freedom*, Mage-Captain Katica Altimari of the destroyer *Sonnet in Springtime* and Mage-Captain James Anholts of the destroyer *Wolfheart*."

He smiled slightly, suggesting—to Kelly at least—that he didn't expect anyone to remember anything from that list of names.

"For anyone who wasn't paying attention, Major Verdandi Trengove, Officer Teodor Ragno and Captain Sharon Deveraux are the senior officers of *Ring of Fire*, a Legion assault transport that has now officially defected to the Protectorate."

"We made a deal," Deveraux's smiley-faced avatar said calmly. "So long as the Protectorate honors that deal, we're good."

"And I have every intention of doing so," Jakab replied. "If one of you would care to lay out the situation in Legion space, however, I would appreciate it."

"Trengove?" Deveraux suggested.

"Of course, Captain." The ex-Legion Major looked thoughtful for a moment, then glanced at Jakab. "May I have control of the table projector, Admiral?"

"Of course," Jakab echoed. "Kumar?"

The Flag Lieutenant wasn't present in the room, but was clearly running tech from just outside. Jakab's single-word inquiry was enough for the holoprojectors to come alive with an image of the 95A-36R System.

"We are here," Trengove told them. The hologram zoomed out, reducing 95A-36R to a single icon. Five more then appeared glittering around it, one on a nearly straight line out from Earth and the other four to the side and "down" relative to that icon.

"These are the Legion's five primary systems," she continued. "Agikuyu, Aquila, Mackenzie, Pharaoh—and Exeter."

It seemed that Jakab's word was enough for the mutineers to provide the full databases they'd threatened to hold back.

"Agikuyu, Aquila, Mackenzie and Pharaoh are all rogue colonies," Trengove noted. "Settlements created by factions inside the Protectorate that decided, for whatever reason, that their desired societies weren't acceptable inside the structure of the Protectorate."

"I thought we didn't really enforce any structure on the individual systems," Benjaminson replied.

"There's enforcement and then there's unacceptable," Jakab told the Martian officers. "With the notable exceptions of the cooperatives of Amber and the Kingdom of Mars, almost every planet in the Protectorate operates some form of federal republic. Usually derived from either the European Union Parliament or the United States Congress.

"While neither the current Constitution nor the Charter that preceded it *require* that—the Kingdom of Mars itself is a constitutional monarchy, after all—it is very much a fixed reality of our system."

"And Aquila, for example, was founded by several different groups that felt a more explicitly hierarchical structure had a benefit for everyone," Ragno told them. "Most of that structure is currently in a state of chaos due to the invasion, but I was born to the equestrian class—the second-highest of six tiers in our society, with both options and responsibilities that a member of a lower tier would not have."

"Exactly," Trengove agreed. "Pharaoh, on the other hand, is a confederation of theocracies based around, I believe, nine different religions. The first among equals and official ruler of the planet was the Horus of

Cairo, but while her secular authority was real, her *religious* authority was restricted to the Cairo Principality."

"So, these were people on the fringes of Protectorate society who decided they wanted to create their own perfect worlds," Jakab concluded. "Much what we figured once we realized these kinds of colonies existed at all."

"All of their structures are currently, as Teodor noted, in chaos," Trengove reminded them. "The Legion...Admiral Muhammad did not care about local structures at all. He imposed military rule at a planetary level and broke any structure that resisted Legion control."

"Which was most of them," Ragno said quietly. "Our grandparents did not come here to live to someone *else's* ideals, after all."

"All told, the Legion's territory has about ninety million people," Trengove said. "Forty million of those people are in Mackenzie, a system that has two habitable planets and has become the center of the Legion government.

"Mackenzie contains one set of refit yards and is where Muhammad keeps his battleships and carriers. It is not, however, where the Legion has set up their primary shipyard."

"That is Exeter?" Kelly asked.

"Exactly," the Legion officer confirmed. "Drafts of forced laborers have been moved from every world in the Legion's empire to the Exeter System to work on constructing first a major shipyard and, now, a series of Republic Model Two hulls."

"Once complete, those hulls are intended to become two battleships and six cruisers," Deveraux told the gathered officers, the smile on her avatar incongruous with her words.

"That information wasn't available to Major Trengove," the Promethean noted. "It was in *Ring of Fire's* files. Not everything the Legion was doing was," she warned. "Certain information was only held in the implants of senior officers.

"For example, Major Trengove would be vaguely aware of the threat the Legion calls the Chimerans," Deveraux said. "The ship's XO, Lieutenant Colonel Rooijakkers, helped me put together the mutiny before her death—and even she didn't know who the Chimerans are.

"My *belief* is that Colonel Ajello did know, but that information was solely in his implants, and I don't believe that it was the only information that was kept outside of *Ring of Fire*'s files."

The Promethean's avatar shook her head.

"The Legion is extremely paranoid about its information security, and only the fact that *Ring* has visited all five of their systems allows us to know where they are," she admitted. "While I am confident that there are other bases like Sondheim Base here, we are unaware of those locations.

"What we *do* know is that there are one hundred and thirty-five thousand innocent people that were swept up in draft orders, loaded onto transports like *Ring of Fire* and delivered to the Exeter System," Deveraux said grimly. "Those people are being forced to do extremely dangerous construction work with minimal training and worse safety standards.

"It is arguable whether the staff on the surface resorts, who are expected to submit to repeated rapes with a smile, are the lucky or unlucky ones, given that the orbital works have a double-figure daily death rate."

The room was silent as the Exeter System flashed red.

"That brings us to the price for this information," Jakab said quietly. "While Battle Group *Pax Dramatis* lacks the strength to engage the core Legion fleet at Mackenzie, we believe we can engage the defenses of any other Legion system.

"Once Seventh Fleet finishes assembling in a few weeks, even the Mackenzie fleet will be handleable. Right now, though, the Battle Group would be capable of courting a series of engagements and securing the Legion's entire empire outside Mackenzie.

"The commitment that I made to Captain Deveraux and her people is that we will start with the Exeter System and those kidnapped laborers," he said firmly. "So, that is the plan.

"Exeter is fourteen point four light-years and change from this system. A little over a day's travel for this Battle Group at standard jumps. Allowing for some of our ships' having lost their fourth Mage and preparation time one jump away from the system, two days."

"What's the plan?" Altimari asked.

"That is part of why Captain Deveraux and her people are here," Jakab replied. "They recently left the Exeter System and can give us the layout of what we're looking at."

"I appreciate that, Admiral," Deveraux said. "Major Trengove, I have used the relay to take control of the holoprojector."

The Legion officer simply nodded and leaned back in her chair. Kelly shivered at the casual manner in which the Promethean handled computers. Even the neurally implanted people she knew—including herself!—weren't that smooth.

The holoprojector zoomed in on the Exeter System, revealing a small MV-class star with two gas giants.

"Exeter has six planets," Deveraux told them. "The only two of relevance to anyone are Exeter-I and Exeter-V, the gas giants. Exeter-V is a frozen ball of garbage a billion kilometers from a tiny sun.

"That leaves Exeter-I, a close-in giant with eight major and eleven minor moons, plus a ring of debris surprisingly rich in useful metals," she continued, zooming the hologram even farther in.

"The pièce de résistance is the ecological fluke of Exeter-I-Seven," Deveraux said, highlighting the moon. "At approximately sixty percent of Earth's radius and eighty percent of Earth's gravity, Seven has managed to hold on to enough atmosphere to have surface-level pressure equivalent to Earth."

"Breathable?" Narang asked, his tone surprised.

"Sufficient oxygen but too much CO_2," Deveraux replied. "The Legion has used light inflatable domes with appropriate filtration systems to create surface resorts for rest and recreation for their personnel.

"Most of Seven is on the chilly side, but the equator is quite pleasant—I'm told. My assessment is no longer standard."

"So, the Fleet Base is anchored there?" Kelly asked, studying the iconography of the projection. It looked like it to her.

"The core stations use Seven as their gravitational anchor, yes," Trengove confirmed. "There are mining ships and so forth scattered throughout the planetary system, but the major base is in the same orbit of Exeter-I as I-Seven, just leading by about fifty thousand kilometers."

"There are approximately fifty-five hundred workers on the surface of I-Seven," Deveraux continued. "Another eighteen to twenty thousand are in working ships through the rings and the mining outposts on I-Five and I-Seven.

"The majority, approximately one hundred and fifteen thousand forced laborers, live and work in the Exeter Fleet Base itself."

The conference was quiet for a few seconds, then Jakab cleared his throat.

"There are other locations in Legion space where they are using forced labor, as I understand it, but this is the largest concentration, correct?"

"Correct," Deveraux told him.

"Then even putting aside our agreement, I would want to move against it immediately," he told everyone. "What is the status of the defenses?"

"While Muhammad keeps his heaviest ships with him in Mackenzie, Exeter is probably their second-most important base," Deveraux noted. "There are four cruisers permanently stationed in the system, along with several flotillas of gunships.

"Exeter is home to the Legion's sole construction-and-training facility for new gunships, so those gunship flotillas may not be as honed as the ships flying off the Legion's carriers, but they are present. There were sixty-five of them present when we left, but the production plant was online and expected to produce six gunships a week going forward."

"So, call it a hundred gunships and four cruisers," Jakab said thoughtfully.

Kelly was running the math in her head. She wasn't a naval officer, but she'd been around them enough to know that the straight mass comparison was often valuable.

Battle Group *Pax Dramatis* had forty-two million tons of cruisers and a sixty-million-ton battleship. Even without the destroyers and assuming that all four Legion cruisers were *Benjamins*, they had the Legion forces outmassed five to one.

And her understanding was that the Legion ships' need for internally rotating pseudogravity hulls reduced their weapon-to-mass ratio, leaving them inferior to their Martian counterparts on a ton-for-ton basis.

"We can handle that," Benjaminson said aloud, clearly voicing the thoughts of the other officers in the room. "A straight-up fight with four cruisers is well within the Battle Group's capabilities. What about fixed defenses?"

"That is where we hit the wrinkle in the equation," Trengove said grimly. Something in her tone drew Kelly's attention instantly.

"It isn't that the fixed defenses are particularly impressive," she explained as everyone looked at her. "The Legion had a stockpile of Battleaxe VIs but hasn't manufactured more of them. There are thirty of them positioned around Exeter Fleet Base, combined with, I believe, fifty fixed missile-launcher emplacements on five improvised forts."

The forts and satellites flashed in the hologram as Trengove mentioned them, Deveraux clearly letting her senior ex-Legionnaire give this spiel.

"The forts also have standard Republic twenty-gigawatt lasers," the Major continued. "But their *weapons* aren't really the concern. It's their *orders*."

Kelly swallowed.

"Admiral Muhammad knows his enemy," Trengove said quietly. "He *knows* the Royal Martian Navy, a knowledge bought in the invasions and counter-invasions of the war and paid for with blood.

"He *knows* you will hesitate with innocent lives at stake. He has constructed an entire *fleet* of Zeus-class orbital bombers to hold his conquered worlds hostage—and the fixed defenses at Exeter have similar orders.

"If you jump into Exeter with this Battle Group, those defenses *will* open fire on the worker habitation stations," she said grimly. "Even a single laser hit will kill tens of thousands—and they have had years to work up their targeting solutions.

"There are nuclear warheads positioned throughout the habs, *and* they are locked into the targeting systems of the forts," she concluded. "Admiral Muhammad's local commander will hold them hostage until you either withdraw or she kills them all.

"Vice Admiral Dunajski is Admiral Muhammad's most trusted right-hand woman," Trengove told them. "She will push that button.

"I agree with everyone here," the ex-Legionnaire said. "We need to save those people and we need to bring down the Legion and stop Admiral Muhammad.

"I just don't see how to stop them killing all of the workers at Exeter."

CHAPTER 49

FOR KELLY, AT LEAST, the silence that followed was thoughtful. Deveraux had helpfully zoomed the hologram of the Exeter System in around the Fleet Base, with the fixed defenses highlighted and estimated patrol routes for the cruisers marked.

As the silence continued to drag on, she finally chuckled.

"Am I the only one who thinks the solution to this is obvious?" she asked.

"Yes," Jakab said with a chuckle. "But then, that is why we bring different perspectives. Tell me, Director LaMonte, what does the *spy* see that the rest of us miss?"

She shook her head at him but took the invitation anyway.

"The answer to this is a magic trick," she told them, then held a hand up before anyone could say anything.

"You're all thinking *real* magic," she continued. "*I'm* thinking pre-Mars stage tricks. Misdirection, presentation and lies.

"Even with something like the *Rhapsodies*, stealth in space is hard. We can conceal our presence but not our arrival—and that's only for a handful of very specialized, very expensive ships.

"Real surprise, the kind it will take to save those hab stations, requires the Legion to *see us coming*...and think we're something else entirely."

"A Trojan Horse gambit," Deveraux suggested, the Promethean sounding intrigued.

"Exactly," Kelly agreed. "*Ring of Fire* is a Legion ship—and a badly damaged one, one whose state easily explains her delays. Captain Deveraux and her officers couldn't take her into Exeter without questions being asked—but we can easily provide answers that the Legion will believe."

"We have several of *Ring*'s original bridge officers among our mutineers," Trengove said slowly. "While they weren't originally involved and didn't argue for their authority, they are people that the Legion would expect to take command.

"If they are prepared to take part, then, as Commodore LaMonte suggests, we could easily get *Ring of Fire* to a repair slip."

"But what does that buy us?" Benjaminson asked. "We could stuff *Ring of Fire* full of troops—though our Guard transports are still over a week away—but that doesn't help us against cruisers and defensive forts."

"Deveraux, what is the largest bulk storage space *Ring of Fire* can make available?" Kelly asked.

A hologram of the cylindrical transport appeared above the table, pushing the map of Exeter to one side. The outer hull became translucent, and components began to shift around until the structure became clear.

"Unlike a true warship, *Ring of Fire*'s central keel is only three hundred and fifty meters long," Deveraux told them. "As she's primarily an assault transport, she currently has modular transport pods filling the last hundred and fifty meters of her hull, but those pods are removable.

"That would provide us with a cylindrical storage space one hundred seventy-five meters in diameter and one hundred and fifty meters long."

The room was silent—and this time it was *definitely* thoughtful.

"We can fit a destroyer in there," Kelly told them all. "My preference, obviously, would be *Voice of the Forgotten*—Mage-Commander Chambers knows how I think, how I operate."

"How *you* think, Commodore?" Jakab asked drily.

"We can fit *Voice* and two *Rhapsody*-class ships in there, and there is no way I am sending two of my ships into the lions' den without being in command," Kelly told him. "And this is *my* area of expertise, Admiral."

"That gets one warship to the center of the Fleet Base," Trengove said quietly. "Where she's going to face four cruisers, each fifteen to twenty times her mass, *plus* the forts.

"Surprise won't carry you far."

"No, it won't," Kelly replied. "That's why I said we needed a *magic trick*. One part misdirection—we use a carefully timed arrival by the Battle Group, potentially without *Pax Dramatis*, to lure the cruisers away. We give the Legion a clear threat to focus on, potentially even a threat they'll want to protect *Ring of Fire* from.

"But the last part to all of this is real magic, the kind of stunt that only the Mages of the Royal Martian Navy can achieve. The Legion turned it on us here at Sondheim Base, killing several of our best people, but the idea of teleporting fire teams to key positions is more than worth its weight in gold.

"We have enough analysts in this Battle Group—and Mr. Ragno has enough techs familiar with the hab stations!—for us to identify where the bombs on the stations themselves have to be.

"We land small teams on the habs to neutralize the bombs. Large teams by more conventional methods assault the forts and the main space station."

"And a single destroyer has to handle the massed firepower of four forts and thirty-plus missile satellites until we're in control of them," Jakab murmured. "A newer ship would serve better, Commodore LaMonte."

"A newer ship wouldn't *fit*, Admiral," she replied. "And surprise is the key. We should be able to neutralize the forts before they turn their beams on the habitation stations—and as I understand it, missiles will be slow enough at that range to make them easy targets."

"Potentially," Jakab conceded. "It's a risky plan. We'll want to go over it in detail, and we need some key people to volunteer, it seems, but it has potential."

"The question isn't whether we can defeat the Legion cruisers, after all," Mage-Captain Narang said, his voice considering. "It is whether we can disable the bombs and protect those stations *while* we do so."

"The only way we're going to do that is by misdirection, stealth and surprise," Kelly said simply. "And a Trojan Horse gives us everything we need."

CHAPTER 50

BY THE TIME ROSLYN WAS actually *consulted* on her new suicide mission, the meeting had shrunk to only four people: her, LaMonte, Jakab...and the Promethean, Deveraux.

Despite being a virtual presence in Jakab's office herself, Roslyn found Deveraux's faceless avatar unnerving.

"Sorry for volunteering you, Roslyn," LaMonte said as the connection stabilized. "But if I'm pulling off this kind of hare-brained stunt, I want you with me."

"I'm glad that when you come up with the riskiest, most near-suicidal, outrageous and mind-boggling plan ever, I'm the first person you think of to take with you," Roslyn said drily.

"If there's any question, Admiral, my crew and I volunteer."

She didn't even need to ask her crew. She *would*, she supposed, but she knew they'd follow her into this. With a hundred thousand civilian lives at stake? What else could they do?

"I appreciate that, Mage-Commander," Jakab replied. "I hesitate to order anyone into this kind of...scheme. We'll need to assemble a Marine force from across the Battle Group, but I can't see any difficulties there."

"Marines tend to volunteer when asked," Roslyn agreed quietly. "That is part of why *Voice* no longer *has* any."

"I know," Jakab told her. "We should be able to pull together a strike battalion for this operation. The shortage will be Jump Mages we can spare for the initial strike."

"We have the space for that, even after we discard the modular troop bays," Deveraux's avatar said. She paused. "I don't know enough about true Mages to know if this plan can work."

"It can," Roslyn told the Promethean. "But we are limited in how many Marines each Mage can bring with them. A single Jump Mage can only bring three or four people with them.

"Wrapping Marines and Mages alike in combat exosuits won't help but will be essential for the mission." She shook her head. "We need to know how many bombs we're looking at and, preferably, the location of the command center aboard the main station.

"Surprise will let *Voice* take down the fortresses, but control of the bombs and missile satellites will be from the main station, from wherever this Vice Admiral Dunajski is based."

"That will be Station Alpha," Deveraux told them. "It has limited purely defensive armaments of its own."

"We'll need to deal with those as well," Roslyn noted. "Even RFLAMs are a real danger to the habitation stations at the ranges we're looking at."

That wasn't something she'd expect the Promethean to realize.

"*Ring of Fire* still has most of her missile launchers, and we have two lasers almost online," Deveraux told them. "If you can provide some parts and technical assistance to Ragno's teams, we should be able to bring ten launchers and two lasers to the fight."

"We can do that," Jakab confirmed. "We'll also provide assistance in removing the modular troop bays. We'll need every scrap of space we can free up if we're squeezing in a destroyer and an assault shuttle flotilla."

"We have plenty of space for assault shuttles," Deveraux noted. "In fact, I am checking our inventory, and we have forty Republic-construction assault shuttles aboard already.

"While your flight crew and Marines may find them awkward, the controls are the same standard as Protectorate spacecraft, and they will appear friendly on Legion scanners."

"I'll check with my husband, but I suspect we'll have no problems flying your shuttles," LaMonte said. "And I like the idea of adding more confusion to the chaos. Everything we can do to make the Legion hesitate buys us time to protect the hab stations."

"How many of the workers will be on the habs versus the working platforms?" Roslyn asked. "If they're dispersed across the entire shipyard..."

"I'm not certain, but my data suggests about half are on the habitation platforms at any point in time," Deveraux admitted. "The rest of the shipyard platforms and stations are, at least, not wired to explode."

"Which means that if you neutralize the forts and the missile satellites, they're relatively safe," Jakab told them. "Even the Legion has a limited number of people willing and able to go work-post to work-post, shooting their workers."

"And we won't give them a chance," Roslyn said grimly. "That part will be down to the Marines. Once we've secured the hab stations and the main command base, they'll have to sweep the entire Fleet Base to make sure we bring everyone in."

"The Marines will know the drill," Jakab promised. "I'll speak to Mage-Colonel Dirks and see who she will want to command the operation."

Hagir Dirks was the senior Marine in Battle Group *Pax Dramatis*. Theoretically, her command was the short battalion aboard *Pax Dramatis* herself, but she was over-senior for that role because *Pax* acted as a flagship.

"Understand, people, this plan is a risk," he warned the three women. "While the rest of the Battle Group will be only one jump away, we'll be sending at least a quarter of our Jump Mages ahead with you. We will have less flexibility than I would like, and while *some* people will take close-in jumps with live data, I'm not sure I can justify risking the entire Battle Group."

Roslyn chuckled wearily.

"I'm not sure I could justify it with a destroyer in less...dire circumstances," she reminded him. "Live data from *Rhapsody in Purple* will help, but once we're in, things are going to get messy."

"At that point, the Battle Group is going to come straight for you," he promised. "We'll draw those cruisers away, but once you send up the rocket, we're punching through them and coming to you at full speed."

Roslyn nodded—but she was a starship commander, and she knew the kind of time frames involved in that. For the Battle Group to pull the Legion cruisers out of missile range of the Exeter Fleet Base, they needed the cruisers to be at least thirteen million kilometers away from Exeter-I.

That meant the Battle Group was probably going to be closer to *twenty-six* million kilometers away, well over a light-minute, and potentially unable to jump. That was a *seven-hour* flight.

A lot of things could happen in seven hours. If they got it wrong, a hundred thousand innocents could die in seven *seconds*.

"We can't get this wrong," she said aloud. "LaMonte, Deveraux...it all rides on the three of us. If either of you thinks we can't do this..."

"There is no alternative," the Promethean said calmly. "If I can offload my prisoners and any of my mutineers who are unwilling to take the war back to the Legion, then I am in.

"*My* power delivered many of these innocents into this nightmare. Therefore, it must be my power that frees them from it."

"It's my plan," LaMonte added. "I'm in. You got volunteered for this. Are you sure you and your people are in?"

"We are Royal Martian Navy," Roslyn told them. "If we do not act, innocents will die—and what value is Her Majesty's Protectorate then?"

CHAPTER 51

SHARON DID NOT regard *Ring of Fire* as her body. She did not, in her mind, *have* a body. She was as close to a disembodied entity of pure intellect as was physically possible while still being technically human.

It was still a strange sensation to have the modular troop bays that had been part of *Ring of Fire* as long as she'd been awake removed. Section by section was detached and hauled out the gaping maw of *Ring*'s prow by heavy-lift shuttles.

"We'll have the last of the troop bays out in an hour," Ragno told her. "Then we're going to very carefully bring that destroyer inside, then fit the stealth ships in around her."

"Are you comfortable with that, Teodor?" Sharon asked, most of her attention still on the surgery on her ship.

"We have the space," he replied. "We could, theoretically, fit even one of their *Cataphract*-class ships in the hold once it's emptied, but I think they'd have a harder time squeezing in the stealth ships."

"And LaMonte wants this Chambers," Sharon noted. "Which, given the way the woman keeps getting in the Legion's way, I can see the appeal of. I can't imagine Vice Admiral Muhammad knows many Mage-Commanders' names—but he knows hers."

Ragno chuckled.

"I don't envy her that. But we'll make this work, Captain," he assured Sharon. "The Martian engineer teams know their way around our lasers surprisingly well."

"Two of the destroyers are actually armed with the same lasers," Sharon told him. "Including our soon-to-be passenger, *Voice of the Forgotten.*"

"You know, I was only vaguely aware of the existence of the Protectorate a few years ago," Ragno told her. "They weren't quite a boogeyman back home, but they certainly weren't held up as a shining beacon of liberty either."

"I can't imagine the rogue colonies think much of the nation they ran away from," Sharon pointed out. "I know the UnArcana Worlds didn't— and we technically *were* Protectorate worlds, before the Secession."

They'd been Protectorate worlds when Sharon had died, even. She'd "slept" through the entire war, after all.

"Yeah. But when everything's down to the wire, it's going to be the same white pyramids that our media always used as the bad guys who save us," Ragno said. "Something to think about, I think."

Sharon chuckled.

"As we load a thousand Martian Marines and twenty Jump Mages aboard?" she asked.

"Yeah. First shuttle loads are coming in now," the Aquilan told her. "Trengove and Young are managing them."

"I'm glad Young and Zhao are sticking with us for this," Sharon admitted. "We needed at least one of them for the tale we're going to spin, but neither was involved when we started this whole mess."

"I think...most of the Legion folk are pretty torn up about what they did out here," Ragno said slowly. "I'm not forgiving anyone yet, don't get that idea, but I do recognize that a lot of them didn't have much of a choice. Once their ships ended up with Muhammad, they were trapped in 'doing their duty' under pain of punishment."

"We're giving them a chance to make it right," Sharon told him. "And they will—and *we* will."

"The Martians certainly don't seem intimidated by the Legion. Just worried about saving lives," her engineer said. "I think that's promising."

"Me too. But to save as many lives in Exeter as we can, we have to help. I...don't know how this is going to end for *Ring of Fire*, Teodor," she warned him. "It could get real messy."

"I know," he admitted. "But, frankly, this feels at least as important as sitting on a rooftop, transmitting video of the labor drafts, and I knew I had a good chance of getting executed for *that*."

"Whatever happens, you're in good company, I think."

"That I am," Ragno agreed. "The Legion is going to regret ever waking you up, Captain Deveraux."

Ring of Fire's prow was now wide open, heavily armored hatches swung out to create the impression of a vast, toothy maw. Sharon had access to several thousand sensors confirming everything around those access hatches and their position.

"Captain Chambers, I have the hold as clear for your approach," she told her Martian counterpart. "You should have approximately five meters of clearance on all sides, but..."

"But that is not enough for comfort with a million tons of starship," Chambers finished for her. "I have direct control of *Voice of Forgotten*'s maneuvering systems, and we are running on tertiary thrusters.

"Current relative velocity to *Ring of Fire* is three centimeters per second along the x axis. Our scans show no vertical or horizontal relative to your ship."

Sharon ran over the data she was receiving herself.

"We have the same," she replied. "No offense, Captain Chambers, but where is your navigator?"

Zhao had dropped everything else to take part in this maneuver, even with Sharon's full integration into the maneuvering and sensor systems.

Part of that, of course, was that *Ring of Fire* was still short most of her engines. Her maximum thrust at the moment was only half a gravity, which was going to make everything in Exeter take far longer than anyone would like.

"Mage–Lieutenant Commander Victor died on Sondheim Base, Captain Deveraux," Chambers told her quietly. "I'm what you've got.

"I make the range five thousand, four hundred and eighty-six meters," Chambers continued. "Confirm your vector."

"Lieutenant Zhao?" Sharon asked.

"Transmitting to Captain Chambers," the ex-Legion officer confirmed. "We are solid on course; I have the same range and velocity as Captain Chambers."

"Confirmed, all vectors. Bringing up our engines at one meter per second squared," Chambers reported.

All of this felt slow as hell to Sharon, but she understood the logic. Even a *slow* collision between the two starships would wreck the mission, potentially leaving thousands to die.

Continual communication and slow maneuvering were key. It wasn't how *Voice* would leave when the time came—Sharon was already expecting *that* process to cripple *Ring of Fire* forever.

That was a price she was prepared to pay. Of course, that was a *theoretical* price, and the boredom of the slow and careful maneuvering was very real at that moment.

"Range is one hundred meters, commencing deceleration to contact," Chambers finally reported. "You have a very fine ship, Captain Deveraux, but this still feels vaguely creepy and wrong. Like that's a lot of teeth."

"Consider that *Ring of Fire* is the closest thing I have to a body, Captain Chambers," Sharon pointed out indelicately. "This is *very* different for me."

That startled a laugh from the other woman.

"I can see that," she admitted. "I have, uh... Damn it, Deveraux. I have *entrance.*"

All of the women on the conversation started chuckling as Chambers failed to find a description unladen with innuendo for this part of the process.

"I have your velocity at...zero," Zhao reported. "Distance from inner hull...four point six meters."

"I have the same," Chambers said. "We have a few struts and support bumpers for yard work; my engineering team is heading out to set them up. We appear to be good."

"We appear to be *very* good," Sharon replied. "Don't worry, I'll call you!"

That lost at least ten seconds to both Chambers and Zhao staring at the Promethean's digital avatar in surprise, then the Martian officer cleared her throat.

"And on that innuendo-filled note, I have some goodbyes to make before we leave," she told Sharon.

"*Voice of the Forgotten* is ready for the mission."

CHAPTER 52

"YOU KNOW THIS IS a suicide mission, right?" Ajam asked as Roslyn walked him to the shuttle bay. He'd repacked all of his stuff in the self-driving suitcase that followed him and wore his leather jacket over a standard shipsuit.

"I know it's risky," Roslyn replied. "But we have an obligation."

"And that's what makes you Navy and me a bounty hunter, I suppose," Ajam said drily. A gesture pulled the suitcase over to the wall as he stopped just inside the hallway, regarding her levelly.

"You can't help anyone if you're dead, Roslyn," he told her. "If you keep taking on missions like this and the last one, that's more likely than not."

"That's my job, Nunzio," Roslyn said sharply.

She wasn't sure what she'd expected his response to be, but it wasn't for him to thrust his hands into his pockets and nod seriously.

"I know," he conceded. "And it's what makes you you. It's what makes you...well, more attractive than most people I've met."

Roslyn hoped she concealed her flush at that.

"Behave, Nunzio," she warned.

"I'm leaving your damn ship, Roslyn," he reminded her. "And you're charging off on another damn fool crusade to save the innocent. I'm going to stand back here and cheer for you like my own kind of fool. You're going to go save a hundred thousand people, and I'm going to sit here and feel a bit like an ass because I'm more worried about my own feelings than I am about their lives."

"That would be an asshole thing to do, yes," Roslyn said wearily. "I set my boundaries for a reason, Nunzio Ajam, and I'm not changing them anytime soon.

"Besides, I don't exactly have time to do anything else right now."

"No, you don't," he agreed. "You have to go be the heroine. It's what you do. And some day you won't come back from it."

He paused, regarding her pensively with his hands still in his pockets.

"I don't think it's going to be this time," he admitted. "But I could be wrong. I have always been more careful than most who end up in my profession—but no one ends up a gray-market bounty hunter because their risk-assessment instincts work properly."

"Do you have a point, Nunzio?" Roslyn asked. Despite his self-flagellating tone, she was finding herself very aware of how kissable his lips looked and the fact that it would take less than three steps or a spell to pin him to the wall.

"Go do what you do," he said. "You don't need my permission; that's for sure! I wish luck to you and damnation to the Legion."

"And?"

"And when this is over and you've got leave booked up somewhere, drop me a line," he suggested. "We'll do dinner."

"You have no idea what system I'll be posted in next," Roslyn countered.

"I know," he agreed. "And I don't care. Let me know when you're on leave and I'll make it happen. We'll deal with the details then. For now, I'm going to go back to looking for my ship while you go save the galaxy."

"I don't think a few hab stations count as *the galaxy*," Roslyn said. She was...taken aback by the open-endedness of the offer. He was willing to travel between star systems to have dinner?

That sounded a lot more smitten than she'd expected from a man she'd read as a lady-killer.

In the end, Roslyn wasn't sure *she* was down for that kind of offer.

"I'll think about it," she promised. "Once we've saved these people."

Roslyn was still put off by the whole conversation with Ajam when she reached her check-in meeting with LaMonte. They went through about two minutes of basic updates before the colorfully haired spy paused, studying the younger woman, then chuckled.

"What's on your mind, Chambers?" she asked.

"I didn't realize I was noticeably off, Commodore," Roslyn replied.

"Probably not to most people, but we've walked into hell together, Roslyn," LaMonte said, instantly switching tones to a more personal atmosphere. "*Something* is distracting you."

Roslyn chuckled.

"Personal stuff," she admitted. "I've got it together."

The MISS spy sighed and wiped the data off the screen.

"I am not old enough to be your mother, but I can manage *cool big sister* while we're off duty," LaMonte told Roslyn. "Or even *friend*, for that matter. Like I said, we've walked into hell together."

Roslyn considered it for a moment, then echoed LaMonte's sigh and leaned back in her office chair.

"Fundamentally? Our pet bounty hunter is *really* hot," she admitted. "But I'm not sure I actually see enough more than that in him to do more than jump him like a trampoline."

"Rumor has it that he's made that offer and you shut him down," her friend replied.

"He did and I did," Roslyn confirmed. "He was a passenger and I was in command. It was a risk to my authority I couldn't afford at the time and wasn't willing to take even when my authority over my crew stabilized."

"So, you seem to know where you're at," LaMonte noted. "He might be fun for a roll in the tool closet, but you're not going to risk anything for it. And he's on his way, isn't he?"

"Yeah, just set him on a shuttle off to *Pax Dramatis*," Roslyn said. "So, he's out of my hair. He just...um. He told me to call him when this was over, and he'd come meet me for a date. Anywhere I called him from."

LaMonte was quiet for roughly two entire seconds and then started chuckling.

"*Someone* hasn't got laid recently, and I'm not sure which of you is suffering from it worse," she pointed out. "*He* clearly sees some long-term potential here if he's willing to travel between stars to see you."

"And I...am not so sure," Roslyn admitted. "I think, in my case at least, it is *entirely* that command lends itself to celibacy."

"At least on a warship," LaMonte said in a somewhat self-satisfied tone.

"Not everyone can marry all of their senior officers, and, yes, it's discouraged on warships, anyway," Roslyn replied.

"Honestly, unless you think you *want* to make something more of the pretty bounty hunter, you're probably as well off letting it go," LaMonte advised. "The kind of relationship that starts with one person unsure and one person willing to move stars to convince them...I don't see that ending well."

Roslyn chuckled.

"I'm more weirded out than flattered by the offer," she admitted. "That's probably telling, isn't it?"

"Yup," LaMonte agreed. "If you thought it was a good thing, you'd be flattered and potentially even happy or enthusiastic about the offer. Confused, distracted and awkward? Not the best sign."

She held up a finger.

"Not an absolute deal-killer, either," she noted. "But I'd suggest using it as a metric. What do *you* want?"

"I want this mission to go off without my being distracted," Roslyn admitted. "I am...not certain I actually care either way, at the moment, if I see Nunzio Ajam again. I wouldn't *mind*, that's for sure, but I wouldn't travel between star systems to see him!"

"So, let it go for now and think about it when the dust settles," LaMonte suggested.

"Yeah," Roslyn agreed. She shook her head, trying to dislodge cobwebs. "We were talking integrating fire-control systems between *Voice's* beams and *Rhapsody's* sensors, yes?"

CHAPTER 53

TWO LIVING WOMEN and a dead one surveyed the final status reports, *Ring of Fire* hanging roughly half a light-year from the Exeter System.

"Are we ready?" Sharon asked the other two.

Everything the Promethean could see of *her* ship was as ready as it was going to be. Part of the whole plan relied on the fact that *Ring of Fire* had been shot to pieces by her former gunships. The lack of said gunships, combined with the damage, was going to help sell their story.

"A lot of that is on your Lieutenant Young," LaMonte told her. "She's going to be carrying the key weight of all of this. None of us can talk to Exeter Base Control, after all."

"She wasn't included in the mutiny plans—but *she* was the one who killed Ajello," Sharon reminded the two Martians. "I think we can trust her."

"I'm not concerned about trusting her," the MISS spy—Sharon had finally worked out just *who* LaMonte worked for—noted. "I'm concerned about her ability to deceive and prevaricate sufficiently to pull this whole mess off."

"She hid an inappropriate relationship from every senior officer on the ship while carrying on her full duties *and* keeping said relationship sexually active," Sharon said. "She'll be fine."

"I hope so," Chambers said. "This whole plan falls apart if we can't get into close range of the defensive forts. A million kilometers is good, but fifty thousand is what we *need*."

"We'll take what we can get," LaMonte replied. "How far can the Mages take their Marine teams?"

"That's why we need to get to fifty thousand kilometers," Chambers said bluntly. "We can take out the forts at a million with lasers and magic, but even our Jump Mages can't teleport more than fifty, maybe sixty, thousand kilometers without an amplifier.

"And before you ask, no, we can't use the amplifiers for this," she added. "The Mages need to see and touch the people they're jumping. Can't do that *and* use an amplifier."

"Couldn't you, I don't know, teleport a shuttle you can see outside the ship?" Sharon asked thoughtfully.

"Yes," Chambers agreed. "Probably. Without the Mage bringing themselves along, though, any teleport gets much, much messier. It *can* be done, but I wouldn't trust one Mage in ten to do it with enough accuracy for this."

"So, we do it the hard way, a fire team at a time, and we hope that the Legion doesn't figure out what's going on," LaMonte said. "That last being why we wouldn't send shuttles, too. We don't want to put anything in space that's going to draw people's attention until we absolutely have to."

"What about *Rhapsody*?" Sharon asked. The plan called for the stealth ship to be in space at LaMonte's discretion.

"Opening *Ring of Fire*'s forward bay is more obvious than *Rhapsody in Purple* flying around, Deveraux," the MISS Captain replied. "So long as we can get her into space, we can sneak around pretty handily."

"But not all the way into the Fleet Base," Chambers warned. "Hard limit is, what, five light-seconds? Ten?"

"It depends on how much attention they're paying, but about that," LaMonte agreed.

Even *that* was, well, literally magic to Sharon. It took both a lot of high tech and a lot of magic to let the ships "hide" in space. All it was going to take to hide a Marine strike battalion, a destroyer and a stealth ship in *Ring of Fire* was some fast talking.

It was still a shame they hadn't been able to fit two stealth ships into the cargo bay in the end. The geometry of the ships involved just wasn't right for that.

"If we're ready, the operation is ready," LaMonte finally said. "So, Deveraux, Chambers?"

"*Ring of Fire* is good," Sharon replied.

"So is *Voice*. Shall we go talk to the rest of the Battle Group?" Chambers asked.

The *actual* meeting started about ten minutes later, with Vice Admiral Jakab chairing a collection of the senior officers. Chambers was included among the full Captains due to her key role in the mission, but otherwise, it was much the same group that the original mission had been pitched to.

"The Battle Group is ready to jump in after you," Jakab told the three women in charge of the forward operation. "The cruisers are ready for their distraction, and *Pax* is ready to close the trap.

"Even if the deception fails, we hope to engender enough confusion to allow the Battle Group to close with the Fleet Base and neutralize any attempt to destroy the hab stations," he continued. "The Legion loses this system today, people. That's not in question.

"What is in question is how many innocent lives are lost in the process," he concluded grimly. "Everything we can think of to lower that number is in play, including a few options and a primary plan I wouldn't normally approve.

"If anyone has any ideas, suggestions or last-minute modifications, now is the time."

The conference was silent.

"If everything goes according to plan, we should be fine," LaMonte said.

"I feel very young, asking this," Sharon said slowly, "but do things ever go according to plan?"

The chorus of chuckles that answered her were *not* reassuring.

"They don't, Captain Deveraux, no," Jakab warned her. "But you are taking some of the most competent Royal Marines and Navy officers and personnel I know of into the Exeter System. You have a real-time communication link with us aboard *Pax* through *Voice*'s Link and the twin advantages of surprise and being a vessel the Legion thinks is theirs.

"You will have to think on your feet and adapt, but as you do, you will know that the entire Battle Group has your back," he assured her.

"The rescue of those civilians is the priority," Sharon replied. "We will do what we must."

"As will we all," Jakab agreed. He surveyed the virtual conference. "If that's everything, people...let's be about it."

CHAPTER 54

ROSLYN HAD SPENT so long staring at maps and models of the Exeter System by this point that it was almost a shock to be looking at the real thing. Her current view was relayed from *Ring of Fire*'s sensors as the jump flare faded, but it was still *real*.

"Jump complete," Daniel reported quietly. "On target, ten million kilometers from Exeter-I-Six."

"Understood," Roslyn replied. "Salucci, keep us looped in on *Ring*'s communication with the base."

Everyone was on duty. It would be over twelve hours before *Ring* completed her approach to the Legion base, but this was one of the moments where everything could go wrong.

At least *Voice of the Forgotten*'s magical gravity reduced the impact of the assault transport's acceleration. Roslyn knew the ship was designed for it, but it still seemed odd to her to have to tolerate two gravities of actual thrust.

"Thirty-three-second trip each way for coms," Salucci told her, the big woman looking to have settled in for the long haul at her station. "Lieutenant Young is transmitting."

A small window popped up on Roslyn's screens showing the Legion mutineer. Ramiz Young was staring earnestly into the camera, looking so exhausted, Roslyn wondered whether the woman was actually as sleep-deprived as she was pretending to be!

Adding to the effect was that Young was transmitting from *Ring*'s Ground Operations Center, a section of the ship intended to control her assault troops once they were deployed. It *could* act as a bridge, but it was strictly a backup—and its use implied that *Ring's* main bridge was wrecked.

"Exeter Fleet Base, this is Lieutenant Ramiz Young aboard *Ring of Fire*," Young said in a ragged voice.

"We are in need of repairs and debriefing," she told the Fleet Base. "We came under attack on our approach to Sondheim Base by a Martian destroyer. We defeated her, but not before losing all of Major de la Cruz's gunships and losing the bridge and a chunk of Engineering to enemy fire.

"I am the senior surviving officer. It took us this long to get our engines mostly back online and align the support systems for the PDU sufficiently to jump again."

Young shook her head and took in a long breath.

"We are en route to the base at our current maximum acceleration of one point nine five gravities," she noted. "I am standing by for further instructions."

The message ended and Roslyn smiled.

"Hell, if I'd received that, *I'd* have bought it," she said aloud. "It appears Lieutenant Young has a promising future ahead of her in the media industry!"

That got her a few chuckles, but her crew was focused on the task around them.

"Are we dropping *Rhapsody?*" Claes asked Roslyn.

"That's LaMonte's call, but I'm inclined to hold her aboard until we all break out at the end," Roslyn told her XO. "We're a long way out, still."

They were inside missile range, if someone decided that *Ring of Fire* was a threat—but even the Legion's ex-Republic missiles accelerated at ten thousand gravities.

Not two.

"We have a response from Exeter Base," Salucci reported. "Looks like... thirty-second turnaround on their side."

The message played on the same screen as Young's. A dark-skinned young man in a dark burgundy Legion uniform looked at the screen with a sympathetic gaze.

"Good god, *Ring of Fire*, I'm glad to hear you're okay," he told Young. "You're clear to approach inside the outer perimeter.

"The Fleet Base itself is under high security, however. We're sweeping all approaches to watch for Martian stealth ships. Sondheim Base was overrun by a surprise RMN attack—we think Broomhandle Two has them lost again, but Command is getting twitchy. I cannot authorize you to approach within five light-seconds of the Fleet Base.

"I'll have a final orbit for you in about thirty minutes," he continued. "You'll hear from either myself or the Vice Admiral by then. Stand by, Lieutenant Young."

That wasn't perfect, to Roslyn's mind. She wasn't clear what the "outer perimeter" entailed in this case—the farthest out of Exeter-I's satellites was only two light-seconds from the gas giant, so even hanging out next to a rock on the far side of the gas giant would still be inside the five-light-second line.

"That could be a problem," Salucci said aloud. "Depending on what they want from Young to get close enough to the base..."

"We have nine hours to sort out that problem," Roslyn pointed out. "We'll sort it out as they get us details."

And if the plan was already doomed, well...they'd expected that to happen to some degree.

No plan survived contact with the enemy, after all.

The message that arrived from Exeter Fleet Base, twenty-four minutes later, wasn't from the earnest-looking young officer that had answered Young's original missive.

Vice Admiral Marcella Dunajski was a slim but swarthy woman, her hair shaved except for a pair of pitch-black cornrows that ran perfectly parallel to each other toward the back of her skull.

Her eyes were unnaturally black as she focused on the pickup, and her smile felt false to Roslyn.

"Lieutenant Young, it sounds like you had a hell of a trip," Dunajski said in a warm tone. "As Lieutenant Ansem warned, we're operating with a high security level right now.

"I'd like to bring you in for immediate repairs and debriefing, but we need to be cautious about the security of Exeter Base. You will enter a stable orbit at one-point-eight million kilometers from Exeter-I. My staff will forward exact details.

"One of my staff officers will then come out to meet you with a contingent of Space Assault Troopers and a gunship flotilla. My officer will interview you and the other surviving senior officers while the SATs sweep the ship for potential Martian traps.

"I expect all of that to pass relatively quickly, at which point we will bring you in to the Fleet Base and get your crew down to the surface for some R&R while the yards work out where they're going to put you."

She tried to widen her smile, which only made it look even more fake.

"With everything that's gone down the last couple of weeks, we thought we'd lost *Ring of Fire* with all hands, Lieutenant Young. I know the security means it may not feel like it, but it's damn good to see you.

"Welcome back to Exeter."

Roslyn considered the message for a second, then opened a channel to LaMonte and Deveraux.

"So, what's the chance that we can run through an inspection by a remotely competent team without them realizing there's a destroyer and a strike battalion concealed aboard *Ring of Fire*?" she asked.

"For a lot of stuff, I'd say I'd have to ask Trengove," Deveraux told her. "But in this case, I know the answer: zero. They'll realize that the modular troop bays are missing within twenty minutes, and at that point, all it will take is someone sticking their head in the cargo hold to see what's there."

"So we have a problem," LaMonte said grimly. "Let's see what the details of the orbit are, but I'm guessing it will keep us five light-seconds from the base itself."

"Our Mages can't make the jump at that range," Roslyn warned. "*Voice* can probably take out the forts before they can fire their lasers, and we have a decent chance of shooting down any missiles they launch—but I can't do anything about remote-controlled nukes or RFLAMs at that distance."

She could probably manage a *few* tricks against the RFLAMs, if she was being fair. Five light-seconds was inside any Mage's reach with an amplifier, let alone Roslyn's.

"We still have over five hours until turnover," LaMonte pointed out. "We can think on this. How obvious will it be if we blow past turnover?"

"Obvious," Deveraux said instantly. "*Ring of Fire* is huge, LaMonte. It's pretty obvious when twenty-ish million tons of starship flips. Thirty-second turnaround on coms might buy us a minute or two of confusion and orders, but we'd need thirty to be coming in to the base at zero vee."

"What if we don't come in at zero?" Roslyn asked. "*Ring of Fire*'s engines are damaged. Can we fake a blowout at turnover, slide the rest of the way in at the four hundred–odd KPS we'll have at that point?"

"They have tugs to send out...but their first priority would be to stop us *hitting* anything," Deveraux said slowly. "We can get closer—and we'll get closer *faster*, but four hours is enough for Dunajski to decide *Ring of Fire* is expendable and blow us to pieces."

"It's not a bad plan," LaMonte said. "Can the Jump Mages make the teleport at that velocity?"

"It's harder," Roslyn admitted, thinking it through. "But if we give them the warning about what kind of velocity we're using, they can update their calculations. Nothing in space is ever truly immobile, so the calculations have to account for some velocities anyway.

"We can make it work," she concluded. "Better than we can make jumping an extra half-million kilometers work, anyway."

"Then that's the plan. Deveraux, talk to your people," LaMonte ordered. "Chambers, lend her *your* people if they need them. I'm not convinced Ragno has enough hands in *Ring*'s Engineering to pull off that kind of stunt."

"All we need is for him to blow up an engine," Deveraux said brightly. "That part's easy. It's doing it without blowing up the whole ship that's hard!"

CHAPTER 55

"WE SPENT *WEEKS* rebuilding the engines, and now you want me to blow one up?" Teodor Ragno asked when Sharon told him the plan.

"You don't actually have to blow up one of the ones we *fixed*," she pointed out. "Exeter Base won't be able to tell which engine explodes, not if we do it right."

The Aquilan engineer sighed and pulled up schematics on the wall-screen in his office.

"We have three of six engines running right now," he told her. "If we lose even one, we're down to a single gravity of acceleration. We're sustaining our current thrust by alternating which engine is carrying full power."

"All we need to do is fake an engine failure," Sharon said. "I don't really want to give up half of our acceleration or a third of our engines. Ideas?"

"Faking a main engine failure is overkill, boss," Ragno replied thoughtfully. "And a bit unbelievable. After all, by the time we make turnover, they'll have seen us accelerating for over five hours. They'll have a decent idea of what I'm doing to keep the engines stable, and they'll know we've got a handle on it."

"I don't know if rotating three engines to balance thrust counts as *stable*, Ragno," Sharon pointed out. "But I'm guessing you have an idea."

"Yeah," he confirmed. "To make turnover, we have to physically rotate the ship. The engines we've fixed? They can't do that. We balanced them to provide thrust. We don't have the flexibility to turn them enough to rotate the ship.

"*Ring* is designed with six mid-ship maneuvering thruster pods," he explained. "We've been maneuvering with those when we've needed to."

"I knew that," Sharon said. "I hadn't thought about it in this context, though... We've only got three of them left, right?"

"Four," he corrected. "The Martians got one more online for us before they sent us into the belly of the beast."

"You're thinking fake a maneuvering pod failure?" she asked.

She had video into his office and saw the Aquilan agitator grin wickedly.

"I'm reasonably sure Zhao can maneuver the ship with two thruster pods," he pointed out. "And Exeter Base doesn't have the resolution to physically see how many we have left.

"I'm thinking we fake a failure on one of the pods—hoping it survives, but knowing that the odds are only fifty-fifty—and we blow a second to kingdom come."

"There isn't going to be much question of whether we're actually crippled when a pod actually blows up, is there?" Sharon asked. "Can you do it without damaging the ship?"

"They're outside the inner hull, so I should be able to contain the damage away from any of the Marines," he said cagily. "We'll probably end up with a breach through the armor around where the pod I'm blowing is, but unless someone gets real lucky shooting at us..."

"It's not likely to be a problem," Roslyn finished. "Okay, Ragno. Set it up. We need to get closer and faster than the Legion wants us to for the plan to work."

"I'm on it, boss, but..." He trailed off.

"What?" she asked.

"I don't know enough about this magic shit," he admitted. "I don't like hanging a hundred thousand lives on some woo-woo bullshit."

Sharon laughed.

"The only reason humanity ever made it to Aquila and the only reason any of us are here at all is that *woo-woo bullshit*, Ragno," she pointed out. "I may be a brain in a jar, but what I do to move us between the stars? It's still magic.

"More, it's the *exact same magic* that the Marines are going to use to save those people, just on a different scale. If you trust me to jump us between stars, trust those Jump Mages to deliver the Marines to their targets."

There was a long, pregnant pause.

"What if we gave them the wrong targets?" he whispered. "The locations of the bombs are guesswork and estimates, Deveraux. We don't *know* anything."

"That's why the Augments are going for Dunajski herself," she reminded him. "Even if all it takes is the push of a button, she can't push a button if she's tied up with her implants jammed."

Or if she was dead, which Sharon suspected was more likely. She didn't have the impression that the Martian Augments—the Bionic Commandos, they called themselves—were planning on taking prisoners until *after* they'd secured the command center.

Even if Sharon had normally been able to sleep, she was sure she wouldn't have been able to during the five hours they'd been in Exeter. She knew Trengove was taking catnaps, for example, but had woken up for the next evolution of the plan.

"Turnover is in fifteen minutes," Zhao reported, the navigator never quite looking comfortable on the bridge since the mutiny. Her lover squeezed her shoulder, and she forced a smile at Young.

"I'm fine, Ramiz," she assured the tactical officer. "It's just all strange, you know?"

"I know," Young agreed. "I'm mentally rehearsing what I'll tell Dunajski after our turnover fails."

"Glad that's you and not me," Zhao said.

"The Martians will stage our distraction in about ninety minutes," Trengove told the two juniors. "Zhao, are you good with Ragno's plan?"

"Yeah," the navigator confirmed. "We'll cut the main engines as soon as the thruster pod goes. I'd preprogram it, but it needs to look like a panic reaction, right?"

"Right," Sharon agreed. "And you're good?"

"Believe me, Deveraux, I can manage to make it look like I'm a panicking ball of stress with a starship's body language," Zhao said wryly. "Just have to fly like I'm feeling!"

"Be careful," Sharon told the navigator. "We need to break the ship a little for this, but we don't want to break her much. And we need it to be convincing—"

"Jump flare!" Young suddenly interrupted. "We have a jump at three light-minutes."

"I thought the Martians weren't due for over an hour?" Trengove demanded.

"They aren't," Sharon replied. "Plus, that's just one ship."

She was digging into the data as quickly as Young was, but the tactical officer was faster than she was.

"Twenty megatons, fusion engines, she's maneuvering to orbit Exeter itself at four light-minutes." There was a long pause. "She's a *Benjamin*-class cruiser. I'd say she's Legion, but..."

"She isn't maneuvering like she belongs here," Trengove finished for Young. "She's maneuvering like she's on a scouting run."

"Dunajski's cruisers just lit up like firecrackers," Sharon warned her officers. "Engines online at full power, accelerating to intercept the stranger at eight gravities."

"Huh. I thought we were expecting four cruisers?" Young asked as she caught up on the data and began running through it. Sharon could see more of it at once, but the mutineer tactical officer definitely knew what she was looking at.

"We were," Sharon replied. "And now...I see three. Did they leave one behind?"

"Doesn't look like," Young said. "Looks like either Dunajski lost a ship somewhere or it got called away. I make it two *Andreas*es and a *Benjamin*. Mmmm... *Audacious*, *Awakened* and *Basalt*."

"None of them have full Prometheans," Sharon noted. "But who the hell are they chasing?"

The answer came from the inevitable source—Vice Admiral Dunajski herself.

"Incoming transmission," Sharon said aloud as the icons pinged on her virtual screens. A moment later, she'd looped in LaMonte and Chambers as she played the Legion flag officer's message.

Lightspeed delays meant that the recording was twenty seconds old— but so was every piece of data they had on the Legion cruisers.

"Lieutenant Young, I don't know how well your sensors are functioning, but we have a problem," the small Admiral told their figurehead. "A Chimeran cruiser has entered the system, and we are at risk of a serious security breach.

"All mobile combat units in the system are being deployed in pursuit of the Chimeran in the hopes that she can be destroyed or captured before she can jump away. We have no personnel available for the sweep of your vessel."

Sharon dared to hope that meant they'd be allowed straight in, but she knew it was in vain even before Dunajski continued.

"We're transmitting a new course to you, Lieutenant Young. You will adjust your vector to bypass Exeter-I entirely and enter a leading orbit well ahead of the gas giant.

"Once the security situation has resolved, we will look to get the inspection of *Ring of Fire* complete and get your people somewhere safe to rest. Right now, we must protect the Legion."

The message ended and Sharon wanted to curse.

"I have their new course," Zhao reported. "We're to maintain acceleration and adjust our angle five degrees outward. New turnover is in three more hours."

"Okay," Sharon replied. "Hold that thought for the moment."

She switched her attention to the "command council" with the two Martian officers.

"What do we do?" she asked bluntly.

"We have our distraction," LaMonte pointed out. "We need those cruisers out of missile range, and they are burning *hard*. At eight gravities, they're completely out of the equation in five hours."

"The original plan relied on them not being able to shed velocity to engage the base before *Pax Dramatis* dropped on them," Chambers agreed. "We weren't expecting them to push this hard."

"These Chimerans have the Legion spooked—but who the hell *are* they?"

"The only place that information was stored aboard *Ring of Fire* was in Ajello's head," Sharon admitted. "Right now, though, we're being ordered to divert our course to sweep past the planet. We're not going to get within two million klicks of the Fleet Base.

"If we blow the maneuvering pod as planned, we'll still be on course for the base at four hundred KPS..."

"But they're a lot more likely to decide that one officially undermanned assault transport is expendable now than they were before," Chambers said grimly. "And while those cruisers will be out of the equation in four or five hours, we are right in the middle of their fields of fire at the moment."

"If Deveraux diverts, what are our options?" LaMonte asked. "We're already close enough and closely enough watched that launching *Rhapsody* may draw too much attention. We might have been better off launching her early, but...I wanted options."

"And now we're out of options," Sharon said grimly. "We can probably spin out not changing course for a few minutes, but not for long without blowing the thruster pod. Once we do that, we start looking like a threat that Dunajski has to assess risk for."

There was a long silence.

"What about a microjump?" LaMonte said quietly. "Chambers, you Picard-maneuvered that cruiser at DEL-Three-T-Three. Can you set up a jump to bring us *back* to the Exeter Fleet Base after we pass her on their course?"

Chambers sighed audibly.

"I could do it," she confirmed. "With *Voice*. Not with *Ring of Fire*. Her matrices aren't designed to let anyone who isn't in a Prometheus Drive Unit make a jump."

Sharon considered the situation and what the RMN Mage was saying.

"So, I have to make the jump," she told them.

"Have you ever made a sub-light-minute jump, Deveraux?" Chambers asked.

"There's a first time for everything, isn't there?" Sharon asked. "You can do the calculations and run me through it."

There was a long pause.

"It's risky," the Mage-Commander said. "It's risky as all hell...but it might work. It'll work *better* if we have real-time data from the emergence zone."

"That will require us to sneak *Rhapsody* out," LaMonte said. "I can get... close. Not close enough for real time, but enough to give you data that's a lot fresher. But they will *see* us popping *Ring of Fire*'s forward doors."

"Not if we provide the right distraction," Sharon told them.

CHAPTER 56

IF *RHAPSODY IN PURPLE* had been a Navy ship and Kelly LaMonte had *actually* been a Commodore, there would have been a list of rules against how she was taking part in the operation as long as her arm.

The Martian Interstellar Security Service was *far* more flexible—and no one aboard Kelly's ship was going to argue the fact that Kelly was, without a doubt, the best hacker and computer systems expert aboard.

That meant that she was wearing body armor as she stood on *Rhapsody*'s bridge, listening to Liara Foster mutter.

"I cannot *believe* I let you all talk me into shit like this," the Mage told her.

"I wasn't under the impression there was much convincing," Kelly pointed out. "More along the lines of *orders* and *enthusiastic* compliance."

Foster chuckled and checked another set of numbers.

"We're good," she replied. "Just waiting on... There we go. The signal from *Ring of Fire*. Doors are opening and we are maneuvering."

Rhapsody had cold-gas thrusters for just this kind of movement. Liara's magic was wrapping the ship in a muffling field of silence and chill as well, but the thrusters also protected the assault transport from the damage the main antimatter engines would do.

"We are going to be really visible to anyone looking," Foster noted.

"Deveraux has a plan for that. Watch for unexpected movement on *Ring*'s part."

"Unexpected movement?!" the navigator snapped. "She's already supposed to be turning while we dro—"

And *then* the thruster pod exploded, a spray of debris covering the fact that the bow doors were open and a wave of energy concealing any leakage from *Rhapsody in Purple's* stealth systems.

Foster, who was *exactly* as good as Kelly thought she was, had the ship in motion before she'd finished her complaint. For a fraction of a second, even the antimatter engines unleashed a carefully measured pulse, and *Rhapsody in Purple* flung herself clear of the assault transport.

"Well, that was a convincing disaster," Shvets said mildly, the enby tactical officer looking over their scanners. "*Ring's* doors are closed up and I'm pretty sure the blast covered anything that might have drawn suspicion. I'm watching the cruisers for reaction, but I think we're clear."

"And *Ring of Fire?*" Kelly asked.

"On the new course a few seconds later than expected, trailing debris like a wounded deer," Shvets told her. "And, of course, because she *is* on her assigned course, it just looks like she's having a real bad day."

"Good. Then no one is going to be expecting things to get wonky," Kelly replied. "Our ETA to zero-vee to Exeter Base?"

"Two hours, fifty minutes," Foster told her. "At that point, the Legion ships will only be four million klicks out. Are we better served waiting here or there?"

"Let's give them their five hours to get well and truly stuck into the chase," Kelly ordered.

"Understood. Adjusting acceleration for a five-hour arrival," Foster replied. "We'll have all of the data for our friends' jump, too."

"And we'll need our own, too," Kelly warned. "We still need to make the run for the command center."

She was going in with Xi Wu and the two junior Ship's Mages. Between the three Mages, they'd bring all twelve of Vidal's Bionic Commandos plus Kelly herself into the heart of Exeter Base's Station Alpha.

If everything went right, Kelly's husband would pick them all up after the work was done—but the assault shuttles had another job before that. Their weapons were about right for carefully taking down RFLAM turrets before they could threaten the hab stations.

"When the penny drops, I'll put us right on top of Station Alpha," Foster promised. "But I don't think we're going to get the quiet moments we were counting on."

"No," Kelly agreed. "When the penny drops, *everybody's* going to jump. Including the Battle Group."

She wasn't worried about the Legion cruisers. They'd already fed enough information to Battle Group *Pax Dramatis* that the cruisers were doomed. Everything now was down to a handful of Jump Mages and whether they could save the hab stations.

"Get some rest if you can," she ordered everyone around her. "Grab a meal and a coffee if you can't.

"Five hours until we ruin Vice Admiral Dunajski's day."

CHAPTER 57

"LEGION CRUISERS are firing on the Chimeran scout."

Roslyn nodded silently at Claes' report. There wasn't much else she could do. The Legion ships were now at extreme range for *Voice of the Forgotten*'s Phoenix IX missiles even if both ships had been immobile. Given that *Voice* was concealed inside *Ring of Fire*'s cargo bay, heading along Exeter-I's orbit, and the Legion cruisers were accelerating perpendicular to that orbit to close with the scouting cruiser...

She was out of their range and they were out of hers. That was just *fine* by Roslyn's books.

"Any chance they'll hit?" she asked her XO.

"Low," he estimated. "They're at maximum range, and the Chimeran knows *exactly* what she's doing. The Legion ships know it too—there won't be a second salvo. Everybody out there is a veteran."

"I'll admit, I'm not enthused to learn about *another* group of veteran Republican Navy warships out there," Roslyn said. "Any idea who we're looking at out there?"

"Not a clue," Claes said. "I didn't think there were any more *Benjamins* unaccounted for."

She grimaced.

"Neither did I, but we were obviously *wrong*," she told him. "So, get as much data on that ship as you can."

"Well, that's going to be whatever we've got," Claes replied. "She just jumped. Did a pretty decent sensor sweep of the system, got a good look at the Legion's mobile defenders *and* got them to launch missiles so she could assess their current firepower."

Roslyn exhaled and nodded.

"Veterans, like you said," she noted. "That's a pain in somebody's posterior but a problem for another day as well. Do we have the gravity data from *Rhapsody in Purple?*"

"We do, sir," one of Daniel's chiefs confirmed from Navigation. "We're also linked in with *Ring of Fire* to coordinate punching out."

İsa Daniel himself was taking on the same role that had killed Roslyn's last navigator. Claes was supposed to do the same, though he appeared to still be in the Combat Information Center.

"All right." Roslyn said calmly. "Claes, get to the Marines."

"Hop, skip and a jump, Captain."

"Then hop, skip and jump, Commander," she ordered. "The clock is ticking."

"Understood."

Claes and Daniel were still aboard *Voice of the Forgotten*, working with Marine fire teams who'd come aboard for just this purpose. Another thirty Jump Mages were aboard *Ring of Fire*, standing by to deliver ninety exosuited Marines to key locations throughout Exeter Base.

There would be no moments of secrecy. No hope for confusion to allow the Marines to work before the Legion realized they were under attack. The moment they pulled the trigger, the Legion would *know* things were going wrong.

"Ready," Claes reported.

Roslyn nodded silently and tapped a command, opening a four-way conversation via the Link.

"*Voice of the Forgotten* is ready," she reported.

"*Ring of Fire* is ready," Deveraux's generally calm computer-generated voice said.

"*Rhapsody in Purple* is ready," LaMonte said.

"Good," Jakab replied. "The Battle Group's Captains were getting impatient. Captain Deveraux—the call is yours."

There was a long pause. Roslyn took the moment to triple-check the calculations she'd made and sent the young Promethean. They were fully updated for all of the information LaMonte's people had sent them.

Thirty-five Mages were about to take over a hundred Marines and commandos into hell—but it was down to Sharon Deveraux to get them close enough to make that jump.

"I am ready," Deveraux said quietly. "Jumping in three. Two. One. "Jump."

The world flashed around Roslyn, though the direct view from *Voice of the Forgotten*'s external sensors didn't change. All she saw from the hundreds of pickups that fed the destroyer's simulacrum chamber bridge was the interior of *Ring of Fire*'s cargo hold.

She couldn't even feel the rapid sequence of pulses as dozens of Mages teleported around her. The only sign she had that the main force of the mission was already on their way was an update board marking that the fire teams were on their way.

She was receiving sensor data from *Ring of Fire*, however, and could see the hornet's nest they'd just leapt into. Dunajski hadn't kept any of the gunships back to protect the Fleet Base, but that was because the Fleet Base was *quite* capable of defending itself.

"Bow doors opening, bow doors opening!" Salminen snapped.

The maneuver to extract the destroyer had been preprogrammed, but Roslyn still had to hold her breath as her ship flung itself forward at the still-opening forward bay of the assault transport.

Engines flared from cold to gentle to full thrust as they went, a measured pace that spared *Ring of Fire* the worst impacts of the massive antimatter rockets that propelled Roslyn's ship.

Not all of them—that was impossible without spending more time—but enough that the Legion transport was intact enough to roll to evade incoming fire as the forts near-instinctively lashed out.

Roslyn was already designating targets as laser beams punched through where *Ring of Fire* had been. *Voice's* twenty-gigawatt beams spoke in rage and a fort died. Then another.

But she was watching her enemies like a hawk, and the third fort had clearly received orders from Dunajski. Instead of firing on the starships, it was turning to fire on the hab stations.

Roslyn's magic lashed out a moment too late and the beams fired into the void—only to hammer into *Voice of the Forgotten's* hull. She hadn't even realized the chief navigating her ship had made the maneuver, but she'd have given the order without hesitation.

Massive gouges tore through the destroyer's hull, stripping away weapons and armor alike. Linked into the simulacrum, Roslyn felt the strike like it was cutting into her own flesh.

But she was already unleashing her magic. The fort died even as it tore into her ship. The other fort landed a second glancing blow on *Ring of Fire* before she pulsed a massive blaze of magical fire into it.

The forts were gone, but there were other weapons in play. Roslyn could hear the damage reports being shouted around her, but she knew the key point.

Dozens of her people were dead and *Voice of the Forgotten's* weapons were gone. The only hope anyone now had was the amplifier and the magic at the command of a scion of the First Families of Tau Ceti.

And Roslyn Chambers would allow no one to die because *she* failed.

CHAPTER 58

IN THE THIRTY SECONDS after making the microjump, Sharon Deveraux realized just how far short her fragmented education and strange library of tutorials left her compared to the power of a fully-trained scion of the First Families of the Protectorate.

Voice of the Forgotten's beams tore apart two of the four half-megaton fortresses, but it was Chambers' *magic* that tore apart the last two. Lightning and plasma arced across the battlespace—but the Martian destroyer had drawn the attention of the forts as well and paid for it.

An entire chunk of the destroyer spun off into space as Sharon loosed her own magic into the space surrounding her, blasting through the missile satellites still threatening the people they'd come to save.

"RFLAMs from the main station are firing on the habs!" Young barked.

"Get us in the way!" Sharon ordered. She didn't even think about what she was saying, not until Zhao was already bringing up the engines.

Ring of Fire was built on the same core hull as a *Benjamin*-class cruiser, but she didn't have the same armor. She was still better armored than the intentionally defenseless residential platforms, and Sharon's ship swung into the path of the anti-missile lasers.

Damage reports flared across her screen as the lasers burnt into *Ring's* hull, but the transport survived.

Now her magic lashed out at Station Alpha, the handful of attack spells she'd learned from the strange database in the Prometheus Interface answering easily to her will.

She couldn't destroy Station Alpha—there were innocents trapped aboard *every* station that made up the Exeter Fleet Base—but she could slice away the Rapid-Fire Laser Anti-Missile turrets tearing into her ship and targeting the hab stations behind her.

Ring of Fire had delivered many of those innocents into their torment. Now her hull melted away under the fire of their captors as Sharon and her crew fought for redemption.

"*Missiles,*" Young snapped. "Engaging!"

They didn't have that many anti-missile turrets, but every one helped. Sharon turned her own magic to the same task as well, now unleashing her attacks on the multi-gigaton warheads.

The RFLAM beams could hurt *Ring of Fire,* but the missiles could fly *around* her—or vaporize a massive chunk of the ship.

"Assault shuttles sweeping Station Alpha. Warheads appear disarmed," Young reported. "Second missile salvo inbound!"

Sharon saw Chambers' magic and the last few weapons the Martian destroyer had tear into the remaining Battleaxe platforms. Every satellite that died before it launched meant multiple missiles that weren't fired at the hab platforms.

And if not all of the missiles were aimed at the hostages, *Ring of Fire* and her passengers had known their mission when they arrived.

Rhapsody in Purple flashed "above" *Ring of Fire,* the stealth ship flaring waste heat from her stealth systems as her anti-missile turrets cut down missile after missile aimed at the hab platforms—and then everyone missed one that *wasn't* aimed at the stations.

The two-gigaton explosion was close enough to shake Sharon's ship, the massive transport thrown away by the shockwave of radiation and debris... Debris that *had* been one of the Protectorate's veteran stealth ships.

"*Rhapsody* is gone! More missiles heading high!" Young barked, panic underlying her voice as she desperately ran her handful of weapons. "*I can't stop them.*"

"I can."

Zhao's words were flat and calm, a warning that Sharon processed... and did nothing to stop.

Only three of *Ring of Fire*'s engines had been repaired, but the other three still existed. They just weren't safe to use for more than a few seconds.

And a few seconds was enough.

Alex Zhao fired every engine the assault transport had at full power. Fifteen gravities hammered the entire crew to the deck—and imposed a half-kilometer-long starship in the way of the last missiles.

Zhao's desperate maneuver hurled *Ring of Fire* into seven missiles— and a new sun swept Sharon Deveraux and her crew into darkness and legend.

CHAPTER 59

THE DOWNSIDE of having a full communications suite inside her head was that Kelly LaMonte *knew* how badly things were going outside Station Alpha—right up until the moment that *Rhapsody in Purple* took an antimatter missile amidships and many of her dearest friends in the universe ceased to exist.

Unfortunately for her grief and her distraction, they had never had a proper set of schematics for Station Alpha and had assumed the Legion had used standard Republic configurations.

That meant that her three-Mage, twelve-commando, one-spy strike team was not, as planned, directly at the entrance to Station Alpha's command center. They were instead in what appeared to be the station's FTL communications node.

Well. Kelly could work with that.

"We're in deep shit," she said aloud. "But I'm into the coms node and..."

Her implant whined internally as it lost what communications it had.

"Dunajski isn't sending any orders to the hab stations now, even if we missed some of the nukes," she told her companions. "The transceivers this node controls are now separate from the rest of the network and acting as high-power multi-spectrum jammers.

"No one is transmitting anything in or out of Station Alpha until I turn them off."

"What about—"

"A problem for later," Kelly cut off her wife swiftly. She held Xi's eyes and prayed that the Mage understood. "We have to focus on *our* mission.

"Vidal, pick a team to stay here and guard the com node," she continued. "We have line-of-sight coms only now, but if anyone gets to this spot, they can undo what I did."

"Dodger, Melian, Coors," the BCR Lieutenant snapped. "Dig in and hold until relieved."

"Who are we expecting to relieve us?" the senior commando asked.

"The Marines," Vidal replied. "The Mages put a hundred of them on the hab station, but that's still four *companies* of exosuited badasses headed our way. Either they'll relieve you or *I* will. Understood?"

"Una salus victus, sir," Dodger replied. "We'll hold."

Kelly wished she didn't have a translator in her head. She was aware of the motto of the Bionic Commando Regiment—one shared by most Protectorate Special Forces.

Una salus victus: the last hope of the damned.

Right now, until she learned whether or not her husband was alive, *Kelly* was the damned—but the lives of a hundred thousand innocents depended on her doing her job.

"I have schematics of the station now," she told the team coming with her. Three Mages and nine Bionic Commandos. They could do this.

"We're not as badly out of position as I feared, but we've got some hiking to do and they *are* going to throw bodies at us.

"Marcella Dunajski is the only person who can order the Exeter Fleet Base to surrender. So, let's go convince her to give that bloody order!"

Jamming all communications inside Station Alpha rapidly increased the amount of chaos in play. Even knowing that the RMMC assault shuttles were supposed to be hitting the exterior of the station and deploying reinforcements, Kelly had to assume that anyone she was encountering was hostile.

The defenders *didn't* have that necessity—or luxury, depending on the perspective—and that moment of hesitation carried her tiny assault force through the first knots of resistance.

"Schematics show the command center surrounded by an armored citadel," she warned her team as they reached the edge of that defense. "Two entries, one to clockwise and one to counterclockwise."

Like most space stations in the known galaxy, Station Alpha was a rotating ring creating pseudogravity. Protectorate stations often had a central spindle with magical gravity, but Station Alpha lacked that.

"Citadel covers four decks and is proof to any weapons we have," she continued. "We *have* to hit the entryways, and they're going to have their best troops there."

"That's what we were trying to teleport past," Xi Wu said grimly. "Best way through is still us Mages. The citadel might be proof against our *weapons*, but is it going to stand against our *magic?*"

Kelly paused thoughtfully. They were still a floor up and about fifteen meters over from the entryway she'd been aiming for. She'd been considering blasting through the floor with explosives, but the citadel's meter-thick armored walls would resist her mundane gear.

"It's warship armor, rated for antimatter explosions," she told her wife. "A meter thick. Tougher than the outer hull of a *Benjamin* and, well"—she gestured—"on the other side of that bulkhead."

Xi Wu shared a long glance with Samantha Traynor and Jong-Su Alekseev, then the three Mages stepped up to the bulkhead together. Power flared brightly in the claustrophobic corridor, and the unarmored wall disintegrated into fine powder.

"Cover us," Xi Wu ordered as she stepped forward to examine the armored wall. "This may take a few minutes. Once we're through, what's the path?"

"Schematics of the interior are vague," Kelly admitted as she checked the ammunition status on her rifle. She was still unused to both the exosuit armor Vidal had stuffed her in and the heavy anti-exosuit penetrator rifle she'd been given.

The rifle's discarding-sabot tungsten penetrators were the premier armor-piercing weapons available to the Protectorate, but she was used to far lighter weapons.

"I *think* the command center is at the exact center, so we're on the right level and it should be straight ahead," Kelly admitted. "We can probably roll out the explosives at that point. Bulkheads inside are tougher than regular, but they're not warship armor."

"We can handle those," Vidal said firmly. "If Mage Wu and the others can open the citadel, we can get the rest of the way."

Each of the Mages had placed their hands on a section of the armored panel and acquired a look of hard focus. For a moment, Kelly saw nothing—and then she saw more fine powder spill away from her wife's hands as the complex layers of ceramics and energy-dispersal webbing began to disintegrate.

"They'll get us through," Kelly confirmed, then grimaced as her link to everyone's suit scanners gave her a warning. "Incoming!"

The commandos were even more augmented than she was, and gunfire was sounding even before she'd finished the warning.

"Three Assault Troopers," a commando reported. "Scouting party."

"Time to dig in, folks," Vidal ordered grimly. "It looks like trouble is on its way."

Barricade grenades emerged from storage compartments. Each expanded into a chunk of foam at about chest height, then flash-solidified into a barrier that would stop most bullets. It wouldn't stop a penetrator round, but it would slow it down enough that the exosuits should survive it.

Commandos took their positions behind the barricades and Kelly joined them, aiming down the hallway that led to them.

"One way in, one way out," Vidal murmured. "If the Mages can't get us through the citadel..."

Kelly glanced back over her shoulder to where a small artificial wind swept away a growing pile of dust. The gashes in the wall were large enough to meet each other now, forming a rough triangle that looked like it was large enough for even an exosuited solder.

That triangle had only cut a few centimeters deep into the armor, though. It was going to take time.

"They can get us through," she promised.

"Incoming!" someone else shouted, and Kelly turned her attention to the deadly work of staying alive.

Gunfire echoed down the corridor as the Legionnaires tried to storm the position. Whatever coordination they had was good enough to field a full platoon of Assault Troopers to prevent them breaching the citadel.

Kelly wasn't nearly as good a shot as the commandos, but she contributed to the hail of fire they threw down the corridor. They had the only cover, and both sides had exosuits.

She took careful aim, linking the scanners and the gun to her implants, and opened fire as another group of Legionnaires made a rush.

Kelly's fire took down one attacker. The commandos took down two more, but the surviving pair managed to achieve their objective: deploying their own barricade grenades to secure part of the corridor.

"That's too damn close," Vidal muttered. "We're running out of ti— *Down.*"

Kelly had missed the heavy weapon being brought up behind the cover of the rush with the barricades. Crudely known as simply a "blaster," it was one of the few effective plasma weapons to exist—and its ball of super-heated energy hammered into the front line of their defenses.

She barely realized what Vidal was doing when he grabbed her armor and flung her backward. Instincts and cybernetics alike allowed her to adjust and land on her feet like a cat—in time to realize that Vidal *hadn't* moved fast enough to save himself.

Half of her commandos were gone in a single instant of fire. The Legionnaires didn't have a second blaster, but a dozen of them came swarming down the corridor in the wake of the plasma burst, and Kelly's people were scattered from avoiding the blaster's fire.

For a moment, she thought she'd failed—and then an arc of sharp blue lightning flashed past her to hammer into the first Legionnaire. It carried forward from attacker to attacker, leaving a dozen exosuits collapsed on the ground in an eerie macabre display.

"We're through the citadel," Xi Wu told Kelly, standing over one of the injured commandos as her magic drove the Legionnaires back.

"Shall we finish this?"

Kelly was the second person through the door of the command center, tracking for the inevitable idiots—probably Augment Corps, this close to the heart of a Legion facility—trying to pull something stupid.

She wasn't wrong. A burst of penetrators hammered into the wall above her head as she ducked down and to the left. She almost-automatically returned fire, and her target *wasn't* wearing armor.

Augment muscles could carry a heavy penetrator rifle and allow the cyborg to threaten an exosuited soldier. They did nothing when five-millimeter armor-piercing darts tore through the woman's torso.

"Are we *fucking* finished?" Kelly barked. "Or is anyone else going to die for some bloody foolish concept that this isn't over?"

Silence fell over the room as her Mages entered, followed by the remaining commandos.

"Marcella Dunajski," Kelly continued when no one said anything, pointing her gun at the swarthy Admiral.

Dunajski didn't say a word, lifting black eyes to meet what Kelly knew was a featureless faceplate.

"If things have gone according to plan, you *haven't* committed a war crime today," Kelly said drily. "I suggest you order your people to lay down their arms before anyone else gets killed."

"Even if I were prepared to do so, I do not have communications," Dunajski told her. "I am not subject to the orders of—"

One of the commandos had the Admiral by the throat before Kelly, pulling her from her chair and dangling her in the air, detached from the strange pseudogravity of the rotating station.

"Put. Her. Down," Kelly ground out. The soldier hesitated for a moment, but Kelly growled in the back of her throat, and Dunajski fell to the ground at an angle.

She crossed to the Admiral's station, removing a connecting cable from her armor, and linked herself into Dunajski's systems.

"There. Now you have coms," Kelly told the Legion Vice Admiral. "Tell your people to stand down, Admiral."

"And if I refuse?" Dunajski asked, lifting herself carefully from the floor.

"There is a very good chance you killed my husband today," Kelly told her, leveling the penetrator rifle on the Legion flag officer. "So, believe me, Admiral, *I* am considering some war crimes of my own.

"Am I clear?"

Dunajski stared up at her in silence for a seeming eternity, then nodded once.

CHAPTER 60

"ALL LEGION FORCES, this is Vice Admiral Dunajski. Stand down. It is over."

The message, Roslyn reflected, wasn't really meant for the space forces around the Exeter Fleet Base itself. The price had been horrific, but *Voice of the Forgotten* controlled the region around the Fleet Base.

Every fortress was gone. Every missile satellite was gone. Between Roslyn herself and the Marine assault shuttles, every RFLAM turret on *any* station in the Fleet Base was gone.

Somehow, the hab stations were even intact.

"Salucci," she finally said. "Link in with the jump strike teams and confirm who's still with us. We're coordinating until the Battle Group gets here."

There was no question on whether the Battle Group would get there. The Chimeran cruiser—and Roslyn still had more questions than answers there!—was long gone, but *Pax Dramatis* and her escorts had emerged from their own jump at close range of the Legion ships.

It hadn't been a battle so much as a massacre.

Unfortunately, the struggle around Exeter Fleet Base hadn't gone much better for the Royal Martian Navy than the fight in deep space had gone for the Legion. *Voice of the Forgotten* was the only remaining ship, and as Roslyn finished withdrawing her consciousness from the amplifier matrix, she became more and more aware of just how badly her ship was damaged.

"CIC, give me a damage report," she murmured into her link with the CIC.

Only silence answered her.

"I've got those links with the Marines, sir," Salucci reported softly. "External standard coms are fine. The... The Link is gone, though. The internal network is...shot to hell."

Roslyn nodded slowly, keeping her face a mask of iron as she pulled up what damage reports she could find.

There were no reports from CIC. At all. Or most of the ship, for that matter. A damage-report display that was supposed to automatically update from the damage-control teams and Engineering was almost entirely blank.

"Salminen, do we have any links with Engineering or the Damage Control Center?" she asked.

"No, sir," the tactical officer replied. "We...were focusing on the battle."

Which was as it should have been, but now Roslyn couldn't see *anything* of what was going on in her ship.

"You're damage control now," she told Salminen. "Start raising departments, section by section, and identifying survivors and intact systems."

The simulacrum was directly in Roslyn's line of sight, and it told her enough of the story. A massive piece of her starship was *missing*. Gouges and holes marked much of the rest of the ship.

"What about you, sir?" Salminen asked.

Roslyn rose, testing her movement. The gravity runes were intact enough so far.

"We have power," she noted. "That means we have at least one fusion reactor online, which means *someone* in Engineering is still with us. I'm going to go link up with them."

The tactical officer coughed.

"Shouldn't *I* do that, sir?" he asked.

"If you were a Mage and could teleport across areas without atmosphere, yes," Roslyn agreed. "Since one of us can do that and one of us can't... We also serve who call everyone and see who's all right, Lieutenant Commander."

"Yes, sir."

Getting to Engineering didn't end up requiring magic, but it did require Roslyn to reroute past a hole clean through the ship that she eyeballed as having run through the Combat Information Center.

Given that the hole was the original twenty-gigawatt laser hit that had shut down their main weapons, she suspected the CIC crew had never even known what had hit them.

Only the fact that her XO was currently on one of the hab stations would have saved his life. At that moment, Roslyn was the only Mage on her ship—and as she reached her second intended entrance to Engineering, she realized that was going to be critical.

A secondary hit—potentially either a debris strike or even an RFLAM beam that had hit inside the hole from the original heavy laser impact—had turned the entire section next to the lightly armored casing around the Engineering section into a nightmare.

Key cables, like the main Engineering section around the power cores, had their own armor. But communications cabling and access conduits had been torn apart and scattered across the entire inner side of the armored casing.

Further damage had sealed the area again, allowing a partial atmosphere to return, but there was no getting into Engineering without heavy power tools or magic.

She was close enough, though...

"Dresdner, this is Chambers," she said, activating her wrist-comp. "Please respond."

There was a long-enough silence that she was afraid Engineering had lost atmosphere, then the channel chirped alive.

"Captain, this is Lieutenant Agli," a young feminine voice replied. "Commander Dresdner is..."

Agli choked off.

"She's the only reason any of us are alive, sir, but she's gone," the junior engineer whispered.

"Status report, Agli," Roslyn snapped, hoping the order would knock some calm back into the younger woman.

"Sir, yes, sir!" Agli replied sharply. "Reactor one is online, but most of the engineering core is lacking in atmosphere and flooded with radioactive coolant."

Roslyn winced.

"Commander Dresdner manually vented the coolant and fuel valves into the main void to prevent an overload on reactor three," the engineer continued. "I have...fifteen of the engineering staff crammed into two of the offices.

"It's cramped, but we have air. I don't know how long reactor one will remain stable, but we don't have the safety gear to attempt to leave the offices."

There was a pause.

"Most of the survivors require medical attention, sir," she admitted. "Lethal or near-lethal rad doses."

"And Dresdner?" Roslyn asked gently.

"The controls on the valves jammed," Agli said. "She vented them with a wrench...but there was already an atmosphere leak."

And the coolant would have been superheated, especially if Dresdner had been venting an active reactor to prevent an overload.

It would have been quick.

"All right, Agli," Roslyn told the junior engineer. "I need to know which offices you're in."

"Dresdner's and mine," Agli said slowly. "Why?"

"I'm going to open entrance Charlie and create safe tunnels to the doors," Roslyn replied. "When I give the word, you'll open the door and make a run for it."

"Sir, yes, sir!" the engineer replied, her panicked faith both terrifying and heartwarming.

Roslyn Chambers inhaled, weaving magic around herself once again to create a safe bubble on her side of the door. Once she did that, she cut a person-sized hole through the debris covering Engineering's entrance C and pushed the safe bubble forward.

She had to hold the plug to keep the coolant in, and she had to run tunnels through Engineering by memory. She'd already burned a lot of power fighting the battle, but she would *not* lose the last fifteen members of her engineering crew when they could be saved.

"Oh, Apollo Phoebus, I see the tunnel," Agli told her.

"Good." Roslyn focused, weaving the magic out farther and farther. She exhaled heavily. "Is it linked?"

"We're linked, we're linked," Agli replied. "Both offices! We're clear, we're opening and we're coming!"

Roslyn fell to one knee, her power flowing out of her like water as she held the tunnel open. It seemed like an eternity until a voice spoke next to her.

"We've got an emergency seal ready to close to the entrance, sir, but your tunnel is blocking it," Agli said urgently. "We're clear. We're all clear!"

"Oh," Roslyn said faintly. "Thank you."

She collapsed as swiftly as her magic did.

CHAPTER 61

THE MARINES TOOK OVER Vice Admiral Dunajski's imprisonment before Kelly or her commandos gave in to the temptation to do anything immoral, illegal or outright wrong.

She considered that a solid victory of self-control on the part of her team. Even the commandos of her squad had been aboard *Rhapsody in Purple* for at least two years apiece now.

With the commandos they'd lost in the operation, Kelly was down to herself, three Mages and five members of the Bionic Combat Regiment. She'd started the morning with a crew of over fifty.

Enough of the news had traveled the rumor mill that the Marines escorting her to the shuttles paid no mind to the fact that she was clinging to Xi Wu's hand just as hard as her wife was clinging to her hand in turn.

The reports she was receiving were chaos and garbage. There were over two dozen assault shuttles flying around outside the space station, and *all* of them were stolen Legion ships.

No one was sure which one was which. No one was sure which half-dozen shuttles *hadn't* made it off *Ring of Fire* before she'd been vaporized.

No one could tell Kelly LaMonte if Mike Kelzin was alive or dead, so she clung to Xi's hand and forced as calm a mask onto her face as possible.

"Commodore, Commodore LaMonte!" a vaguely familiar voice shouted. Kelly turned to see yet another featureless faceplate coming toward her—and then Mage-Colonel Hagir Dirks opened her helmet and waved Kelly over.

"Are you okay, Commodore?" the Colonel asked.

"I don't know yet," Kelly admitted. "The operation?"

"Successful," Dirks said bluntly. "Not cheap. *Ring of Fire* was lost. Your ship was lost. We're still reestablishing contact with the Marine strike teams, but it looks like we lost at least a half-dozen teams in their entirety before Dunajski ordered the surrender.

"But we got all the bombs disarmed in time." The Marine grimaced. "It was nearer-run than I'd like, and your idea to jam Station Alpha's coms likely saved the day there, sir."

"So, we did it," Kelly murmured. "A hundred thousand people saved."

"More," Dirks told her. "There were a hundred thousand on the hab stations alone. They'd clearly brought more hands in; we're expecting to find fifty thousand in the working stations and at least twenty thousand on the surface and scattered through the mining facilities.

"Sorting everything out is going to take *days*, Commodore, but we did it," the Marine continued. "Come on; this way."

Kelly arched an eyebrow behind her own faceplate but followed the Marine Mage-Colonel. With her own ship gone, she wasn't quite sure what the plan was.

"We took over the main shuttle bay on Station Alpha to coordinate," Dirks told her as she led them onward. "We're trying to keep all of the birds in the air, *and* we're hot-wiring the local craft to add to the numbers, so I'm afraid it's a chaotic mess but—"

"Mike?"

Xi Wu had seen the pilot before Kelly had. Mike Kelzin was standing in the middle of a cluster of technicians poring over what looked like the control console for an assault shuttle—a console notably missing the *assault shuttle* component.

Kelly's wife was gone a moment later, running across the bay deck. Her exosuit boots made a cacophony of metal on metal.

"Your husband is walking my techs through the hot-wiring process," Dirks said softly. "*He* knew *you* were okay, so...I don't think it occurred to him to check in, and we're not doing a great job of keeping personnel assignments up to date."

Xi Wu had removed her helmet and was clearly not sure what to do about embracing their husband while still wearing a combat exosuit.

"I lost most of my crew today, Colonel," Kelly said, her voice wooden even to her. "But...until a second ago, I also thought I'd lost our husband, and I didn't know if my wife would ever forgive me."

"I'm in a line marriage," Dirks murmured. "We lost our senior husband at the Battle of Nia Kriti, and I think my eldest sister-wife still blames every one of us in uniform, just a little bit.

"So, I get it. Go," the Colonel told her. "You're not going anywhere until the Battle Group arrives, and I think my people have worked out the shuttles.

"We'll be fine without you all for a bit."

When the metaphorical dust had settled, Mike flew his spouses and their surviving commandos over to *Rhapsody in Vermillion*. It was a strange feeling to Kelly to be landing on a stealth ship that *wasn't Rhapsody in Purple*.

The ships looked almost the same, but she didn't recognize the crew she saw and, well, it wasn't *her* ship.

Yvonne Ó Cearmada was waiting for them, giving Kelly a passable attempt at a salute as she and her spouses crossed the shuttle bay.

"Welcome aboard *Vermillion*, Director," the redheaded spy ship captain told her. "I wish we were welcoming you under better circumstances."

"I wish I fully understood what this was going to look like, going forward," Kelly admitted. "I'm not going to steal your ship, Yvonne. I just need somewhere to hang my hat that isn't a Navy ship."

"We have a little bit of space, assuming your commandos are fine bunking with my commandos," Ó Cearmada replied. "We've cleared a room for you and your spouses. It won't work for the long term, I'm sure, but we'll make it do."

"I won't stay on your ship forever, Yvonne," Kelly reiterated. "What exactly that looks like—a new ship for me, or even a damned desk—but *Vermillion* isn't designed to haul supercargo."

"Maybe, but we've still got work to do out here," her subordinate replied. "Got any brain to spare?"

Kelly arched an eyebrow at that.

"Xi, take Mike and our bags and get us situated, please," she murmured to her wife.

"Got it," Xi Wu said, pressing a kiss to Kelly's cheek. "Don't work *too* hard."

Kelly's spouses followed Ó Cearmada's XO, leaving Kelly and Ó Cearmada standing alone in a corner of the shuttle bay.

"What did you find?" Kelly asked grimly.

"We had a few less distractions, sitting with the Battle Group," *Vermillion's* Captain pointed out. "Our commandos were with the Marines providing extra fire support, so we even had extra space to think."

"Your point?" Kelly replied.

"We had the time to run the data you sent us on the Chimeran ship," Ó Cearmada told her. "Adding the data we picked up here, we *should* have been able to find her in the Styx files."

"Should have," Kelly echoed. They'd pulled the full administrative files of the Republic Interstellar Navy out of Styx Station. The last throes of the Republic's government—and the station's savaging at the hands of Roslyn Chambers and Jane Alexander—had meant the data was inconsistent and incomplete, but they'd *thought* they had a full list of the RIN's ships.

"But we didn't," Ó Cearmada told her. "Except one of my junior analysts had a brainwave and ran the emissions schema against the *other* list we have of RIN warships."

"The other list?" Kelly had to roll that around in her head for a moment. "From Legatus?"

"Our Chimeran is the *Benjamin*-class cruiser RINS *Barracuda*," Ó Cearmada said calmly. "Commissioned prior to the war, assigned to Republic Home Fleet. She was there when Montgomery told the RIN just what the hell was powering their starships.

"And she's missing from all Republic records after that. I believe, with the benefit of hindsight, that she was one of the ships that deserted after that revelation."

Kelly nodded slowly. Damien Montgomery—with help from one Kelly LaMonte, among others—had arrived at the Siege of Legatus with undeniable proof of the nature of Project Prometheus and just how RIN starships worked.

The fact that RIN command had tried to deny that in the face of the truth, to the point of self-destructing several ships that had poked too hard at their Prometheus Drives, had turned hesitation into mutiny and desertion.

Between surrenders to the RMN and ships that had eventually returned to the RIN, she thought they'd accounted for them all. Except...

"How many ships did we miss?"

"The Republic officially listed every ship they didn't find again as 'defected,'" Ó Cearmada told her. "And I guess we figured every ship that was missing from that particular stunt either went pirate or was scuttled by her own crew—we certainly knew about a bunch of the latter."

"So, how many?" Kelly repeated.

"Don't know," Ó Cearmada admitted. "No more than thirteen, at a guess—because going back through the records of the Siege of Legatus, that's how many ships followed the heavy carrier *Chimera* out of the star system."

Kelly caught the name and realized she'd growled in the back of her throat.

"*Chimera*," she repeated.

"The Chimerans are Republic deserters, people who broke with Legatus when they learned what the Prometheus Drive was," Ó Cearmada told her. "I don't know what that means or why the Legion didn't know where they were...but that's a wrinkle we weren't expecting, isn't it?"

CHAPTER 62

"**MAGE-COMMANDER CHAMBERS.** Take a seat."

Roslyn relaxed from an unnecessary parade rest and obeyed. She knew she was still excessively rigid as she took the chair in front of Mage–Vice Admiral Jakab's desk, but rigidity helped keep the mask in place.

Without it, she would cry.

Voice of the Forgotten had a listed crew of three hundred and fifty-eight, including the Marines who'd died at Sondheim Base and never been replaced.

In the aftermath of the Battle of Exeter, seventy-three of her people were still alive.

Every volunteer and mutineer aboard *Ring of Fire* was gone. Forty MISS officers and crew aboard *Rhapsody in Purple* were gone.

"How are you holding up, Chambers?" Jakab asked gently.

"With difficulty, sir," Roslyn said carefully. "But duty remains."

"That it does," he agreed. "The situation here in Exeter is still fluid, but things are stable enough that we can begin memorial services for your crew members.

"What is *Voice of the Forgotten*'s status?"

Roslyn inhaled slowly and focused her will to get through this meeting.

"We have completed the evacuation," she said, as calmly as she could. "Depending on the next steps, we will need to send people back aboard in small groups to retrieve personal effects before or during the engineering survey."

Jakab just looked at her in silence for at least ten seconds.

"Mage-Commander, can *Voice of the Forgotten* even jump in her current state?" he asked gently.

Roslyn looked down at her hands. Like most Jump Mages, she wore thin gloves to conceal the silver runes inlaid into her palms. Those runes allowed a Mage to jump, but only by completing the matrix woven through the ship.

If the amplifier or jump matrix was too damaged, jumping became unsafe—or even suicidal. *Voice* was unquestionably in the latter state.

"No, sir," Roslyn admitted quietly. "Not without material repairs here in Exeter."

"Your ship's weapons are nonfunctional," Jakab reminded her gently. "Only twenty percent of your crew remains, and you commanded one of the oldest destroyers still active in Her Majesty's Navy.

"*Material repairs* cannot be justified on *Voice of the Forgotten*, I'm sorry. There isn't, so far as my staff can tell, even a purpose in carrying out an engineering survey. She is too old, too small, and she has given too much."

Roslyn was silent. What could she say to that? She'd suspected that was going to be the verdict, but she'd expected it to *take* that survey, to let her carry on the belief that she still had a command.

"What now, then, sir?" she asked softly.

"Right now? We're all waiting for Mage-Admiral Medici," he admitted. "While I have the firepower to challenge most of the Legion's defensive forces, I don't have the troops to secure a planet.

"In truth, I barely have the troops to handle what we're facing here in Exeter." He spread his hands wide. "I know the cost hurts, Mage-Commander, but I want you to fully understand what you achieved.

"The Royal Martian Navy now controls the Exeter Fleet Base. That includes six surprisingly modern shipyard slips that can be easily converted to the construction of our cruiser designs. I have already submitted that the base will be renamed *Deveraux Base*, which I expect to pass muster with High Command.

"But, more importantly, it means that your forward element is directly responsible for the liberation of over *one hundred and eighty thousand* forced laborers."

Roslyn had known there'd been more prisoners than expected, but she hadn't realized there'd been that many workers.

"The cost was still high," she admitted softly.

"It was," Jakab said levelly. "Director LaMonte has moved her remaining people aboard *Rhapsody in Vermillion*. I don't know if she'll continue operating out here with us, but there are definitely questions that will entail MISS involvement for a while yet."

"Yes, sir. And my crew, sir?"

"Once Admiral Medici arrives, your crew will be transported back to Tau Ceti," Jakab said firmly. "I have already signed orders for all of *Voice of the Forgotten*'s survivors to be sent on six months' stress leave.

"If I had the authority to make Director LaMonte take that leave, I would," he noted. "As it is, I will quietly encourage her when the opportunity arises."

"And myself, sir?" Roslyn asked.

"Are you or are you not part of *Voice of the Forgotten*'s crew?" he asked drily. "You have some duties remaining with regards to the memorials and funerals for your people, but you will report aboard that transport home.

"You *will* take those six months to rest, Mage-Commander," he continued—and his tone was iron. "I have my guesses about the tasks we'll put you to after that, but you are taking those six months."

"We are at war!" she protested.

"A war that Seventh Fleet is now well equipped and well informed to fight—thanks to you and thanks to Sharon Deveraux. A war, bluntly, that I do not expect to take six months to finish."

"I can't..."

"You *need* to rest," Jakab told her. "In six months, when our doctors clear you, you will be in the Tau Ceti System and available when they start looking about for instructors for the new Academy semester.

"My *personal* recommendation to the TCNA administration will be to snap you up before the rest of the Navy does," he concluded. "It is, to be fair, the last check mark you need to set your feet irrevocably on the path to flag rank."

Roslyn looked down at her hands again. That didn't feel right to her at all.

"You're probably going to get another medal out of this, but that's for another conversation," Jakab told her. "The only reason you aren't already a Mage-Captain, Chambers, is that you are simply too damn young.

"Six months of leave. A year as an instructor. Potentially another tour as a staff officer after that, and you'll be ready for that leap," he continued. "The Navy wants you to get that seasoning, Mage-Commander, but we also would prefer that you stop trying to *die* getting it.

"Do you understand me?"

"I lost my ship and most of my crew, sir," Roslyn told him. "I feel like I need more than *seasoning*."

"Do you know what the most difficult skill an officer must acquire is, Mage-Commander Chambers?" Jakab asked.

She blinked at the non sequitur.

"Sir?"

"It is not courage," he told her. "Courage is surprisingly easy to find, in the end. It's not compassion or empathy—we have two centuries of experience teaching those and weeding out those who cannot learn them.

"It's not even tactics or leadership. It's one we cannot teach, because no lesson truly prepares you for it."

"I don't understand, sir," Roslyn admitted.

"It is the ability to give an order where you *know* some or all of the officers and spacers you are ordering into battle will not come back," Jakab said gently. "And to assess that you are spending their lives for a purpose worthy of them.

"You knew when we put together this operation and you helped plan it that many of the people you led into this system would not come back. You led them here anyway, because a hundred and eighty thousand innocent lives rode on your success."

He raised a hand before she could speak.

"And every officer, spacer, mutineer, Marine and spy you brought with you knew the risks. Many of them had the chance to back out—and did not. The price was high—but it was worth it."

"I hope so, sir." Roslyn shook her head. "I don't know if I truly believe it yet, though."

"That takes time, Commander," he conceded. "That is why you need the break I'm ordering you to take. Paperwork and medals will follow, but I know damn well you don't really care about the medals at this point.

"By the time I'd hauled Damien Montgomery around for a year, I'd picked up my own drawer-full of the things. They're just reminders to the people who weren't there."

"Those of us who were don't need the reminders," Roslyn murmured.

"No. And you know that." He shook his head gently. "But I want you to know something else, Roslyn."

His use of her first name took her by surprise, and she raised her gaze to meet his.

"The Legion had been stripping Prometheus Interfaces off their starships for years. Many of those were stored here," he told her. "We also retrieved two Interfaces from the cruisers we engaged before their life support ran out.

"Twenty-nine Prometheus Interfaces and their captive Mages will be returning to Tau Ceti with you, Mage-Commander Chambers. A laboratory is already being set up to see if we can duplicate what the Legion did with Captain Deveraux."

Jakab smiled.

"She died attempting to right a wrong she'd helped commit, but she also showed *us* a wrong we committed on our own," he told Roslyn. "We can't undo what has been done—but thanks to Sharon Deveraux, we can do better by those who come after.

"They, too, are victims of the Republic and Legion."

Roslyn nodded with a long sigh.

"I appreciate that, sir," she admitted. "I'll see them safely to Tau Ceti. Regardless of orders or duty, I owe *that* to Captain Deveraux."

ABOUT THE AUTHOR

© Art and Soul Photography

GLYNN STEWART is the author of Starship's Mage, a bestselling science fiction and fantasy series where faster-than-light travel is possible–but only because of magic. His other works include science fiction series Duchy of Terra, Castle Federation and Vigilante, as well as the urban fantasy series ONSET and Changeling Blood.

Writing managed to liberate Glynn from a bleak future as an accountant. With his personality and hope for a high-tech future intact, he lives in Kitchener, Ontario with his partner, their cats, and an unstoppable writing habit.

CREDITS

The following people were involved in making this book:
Copyeditor: Richard Shealy
Proofreader: M Parker Editing
Cover art: Jeff Brown Graphics
Layout and typesetting: Red Cape Production, Berlin
Faolan's Pen Publishing team: Jack, Kate, and Robin.

OTHER BOOKS
BY GLYNN STEWART

For release announcements join the
mailing list or visit **GlynnStewart.com**

STARSHIP'S MAGE

Starship's Mage
Hand of Mars
Voice of Mars
Alien Arcana
Judgment of Mars
UnArcana Stars
Sword of Mars
Mountain of Mars
The Service of Mars
A Darker Magic
Mage-Commander
Beyond the Eyes of Mars

Starship's Mage: Red Falcon
Interstellar Mage
Mage-Provocateur
Agents of Mars

Pulsar Race: A Starship's Mage Universe Novella

DUCHY OF TERRA

The Terran Privateer
Duchess of Terra
Terra and Imperium
Darkness Beyond
Shield of Terra
Imperium Defiant
Relics of Eternity
Shadows of the Fall
Eyes of Tomorrow

SCATTERED STARS

Scattered Stars: Conviction
Conviction
Deception
Equilibrium
Fortitude
Huntress *(upcoming)*

Scattered Stars: Evasion
Evasion
Discretion *(upcoming)*

PEACEKEEPERS OF SOL

Raven's Peace
The Peacekeeper Initiative
Raven's Course
Drifter's Folly
Remnant Faction *(upcoming)*

EXILE

Exile
Refuge
Crusade
Ashen Stars: An Exile Novella

CASTLE FEDERATION

Space Carrier Avalon
Stellar Fox
Battle Group Avalon
Q-Ship Chameleon
Rimward Stars
Operation Medusa
A Question of Faith: A Castle Federation Novella

Dakotan Confederacy
Admiral's Oath
To Stand Defiant *(upcoming)*

AETHER SPHERES
Nine Sailed Star *(upcoming)*

VIGILANTE
(WITH TERRY MIXON)
Heart of Vengeance
Oath of Vengeance

**Bound By Stars: A Vigilante Series
(With Terry Mixon)**
Bound By Law
Bound by Honor
Bound by Blood

TEER AND KARD
Wardtown
Blood Ward

CHANGELING BLOOD
Changeling's Fealty
Hunter's Oath
Noble's Honor
Fae, Flames & Fedoras: A Changeling Blood Novella

ONSET
ONSET: To Serve and Protect
ONSET: My Enemy's Enemy
ONSET: Blood of the Innocent
ONSET: Stay of Execution
Murder by Magic: An ONSET Novella

STAND ALONE NOVELS & NOVELLAS
Children of Prophecy
City in the Sky
Excalibur Lost: A Space Opera Novella
Balefire: A Dark Fantasy Novella

Made in the USA
Monee, IL
25 May 2022

· 97019508R10225